THE
MERMAID'S
WRATH

ANDIE HOLMAN

Copyright © 2024 by Andie Holman
All rights reserved.

No part of this publication may be reproduced, distributed, or transmitted in any form or by any means, including photocopying, recording, or other electronic or mechanical methods, without the prior written permission of the publisher or author.

This is a work of fiction. Names, characters, and incidents are products of the author's imagination. The scientific suggestions are based on current research.
For permission requests, contact the author at www.andieholman.com.

Book Cover by Richard Ljoenes
Edited by Kenneth Zink
Formatting by Lorna Reid

Edition One 2024.

This book is dedicated to octopuses.
With three hearts and eight arms, surely they are the
embodiment of love.

ONE

JELLY

"They're getting worse," I croaked, rubbing the residual fear from my eyes. I groped for the double-shot coffee Nell offered. I'd had nightmares my whole life, but they'd recently become hyperintense. I was always too late, arriving at the end of the slaughter. I was swimming in an ocean of blood, dolphin cries ringing in my ears.

I shivered with a sigh as the cool breeze dried the sweat from my skin. Nell settled at the foot of my bed, squeezing my ankle. Her mouth turned down. "Your yelling was loud enough to wake the dogs. Want to talk about it?"

I frowned into my mug. "Not really."

"Well, you're going back home in a couple of weeks. Maybe they'll settle down when you're in your own bed." She paused, tapping her toes on the wood floor, the base of her slipper slapping. "So tell me, Jelly, what's the point of all your visits? What good does it do when you return to the reef? To make a difference, you need to be here, with the humans. They're the ones who need help."

I groaned. "Nell, we've been through this. I belong to the

ocean. No one else cares for the sea life like I do. I can't abandon them."

The Pacific Mers, my people, lived below the East side of a swamp of pollution known as the Great Pacific Garbage Patch. We simply called it the Patch. It covered 1.6 million square kilometers, almost a million miles, and despite my best attempts, swimming for hours without a break, I hadn't been able to find an edge.

Nell crossed her arms and scowled. "At some point, they'll figure out you aren't trying to get knocked up. They must be getting suspicious by now."

The incessant ocean pollution destroyed our ability to reproduce naturally. Grappling with infertility, mermaids went to the surface to mate with human males on Procreation Missions. The humans had adapted to plastics better than we had, albeit not by much.

I scrubbed my palm over my cheeks. "Yes, I know."

Nell was a Walker, my contact on the surface, and had lived here since the seventies, one of the first mermaids to undertake a mission. After swallowing a potion to change her tail into legs, she swam for the surface, with no support once she got there. No clothes, no money, and no clue of what to expect. It must have been terrifying. Fate intervened, and a storm consumed her, throwing her off her route.

Jack found her while deep-sea fishing. He spotted her frantically waving, naked and floundering, clinging to a buoy on a drift net. He puttered up in his boat and hauled her in, shivering and shaking. When she wouldn't tell him why she was half-dead in the ocean, he insisted he take her to the hospital. She weighed her options in a split second. Frightened of exposing the Mers to more than one human, she told him what she was.

Jack was over the moon. He'd seen the wasteland of the ocean and wanted to help.

She made a case to our government, the Trident, that the mermaids needed support, someone familiar with the surface. They saw the benefit in her plea, granting her amnesty and the title of Walker. However, as penance, she could never again visit the reef. She could still talk to the sea life and swim like the dickens, but she'd lose her beautiful tail.

Whenever I'd visit, she'd ask me for gossip and laugh at my stories, but her eyes were never wistful. She was happy. She'd made a home for herself here.

Nell's knee bounced as she ran over our looping argument. She wanted me to stay. I couldn't. "Jelly, they'll stop you from coming up. That's after they punish you for deceiving them. You've been here seven times. They'll either think you have a faulty womb, or put it together that you're lying. You only have two weeks left of your month, and I'm not allowed to give you more transformation potion." Nell ran a hand over her long, twisted locs, twirling the end of one through her ebony fingers. She said quietly, "Stay. You and Simmi could do so much together."

I'd met Simmi a year ago. Today, she was in Mexico supervising a baby turtle project. The timing was terrible, but Nature had her schedule, and the eggs were due to hatch any moment. Since only one in a thousand hatchlings survived to adulthood, Simmi did all she could to help them get started, patrolling the beaches for predators, chasing off ghost crabs and birds.

I spoke in a gentle, yet firm, voice. "Nell, you're breaking my heart. You know my position is impossible. If I had my way, I'd come here freely and help you, help Simmi, yet still go back to the reef to support the sea life."

Nell snorted, "Don't hold your breath, Jelly. They'll never allow you to do that."

A bark of laughter escaped me. "And so, here we are. As I've told you, until their protocols change, I'll do what I can to come up here, but otherwise, my home is the reef."

She hauled off my bed and slapped her hands to her ample hips. "Fine. I'll just keep pestering you until you give in." She grinned, and I laughed. Her face sobered. "Are you sure you want to go today?"

Caffeine lashed my tongue with a longer sip, waking me fully. I set the mug on the bedside table, combing strong fingers through my long, blue hair, airing out the back of my neck. "I need to see it, Nell. I can handle it alone."

Nell's dark eyebrows drew together as she frowned. "I have a weird feeling, Jelly. I don't think you should go."

I'd never been to the superstore. I was familiar with the small village with its farmers' market, the refill store for soaps and nuts and rice, the dojo, the coffee shop, and, of course, the library, but never the looming monstrosity the humans frequented in droves.

Turquoise eyes rolled in my head. "Goddess, Nell, it's fine. It's just a store."

Nell conceded reluctantly. "Suit yourself."

I finished my coffee and swung my legs over the side. With my feet on the floor, I shook my head, grateful the dolphins were finally quiet. Nell rested a heavy hand on my shoulder. "Jack and I are here for you if you change your mind. We'll help you find your feet."

I nodded. "Thank you, Nell. I appreciate that."

She changed the subject. "What are you doing before the store? Library or Mew?"

I rubbed my hands together. "Mew. We're practicing

roundhouse kicks today." Nell had introduced me to Bartholomew, or Mew, to help me learn my legs. He ran the dojo in the village and trained me to fight on land. He insisted I lift weights to build my muscles, and with each return to the reef, I was leaner and meaner, wielding new skills that shocked my opponents. Mew was an expert in all things violent. I liked him.

I squeezed Nell's shoulder reassuringly. "I'll see you when I get home from the store. Maybe you can teach me how to make a pineapple upside-down cake."

She nodded with a tight smile and left.

Mew barked, telling me to aim higher for his head, and I strained to reach my heel for his jaw. I kicked at my growing anxiety, and while sparring offered an excellent distraction, I couldn't linger. I had to go. I washed the sweat from my skin and sighed, slipping on a sundress and tying my long hair into a messy bun. Mew walked with me down the tree-lined street. I paced at the bus stop, chewing my bottom lip. "I can join you," Mew soothed, his voice kind. "You might want company for your first time."

"No, I'm good. You've got the girls coming later."

"I can reschedule them." His broad face etched with concern. "It's going to be a shock, Jelly. It's like nothing you've seen before."

"Thanks, Mew, I appreciate it, but I've got this, unlike the ten-year-olds learning to punch. Have fun with them. I'm sorry I'll miss the class. I love watching them express their fury at you."

"Okay, then," he said. He clamped his massive hands on my shoulders, turning me toward him as the bus trundled up. His rich brown eyes were solemn as he said, "Good luck, Jelly."

The bus hummed and bumped down the road, away from

the village and into the city. I watched as the humans boarded, observing their habits and mannerisms. My jaw clenched when they whipped out plastic bottles, careful not to spill on themselves as we hit potholes large enough to compress my spine. Squat buildings, neon signs, and gridlock traffic replaced trees and vibrant green fields. So many cars idled in the sun's blaze. The occupants fiddled on phones while sitting comfortably in their cool, climate controlled boxes.

Sweat beaded on my upper lip and slipped between my breasts, partially from the stuffiness of the bus, but mostly from anticipation. I suppressed a snarl as we paused outside the dump; the stench overpowering. Bulldozers spread the filth into ever-growing piles while cars and trucks waited to unload. Familiar plastic jugs spilled and rolled along the rot, not recycled. They could have been.

We lurched forward, the smell of exhaust replacing the garbage. I closed my eyes, mentally preparing myself. Soon, we pulled outside a building that swallowed an entire city block. People brushed past me in a hurry to get to the air conditioning. I lingered, hesitating. Outside the store, a non-profit had set up a picnic table draped with a banner emblazoned with SAVE OUR OCEANS.

Two cute and scruffy guys waved fliers and called to shoppers, who avoided their eyes as they hurried past. I stopped, curious. "What is this?" My fingers grazed over a clear ball set in a cheap black base. Inside was a small plastic turtle perched on a rod, surrounded by garishly colored coral.

The young blond with a goatee smiled. "It's a snow globe. We're selling them to raise money for the ocean." He tipped his chin at me. "Go on, pick it up and shake it."

When the turtle became obscured by tiny white specks of plastic, I dropped it with a shriek. We watched it bounce, spinning until it rested against the table leg, scratched but indestructible. I spat, "Is that a sick joke?"

He looked at me, confused, bordering on apologetic. "What? No. Everyone loves snow globes." I stepped back, staring furiously at the row of captured turtles, forever swimming in filth. He said, "Hey, why are you so mad? It's just a snow globe."

I bit my cheek. The thin taste of copper hit my tongue like a balm. I muttered, "You wouldn't get it. Here's a twenty."

He offered me a new one. I shook my head. "No. I don't want that. I want nothing to do with that." I paused. "If you're trying to help the ocean, canvas bags or linen dishcloths would be better." He blinked, realization blooming across his cheeks.

I walked toward the playground, jangled by the plastic pieces of the snow globe. I needed to calm myself down. Sweaty children played on slides, swings, and a jungle gym, planted on a concrete slab. A drooling baby gnawed on a bright blue ring, screaming toward a toddler who rocked on a yellow seahorse; the heavy-duty plastic faded and cracked along its face.

I watched the broken eye swing back and forth. The girl noticed my blank stare and waved at me, squealing as she resumed her play, the thick, rusted spring squeaking under her weight. I gave her a half-smile, raising my fingers in response. I willed my racing heart to settle. It was just a store, a place where humanity shopped. Nothing more.

To my left was an entrance through the garden center, manned by stacks of plastic pots of varying sizes and colors. I'd start there. I murmured aloud, "You are a Warrior. You have seen unspeakable horror. You can handle this." I steeled myself and walked inside, bracing for the onslaught of human ignorance.

The shelves groaned with tchotchkes of gnomes hugging red and white mushrooms, and frogs smoked cigars, while fairies waved their sparkly star wands. Young plants wilted in their fabricated pots, desperate to feel cool earth on their roots. Further along, I paused at the dedicated aisle of bottles and massive containers of weed killers, insecticides, and pesticides, all decorated with skulls and crossbones. Growling at them, I stomped toward the main entrance.

As people passed through the automatic doors, cold air whooshed into the open garden center. Open. Closed. Open. Closed. Out of habit, I slid my teardrop pearl pendant along its chain, comforted by the action and the rasping noise. I let it drop at my throat and fisted my hands. Swallowing, I stepped into the cold, determined to see this through.

It was worse than I'd imagined. Everywhere I looked, plastic dominated. Monuments of nestled buckets stood guard at the ends of each aisle. Flocks of people pushed overflowing carts, grabbing things without glancing at the packaging. It was chaotic, overwhelming, and I almost chickened out.

I must have looked lost or stunned. A kind older lady wearing the store's colors asked if I needed help. I blinked at her. My voice was shaky. "I need to see the laundry jugs, please." She pointed me in the correct direction, just four more aisles to the right. I nodded my thanks and set off. Goddess, it was freezing in here. I shook my hair free from its bun and let it fall over my back like a blanket.

I wandered down the first aisle—food, if you could call it that. Obnoxiously colored packaging held candy in combinations of sugar and artificial chemicals. Labels proudly proclaimed, "Contains 2% real juice" and "No added sugars." I picked up a package of fish-shaped gummies and scanned the back, searching for something I'd know. I couldn't pronounce half the words.

There were rows of drinks in plastic bottles, in hues I'd never seen in nature. Some touted energy, others promised calm, making the liquids seem almost magical. Then, the bottles of water, at least a dozen versions, stewed in their disposable plastic, shrink-wrapped tight for good measure. My blood heated. Idiocy.

I walked faster and rounded the corner, skipping the toy aisle. This section had lotions, potions, and powders, all in plastic bottles or tubes. A small bottle of sparkly blue nail polish read, 'Try Me.' I opened it, curious, and choked on the fumes. I twisted the top on and rubbed my nose to stop from sneezing.

Distracted, I turned the corner without thinking, trying to get the acrid taste of the nail polish out of my mouth. My breath escaped with a whimper as horror weakened my knees. A towering wall of neon-colored jugs stretched before me. The shelving loomed at least twenty feet high, and the aisle was seemingly endless. My eyes darted across the shelves; each crammed eight deep, the jugs lined up like soldiers.

"Oh, my Goddess," I gasped. These were the exact ones I'd seen floating at home, so carelessly and callously discarded, only these were shiny and so much brighter. I crept past them as if they could bite. I barely breathed, my voice hoarse as I whispered, "There are so many." My stomach rolled from the smell as sharp fragrances vied for my attention.

The kind shop assistant from before met me down the aisle. "Good!" she chirped, "You found it. Gosh, honey, you look a little shell-shocked. Not sure which to choose? We have them categorized. These have fresh flower smells like lavender, or apple flowers, or honeysuckle. This one here is pricier, but look what it has: rose, lychee, cedarwood, and white musk. Fancy, eh? These are citrus. Let's see, we have lemon, orange blossom, or grapefruit. Or this one is ginger mango. Or, ooh, I like this one—crisp linen with ylang ylang and bamboo. And this one over here smells like mountain rain."

My mind spun. What did bamboo smell like? Mountain rain? She droned on. "And those are for sports. They will overpower *any* funky sweat, guaranteed. Have you ever noticed how the stink clings to sportswear?"

I muttered without thinking, "Synthetic fibers trap bacteria. It reactivates with body heat, creating the smell. Natural fibers like wool or cotton won't stink."

"Ah! Well, learn something new every day." She lured me along the aisle, pointing and explaining. "These here have extra bleach plus a booster to get out invisible stains." I blinked at her. Invisible stains?

"These over here are on special. Two for one." She winked and whispered conspiratorially, "Can never have too much laundry soap." Her smile was too bright and forced. "What kind are you looking for, sweetheart?"

I ignored her question and gaped at the wall of jugs, my eyes scanning back and forth. My heart pounded as I imagined their future, weather-torn and deteriorating under the sun and the battering waves. My head swam. The massive space was suddenly too confined, and the artificial air was stifling.

A frazzled woman pushed past us with an enormous toy car containing two restless children. I stared at the next generation of plastic consumers. The girl chewed the foot of a female doll while the boy aimed at jugs with his pretend gun. The exhausted woman grabbed a jug, the one for invisible stains, and wordlessly plopped it on the boy's lap. He whined. The girl swatted him with her doll, and he broke into a shrilling noise. It sounded like a dolphin in pain.

My pearl pendant pressed hard into the notch in my throat, and I struggled to breathe past the sensation. The mother yelled at the boy to hush. He smacked his sister, and she started wailing, high-pitched and keening, remarkably similar to a distressed whale. The children unwittingly performed a two-part harmony of ocean distress, and my nervous system flew out of control.

I panicked. *Abort! Abort now!* But my brain overwhelmed my internal survival, showing me the consequences of human ignorance. It flooded my mind with abandoned fishing nets, heaving with bloated, dead bodies. Gentle giants reduced to bones from tenacious ropes trapping their jaws shut. Strangled sea life spun through my mind next to plastic bags, bottles, and six-pack rings. I choked for breath.

The music overhead tripped into a song telling me not to worry and be happy. The pearl snapped at my heartbeat, which rocketed higher and faster. I fell into my comfort zone. Anger. I bared my teeth and glared at the fortress of plastic. I fisted and released my hands, trying to shake off the rage. The harried mother glanced at me when I growled in my throat and put pep in her step, hurriedly pushing her squalling car.

The store assistant frowned. "You don't look so good. Are you okay? Can I get you some water, sugar?"

The music scraped against my nerves. The harsh fluorescent lights blurred my vision as the jugs shone brighter, as if backlit. The overpowering scents assaulted my nose, making me nauseous as flowers and lemons collided. "So much waste," I gritted through clenched teeth. "What is wrong with you people? Why do you use so much plastic?" Sweat prickled my skin, sliding past my ear.

Her kind face creased with concern. "Sweetie, it's no big deal. It's just plastic."

I bit on my cheek to startle myself and rein in my anger. It didn't work. I mimicked her in a deathly tone, pacing toward the jugs with tight fists, my nails cutting into flesh. "No big deal?" My voice strained, edging with panicked laughter. "No. Big. Deal?"

I bit down again, harder, and blood poured from my cheek, staining my teeth as I snarled, "You humans. You only think of yourselves. You are reckless and selfish, needing more and more and more."

My breath came in harsh pants, and my heart hammered my ribs. The pearl jerked on its chain, pulling hairs from my neck before it hovered and tugged away from me, straining toward the detergent. The lady's eyes bulged like she'd seen the devil, and she spun away so fast she stumbled. Running, she yelled for assistance on aisle six.

I glowered at the jugs and hissed like a feral cat. "It's just plastic?" My vision swam and tunneled to white, and a searing pain flared through my sternum. I couldn't catch my breath, couldn't see, couldn't… Something terrible was about to happen, and I was powerless to prevent it. The pearl had taken control. My fists were so tight they hurt.

The pearl yanked, jerking me to step forward. My heart thundered as the scream inside me built, the pressure in my body insurmountable. My arms lifted wide like a puppet, and my hands flew open. I threw my head back and *roared,* "This entire world is plastic!!!"

With a horrifying boom, the entire fortress of jugs detonated. Sharp fragments of plastic sliced through my skin, and noxious blue soap drenched me like a tidal wave, plastering my thin dress to my body. I swiped at my eyes, stunned at the volcanic destruction. I looked up at the flashing red light of a camera. People screamed. An alarm went off. I turned tail and fled, shrieking in my head for Nell.

TWO

JELLY

My emergency extrication was frenzied. I understood there would be consequences, but I expected a trial, or at least a chance to explain. It hadn't been me in control. But sour-faced guards met me at the surface, their faces disapproving as they ushered me down to the reef.

They threw me into the hole, a deep, black abyss submerged into the bottom of the ocean, the top covered with a cage of bones. No matter how hard I shook the bars, they remained firmly sealed with magic.

At first, I spewed profanities at my jailer, my fingers clinging to the bones as I screamed I needed to talk to the Trident to tell them what happened. Gorn, a fellow Warrior but no friend, smirked and stayed silent. After a time, tired of my slurs against his person, he spat, "You made a mess on the surface! Just another stupid mermaid! Now, shut up before I make you!"

I sank to the bottom of the hole. It was just wide enough for me to stretch out from head to tail. I lay on my back, my fin flicking with irritation. Three days. I could do three days. It was a vacation, a reprieve from my responsibilities. I closed my eyes.

A short time later, the Shaman yelled from above, "You don't understand! She can't be in there! I need to talk to her! Now, soldier!" With her urgent and panicked voice, she promised violence, but Gorn was a soldier who obeyed orders. Plus, he despised me. I'd beaten him every time we sparred, and this was his sweet retribution for his bruised flesh and ego.

He grunted, "No one sees the prisoner. Not even you, Shaman. Trident's orders."

She threatened him, cajoled him, and eventually pleaded to no avail. I was in trouble if the Shaman couldn't talk to me. She shouted in my direction, "Hold fast, Jelly!"

The next visitor, who came minutes or hours later, it was hard to tell in the pitch black, tried a different persuasion. Her familiar voice was soft and beguiling. I couldn't make out the words, but I was familiar with the tone.

I bellowed, "Mori, don't you dare!"

She yelled, "We're working on getting you out!"

I cradled my head in my hands and stared up at the bones. My stomach growled. When had I eaten last? The teardrop pendant at my throat purred, sending vibrations across my skin. I stroked my fingers over it, curious, remembering how it behaved in the store. It had never done that before.

I squealed as magic snapped through my blood, and the pearl jerked, rising from my throat like a bubble, just as it had before. My eyelids slammed shut, my hands pinned down, and my body froze. I struggled to move, to call for help, but I was paralyzed, locked in my mind.

At first, the image was fuzzy. It was a peaceful reef scene with scores of fish and corals going about their business, searching for food, and playing with friends. With no warning, I saw a blinding flash, followed by a fireball. The ocean boiled and turned to steam. A mushroom cloud bloomed like a curse. Recognition stalled my breath. I was seeing nuclear bombs.

Everything evaporated in the space of a heartbeat. With an ungodly roar, a shock wave rose to a hundred feet high. A column of water erupted into the sky, so tall it touched the clouds. Violent waves followed, moving from the center of the explosion to rip across the ocean, crushing sea creatures for miles.

The smoke cleared, and the ocean calmed, but poison replaced the salt. Sea eggs and larvae choked on it, mutating and changing forever. I sped through lifetimes of sea life. Unable to tolerate the toxins, they struggled with birth defects and strange diseases that ate them from the inside out. They wailed with terror and grief.

I joined their cries. My voice was the only thing that worked.

Over and over, on an endless loop, fireball after fireball screamed through my mind. I stopped counting at thirty-two, but they went on and on, each ravaging the ocean, shredding it further like wet tissues. When the visions ceased, my throat was raw, my mind blank and shattered. As I regained agency over my body, I vomited bile, sobbing until I couldn't draw breath. Drained, I curled into a ball.

Minutes later, the pearl hummed at my throat. I whispered, "Please, no. No more." The pearl did not listen, restarting the monstrous vision. The Shaman came again, pleading with tears for my release. She could hear my screams of anguish. By this point, the whole reef could.

Again, Gorn turned her away. Even Fillian, my off-and-on lover, couldn't interfere. The Shaman must have sent him, thinking he could convince Gorn to stand down. He and Gorn listened to my broken wails until my voice gave out into sobs.

Fillian asked, "Any chance you'll let me talk to her? This is beyond the normal. Something's wrong."

Gorn replied, "No. The Trident ordered complete isolation to make her reflect on her choices. I can't break it. Not even for you."

Fillian's voice was loud enough for me to overhear. "Well, she was always a little unstable." Gorn laughed and muttered something I couldn't catch. It was a knife to the heart. Fillian could have intervened. He was Gorn's superior officer and could have made a deal or bribed him. Instead, he mocked me and left me to suffer.

For three days and nights, my only companion was the pearl. It hummed and twitched as my soul bled from the torture of the ocean. I was half-crazed from the visions. Finally, it stopped and lay still and cold at my throat. I felt desolate and vulnerable, exhausted from all I had witnessed.

From nowhere, a deep, silky-smooth voice dripped and coated my mind. It was soothing and sensuous after the screams of the sea life. I flinched, on edge, as it cooed to me.

Hello, darling. I've been waiting for you to wake up. It's been almost seventy years. My, my, what a state you must be in. I can't stay long, but I'll come back soon. I promise.

Who was that? The voice was comforting, like a lover's croon, yet it held a sinister edge. The pearl weakly thrummed against my throat, as if alarmed, before falling still again. Depleted, I was too tired to give it much thought.

Gorn's voice came down from above. "Time's up." The bones of the cage groaned as it opened. Tucked in a ball with my arms wrapped around my head, my name echoed down the walls of my prison.

I lifted one finger and wiggled it, followed by a deep, broken sigh. It was the Shaman. She said, "Oh, Jelly. Can you swim up?" I pulled my hands from my ears and pumped my tail, dragging myself up by digging my fingers into the holes in the walls. She scowled above me. "This is barbaric! You should be ashamed!"

Gorn grunted, "Not my call." When I reached the top, I hovered and blinked in the light, noting Gorn's sneer. I wanted to punch his smug face, but I could barely breathe. The Shaman pulled me out, grunting under my dead weight. "I'll be seeing you, Warrior Jelly," Gorn sang in a syrupy voice. "It was wonderful listening to you scream."

The Shaman created a whirlpool to save me from swimming and shuttled me straight to my bedroom in our shared cave. I'd lived with the Shaman since the age of seven. She handed me a tonic, the liquid pink and tart like sour lime. "It will knock you out and let you rest." She pursed her lips. "Jelly, do you want to talk about it?" I remained mute. She persisted, "What did you see?" I curled in on myself when she scowled. "At some point, you'll have to tell me."

I croaked over my broken throat. "Later." She fussed, fluffed my sponge pillow, tucked the kelp blankets, and sat in the chair by my bed. I looked over and frowned. "You don't have to stay."

Her milky-blue eyes softened as she whispered, "Oh, but I do, Jelly, I do."

As my eyes drifted shut, she muttered about the curse of the pearl, but my world faded to black as the potion kicked in. I struggled to ask her what she meant. "Wha cur…?" My tongue fumbled and sleep consumed me.

I woke early, donned my armor, and left before the Shaman could interrogate me. Since the Trident hadn't summoned me, I assumed they deemed the hole was a suitable punishment. Mori and I finished a perimeter patrol and swam to our secret spot, hidden by an enormous cluster of orange fire corals. We'd played here when we were young and the corals were small. They knew us and retracted their venomous polyps to let us pass. Silence rang between us before Mori broke it.

"Do you want to talk about it?"

I involuntarily shivered. "Not really."

"I tried to see you. I even cozied up to Gorn." She made a gagging noise, attempting to lighten the mood. It didn't. "But then you shouted at me loud enough to burst my eardrums, so I left." I remained silent. She shrugged her shoulders. She made a sandcastle with her fingers before waving it away. "Well, okay, I'm here when you're ready."

I stared over her shoulder. This close to the bubble, I could see the trash outside. It wasn't always like this, or so I'd been told. Once, the water had been pristine, but over the past fifty years, it had clouded with swirls of pollution. The Mers survived, but at a heavy cost.

"Mori?" I asked. "Do you think the bubble is weaker?"

She nodded. "I do. Has the Shaman mentioned she's struggling to weave the donated magic?" All Mers except Warriors gave a hefty part of their magic to the shield. That's why Mori and I joined the force. We wanted whatever freedom we could grasp.

I frowned. "No. She hasn't. But it doesn't have the same snap it used to."

Mori tugged at her corrosion-resistant metal chest plate and grumbled about it being too tight, changing the subject. "The Shaman had this made to fit my boobs and all, but seriously, would it hurt to put some kind of stretch in it?"

I muttered, "That would require plastic. Stretchy fabrics like elastane or spandex are elastic polymers derived from petroleum."

She rolled her eyes. "You are a treasure trove of delight." I chuckled, and she grinned. She loved my walking-encyclopedia personality. She was one of the few who did.

Tugging off her chest plate, she wiggled her breasts with a sigh of relief. We shared her breakfast of coho salmon wrapped in dark green seaweed. Thoughtful, I swallowed and said, "This reminds me of the food up top. They call it sushi. Did you try it?"

She shook her head, shuddering from the reminder of her only mission to the surface. It hadn't gone well. We had dubbed the misadventure Garlickia. As soon as the human male put his hands on her throat, expecting to give her a thrill, he found himself flat on his back with her knife at his jugular. For a good twenty minutes, she scolded him, schooling him about consent, respect, and that any kinks needed to be discussed and agreed upon before sex began.

When she pressed the knife too hard, yelling about safe words, the man peed himself and passed out from fright. Unfortunately, he'd eaten garlic, and the pungency escaped his skin, mingled with the oily scent of terror and urine.

She'd immediately contacted Hannah, the dolphin who guided mermaids on their missions, calling for extrication. She could have stayed and tried again with another man, but she abandoned her task, saying she didn't have time to educate idiot males. Every mermaid worth her salt knew to avoid foods that came through the skin.

I continued, "Besides fish, it has some sticky white stuff called rice. If you ever try sushi, watch out for the green spicy blob they serve with it. I ate the whole thing, not knowing better, and my eyes didn't stop watering for an hour. It gave me the same burning feeling as when a sailfish drags you and water shoots up your nose."

Mori laughed, "I'll keep that in mind." She took my offering of small, oily surf smelt for dessert. "What are you doing today?"

I replied with a frown, "Teaching the turtles to differentiate between jellyfish and plastic bags."

"That's depressing," Mori commented, "But your entire job is depressing. Every day, there's a fresh horror coming from the humans." She tipped her head. "But there's good stuff too. Don't forget that." I harrumphed.

My education had been self-directed, overseen by the Shaman, as One Reef University didn't offer my subject. I studied ocean environmentalism. It was a fruitless obsession. Magic couldn't stop the pollution, and the ocean and its creatures were dying. They could never relax and just be.

She crunched down on a surf smelt, and said, "I'm finishing my thesis on the ethics of the Surfecti, using their magic to influence human behavior. The humans desperately need guidance. The Surfecti could do it. I find their inaction maddening."

I said, "I thought the Surfecti lost part of their magic if they interfered. Maybe that's why they don't get involved."

She admitted, "That's true, and I can appreciate that, but they could donate a little to the cause." She spun toward me, anger flashing in her hazel eyes. "Seriously, humanity can do it. They just need a push."

She and I differed in our perspective on humans. She believed they were salvageable. I was certain of their doom. I licked my fingers and hesitated. "Does that mean you'll go back up? Nell knows Surfecti. She'd introduce you."

Mori's freckles overlapped as she scrunched up her nose and stuck out her tongue. "I'm not over Garlickia yet." She looked at the angle of the sunlight hitting the cave wall and changed the subject. "Don't forget to double your face cloth. Some pieces got through mine last time, and it was horrible. I could taste it for days."

I nodded, letting a silence fall between us. She hedged, "Have you met with the Trident yet?"

The Mers had initially had a queen regnant. After she died with no heir, the Mers formed the Trident. Only two of the seven liked me. They provided my only means to go to the surface, and so far, I had them fooled, but I'd never touched a human's skin with loving hands, preferring to graze my fingers on paper.

I answered Mori. "No, not yet." I scratched my head. "I'd like to see the video of the explosion. My memory is fuzzy, like I blacked out. I remember coming out of a trance and being covered in soap." Spinning the pearl in my fingers, I looked at Mori from under my eyelashes. "I think the pearl did something."

"The pearl? How do you mean?"

I chewed on my lip, trying to figure out how to phrase it. "It's like it had a mind of its own. It took over. I was angry at the laundry jugs, but blowing it all up? I've never done that before. My skills are water manipulation and glamor, not explosions."

"Nell says you glamored yourself so well you disappeared."

I kicked at the sand with my turquoise tailfin. "Really? See! I've never done that before either!"

Mori chewed on her thumbnail. "Try it now. See if you can go invisible." I shrugged and concentrated, imagining myself as nothing. She laughed and said, "I can still see you. You're a big blue blur, but you're still there. Maybe it was the pearl. Maybe it juices your magic."

I muttered, "Yeah, it does more than that." The words hovered on my lips. I wanted to tell her that the pearl had shown me the endless nuclear bombings. But I didn't. She didn't need my nightmares in her psyche.

I looked at the sun filtering through the microplastics. "I have to go. The turtles will be waiting." I tapped my temple. "Call me later."

THREE

JELLY

I pressed through the bubble, the magic snapping against my skin. I hovered in the protection zone, a secondary area for Warriors to prepare for the outside. It wasn't as robust as the central bubble, only a few feet deep, but it shielded us from the larger pieces of plastic and abandoned nets.

I wrapped a thick cloth around my mouth and ears twice, securing it inside the high neck of my armor, and pulled down my goggles, my only concession regarding plastic. It made me feel like a hypocrite, but the Shaman insisted we use them after a straw blinded a Warrior.

I left the zone and swirling bits of plastic engulfed me. I shuddered, remembering the snow globe from the store. Few humans saw how bad it was, either unable or unwilling to visit the Patch in person.

I swam through the garbage to meet a bale of Leatherback sea turtles at the request of their matriarch, Juniper. She'd just lost another teenager, Sola, to a plastic bag. It lodged in her digestive system and she'd stopped eating. Juniper turned sorrowful eyes to me as I approached the group.

I greeted her and the boisterous crowd of youngsters. "Good morning, everyone! Who's excited to learn?" Turtles were gelatinivores and favored lion manes and moon jellyfish. The lion manes were easier to spot, as they had showy, trailing tentacles. Moon jellies were far trickier. They had hundreds of short, delicate tentacles lining the margins of their round bodies, looking far too similar to the plastic bags. The problem was that turtles swallowed dozens of jellyfish in one feeding, so knowing the difference between food and plastic was a critical skill.

I said, "Before we start, I want you all to thank our volunteers." The jellyfish were old, near the end of their lives, and volitionally sacrificed themselves for our lesson. Sea creatures accepted they were part of the cycle of life, either hunter or hunted, and these older jellyfish offered to teach the baby turtles how to survive. Dutifully, the turtles called out their appreciation.

The jellyfish hovered beside plastic bags on the surface. I did a show-and-tell, pointing out how to tell them apart. One of the youngest dashed for the easy snack, and shock lit her face when I pushed her back into position with a gentle whirlpool, softly scolding, "Phoebe, they're here to help us. You can't eat them. Not yet, anyway." Phoebe rolled her dark brown eyes before grinning at me.

"Okay, dive deeper while I set up the ultimate test," I said, my voice muffled through the cloth. To confuse the young turtles, I placed discarded balloons next to the jellyfish, bunching the long strings to mimic tentacles. I met the turtles further down. Juniper laughed when a sweet turtle named Lily scowled at me, accusing me of playing dirty with the balloons.

Soon, thankfully, every juvenile turtle could spot the differences. I told them, "Remember, look before you swallow."

As they rushed toward their sacrificial breakfast, I turned to Juniper. "Any boys yet?"

For turtles, gender was determined after fertilization. The temperature of the developing eggs decided whether the offspring would be male or female. If the sand temperature rose to eighty-eight degrees or higher, all the hatchlings would be female. Juniper shook her head. "No. I'm not sure what to do. We've tried digging deeper to get to the cooler sand, but it's too hard for the children to climb out and get to the sea."

Worry creased her face, and her amber eyes shadowed with grief. "If it gets much hotter, I'm not sure the eggs will even survive." I thought of Simmi in Mexico and hoped the climate cooperated to give us males. We needed them. With a sad and resigned smile, she said, "Thank you, Jelly, for teaching my girls today. It seems futile, but we appreciate all you do for us."

As Juniper swam away, I returned to the bubble to catch up on my research at the library. I only had part of what I'd planned to bring back. Nell burned the information onto algae paper and gave me what she'd completed on the boat. She'd been doing it leisurely, thinking she had two more weeks to process the studies. Luckily, Synchi had been at the gate on my arrival, and I'd thrust the papers at her for safekeeping.

I read until my eyes crossed, trying to make sense of the mess up top. Some humans pillaged the planet, while others battled to defend it. The problem was that the pillagers had money and resources. Mori was right. If the Surfecti didn't get involved, the planet would collapse. Maybe I could meet the Surfecti and inspire them. I chewed on my lip. After the explosion, the Trident would probably ban me from the surface for life. I'd be stuck here watching the ocean worsen, helpless to do anything about it.

As if she were psychic, Mori's voice sang through my head.

Fancy a puff tonight? Neither of us has to work tomorrow. My adviser liked my thesis, and I'm celebrating.

I replied *I'll meet you at The Dive at nine.*

For once, I arrived before her. The massive bouncer at the entrance straightened as we approached. When we reached him, he bowed at the waist respectfully. "Warriors," he said in a deep voice, opening the stone door with a flourish.

The interior of The Dive was vast and dim, lit by muted glowworms. Tightly pressed schools of male Tosanoide fish swam together and flashed their bright pink bodies, pulsing to the music like traveling disco balls. There were nooks everywhere, with many occupied tables. We swam through the crowd, ignoring the stares from the Mers who didn't think mermaids should be fighters. We settled at a table overlooking the dance floor.

The server came to our table. "What can I get for you tonight?"

Mori said, "We'll start with four tetras, please."

"Four?" My eyebrow arched.

"Yes, four. You need it after three days locked in the hole, and I am celebrating. If I want to make a difference, I'll need to go back up." She dropped her voice. "I want to find some sympathetic Surfecti. I figure I can do what you do. Go up and pretend to be seducing men." She tapped her fingers on her lips. "Although…I could have a little fun if I find the right guy." She winked at me. "Ideally, someone allergic to garlic."

We leaned on our elbows to watch the band play. The bassist pulled on strands of seaweed attached to an enormous clamshell, the deep sounds humming through the water. A handsome merman slapped his hands on drums, fish skin stretched taut across a frame. He smiled at a mermaid, who tapped together shells on her fingers and shook bells on her tail while she sang. Another mermaid joined her, blowing into a hollow shell for harmony.

"They're good tonight," I commented. "Wait, he's new. What happened to Clyde? This guy is much faster." She followed my pointed finger, and we watched a sexy, long-haired merman swim at a frenzied pace, knocking his mallets against the teeth of a long-dead whale. The whale's jaw was enormous, and the merman's speed showed his impressive skill.

"Clyde was…retired. That one's a fresh addition to the band," she said with a sly smile. "His name is Joshua."

"Mori? What aren't you telling me?"

She grinned. "I met him two nights ago. He works at the armory. I was trying to get my chest plate altered, and when he started clinking his tools on the counter, I told him to call Dani for a side gig. She met him, he played for her, and she replaced Clyde, who, let's be honest, wasn't very good."

"Here you go, Warriors. Four tetras," called out our waitress, setting down a plate with four fat, round fish. Mori clapped her hands together and lifted one of the pufferfish. I joined her, careful to avoid the spikes, and we tapped them together before squeezing with light fingers, shooting the neon green liquid into our mouths. Relieved of their toxins, the pufferfish swam to the bar to refill.

The sedative effects acted quickly, smoothing out our psyches. Mori slumped, her face slack. "I needed that. Now, Jelly, I'm your best friend."

I interrupted her with a snort. "Mori, you're my only friend."

"That's not true! There's me and…and…" She rolled her eyes and waved her hand through the water. "Whatever. Tell me what happened in the hole. I overheard the Shaman and Toto talking about your screaming, but they clammed up when I came in."

The pufferfish loosened my reluctant tongue. I leaned in closer, dropping my voice. "Okay, but it's awful. Remember how we learned about the nuclear testing at the Bikini Atoll?" She nodded. "I saw them, Mori. Every single bomb, one right after another. By the end, they were blowing up sand. The effects on the fish were devastating."

I leaned closer. "It went on for three days. I thought I was going to lose my mind." I picked up my pearl and held it out. "This. I'm sure the pearl caused it. It started with the explosion in the store, then the visions. Something is wrong with the pearl."

Mori whispered, "It wouldn't be the first time. The Surfecti have all kinds of amulets and talismans that act as conduits for powerful magic. But why now?"

I shook my head. "I have no idea."

"Have you asked the Shaman?"

"No. I wanted to tell you first."

She held up the second pufferfish. "You should have told me earlier. You shouldn't keep that stuff bottled up. I appreciate you don't like to be the bearer of bad news. But keeping it inside is not healthy."

"No one's interested, Mori."

"Not true. I am. I'll always listen, no matter how grim the facts are."

"You're the only one." A pang of resentment shot through me. I was so ostracized, alone in my knowledge. Of all the Mers on the reef, only Mori, her father, and the Shaman understood my plastic obsession. None of the other Mers realized how awful it was outside the bubble except the Warriors, and they didn't care, always telling me to stop with my depressing facts.

Mori said, "Well, here's to the pearl being quiet from hereon." We swallowed our second puffers and sent the fish on their way. We stared at the dancers below. "So," she started, her voice cagey, "Want me to change the subject?"

"Please," I replied.

She looked at me with excited eyes. "Lady Salmy is throwing a ball next week."

I looked at her through squinted eyes. "And why should I care?"

She shrugged. "You should come."

"No one invited me."

Emboldened by puffers, she said, "Everyone's going. Come with me. Come as my date."

I cocked my head toward the band. "You'd have a lot more fun with Joshua."

I'd rather get a tooth pulled by a shaky-clawed lobster than go to a ball at Lady Salmy's. Or a ball anywhere, for that matter. I understood the Mers needed distractions. After the bubble took its share, they used up what magic they had left on lavish parties. But I couldn't pretend the world wasn't falling apart around us and be frivolous.

Mori grabbed my hand, "Maybe you're right," she giggled, "Let's get closer." She couldn't take her eyes off Joshua's tight back and arms and the powerful thrust of his tail. She danced behind him, throwing a coquettish smile whenever he glanced over his shoulder. As the night progressed, the crowd grew rowdy, and when Mori ordered more puffers, I bowed out, hugging her and leaving her to flirt with the musician.

Outside The Dive, the line stretched long, mermaids and mermen waiting to enter. Still a bit inebriated, and knowing sleep would elude me, I swam to the eastern side of the bubble. I hadn't been this way in ages. Still in my armor, I wrapped up my face and pushed through the bubble.

It didn't take long to find an old net. It was fortunately

empty, as I didn't have the stomach to discover a body tonight. I took out my knife, a standard-issue switchblade, and began cutting and slicing through the strands, cursing the nylon for its durability. I secured the remnants in the back of an abandoned cave and rolled a rock across the entrance. My fingertips were raw from working the netting, and I hissed as I rubbed them over my cheeks. Judging by the light that pierced the water, the sun was rising. Perfect. My favorite spot at the library would be free, and I could finish last night's reading.

I swam back toward the bubble, almost reaching it, when a school of Pacific Lingcod swarmed me. They surrounded me, pulling back their lips and snarling. Puzzled by their behavior, and groggy from the lack of sleep, I stopped short in the water. The pearl pulsed twice, as if warning me.

The fish leered, each baring five hundred pointy daggers in multiple rows, perfect for latching onto prey and shredding it. They looked at me strangely, as if they couldn't focus. Something was wrong with their eyes. I turned in a circle, looking for the leader. "Do you need help with something?"

I received no reply and no warning as they viciously attacked. Half the school went for my tail, gouging out chunks of flesh, some hanging on and ripping. Despite chain-mail protecting my lower half, their multiple teeth dug through the gaps and inflicted considerable damage. I thrashed my tail at them, punting several of them away, but they turned and came right back. I yelled, "What the hell?"

The other half attacked my neck and chest. My chest plate protected my torso, but not my arms or the top column of my neck. I twisted away and shouted, "What are you doing?" but no one answered.

Teeth, so many teeth, snapped and tore at my body, and my blood bloomed in the surrounding water. A pulse in the hollow of my throat made me worry they would hit my jugular. I created a turbulent whirlpool, stronger and faster than I'd ever been able to manage before, and sucked them into it, their teeth shredding as I pulled them away from my skin. "Sorry guys," I muttered, "but you asked for it."

I shot the whirlpool away with unprecedented force, and the fish turned on each other in their frenzy. Shaken, I checked myself over for injuries. The shallow wounds were closing, but regrowing my damaged tail would require time. I was grateful for the bitter healing tonic the Shaman made the Warriors regularly take.

I stroked my neck, relieved I didn't find more damage. With a quick glance over my shoulder, I saw the school in the distance, regathering and charging for the bubble. If maliciously inclined, they would bounce off it, as the Shaman had woven that into her magic.

I hovered in the protection zone only long enough to shake off the tiny plastic particles that clung to my tail and hair before pressing through the bubble. The fish gnashed and snarled, throwing themselves toward me. They hit the shield so hard they knocked themselves unconscious, and soon, all those teeth lay in slack jaws as they floated away, stunned.

This was not normal fish behavior. Something was amiss. I had no idea what was wrong with them. Sure, the odd creature might try to take a nibble, but not like this. I stretched my tail cautiously and winced as my injuries pulled, releasing a small cloud of blood. The lingcod had been savage.

My tail ached as I took the back streets to Warrior Headquarters. I needed to file a report on the confrontation. Mori's father, Lord Tro, commanded the Warriors and served on the Trident, and he always started the work day early.

I nodded to the guards on duty and blew out an impatient

bubble as they ignored me. Typical. They resented me for a few reasons. One, I was female; two, I had potent magic; and three, I'd kicked their tails in training at some point. Thanks to my work with Mew, I had moves and tricks that no Mers warrior had seen. I knocked on the Commander's door, sucking in a breath as a bite on my shoulder pulled taut. His deep rumble vibrated through the water. "Come in."

Entering, I thumped my fist to my chest and bowed, wincing from the effort. With concern in his wide eyes, he swam around his desk and reached out to touch me before pulling back from the wounds on my arms. He exclaimed, "What in the oceans happened to you?"

He rushed to close the door before turning back to me with alarm. I sagged onto a stool. "Morning, Tro. I want to say it's good, but obviously, it isn't." In private, I called him Tro, unwilling to refer to him as Toto, Mori's pet name for him. He'd offered me the same intimacy, but it seemed a step too far despite knowing him all my life. He and my father had been inseparable, the closest of friends at work and play.

My eyes drifted over the familiar space, having played in here with Mori as a girl. The array of weapons had fascinated us, especially the impressive swordfish bills, with sturdy seaweed wrapped around the ends for handles. The swords on display were ten feet long. We pleaded to touch them, but Tro insisted we become Warriors first, his face and voice stern.

I hissed through my teeth as I pulled off my sword, whittled and shaped to suit my size, and set it next to me. Tro floated in front of me, crossing his arms. "What did this?"

"Lingcod. They came out of nowhere and wouldn't answer when I asked what was wrong. They just attacked."

"Where did this happen?"

"Near the East Gate. I was coming back from cutting up

nets. I've never seen anything like it, Tro. It's like they were…" I shrugged, wincing as a larger wound stretched, "possessed or something. It was bizarre." He swam to a large stone cabinet and took out a box. I recognized the dark vial he passed me and scowled. It tasted awful. I shook my head, "No, I'm fine, Tro. I'll heal."

He frowned and shook his head right back. He used his Dad voice. "Drink it, Jelly." With a shudder, I downed the pungent healing tonic and shivered as my wounds sealed up, grimacing at the taste of rotten fish lingering on my tongue. We watched my turquoise tail fill in the holes and gouges left by the lingcod, and he nodded with satisfaction. "Did anyone see you like this?"

"Just the guards at the door. I took the back streets."

"Good. We don't want to panic the public. I'll have to report this to the Trident." He looked at me in a fatherly manner, his face softening. "Be careful, Jelly."

I crossed my arms and said, "I am, Tro."

He ran a hand through his shoulder-length red hair. He frowned. "Jelly? Are you really okay? Gorn reported you screamed about melting faces and dead fish while in the hole."

"I'm fine, Tro. Please…I'd like to put it behind me." I wasn't willing to share, and he knew better than to push.

"They outvoted me," he stated without emotion. "When we found out you'd blown up the store, I voted for listening to your version first, but the majority decided to send you straight to solitary."

I scoffed, "What a surprise. I'm fine, honestly. It wasn't anything I can't handle."

He gave me a long look. "Avoid doing anything that would put you back in there. I mean it, Jelly. I don't hold the sway I used to."

My brow wrinkled. "Understood." Disheartened, I strapped on my sword and swam to the library.

FOUR

JELLY

I sat in my favorite spot and flipped over the algae paper, studying the human male infertility crisis. If they had problems, we had problems. Some scientists blamed it on decreased physical activity. Others pointed fingers at the unnatural things they ate. I was investigating endocrine-disrupting chemicals, such as those in plastics and pesticides.

My scowl deepened as a shrill feminine voice from the adjacent table sneered. "Uh, oh, Jelly's got company. And he's in his official uniform, so she must be in trouble…again." Nasty giggles broke out. "You'd think the hole would have taught her a lesson."

A second mermaid mocked, "I wonder what she did. Did she scare someone to death with her facts?"

Another voice, furtive. "He's so hot. I can't understand what he sees in her."

I peeked over my shoulder at the merman heading toward me, resplendent in his armor. He nodded to me, and I bristled at the interruption, knowing I would lose my coveted space near the cavernous hole that allowed me to watch the street. I shuffled my papers together dramatically and glanced outside. The sun had spilled over, showing it was later than I thought.

The approaching guard was Fillian. He was the last Mers I wanted to see. We were currently on the rocks. After seven years together, we still hadn't found a smooth path forward. He was desperate for a family, and I… wasn't.

He had a square face with a broad jaw. His energy carried an intensity that promised retribution if crossed. He wasn't particularly handsome. He wasn't ugly, but he wasn't special. His chief attraction was that he tolerated me. I looked at the set line of his lips, turning down at the edges. It told me he was irritable and itching for a fight. Great.

He announced, "The Trident wants you." He scanned the space and dropped his voice to one that was low and urgent, his green eyes lit with barely repressed anger. "You've been avoiding me since the hole. Why didn't you come to me after getting out? I could have helped you."

I stared at him with obvious displeasure as I rose from my seat. He gripped my upper arm as I turned away from him, and I gasped as he squeezed over a lingering bruise from the lingcod. Healing potion was good, but not miraculous. I yanked away my arm and crossed it in front of my chest, inclining my head to draw him away from the eavesdropping ears around us. We hovered in a small alcove for privacy, his thick back providing a wall from curious eyes.

I snapped, "You have a lot of nerve. I heard what you said to Gorn."

He ran his fingers through his dark green hair, pulling at the roots in frustration. "Jelly, that was for show. I didn't mean it."

I snorted. "Hell of an apology. Thanks for that."

He sighed and switched subjects. "Did you get pregnant at

least? Before you blew everything up? All your problems with the Trident would disappear if you had a merbabe."

My jaw dropped open. I seethed, "Really? No, hey Jelly, are you feeling okay after being in the hole, after you exploded the surface? Or, maybe, hey Jelly, someone told me you screamed until you were hoarse, and I'm worried? Seriously, Fillian? You're jumping straight to babies? Thank you *so much* for your concern. I'm touched."

He ignored me, barreling on. "If the Trident wants to see you, maybe they're sending you on another mission. You've been up so often; surely you've found a good specimen by now, or at least filtered out the duds." I turned away from his rugged face, but he grabbed my chin to spin me back. "Make sure he's young. Less chance of polluted sperm." He choked on the words, "And pick a virile one. More action means more chance of conception."

A muscle in my face ticked as I ground my teeth together. I clenched my fists so I wouldn't slap him. Once again, advice from a merman on how to use my body. I hadn't trusted Fillian with the truth. I'd never even kissed a human.

My fists settled on my hips. "Be honest. You would be happy if a human impregnated me? You so often like to claim that half-Mers babes have diluted and inferior magic."

He shrugged. "We've tried on our own. Something's wrong with me."

I kept my mouth shut, not correcting him. He wasn't aware that the Shaman had given me a magical contraception to prevent pregnancy, offering it at my ripening. Everyone assumed mermaids yearned for a family, and if we didn't yearn, we performed our duty. The Shaman had given me an out, and I snatched it.

He clenched his jaw. "Jelly, you're the strongest mermaid

on the reef. You're a Warrior. Your merbabes would be formidable." He lifted a tentative hand and stroked my hair. "Find a human with blue eyes. That way, your coloring will dominate."

I pulled my head back. "Stop looking at me like that."

He leaned closer, his lips near mine, tempting me to give in to his charm as I had so many times before. "Like what?"

With an impatient tail flick, I pushed away, scowling as my deepest injury yanked. "Like I'm a tool. I'm more than that. And what about their lives, their future? What's the point of having babies if we leave them to suffer in a swirl of trash?"

He lost his composure and snapped, "Few purebloods are being born anymore, and the mother's strength determines the merbabe's value. As Trident members die off, someone will replace them. And having children elevates your societal position and will increase my chance of getting a seat. But I have to get there first! Why can't you see that? Why don't you understand what I need?"

I recoiled. He quickly tempered himself, shifting his face into a beguiling mask. He flirted and stroked his tail-fin against mine. Shocked, I pushed him away. "So, that's it. You want power." I spun away and gave him my back, biting on my cheek to calm my racing pulse. "All this time. I thought you respected me. I'm just an incubator to you."

He swam to face me again, apologetic. I shook my head, my long blue hair swirling from the motion. He reached for me with hands I'd once loved, and I slapped them away. I growled, "No. I'm a little unstable, remember? Screw you, Fillian. We're done. It's over. Find another mermaid to make your power babies for you."

"Just think about it, Jelly," he pleaded.

I shook my head, tightening my grip on my crossed arms

as if shielding my heart. "No. There's nothing to think about. You've made yourself clear. You want me to stay home, be a good little mermaid, and ignore everything that matters to me."

"I never said that," he replied, his face getting red.

"You didn't need to."

The Shaman's sharp voice cut through my mind. *Jelly, where are you? Fillian left here ages ago. The Chairfish is getting impatient.*

I muttered, "I have to go. The Trident is waiting. Don't follow me, Fillian."

I pushed past him with a shove and glanced over my shoulder as I left the library. His green tail agitated the water, and his face twisted in discontent. He'd lost me for good. I floundered between hurt and anger, furious that I'd wasted so much time with him. I turned down the main street of the reef, putting speed in my swim as he'd stalled my departure, and the Trident hated tardiness.

It was market day, and stalls crammed the primary thoroughfare. Merchants sold shell combs and jewelry, decorative shawls spun from the finest and softest algae, and home items, such as stone and shell furniture, various sponges, and kitchen knives. One merman shouted, "Pufferfish! Get your pufferfish!" Two pretty mermaids worked the stall, hawking the only legal sedative on the reef.

The sentries at the purple sea fan gate verified my credentials, gaining an eye roll from me, and allowed me to pass. As always, my breath escaped as I entered the Grand Hall, the high ceilings lit by dozens of lanternfish, who brightened at my presence and guided me through. I called out a greeting, and they flickered in response.

Kelp and seaweed banners of the Trident Families swayed in the current, Tro's words echoing in my mind. Few of the

Trident were my allies. I cruised through a circular gateway and entered the Trident's official area. Large openings in the cave walls allowed a view of the greater reef outside, but magic protected them to keep prying ears and eyes away from the Trident's business. Once, after submitting a contentious report, I hovered outside to spy on their discussion, and found myself painfully zapped when I came too close.

In the center of the room was a circular stone table, surrounded by stools with backs, providing comfort for the long sessions spent ruling the Mers. The assembled gathering was smaller than I expected, and I sagged with relief. I bowed to Lady Amphi, then Tro, who kept his face stoic, and to the Shaman, who shot me a dark look.

My shoulders relaxed. Lady Amphi had been the queen's right-hand Mers, and when the Trident formed, she assumed the role of Chairfish. She kept the ethos the queen had embraced, but had no power to determine who else sat at the table. The most influential families on the reef had muscled their seats. Lord Tro nodded to me. "Jelly, this is a private meeting. Keep our conversation here confidential. Understood?"

"Yes, sir."

He nodded to Lady Amphi and said, "A strange occurrence happened outside the bubble this morning. I consulted Shaman Synchiropus Splendidus to ask if someone had breached her protection. My question alarmed her and she insisted she attend this meeting. I wanted to bring it to your attention first. Jelly, tell us."

"I was returning from a perusal of the eastern waters when a school of lingcod attacked me. They were vicious and unrelenting. They slammed against the bubble until they passed out, trying to get at me."

The Shaman cocked her head, making her sleek bob of

black hair swirl from the motion. Her youthful face looked bewildered as she lilted, "But the fish adore you."

I nodded, "They do. That's why I reported it to Lord Tro. It was completely out of character. When I confronted them, their eyes were…dead, like they couldn't focus. None of them replied when I asked what was wrong. I had to suck them into a whirlpool to get them off of me."

Lady Amphi turned to the Shaman with concern. "Is there something wrong with the bubble?"

The Shaman scoffed lightly at the insinuation. "Of course not. This happened outside of my magic."

I cleared my throat. "But only just. They approached me right before I entered the safety zone. Like I said, it's as though they were dead inside."

Tro asked, "Do you think they were trying to attach to you and enter the bubble?"

I frowned. "I'm not sure, sir, but it was unnerving."

The Chairfish drew a deep breath and nodded to us, dismissing us. "Thank you, Jelly, Shaman. That will be all."

We bowed to them and swam for the doors. The Shaman hissed, "Did you not think it important to tell me? Give me a little heads up?"

I whispered, my voice tart, "I haven't been home. When would I have had the chance?"

She scowled and urged me into one of her whirlpools, cutting down our swim time. We approached the door to our cave, and she waved her hand through the water to release the lock. She spoke with a measured voice. "Jelly, you should have informed me about the attack. You still haven't talked about what happened in the hole. Tro gave me the report. Don't think I haven't noticed you've been avoiding me."

"I said I wasn't ready to discuss it, Synchi."

"Well," she huffed, "you are now. In."

FIVE

JELLY

As the sun faded for the day, glowworms lit up our cave, casting a soft light across the walls containing rows and rows of shelves, heaving with amulets, bottles of potions, shells, and live creatures the Shaman kept for her magic. I checked on the shelf of oysters, busy creating magical pearls.

The oysters would coat an irritant with nacre, the same material as their shells. Synchi would fuss over them, ensure they had the best phytoplankton to eat, and keep the surrounding water at the perfect temperature. It took a year for each animal to create a pearl, and when it was ready, to Synchi's precise specifications, the oyster would release it. Synchi would swallow the pearl to get an influx of magic, helping her manipulate the matrix that held the bubble together.

I waved my hand, frowning at the water surrounding them. It wasn't as cool as it should be, and the oysters would struggle. Synchi hovered next to me as I whispered. "Synchi, you're spending energy manipulating the temperature, even here in the cave. The ocean is getting too hot and too acidic." I chewed on my lip. "It's getting harder for you to keep the shield up. I can sense it when I go through it."

Synchi tested the water and frowned. "Our magic is getting weaker."

Eight arms interrupted my sour thoughts by wrapping around my torso, greedy suction cups kissing my skin. His jet propulsion was so swift that I didn't see him coming until he latched onto me. I laughed, "Oof, Oggie, easy boy!"

The young octopus chittered and loosened three arms, reaching to stroke the Shaman's smooth face. His suckers stuck on her cheek, and she petted his head with affection as she stared at her oysters. Oggie followed her stare with yearning eyes, but a sharp glance from me made him blink. If he had his way, he would snarf them all.

I told him, "We'll go find you some crabs and clams later, okay?" He squeaked with excitement. I'd found Oggie as a baby, helplessly tangled in rope and netting. When I freed him, expecting him to swim away, he curled around my neck with tentative tiny arms and sucked on my earlobe. Of course, I brought him home.

He was a Giant Pacific octopus, his skin a reddish pink. Once fully grown, his largest suckers would be two and a half inches in diameter, able to support thirty-five pounds each. The largest octopus I knew was a beast, probably weighing two hundred pounds, with an arm span of twenty feet. Considering how well we fed Oggie, there was every chance he'd become enormous.

That was tomorrow's problem, and I didn't believe in borrowing them early.

He still hadn't spoken, too traumatized, and we hadn't pushed. Oggie had the freedom to leave, but he stayed. He settled on my head like a hat, using his chromatophores, pigment-containing cells, to change his body blue to match my hair. Considering he was color blind, he was remarkably accurate and made my head look misshapen, with his long arms dangling down.

I turned to Synchi with a grin. "Look, I have locs like you."

Synchi snorted before groaning, "Speaking of which, this glamor is cutting off my circulation." The water shimmered as she dropped her magic. She reached behind and rammed her knuckles into her lower back, stretching with a sigh. She was in her natural face and body when she straightened, older than sand.

Her pristine white tail took on a softer hue, the scales dull and worn. The tidy black bob became a thick jungle of white, matted locs, shells strung throughout. Wrinkles lined her face, while her dark skin hung over loose muscles. She pulled on the long, white braid from her chin, tapping her nail on the shell on the end.

I smiled at her relief from releasing the glamor. In the past, when I'd asked why she bothered with it, she'd replied that looking youthful made others more comfortable. I thought it was ridiculous, but it wasn't my body.

I plucked a minnow from the school swimming in the cave, offering themselves as snacks. My teeth crunched down on delicate bones, and I smacked my lips with the salty taste. Feeding a minnow to Oggie, I hoped he wouldn't get fish guts in my hair. I flopped onto the chaise; the sponge giving a puff, which the minnows devoured. Oggie, disturbed from his perch atop my head, swam off to his sleeping hole.

I pulled at my pearl pendant, sliding it back and forth across the chain. The unique pearl was irregular, not round, meaning it had formed in the animal's muscle, squeezed and molded by pressure. Mine resembled a teardrop, and given its black color, a *Pinctada margaritifera*, or Black-Lipped Pearl Oyster, had likely created it.

I could sense her staring holes into my skin. There was no avoiding this conversation. I lifted my eyes to the Shaman. "The pearl pulsed during the lingcod attack. I thought my heart was in a panic, but now, I think it was the pearl. I was too busy getting the fish off me to question it."

Synchi scooted my tail off the chaise so she could sit next to me. Her milky-blue eyes scanned mine. "And when you blew up the store? Did you sense it then?"

In my mind, I returned to the scene, reliving the raw, bubbling rage, and rubbed a hand against my sternum. I said, "My only warning was a burning sensation in my chest. I couldn't breathe." She watched me with sharp eyes. "The pearl lifted, pulling on the chain, straining to get to the soap. It tugged so hard I had to take a step or lose my head. I thought the chain would slice through my neck."

She sagged, her spine curling forward as though the weight of the ocean rested on her shoulders. She sounded haunted. "The report said you were having terrors while in the hole."

I bit my lower lip, my skin turning cold. I whispered, "I saw the bombs. All of them. I'd get about five minutes of peace, and it would start again. Why would I see that?" My eyes filled with tears.

She took my hands; her gnarled knuckles firm as she squeezed. "Those were the pearl's memories. I believe you activated the pearl. While plastic is only one of many threats, it is the one you blame for your mother's death. When you were in the store and faced with it… You saw how blithely the humans treat it. It brought out your trauma. If I am correct, seeing the plastic woke up the pearl."

"Woke it up?" My teeth played over my lip. "How do I turn it off again?"

Synchi croaked, half laugh, half groan. "That is beyond my understanding."

I bit too hard and jolted. "Has this happened before? Have you seen it become active?"

"Twice. In my time alive, the pearl first woke during the Industrial Revolution. Sea levels rose, upsetting the tides and the stability of the sea life. We suffered from awful ocean noise from motorized ships. We went further away from the humans to escape the clamor and also to avoid discovery. As they explored the oceans, we were at risk."

She let go of my hands. "It woke again during the height of the whaling industry, or so we thought. Humans had steamships with gun-loaded harpoons, and they decimated the population. The Surfecti stepped in and influenced the humans, prompting them to form the International Whaling Commission. I thought the pearl would settle again. I was wrong."

She pulled on her braid thoughtfully. "I now believe the pearl activated too early for us to understand the bigger threat. At the same time the IWO formed in 1946, the humans performed the first underwater nuclear testing. The bearer of the pearl, your grandmother, begged me for help. Most Mers believe I created the bubble to protect us from plastic. But I first made it to save us from radioactive poisoning."

"My Grandmother?" I remembered my mother speaking of her in a reverent tone, telling me she'd saved the Mers from annihilation. I'd sat on Mama's lap, dragging the pearl across her chain, comforted by the sound and action.

Synchi nodded with a sad smile. "She was a dear friend and an incredibly brave mermaid. But she stayed far too long at the bomb site to move the victims. Thyroid cancer struck her. It was the first time I'd seen the disease." She shook her head. "And sadly, not the last."

I frowned. "And when she died, the pearl went to Mama, right?"

"Yes. And your mother's life was peaceful. The pearl never called her."

I swallowed over the flare of grief that clogged my throat. My mother had been everything to me. She would make up silly rhyming songs, always starting with 'Jelly, Jelly, eyes so blue.' She'd make up the second part. 'No one is as smart as you,' or 'Like the skies where birds do flew.' I'd giggled and told her that didn't make sense. She described the birds she'd seen, and I'd marvel at the thought of feathers and flight.

My favorite was the simplest. 'Jelly, Jelly, eyes so blue, no one loves you like I do.'

We'd watched my vibrant mother deteriorate at an incredible pace. The Shaman's magic had been useless against the cancer as something beyond the natural world caused it, something the humans dumped on us. All Synchi could offer was pain relief. I was seven when she died.

To make things worse, my father changed overnight, becoming reclusive and spending most of his time outside the bubble. A week later, he went missing. I remember Tro sending search parties far and wide, looking for him. A pod of dolphins found his body deep in a cave, ensnared in a fishing net, so tangled and tight that he couldn't reach the knives on his belt. It remained a mystery how it happened.

She stared at me before she released my hands to waft across the room, her rough white tail disturbing the sand on the floor. She paused at the largest window and said, "You were so young when I gave you the pearl. After your parents died, I insisted you live with me. It was essential for me to monitor your childhood nightmares and see if they developed into visions."

I raced the pearl across the chain, then dropped it as if burned. I chewed on my cheek, desperate to keep the tears out of my voice. "Did Mama have visions?"

The Shaman pulled on her braid, her eyes sad. "More like potent dreaming. She shared one dream in particular just before she died. You were in armor wearing the pearl, a warrior. She loved you so much, Jelly. She didn't know if the pearl would call you, but she wanted you as prepared as possible."

"Warrior? Does Tro know too?"

She had the grace to look sheepish. "He argued to adopt you after your parents died. We had quite the brawl over it. He thought you'd be happier living with him and Mori, especially as she had just lost her mother. He was likely correct, but I had to observe you. Once I told him about the pearl, and your mother's dream, he dedicated himself to training you and Mori."

I'd spent my childhood with either a knife or a book in my hand. I blinked. Synchi and Tro had orchestrated every aspect of my life. "You should have told me sooner, Synchi." I swallowed my anger and hurt, lifting the pearl and turning it over in my fingertips. I asked, "What about the Trident? Should we tell them?"

Synchi scowled, "Not yet. I don't trust them. They will try to manipulate its magic and turn you into a weapon. I want to keep it from them as long as possible."

"Does anyone else know about the pearl?"

"There is one other. When I created the bubble, I told a Surfecti, a Witch. I said we were withdrawing from the world for our protection. She was upset and said we had a responsibility to the planet." She looked at me with twinkling, yet regretful, eyes. "I, in so many words, told her to piss off. We haven't spoken in a long time, almost seventy years."

Something jiggled in my memory. I blurted, "The voice said that!"

Synchi swung her head so fast she almost kinked her neck.

"Voice? What voice? What did it say? Male or female?" I closed my eyes to concentrate and try to remember. I'd been so shattered that I had paid little attention.

"Male. Singsong. Very seductive. Something like, 'I've been waiting for you. It's been so long—seventy years, and I'll come back soon.' Any idea who it might be?"

She stroked her fingertips down her chin braid. "There are many possibilities. You wear a coveted item now, a magical phylactery with great power." She shook her head. "Someone wants it and sent the lingcod. You're adored by the sea life. Someone else was pulling the strings." She scowled. "I can only think of one race strong enough to overpower Mers' magic. Even then, it would be difficult, but I suppose…" Her voice drifted off, not finishing her thought.

I rolled my eyes in exasperation. "Who, Synchi? Who would want it?"

"The Fae. They gifted the pearl to the Mers. The details are cloudy. There was tension in the Royal Family, and the Fae King gave it to the Mers to keep it away from his squabbling children. It enhances magic, Jelly, and once it activates, it makes the bearer incredibly potent." That explained the powerful whirlpool that sucked away the lingcod. She rubbed her knuckles over her eyes and sighed, "Well, let's go meet the Sea Goddess."

The Sea Goddess? My heart beat faster as anticipation jumped around my body like a live wire. I asked in a rush, "What? Why?"

"Because the pearl is awake and because someone sent a school of savage fish to attack you. Come. Don't look so scared. She doesn't bite." She shrugged, "Most of the time."

While my bedroom was stark, as I liked it, Synchi's was opulent. Suspended from the ceiling, the tendrils of a massive, glowing jellyfish cast a gentle light. Synchi waved at it, and its body pulsed, illuminating and exposing the rest of the room.

The walls were coated in bioluminescent creatures, shimmering a deep turquoise color. A large circular stone lay to one side, and the sponge on top was thick and meaty, covered in a dense, knitted kelp blanket. Next to the bed were small alcoves in the wall, where sleeping lanternfish hovered beside a singular chaise, ideal for reading. I snorted at the algae book on the table, a bare-chested merman on the cover. The far wall was floor-to-ceiling books, charms, shells, glittering stones, and statues carved from bone. Every piece sparkled, not a speck of sand to be seen.

Synchi gave me a moment to gawk before shooing me into a dark tunnel. We popped out the other side into a smaller cave, lit with soft, cream-colored glowworms in the high ceiling. Along the deep shelf that cut into the back wall lay odd bones, small colored shells, and assorted pebbles next to a large, luminescent abalone shell. A circle of heavy, irregular rocks was the only other feature in the cave.

Synchi observed my wide eyes and said, "Wait there, inside the stones." The smoothed rocks glimmered and shone in the glowworm light, and I did as she asked. She waved her hand through the air, sealing off the entrance with an illusion, making it appear like the walls. She winked, "In case Oggie comes looking for you."

I fidgeted, cracking my knuckles while she prepared. She placed the small bones and stones inside the abalone shell and shook it, adding the smaller shells one at a time. When she cleared her throat and sang, the water swirled around us, picking up speed and sending my hair above my head. I grasped it and held it to my chest, watching Synchi as her white locs flew around her dark, wrinkled face.

Goosebumps broke out as the haunting melody prickled my skin. The pearl vibrated and pulsed as if waking up. My vision blurred, and I blinked, trying to focus. I yelped and jerked back as a body shimmered into being. Synchi fell silent and bowed her head. I copied her.

The Goddess's face was so stunning and terrible that my jiggling energy stilled in equal amounts of respect and fright. Her hair was a writhing mass of sea serpents, their forked tongues flicking to taste the water. Dark green eyes, like algae, peered at us, brimming with ancient intelligence. Her skin was as pale as the moon, and her tail color matched her eyes. I controlled a shudder as her long spiky fangs pulled into a smile.

Parents threatened naughty children with Goddess Kelbazi, warning that her snakes would eat your soul if you didn't behave. On seeing her, I believed. I dipped my head and whispered over a faint breath, "Goddess." I swallowed and raised my eyes again.

"Sssssssoo, it beginsss," Kelbazi hissed, or perhaps her snakes hissed. I couldn't tell the difference. Her serpents swam around her face, their tongues scenting, reaching out toward me. I stayed deathly still as flickers touched my face and neck. "She isss hunted. Who harmed you, Sssssscyphozoa?" My eyes flew wide when she said my name.

I cleared my throat, which had gone bone-dry from the snakes tasting my skin. "A school of lingcod attacked me. They couldn't speak, their eyes were black, and they latched onto me and wouldn't let go."

Synchi said, "I believe they tried to bite through the chain to get the pearl."

I held my breath as a snake squirmed for my throat, its tongue licking, fangs grazing. The Goddess recoiled, her serpents snapping and writhing around her skull. Her green eyes blinked and narrowed. Her voice was slick and smooth, sliding over my skin. "There issss a power, dark and hungry. It huntssss you. It will not stop until it hasss the pearl. The Merssss are under threat."

"Sorry?" I asked in a small voice, hoping her words would change if she repeated herself.

"Sssssurface. You will need the Ssssurfecti to ssssurvive."

I stammered, "Surfecti? How will they help me?" I turned to Synchi. "They won't assist the Mers. You said that you and the witch parted badly."

Kelbazi quietly hissed, as if disappointed she couldn't give me more guidance. "Make hasssste, Sssscyphozoa, you don't have a moment to wassste. Hurry."

She blurred in the water, and I called out, "Wait!" Synchi bowed at the waist, and after she jabbed me with her elbow, I did the same, my forehead on the sand. I stayed as still as a statue until Synchi touched my arm and startled me.

She looked drained. "The Goddess does not give straightforward advice. We'll have to piece it together." She returned the shells and bones to the shelf. Turning to me, she said, "Dark and hungry power threatening the Mers; you must go to the surface, coordinate with the Surfecti to survive, and hurry. How can we bypass the Trident? I'd bet my pearls they want to keep you away from the surface."

"But aren't we enemies with the Surfecti? That's what we were taught in school. They abandoned the ocean and betrayed the Mers."

Synchi's face scrunched up. "It's complicated."

"Well, uncomplicate it for me."

"It's not that simple."

I crossed my arms. "Try, Synchi."

She nodded and whispered, "We were allies once. During the First World War of the humans, the Surfecti guided the

Mers to evacuate as many sea creatures as possible. All the clans worked together. Collectively, the Mers used extraordinary amounts of magic and suffered many losses because of exhaustion and the dangers of vast ocean crossings."

I sucked my teeth. "Yes, yes, we're all taught of the sacrifices from the Mers. Why the dissonance with the Surfecti? What caused the rift?"

Synchi's face pinched. "When the United States began nuclear testing in the Marshall Islands in 1946, the Pacific Mers, mostly through me, begged the Surfecti to intervene and stop the humans. The Surfecti vetoed direct aid, saying they were too frantic managing the overall chaos on the surface. Every continent, except Antarctica, faced war or its imminent threat. Relations between the nuclear powers, the United States and Russia, were icy with espionage, proxy wars, and political subversion. Scrabbling to keep the planet intact, the Surfecti influenced human politicians, forming NATO. They drained their magic and had none left to help us."

"And because they refused to help, we now hate them. Correct?"

"Well, that's what they teach in school. But Jelly, understand, they had no magic to give us. The Fae withdrew to their alternate dimension, leaving the Surfecti to handle the human chaos. And then, when I created the bubble and taught the other Mers clans how to do it, we also vanished, leaving the Surfecti alone. From the Surfecti's point of view, we abandoned them."

I slid the pearl on its chain, grasping to understand. "So the only reason we are enemies is because both sides feel forsaken."

"That's right," sighed Synchi. "If I could do it again, I would choose differently. Our inaction has resulted in being swamped by pollution. The Surfecti can only do so much to influence the humans. They should have had our support after the wars, but the Mers retreated, especially after the Russians began nuclear testing on Novaya Zemlya."

"That's the bombing that decimated the Artic Mers, correct?"

"Yes. The humans exploded two hundred and twenty-four nuclear bombs there. The last one was in 1990."

I paled. "And the radiation has poisoned the ocean. Are they getting cancers like us?"

Synchi sighed heavily. "Worse. Rusting radioactive debris, some seventeen thousand pieces, litters the ocean floor. It's a disaster waiting to happen. And the Arctic Mers are a fraction of what they used to be. Those remaining few do their best to protect the Beluga and Bowhead whales and the Narwhal and Greenland sharks, but their time runs short."

She ran a hand over her eyes. "We should have helped the Surfecti. We are no better than humans, fighting instead of collaborating."

She and I sat without speaking for a while, mulling over her words. I changed the subject. "I could just leave. Not tell the Trident."

She shook her head. "You'd only have a month with the transformation potion. Finding this hungry power might take longer than that." She shook her head. "I don't like our options. But before we do anything, we need to test your magic. The pearl will have changed it, as evidenced by the explosion. You need to appreciate what you're working with before you go up top."

I floundered in a tremor of nerves. "What does that mean? Can I do new things?"

She shrugged. "Normally, it's your standard magic but stronger, but you blew up a wall of plastic jugs. That's new. We need a bigger space." With a snap of her gnarled fingers, the small cave became massive. Five piles of stones lined the outer walls, about ten feet apart. She turned to me. "The pearl took over in the store. You must harness it."

"How?"

Synchi coaxed me. "Focus on the top rock and obliterate it, leaving the rest untouched. Scream while you do it. Maybe the trick is in the scream."

I lifted my hand and roared at the rocks. Sand flew through the water, and I grinned, smug, thinking I'd succeeded on the first try. Synchi waved the sand away, and the pile remained the same. My shoulders sagged. "Try again," Synchi urged. "Focus." I drove my energy through my hand and yelled with all my might. This time, the entire pile disintegrated into fine dust, leaving a crater on the sandy ocean floor.

Synchi frowned and said, "Well, that's better, I suppose. But now you need to hone it. Direct it." Again, I demolished the pile to sand. Tower after tower of rocks turned to sand. Synchi reset my targets without comment, but I could see the nervousness in her eyes. My throat hurt from all my failed efforts, and I was losing patience with my uncontrollable magic.

Finally, Synchi's head drooped in frustration. "I can't explain how else to describe it, Jelly. See it! Believe it." I tried again and grimaced at the hole in the sand. The pearl was hot and heavy against my skin, and I was getting upset.

"Think of the store! Think of the jugs! Plastic, Jelly! There's plastic everywhere!" shouted Synchi, her long locs swirling as she over-dramatized her gesticulations, arms thrashing through the water. "Save us, Jelly! We're all going to die!" I roared again and flung my magic from my palm. The power was so explosive that it flung us backward from the blast. We blinked at each other in silence, shaking the sand from our ears.

Synchi shouted, "Look! You did it!"

I lifted my head, excited to see my success, and cursed. "Hardly! I still blew up half of them! I can't do this, Synchi." My lower lip might have trembled.

She folded her arms across her chest, refusing to entertain my self-pity. She snapped, "You can't quit, Jelly." Holding her stubborn stare, I took three deep breaths. As breath left my body on the third, I threw my hand toward the next pile and blasted it, my scream shrill from fatigue. Her face burst open with glee when the sand settled. The top third was missing. I dropped my head in my hands.

She patted my shoulder and said, "Well, it's a start. It will need fine-tuning, but at least you can do it on command. Hopefully, you'll never need something so destructive." Synchi snorted with amusement as I gave a loud moan. She said through a chuckle, "Let's move on. I want to test your long-distance telepathy. Call Amira."

I blinked. "Amira? She's miles away on her way north by now. She won't hear me." Amira was the matriarch of the Gray Whale Collective, leading the longest-known mammal migration, twelve thousand miles from Baja, Mexico, to the Bering Sea. One glare from Synchi had me try.

I closed my eyes and focused on the bright, wise eyes of Amira. She was a long-time friend of the Mers. In my mind, I called her, knowing that whales could cover vast distances with their minds. We waited for a reply—and waited some more. I chewed on my cheek, creating tiny whirlpools with my fingers while Synchi meditated, her tail-fin floating six inches above the sand.

After about fifteen minutes, Amira's whale song came back. It trembled through the water like a ghost, vibrating against my ears.

Jeeeelllyyyyyy

I squealed, which roused Synchi, who nodded and smiled at me. "Can you hear her?" I asked.

Synchi shook her head. "She's only speaking with you. Keep talking." I sang in my mind to ask Amira where she was. Her response came faster now that I had her attention.

Essssss Effffff.

I clapped my hands with excitement. "She's in San Francisco! That's miles away!" I asked if there were any babies this year.

Siiiiiiiix.

I gasped, "Six new babies!" I grinned at Synchi and held my hands to my chest. Six was wonderful. Given that all sea creatures were having difficulty reproducing, six was fantastic. I asked if they were healthy.

Yeeeasss. There was a pause, then, *Whassssss Wrooooong?*

I replied nothing was wrong, and that I was testing new magic. I wished her a safe journey and told her to kiss the pod's new babies for me. Her reply stopped my heart and made the blood drain from my face.

Carefullllll. Eeeeeeviiiillllll.

I panicked, looking at Synchi, who raised her eyebrows in concern. "Synchi, call her. My telepathy at this distance is too basic. She says there's evil."

Synchi spun her hands, creating a small whirlpool she used as a telephonic amplifier. She contacted Amira and leaned close, only asking for clarification twice. The keening moans Amira sang at the end of their conversation made the hair stand up on my arms. Maybe it was the look of fear on Synchi's face.

Synchi, distracted, let the whirlpool spin away without closing it. It sucked in an unsuspecting fish and then spat it out. It shook its head and glared at Synchi, who hadn't noticed. She said, "She's noticed odd behavior on her journey. Fish acting strangely, mostly sharks. They've attacked the humans more often. We're at triple the deaths, and it's still early in the season. She says their eyes are dark as a moonless night."

"Black eyes," I confirmed, fear clutching my heart. "That's what the lingcod had. I said their eyes were dead, but they were black. Fully black. Synchi, it's spreading!"

Synchi frowned. "Make me a whirlpool, thirteen feet in diameter, narrowing to one inch."

"What? Amira just told us that something is possessing sharks! And you want me to play with whirlpools?"

"Do it!" Synchi yelled, fury in her voice. I jerked back, shocked. Amira's words must have rattled her. She was trying not to show it. I stung from her rebuke and spun a whirlpool to her exact measurements, my vision swimming from fatigue. The temptation to push her into it and watch her twirl was overpowering. Her voice rang in my ears.

Don't even think about it.

I had to laugh. She commanded, "Make a second, swirling in the opposite direction, then combine them. Let's see what happens."

I laughed harder, delirious from fatigue and fear. "See what happens? Fine." With my other hand, I created another funnel and dragged my fingers together, the pressure making my arms ache. The whirlpools collided, knocking us back with a loud boom and rolling us across the ocean floor.

Synchi roared with glee as she rubbed her hand on the back of her neck, wincing from being thrown. She clapped her hands together. "Magnificent! You can create havoc without your scream. That's useful."

I grinned, pleased that I'd made her smile. Synchi chuckled before sighing heavily. "You need more training before you meet the Surfecti." Her face fell. "Training we don't have time for." She spun to me. "But you can see you're more powerful, yes? You can sense the effects of the pearl on your magic?"

I nodded. "When I concentrate, it's like a hum throughout my body, like a layer of a vibration that I hadn't noticed before."

"Very good, Jelly. Very good, indeed. You need to work on that. You need to control it."

She crossed her arms and said, "One last thing. Your glamor work is excellent, but I'd like to see your speed." As she barked out names, I wove my magic around myself, hiding my true form. A dolphin, a pufferfish, an angelfish, an eel, a snail, a crab, and finally, a sea cucumber. I panted with exhaustion when I was done.

With a wave of her fingers, we were back in the small cave, hidden behind her bedroom. "Right," she sighed, "I'd better call the Witch."

SIX

JELLY

Synchi frowned as she said, "Grab the mirror, would you?" I swam across the cave to the shelf containing Synchi's many potions, careful not to knock any as I lifted the heavy mirror. It was circular, about two feet in diameter, and black shells protected the edges. They were Naticidae, or moon snails, large, predatory creatures from the Triassic era, older than the dinosaurs, and still living on Earth.

I settled it on the sponge cushion she held on her lap. She angled the glass so I could watch from the side. "The Witch and I have a sordid history. Do not interrupt us. We will dance around each other until we get to the meat of it. I need to handle her carefully."

She tapped the cloudy surface three times and whispered a spell. I inched closer as a face illuminated and materialized, the features blurry until they snapped into clarity. A woman stared back, her face sharp and forbidding, with a straight nose, high cheekbones, and a delicately pointed chin. Long, black hair twisted into a tight bun at the nape, and cold, blue eyes narrowed on the Shaman.

She spoke with a clipped and tight voice. British. I'd met an English tourist in Nell's village once, hanging on to every word she said. The witch scowled, "Shaman. It's been some time since I saw your face. Can't say I missed it."

Synchi dipped her chin to the mirror while I bristled at the witch's words. Synchi was unruffled. "You're looking well, Anna. Haven't aged a day. I hoped we might talk. We've had some strange things happening in the ocean."

The woman's thin lips pressed together as her eyebrow arched up. "Are *you* asking *me* for help?"

Synchi fought back a scowl, her voice placating. "I am. There's been…an incident. I wondered if the Surfecti has seen any… unusual events."

Anna frowned and peered closer into the mirror, her expression dark with mistrust, closely bordering on loathing. Her words were as cutting as ice. "You made it quite clear you wanted nothing to do with us, Shaman. But at the first sign of trouble, you call."

"Consider it a courtesy. If we are under attack, you are also, although perhaps you are unaware." Synchi also leaned into the mirror for intimidation, her chin braid swinging forward from the weight of the shell on the end. "Do you need a formal apology before we speak, Witch?" Her tone was mocking, and I wasn't sure it was the best approach when enlisting someone's help. As if hearing herself, Synchi softened. "Fine. You're right. I abandoned you. I hid the Mers and left you to fend for yourselves on the surface. That was wrong. I was wrong, and I am sorry."

Anna blinked, clearly not expecting a confession or apology. She recovered and snipped, "Well, you must be in trouble. What's wrong with your oceanic fortress?"

Synchi rubbed her gnarled fingers over her eyes. "Besides

overcrowding, infertility, and fading magic? Possessed sea creatures. They attacked one of our warriors."

Anna balked, affected by the Shaman's admission. "Possessed animals? I should like to speak with this Warrior, Shaman. Is he available?"

"*She* is." Synchi waved me to her side. "This is Scyphozoa, known as Jelly. Jelly, this is Anna, the Head of the New Forest Coven of Witches." I leaned over Synchi's shoulder, staring at the formidable woman in the mirror. The pearl dropped forward from my throat. Anna's composure shattered when she saw it, her eyes and mouth flying wide open.

"She wears the Vetula Pearl?" she screeched. "We detected the magic. It flung through the ether like lightning!" Her eyes narrowed into slits. "You kept this from us? Some things surpass our disagreements. You should have informed me at once."

Synchi's lips pursed as she exhaled. "Indeed, it seems I need to apologize a second time."

"I should bloody think so," Anna spat scathingly. "This is outrageous, Shaman. The pearl impacts us all, and you hid it. Typical Mers behavior." She inhaled and opened her mouth to continue her tirade.

I cut her off. "Can we stay on point? I got attacked by fish behaving badly."

Anna's mouth fell open from my interruption. She closed her eyes to calm herself and gritted through clenched teeth, "What activated it? Jelly, was it?" Her tone was derogatory.

I cleared my throat. "It happened in a superstore on the surface, and I blew up the laundry detergent aisle."

Anna cocked her head, puzzled. "What on earth drove you to do such a thing?"

I frowned. "It was an accident. I saw all the plastic and lost my temper. The pearl was vibrating and jerked itself up on the chain. When I screamed in frustration, all the buckets of soap exploded. I ran away as fast as I could and came home."

Anna tapped her lips with her fingertips. "You lost control of the pearl?" I nodded. She looked at Synchi with an arched eyebrow. "She lost control? Shaman, you appreciate how disastrous this is?"

I defended myself. "It's not that bad. It was just one aisle. I mean, it's not like I blew up the entire store. And I didn't hurt anyone."

She said nothing. She just stared at me like a bug. One she would like to crush.

Her penetrating gaze left my face to spin to the Shaman. "Something is wrong with the ocean to have woken the pearl so abruptly. Tell me the truth, Shaman."

Synchi was reluctant to answer. Her voice broke when she did. "It's getting harder to hold the bubble. The micro and nanoplastics are almost impossible for me to filter. I can't create pearls fast enough because it takes energy to keep them cool. Anna, I am loathed to say it, but I am failing." Her voice faded to a quiet wobble.

My breath froze in my lungs. If the bubble fell, the Mers and all the animals we sheltered would die. Synchi recovered herself and squared her old shoulders. "We contacted the Goddess, and her message was not what I expected. To paraphrase, there is a dark and hungry power hunting the pearl. Jelly must go to the surface and work with the Surfecti to survive. And we must hurry. Whether it's regarding just Jelly surviving or all of us surviving, I cannot say."

Anna visibly paled. "That is most disconcerting. Any idea who the dark and hungry power is?"

Synchi shook her head. "I was hoping you would know."

I blurted, "The pearl was a gift from the Fae to the Mers. Could the Fae be behind it?"

Anna's eyebrows pinched together. "Perhaps, but it's unlikely. They've been in hiding for years. I can't see why they would get involved now. Shaman, I must consult my advisers and tell them about the active pearl. Then your warrior must meet with us."

I blinked. "But Amira, a humpback, warned us of possessed sharks. They might come here. I can't leave the Shaman undefended." I turned to Synchi. "Surely that takes priority?"

Anna snorted, "Of course, you think of the Mers first."

I swung back to the witch and spoke in a sharp tone, indoctrinated with vitriol. My lip curled as I spat, "I have no allegiance to the Surfecti. You abandoned us before, so, obviously, I'm going to worry about the ocean first. Someone has to guard it."

Synchi, not-so-gently, pushed me away and nodded at the witch. "Until, Anna. We shall speak soon."

The mirror's gloomy surface returned with a pop. Scowling, I lifted the mirror from Synchi's lap and carried it back to the shelf when she stopped me, telling me to rest it against the cave wall. She watched me swim in circles, biting my lip and playing with the pearl.

"I don't like her, Synchi."

"Frankly, Jelly, I don't care. You need her. We need her. Didn't we just speak of this? That we are both aggrieved?"

I scowled deeper and harrumphed. "What about the sharks?"

Synchi tapped her fingers on her shell, thinking. "They're far away." Her milky eyes narrowed. "Call Mori. I'm curious to see if the fish will attack you again."

"What are we, bait?"

"I need to understand the magic behind the possessions. Just go out there and swim around. It's a fact-finding mission. Nothing more. You and Mori will be fine."

I pressed my middle finger and thumb to my temple. *Mori, the Shaman has a secret mission for us. Meet us at the West Gate. Wear your armor.*

Copy that, came her quick reply.

Synchi muttered under her breath and put on her glamor, grumbling and jerking on her tight skin. I kissed Oggie's head and fed him a few more minnows, strapping my sword to my back. Mori was already waiting for us when we arrived, her hair tied back into fighting braids.

Flexible chain-mail encased her dark red tail, and she turned with a smile as we approached. She pulled at her chest plate. "Hey, Jelly. Hi, Shaman. Shaman, did Toto talk to you about adjusting my armor? My boobs are so squished that they're killing me. I think they're getting bigger. These rounded bits are better than they were, but dayum, help a girl out." She shrugged and tugged and stared at my face. "Why do you look so worried?" Mori tipped her head to the side and crossed her arms. "Out with it."

I sighed and scrubbed at my eyes. "Plastics mimic the hormone estrogen. It can trigger a proliferation of cells in breasts." I kept my following thought to myself, but Mori voiced it aloud, her voice hollow.

"Mom died from breast cancer. Does this mean I'll get it, too?"

I rocked my head. "No. It doesn't. It doesn't, Mor. Don't think that." She looked at me skeptically, her freckles bunching together as she scrunched her nose. Sometimes, I hated my advanced knowledge. I looked to the Shaman for backup.

Synchi said, "Mori, we will monitor it. Do your regular checks. If you have any lumps, dimpling, or discharge, you come to me straight away. In the meantime, may I?" She gestured at Mori's chest. Mori nodded, her eyes still anxious.

The Shaman re-crafted her chest plate, expanding the rounded areas to give her more space. Mori sighed with relief as she wiggled inside her armor, readjusting the thick strap that held her hira-shuriken or throwing stars. Synchi sternly said, "I want to see if you're attacked. Be on your guard."

Mori nodded. Even though her father said it was a private discussion, I'd told her about the lingcod attack. I told her everything. I had so much more to confess, but now wasn't the time. We needed to be sharp outside the bubble, especially if murderous fish were on the loose.

We pushed through the barrier to the safety zone. I wrapped my face cloth twice around my mouth and ears, anchoring it. I put on my goggles and then turned to Mori to check her gear. We slid our swords from their scabbards and pressed into the ocean.

Mori coughed, "Gods, Jelly. I can taste it now. It's disgusting. We're going to need better gear. Even doubled cloth isn't enough." My eyebrows knit together. I could barely see in front of me. I created a whirlpool, clearing microplastics before us. "What now?" Mori asked.

"Let's go up and look around." I widened the whirlpool as we raced, our eyes scanning for danger.

Mori's scowl was dark as we reached the surface. She smacked a faded orange jug out of her way. Given time and weather, it would break down into the little pieces that Synchi struggled to keep out of our home. She said, "It's so much worse."

I went into academic mode. "Most plastics used today are virgin. Only six percent of the older stuff gets recycled." I held up a bright green jug, pointing to the triangle on the bottom. "These symbols give false confidence to humans. They're a resin identification code for the material, nothing more."

"No. That can't be right." She looked at my raised

eyebrow. "Okay, fine, whatever. I thought they recycled numbers one and two."

I shrugged. "They're the *easiest* to recycle, but it doesn't mean they are. They burn it in incinerators or toss it in the dump. A lot of it gets shipped off to foreign countries, letting them deal with it. Some humans say that the whole recycling gig is a scam made up by plastic manufacturers, making humans complacent." In one motion, I swept my hand out and gathered two plastic bags, four straws, and a flimsy fork in my fist. I held them up and spat, "Single use."

A loud splash to the left spun our heads. We raised our swords, expecting an attack. "Let's get closer. Drop a glamor on us," Mori whispered. I nodded, hiding us as dolphins as we eased forward, our weapons obscured under my magic.

A flashlight burst through the water, lighting the plastic particles like thick dust in a sunbeam. A solitary male was underwater, slashing at a net with a knife. His dark eyes were furious as he tore at the nylon. Fishing nets used to be made of rope, which decomposed. Nylon plastic replaced it in the 1960s, and it was indestructible.

The man ripped and shredded, dragging pieces to his boat and hauling them up before splashing back into the water to continue. He had long, dark hair, was lean and muscled, and tattoos of waves circled up his arms to crash across his shoulders and upper back. He wore a dive mask and had a cloth tied around his mouth.

Mori raised her fingers to her temple to speak into my mind. *He's not in scuba gear. He can hold his breath for a long time.*

I noticed that. And he's going deep for a human.

She waggled her eyebrows and chuckled in my head, staring at the man's thick thighs. *Those are very pretty.*

His flashlight spun in our direction, and I held my breath as he stared right at me, his eyes widening in surprise. His breath escaped him in a flurry of bubbles, and he kicked for the surface, the long dive fins strapped to his feet bending from his strength.

She giggled, about to comment further when Synchi's voice blared in our heads, her words garbled and laced with panic. *Help me! We're under attack!*

Fear coated our hearts, and we dove at speed, accelerating as Synchi shrieked with stark terror. My tail muscles groaned with effort as we sprinted for the bubble. My eyes sprang wide as a juvenile great white shark bit into the main layer of the shield, having torn a hole in the protection zone. Synchi had dropped her youthful glamor, putting all her magic into defense. Her eyes flashed to mine, bald relief shining through her deep wrinkles when she saw me.

SEVEN

JELLY

The pearl heated at my neck, pulsing in time with my frantic heart. Its magic vibrated and strummed through my blood. The shark stiffened, sensing the subtle change in the water through the small black spots near its nose, eyes, and mouth. It turned with a flick of its tail and stared at us, specifically me.

Great whites spoke through body language, and this one had malicious intent. It hunched its posture, elevated its snout, and lowered its pectoral fin, making jerky side-to-side movements, powering up to attack. The shark was a young one, maybe seven feet long.

The shark came at us like a ghost, its scales allowing it to move silently. I careened to the left to avoid its sharp teeth. Mori locked her arm around my waist, and together, we grunted, delivering a hard blow with our tails, knocking it off course. It twisted, unaffected, and charged for us again. Mori drew her sword and delivered a slice to the belly, blood staining the water, mixing in with the plastic, making it even harder to see.

"Wait!" I cried to Mori. "Let me talk to it!"

I yelled at the shark, "What are you doing? We mean you no harm."

The voice that returned was so flat and cold, it sounded like a corpse was speaking. "Give me the pearl, and I will let you live."

"Why do you want it?"

"Give it to me, or I will rip your head off and take it." Its mouth pulled back in a grimace and three thousand triangular, serrated teeth promised pain. I needed time to think. Time I didn't have. It came at us again, and we ducked away, but it razed against Mori. She screeched as it abraded her skin with its placoid scales.

"Jelly, it's not stopping!" she yelled, wincing at her chafed arm. I turned to the shark and raised my hand. I didn't exactly scream; it was more of a yelp, hitting the shark square on the caudal fin that it used to propel itself forward.

It swam away, struggling, spinning, and writhing as if in agony. Sharks don't experience pain. I'd seen hammerheads prey on stingrays. They could have a hundred barbs in their mouths with no ill effect. Yet this shark was being tortured. I prayed it wasn't my magic causing it pain. It tried to swim away, but turned again as if under foreign control. It blinked, and I saw the cold black eye as it inched through the water to breathe.

I shouted to Mori, "Get inside the main bubble! I'm going to do a stupor!"

She darted for Synchi, and the shark turned all its attention to me. I created a whirlpool and flipped the shark upside down, putting it into a trance-like state. While held in my magic, whatever or whoever controlled it stalled.

It called me in a desperate youthful voice, "It's not me! I don't understand what's wrong and I can't stop it! I'm just looking for something to eat. Everything went black, and I was told to attack you and get the pearl. I don't even see a pearl!"

The pearl nestled underneath my armor, but I wouldn't tell the shark that. I asked, "Who sent you? What's controlling you?"

Its eye was dark blue and frightened as it said, "I don't know! It just happened when I got near the bubble. I swear! Please, just give me the pearl! I don't want to hurt you!"

The pearl vibrated under the strain of holding a three-hundred-pound creature suspended in a whirlpool. The shark's blue eyes blinked before clouding over to black. It lurched and broke through my magic, causing me to flip backward as the energy reverberated and hit me. As I spun head over tail, I tightened my grip on my swordfish blade, halting my tumble with another quick whirlpool.

"Decapitation it is," snarled the shark.

I waited until it was almost upon me and then spun at the last second, slicing it across its side. It gasped through its gills and swam away to recover, and I took advantage of the brief respite to bolt for the bubble.

I rushed to Synchi, her arms raised as she battled to mend the shield. Her milky eyes were furious, and a small but steady line of crimson blood leaked from her nose, swirling and dancing in the water. Without dropping her hands, she gasped, "Its eyes are black. I can't get through to it."

"Synchi, it's being possessed. It was told to get the pearl. Even if it had to kill me."

Her eyes narrowed as she grunted from effort, madly trying to weave her magic. "It told me to give it the pearl, or we all die."

On cue, the shark rammed against the bubble, its skin sizzling under the burn of the repelling magic.

"Scream at it!" Synchi shouted. I raised my hand and dropped it. There had to be another way. Synchi barked, "Use your scream, Jelly! Force it back!"

I shook my head. "I don't want to hurt it! Something's overpowering it!"

She snarled, "Jelly, it will kill us if it gets through!" I glanced at her, frightened to see the blood now streaming from her nose. Her hands shook. The thought of taking an innocent life…it was too awful. But the consequences of the shark breaching the bubble were far worse. Maybe I could still reason with it.

The shark was berserk, slamming into the bubble with its mouth open, ferocious teeth shredding through Synchi's magic. Mori's face was ashen as she floated beside the Shaman, her sword clutched in her non-dominant hand. Synchi's terrified voice splintered my hesitation. "Scream, Jelly! I can't hold it back! Raise your damned hand and scream!"

I bolted away from Synchi and Mori, drawing the shark's attention toward me. The pearl jumped and skittered on its chain, banging against my armor. I lifted one hand, and as the shark sped toward me with its jaw open wide, I tried one last time to reach it.

"STOP! Stop what you're doing!"

The dead eye never wavered, and as the razor-sharp teeth cut through the haze of the plastic snowstorm, I closed my eyes and screamed. I held my breath, waiting for the feel of my flesh being torn from my bones, but it never came. I cracked open one eye and blinked as a kaleidoscope of fish snapped up minuscule pieces of shark. What looked like a cloud of ink faded before disappearing altogether.

Solid arms yanked me into the protection zone before thrusting me beside Mori. Given her injury, she hadn't been the one to grab me. I pulled off my goggles and pushed down my face cloth, turning and raising my eyes to a thunderous Tro.

His brown eyes were electric with terror. He stared at the

cluster of fish outside the safety zone, enjoying their unexpected meal. Just behind him, inside the main bubble, seven guards waited with drawn swords, all glowering at me. They'd seen everything. One of them idled closer to eavesdrop. Tro's voice was dangerously soft, as if it took every ounce of his power not to yell. "What did I just see?"

The edge of his voice cautioned me to be careful with my answer. I hedged. "Where did you come from?" I scanned for Synchi, but didn't see her.

"Answer my question, Warrior." This was my Commanding Officer, not the fatherly Tro who had spun me in circles as a mergirl. Mori swallowed and slipped from under his hand, squaring her shoulders to take my side. Tro asked again, "What was that?"

"A shark under foreign power. It was attacking the bubble. It wouldn't stop." I added belatedly, "Sir."

"Why are you and my daughter alone with a frenzied great white?"

"Synchi…" I started, but Tro's eyes flashed in warning. I amended my statement. "We were monitoring the Patch, and when we returned, the shark attacked. I used my scream to stop it."

I could see the guards' lips moving as they muttered to each other. Their eyes were accusatory and hate-filled, as killing a shark was a serious crime. The humans had decimated their population, and the reef needed them to be healthy. They maintained food webs and fish stocks, cycled nutrients, reduced disease, and regulated invasive species, and I had just annihilated a young one.

I dropped my voice to a whisper. "We need to check on the Shaman. She may be hurt."

Tro closed his eyes for a moment as though gathering

himself. He murmured, "Your scream…the pearl…" His chin dropped to his chest. He twitched like he wanted to hug and protect me, but steadied himself. I could barely hear him whisper. "It's happened, then. The pearl is awake." I sucked my bottom lip into my teeth in reply.

He glanced at the guards. "Prepare for the fallout, Jelly. I won't be able to cover this up for you. There are too many witnesses. We all saw it. The penalty for killing a shark is severe. I'll do what I can, but Jelly, this is bad, especially given the recent explosion. You'll be lucky if all you get is the hole. I will call a Trident meeting in the morning and plead your case. Be ready."

He turned to Mori, the hot fear in his eyes almost blistering. "Get Jelly home, have the Shaman heal your arm, and return to the cave immediately." She nodded, too meek to speak. I didn't blame her.

"Sir." I raised my fist to my chest and bowed my head. He nodded curtly and dismissed us. We remained silent until Tro and the guards dispersed, leaving us alone. My eyes followed the guards, some shaking their heads as they glared over their shoulders. Once they faded from view, Mori turned to me and grabbed my shoulder with one hand, her eyes scanning mine.

"I thought you were dead! Jelly, it was right there! Are you sure you didn't get sliced by its teeth?" She looked me over, searching for cuts and blood.

My throat burned under the high neck of the armor. I needed to check for damage. "I'm fine. But I don't think Synchi is. Where did she go?"

Mori looked around. "She was right here. She must have left. No, she wouldn't do that. She wouldn't leave us alone with the shark. Jelly, it almost got us. I could see punctures in the bubble from its teeth. It would have torn clear through if it had whipped its head. It was ripping through it like it was a jellyfish. The Shaman could barely keep up."

The water behind Mori shimmered, and Synchi appeared, slumping against the bubble wall, her white tail listless on the sand. "I'm over here." She strained to rise, and Mori and I rushed to help her. "I almost lost the bubble," she whispered. "To a baby shark." She wiped at her nose, pinching it at the top to stop the bleeding. "Glamor me. A dolphin. Take me to the cave."

We swam at a slow pace, the reef empty save for us. I opened the door with the releasing spell and dropped her dolphin glamor as we entered. "Fire urchins," she groaned, tumbling into her chair. "Five." Fire urchins helped replenish Synchi's magic, but I'd never known her to need so many. Typically, one or two per week sufficed.

I hurried to the kitchen and reached for a glass jar while my lips sped through the prayer. I thanked the urchins for their sacrifice, slid two knives into their bellies, and tore the shells apart. Without ceremony, I dumped the treasured meat into a bowl, and passed them to Synchi, returning to the kitchen to clean up.

I held the blades and cutting board against the whirlpool next to the shelves. It spun quietly, sucking the guts and shells out to the holding pool that fed the fish beyond our cave. I put everything back in methodical order, attempting to reconcile what I'd done to the shark. Guilt clung to me like perfume.

I pulled off my chest plate and rubbed my throat. It was tender just in the hollow, right where the pearl lay. Mori came close, scrutinized it. "It's a little blue, like the start of a bruise, but the skin is fine."

"Unlike your arm."

"It stings like fire coral."

I nodded. "Abrasions effect nerve endings. Let me get you a tonic before you take off your armor. You don't want to knock against it." I opened the small stone cupboard under the kitchen sink that held extra vials of the healing potion. She tipped it back, grimacing from the taste, and we watched as her skin glowed before mending and knitting itself over.

Oggie, smelling food, crawled out of his hiding hole under the chaise with a yawn. One unfurling arm reached toward Synchi's bowl to smell and taste the delicacy inside. I dragged him away and wrapped him around my waist, ignoring his petulant whine.

Synchi chewed slowly, fatigue painting her skin gray. I whispered, "Do you want a pearl, too? One of them is almost ready."

She rasped, "No. It needs to be at full strength for the bubble."

I rubbed the skin above my eyebrows and said to Mori, "I have so much to tell you."

She hesitated. "Look, Jelly, I need to get home to Toto. I can't remember the last time I saw him so upset. It might have been when you wrestled with that giant squid. When it dragged you for a mile before it let go. You should have some fire urchins, too. You used a ton of magic." She stared at the pearl before tapping her fingers on her head. "Call me later."

I fed Oggie his mixture of fish and crustaceans before checking my throat in the mirror. As Mori said, it looked bruised but nothing more. I lifted the pearl and looked at it in the glass. It was silent and cold to the touch.

I dropped it, staring at Synchi apprehensively. She'd never been so depleted and vulnerable. I always imagined her as invincible, but even the Shaman's magic appeared to have limits. I sprawled on my stomach on the chaise, and lay my face on my arms, agonizing over the shark.

Synchi rested the empty bowl on the shell table and sighed. "That's better."

"Synchi, how did that shark damage the barrier so easily?"

Her milky-blue eyes sparked with anger. "There is only one magic that is stronger than the Mers. With the Goddess as my witness, if those dirty Fae bastards think they're going to take me down without a fight, they have another thing coming."

Fear crept up my spine as I realized there was something that could defeat the Shaman. It had never occurred to me before. I asked, "Why would the Fae attack us?"

"That's what I intend to find out," Synchi muttered. "Mori's right. You need to eat. Maybe call Fillian and see if he can give you a top-up." I made an exaggerated gagging noise.

The Mers used sexual intimacy as a power booster, a way to restore our energy. It was also healing. During the height of my Warrior training, sleep-deprived, hungry, and carrying heavy whale vertebrae to increase the stamina of my tail, Fillian and I had started our relationship. Maybe he'd marked me for my power back then.

I scowled, "Fillian and I are over. Done. Finished. Forever. He told me he wanted my babies because they'd be formidable. His greedy eyes are on a seat at the Trident table. He was using me, Synchi. He never loved me for me."

"Oh, Jelly," she said, her eyes crinkling. "I'm so sorry."

"Once again, my life isn't mine. You and Tro set up my life path from the age of seven. The Trident tells me to get knocked up, and Fillian wants my uterus for power babies. Now, the pearl has me chasing off after some monster. When do I get to choose what I want?"

Synchi didn't respond to my tirade. She held the heels of her hands over her eyes, her voice barely audible. "I would have failed without you there. We would have lost everything."

"I'm the reason it attacked, Synchi. It wouldn't be here if it weren't for the pearl." At that moment, seeing her so desolate, I hated the pearl and the target it had placed on my people.

As if reading my thoughts, Synchi's voice sharpened. "You must never relinquish the pearl! It belongs to the Mers and we need its power. You cannot give in, no matter what." She glared at me until I nodded. "If you won't call Fillian, have some fire urchins and go to bed. I'll see you in the morning."

She swam to her shelf of oysters and waved her hand through the water, cleansing and feeding them what little magic she had to spare. I watched her with worry. I ate two fire urchins before collecting Oggie in my arms and sagged toward my room. Exhausted from using so much magic and adrenaline, I fell asleep in an instant.

Sometime later, my teeth rattled together as I shivered, frozen down to my spine. I was weak, spent, unable even to move my head. It was so cold. I opened my eyes and rapidly blinked as bright light blinded me.

A soft voice rattled across my ears, "Over here."

My head spun as I squinted toward the sound. It was strained and raw. I gasped as my vision cleared. A young woman was bound to a bed with thick leather straps. Heavy metal cuffs chained her chafed and torn wrists and ankles to the rusty bedframe. She'd been struggling.

She was agonizingly thin, her ribs and hip bones showing through the sparse, dirty nightdress she wore. Her dark hair was a tangled mess around her chest. I couldn't see much more, as she had a hood over her face. My eyes strayed and stuck on the thick needle plunged into her arm, hooked up to a tube that dripped her blood into a bowl on the stone floor. I noticed a thin line tattoo on her upper arm that looked like a rolling wave.

I tried to talk but had no voice, becoming frustrated and panicked as my vocal cords refused to work. She spoke through panting breaths, her voice muffled. "He… Wants the pearl… Using my blood… Slaughter. All of you… Us." She used the last of her breath. "Stop him! Find me!"

I tried to move to help ease her distress, to release her straps and whisk her away from whatever caused her rough voice to seize with such fear. In my head, I screamed to her, but no words passed my lips.

A disembodied voice, dark, deep, and sensuously male, spoke next. My blood turned cold. It was the voice from the hole. "Oh! You have a visitor. How wonderful! Your blood *is* useful. Shall I pop the kettle on? I adore fresh fish. It's lovely with those sweet local bananas."

He laughed with menace before hissing, "You got lucky tonight. Last chance, mermaid. Give me the pearl or die."

EIGHT

JELLY

"Merciful Goddess! Jelly! WAKE UP!"

Rough hands jostled me, slamming me into the sea sponge mattress. I rolled away in alarm, disoriented. Scrubbing at my eyes, I tried to calm my thumping heartbeat with deep breaths. A thick, dark cloud engulfed the lanternfish above me. Fingers snapped twice and cleared the room. Oggie stared at me with wide, frightened eyes, eight arms latched around the bedpost. Synchi slumped in the chair next to my bed and wiped at her face with a trembling hand. "You were screaming. I couldn't wake you up."

I smoothed my breath into something less frenetic, and patted my lap. Oggie released one arm at a time before he snuggled in, shoving the end of one into his beak like a pacifier. He made small chittering noises—poor baby. I'd scared the ink out of him.

"Synchi?" My voice sounded broken, rattled by the night terror.

"You're safe, Jelly. I'm right here. Before you wake too much, tell me everything you saw."

I told her about the girl, and dread snaked up my back, leaving behind goosebumps. Synchi's face was impassive as I croaked, "Who is she? We have to find her, Synchi! He's torturing her because of me!"

"Perhaps. You can't be sure."

"Aren't I? Give me the pearl or die? It doesn't get much clearer than that! He was *draining* her blood, Synchi!" I was beside myself with guilt, tears hovering in my eyes.

Synchi hung her head. "Your first true vision, and a terrible one at that. Come, you need to eat." She helped me from the bed, and I leaned on her as we swam for the living room, Oggie repositioning to circle my neck.

After settling me on the chaise under a thick kelp blanket, she lifted sympathetic eyes to mine. "When you detonated the shark, you pulled power from the pearl. Somehow, that is drawing the mystery man to you like a homing device." She shivered. "He is powerful."

"Did she reach into my head?"

Synchi tapped her chin and shook her head. "I'm not sure, Jelly. Maybe he did something. Or she could do it alone. Perhaps it was the pearl. I have little experience with the fine nuances of vision work. And it has been decades since I've had any brush with magic on the surface. To my detriment, it now seems."

She brought me a bowl of fire urchins, and I forced myself to eat. My blood instantly warmed as the spicy meat hit my stomach and their magic unfurled. I pulled the blanket up to my chin. "I couldn't speak or move. It was like that when the pearl showed me the bombs."

Synchi frowned. "Yes. That's an issue, and I don't have a quick answer." She fluffed the pillow behind me and sat in her chair, furtively pulling on her chin braid as she changed the subject. "The guards saw you kill the shark. There will be questions. It's a shame you couldn't have paralyzed it. I would have liked to question it."

I grumbled, "Difficult to do when rows of sharp teeth are coming for your throat. Did you call Tro or did someone else?"

Synchi sighed. "I did. When it attacked, I wasn't sure I could hold the barrier and wanted Warriors there in case you didn't reach me in time. I disappeared using glamor when the guards arrived because... I can't appear weak." Her eyes darted to mine. "You mustn't tell them I'm struggling. We will have pandemonium if they suspect I can't hold the bubble. And the Trident might toss you in the hole for killing the shark."

I groaned, "Or worse. Tro said it might be worse. Synchi, these attacks won't stop. First the lingcod, then the young shark. What if that was a twenty-foot adult? And it wasn't its fault. Something possessed it. I can't indiscriminately kill animals that aren't in their right minds." I worried my lip with my teeth. "I have to go to the surface and find the girl. It's my fault she's being harmed, and she's involved in this."

When I glanced up, I caught her trying to hide her fearful expression. I whispered, "If I leave, you'll all be safe. It's the pearl he wants. Synchi, convince them to let me go to the surface. I have to leave, for everyone's sake." As much as I spoke with courage, my nerves were quaking inside. It was one thing to go on a set mission for one month. This was a completely different kettle of fish.

Her lips pulled down. "Could you tell where he was keeping her?"

I scrunched up my face. "I wasn't paying attention. She was so starved. I was too upset by what he was doing to her."

The first rays of morning light streamed into the cave, washing a path across the sandy floor until it struck the mirror, blinding me until I shifted positions. Mori's worried voice buzzed in my head.

Toto keeps swimming back and forth, back and forth, muttering to himself. He's scaring me.

I replied, *We're kind of in the middle of things over here, like me needing to go to the surface. Synchi doesn't think the Trident will let me.*

What? The surface? Who will kill the crazy sharks? You can't leave in the middle of this.

That's what we're discussing. Seriously, I have to go.

I refocused on the Shaman, weighing my words. "Tro is upset. You're scared." Synchi snorted. I narrowed my eyes. "I can see it on your face. I have to leave. The sooner, the better. If I'm not here, the attacks will stop."

Synchi blinked. Her milky-blue eyes clouded with apprehension, and her lower lip trembled, jiggling her braid. After weighing my words in silence, she nodded her head in resignation. "He will hunt you on the surface."

"But at least you'll be safe. Call Anna and tell her I'm coming. Tell her she has no choice but to help me. I noticed she didn't agree when we spoke."

"You'll need more than just her, but she'll assemble a team. Whatever is possessing the sea life is powerful. You'll be in danger."

"I'm already in—"

An Official Trident Triggerfish burst through the window, able to swim past Synchi's magic. With a voice full of self-importance, it proclaimed, "Shaman Synchiropus Splendidus and Warrior Scyphozoa Vetula, The Trident demands to see you." When we didn't move, it turned in a circle and barked, "Immediately!" Synchi dismissed it, promising we would be swift.

She snapped on her glamor and ran her fingers through her sleek bob. She checked herself over, ensuring no wrinkles remained on her skin. "Wear your full armor. It will look more imposing. Keep your temper checked and do not argue with them. Let me handle it."

I pulled the chain mail over my tail. "What about Anna? We need to tell her about the shark and my vision."

Synchi snapped, "That will have to wait. We have to keep you out of prison for killing a shark first." She muttered the words so softly that I almost missed them. "Keep you alive more like it."

We left the cave and swam for the Great Hall, Synchi too depleted to shuttle us by whirlpool. Mers stopped and stared at us along the way, whispering behind covered mouths, but some were outright brazen. We passed a group of mermaids, ones I'd gone to school with, and they gossiped as we swam past, their voices cruelly mocking.

"Killed an innocent shark. Murdered it in cold blood. She somehow blew it to pieces."

"What's her problem? Why can't she be happy? She's got her precious warrior status and a powerful partner. What else does she want?"

"Didn't you hear? She broke up with Fillian. He's already moved on."

"Really? He's next in line for commander! She's an idiot!"

My cheeks burned with indignation. I held my head high and tried to let their words slip over my skin without cutting. Synchi snarled at them, and they balked before swimming away, tittering. "Ignore them. They're vapid idiots," Synchi growled. More Mers stared, but turned away when I met their eyes.

I dropped my voice. "What do we say to the Trident?"

Synchi stalled as we reached the gates. "You say as little as possible." She shot me a look of warning. "I mean it, Jelly. Hold your tongue." Solemn guards led us into the hall, and I avoided the gaze of those from last night, their expressions hostile. I pushed back my shoulders and swam at the Shaman's side, ready to meet the Trident.

My confidence faltered as we faced them. Instead of occupying the round stone table, they sat at one made of shimmering ivory shell, stretching in a long rectangle along one wall, most of them scowling as we entered. Lady Amphi lifted her hand for silence. In a groggy voice, she said, "Lord Tro called this very early emergency meeting, demanding our Shaman and Warrior Jelly attend. Lord Tro, I hand to you."

Tro floated beside Synchi and me. He had braided his hair in the Warrior style, and trimmed his thick red beard. He, too, wore full armor. With a hardened expression, he addressed his colleagues with authority. "There have been two recent attacks on the bubble, both involving this Warrior," he said, nodding to me. "We believe a sinister force on the surface is testing the strength of the Shaman. Last night, a young shark attempted to bite through the shield, and this brave Warrior destroyed it before it could cause further harm."

He lowered his chin to me and said, "We owe her our thanks."

Synchi nodded. "Indeed, Warrior Jelly did us all a great service, defending the bubble valiantly." I thought we were off to a good start and relaxed my tight shoulders.

They seized up when Lady Salmy's nasal voice sneered, "Trouble follows you, Jelly. How is it you were there?" Lady Salmy had a bright pink tail with matching eyes and hair. Given her coloring, one would expect sweetness and sugar, but she was toxic.

I bowed to her. "Serendipity, Lady Salmy. Right place,

right time." There was no way I would admit that Synchi set it up. Lady Salmy snorted and leaned toward the merman to her right, whispering. Lord Thunni.

He loathed me. He believed mermaids should focus on reproducing. My warrior status vexed him. His gray eyes flashed and his salt and pepper hair floated as he tipped his head with a condescending smirk. His voice was mocking. "What were you doing outside the bubble at night?"

I glanced at Tro, and he gave an imperceptible nod. I answered, "Cutting up abandoned nets, sir."

"To what purpose?" he asked.

My mind blanked. Was he stupid? Nets drowned animals, not to mention Mers like my father. I opened my mouth to respond when Synchi replied, "We are getting off track. What is important is that the sea creatures are under foreign control. Likely initiated from the surface. I believe that Jelly should go up and investigate."

A different merman responded. Lord Manta huffed, "Well, *I believe* that when she's on the surface, she's playing instead of securing a pregnancy. And the last time…" He lifted his hands in the air, "Boom!" My eyes widened.

Tro interjected on my behalf. "Jelly has infiltrated the human world numerous times, brought back useful intel, and, most importantly, has remained psychologically undamaged by the experience. Many of our mermaids return from the surface traumatized. Now, our bubble is under attack. Please, let's stay on point."

Lady Salmy quipped, "Not so sure about the psychologically undamaged part, Lord Tro."

Lord Manta said with a dismissive wave of his hand, "We're secure behind the bubble. I'm sure the Shaman can keep us safe." Synchi's fresh face did not flinch.

Lady Salmy tossed her bright pink curls over her shoulder. She tapped one thin arm with lethally long nails. "I think she's trying to get attention, just like always, with her multi-paged reports on the pollution. Everything is fine. We need to talk about punishment for killing a shark."

The pearl jerked across the chain under my armor, expressing its displeasure. I inhaled a soft wince as it banged against the bruise. Tro dropped his voice, growling. "It has been a while since any of you saw the state of the world outside. The ocean is not as you remember. And if—"

Lord Thunni snorted, interrupting him. "The pollution is a gross exaggeration. We don't need to go outside the bubble. I haven't been in years. The girl likes to make up stories to feed her ego, nothing more. There's no pollution, at least, not to the extent she claims."

"Exactly," said Lady Salmy triumphantly. "That's the perfect word. She's exaggerating."

I stared at the Trident, my blood boiling. The girl? Stories? I gasped, "Wait a minute. You haven't seen the garbage?" The pearl yanked again. These ignorant Mers were no different from the humans. Just swimming along with no consideration of the state of the world around them.

Steady, Jelly, came Synchi's voice as she tucked her hair behind her ear.

I cried, "You think I'm exaggerating?" The pearl lashed under my armor, pounding on the bruise. Blood flowed against my tongue as I snapped at my cheek for control.

Lady Salmy rolled her eyes. Her voice was scornful. "Why would I?" She sat back and looked at her nails. "My life inside the bubble is everything I could want. There's no reason to see the mess the humans have made."

The pearl heated and vibrated with rage. I hissed, "But

you'll treat mermaids as slaves? As prostitutes?" She tossed her hair and muttered something to Lord Thunni that made him laugh. My hands fisted tight, and I bit my tongue over and over. The blood spurred the pearl forward. Hair ripped from the back of my neck as it lurched against my armor, taking vehement command, using me as its puppet.

With a roar, I dropped a heavy glamor on the Trident, encasing them in a snow globe of pollution. I flooded it with nurdles, the lentil-sized pieces of plastic that were the scourge of the ocean, creating a current to make them swirl and blind the Trident. A female voice squealed in shock.

I added dozens of plastic bags, floating to look like jellyfish, disintegrating jugs beat their skin, while plastic cutlery stabbed and sliced them. Bloated fish ripped open, their guts spilling loose with bottle tops. A turtle flailed, strangled from a plastic ring, begging for help. The sounds of hundreds of screaming whales filled the cavernous space, and the smell of melting plastic permeated the glamor, so vile you could taste it. The carcass of a misshapen, small dolphin hovered before them, poisoned before it breathed its first breath.

Shrieks of horror delighted me as I plied them with the gruesome glamor. This was only a fraction of what I'd seen, but these images haunted my dreams. Lord Thunni yelled for me to stop. I didn't. I couldn't. The pearl had taken over.

"Jelly, that's enough!" Synchi shouted.

I threw an imaginary net over Lady Salmy and Lord Thunni, relishing their fear. They thrashed as I entangled their limbs and pulled tight. I grinned maliciously as a plastic bag smothered Lady Salmy's face, indenting when she gulped in a breath. It pressed harder, and her eyes bulged with panic. I let out a cackle of glee.

Suddenly, my glamor broke, leaving the Trident members

blinking in shock. Lady Salmy rearranged her hair with shaking fingers and grasped at her throat, assuring herself she could breathe. Lord Thunni's eyes blazed with enough venom to melt my skin. The Shaman sagged, and the pearl rumbled, displeased. I looked over at Tro, noting the gleam of wicked pleasure in his eyes although he kept his face blank.

I snarled at them. "That's what it's like out there!"

As one, they yelled, their shouts climbing on top of each other, swearing to send me to prison for life. There were cries for torture to teach me a lesson. Lady Salmy snapped her fingers, and guards surrounded me, wrestling my wrists behind my back. I shouted, "You can't do this! You don't understand! We will die if I don't go up!"

The Trident members turned their backs on me, arguing at full volume. Their faces twisted in rage or fear, save for one, Lord Synanceia, who remained blank, as if disinterested in the entire drama. One guard sidled close, shamelessly rubbing against me, invading my space. He growled in my ear, "I can't wait to visit you in the hole, little Jelly. Get it? The hole? Yeah, we'll *all* get to visit your hole. Traitor."

It was Gorn. He'd been a lecherous prick from the day I started training. I struggled as he laughed at his sick joke, the other guards grinning and leering. He licked his lips and moved behind me, claiming ownership of my wrists. He pressed against my back, his arousal baldly apparent. I fought to put space between us, making him move closer and rub against me. He snarled loudly, "I'm going to paint your skin red with your blood and white from my cu—"

"Commander Tro! Control your guards!" Synchi shouted.

Tro barked, "Release her!" I took advantage of Gorn's proximity and slammed my skull into his nose, relishing the crunch and the bloom of dark red in the water. He let go with a jerk and retreated. I rubbed my wrists and straightened, certain I was about to die.

Lady Amphi lifted her hand for silence. Her voice was hollow. "Lord Tro escorted me outside the protection zone yesterday. I wore two-ply cloth to avoid swallowing or inhaling the plastic and keep it from entering my ears. I needed eye protection, which I thought ridiculous, but proved necessary when a plastic knife bounced off the goggles. There is a taste to the water like nothing I've ever experienced. It's no longer salty. I can't quite describe it except to say it tastes like death. The fish are dying. *We* are dying. And now, we are under magical attack. Controlled by something on the surface."

The Trident members mumbled amongst themselves, still throwing barbed glares in my direction. Gorn hovered nearby, his face suggesting he would love to mete out my punishment. I smirked as he fixed his nose with a sharp twist, causing himself to grunt from pain.

Lord Manta smoothed his hands down his black tail, his dark eyes flicking at me with new appreciation. "That was a disturbing and effective glamor, Warrior Jelly, and very jarring. But tell me, what do you plan to do? Wander the Earth in search of evil magic? If that's the case, we'll never see you again. The surface is rife with it."

Lady Salmy shouted, "This is ludicrous! You can't believe she should go up again! The girl is dangerous and disturbed! She's killed an innocent shark, a species we swore to protect! The guards said that she blew it to pieces. Why didn't she take it peacefully? Why kill it?"

Lord Thunni backed her up. "Absolutely right! It was murder! Forget the hole. We should behead her for this crime!"

"That's a touch aggressive," snorted Lord Manta.

Their voices rose into hurricane force, battering and

beating against each other. My eyes shifted to Synchi as I pressed my fingers to my temple. *Tell them about the pearl. They will kill me if you don't.*

Synchi raised her arms and shot a beam of light down from the ceiling to encompass her, drawing everyone's attention and eyes. She waited for silence and thundered, "The Vetula Pearl has activated. Warrior Jelly has had her first vision, and the Mers are unquestionably in danger."

The Trident members combusted.

"The Pearl?"

"The Vetula Pearl?"

"Activated?"

"She wears the pearl? Why weren't we told?"

Synchi explained. "The identity of the bearer is intentionally kept hidden. It is a coveted item, as we now see."

"When?" gasped Lord Manta. His eyes widened as he realized. "The explosion! Why were we not immediately told? Shaman, answer me!"

Synchi crossed her arms. "We have spoken with Goddess Kelbazi. She stated the pearl is being hunted and that Jelly must go up top. I contacted Anna Smith, the head Witch of the New Forest Coven. She is my only remaining Surfecti ally, and even calling her that is a stretch."

Lord Manta paled. "The Goddess?" Even Lady Salmy looked shaken at the mention of Kelbazi.

Lord Thunni turned a sickly shade of purple as his blood pressure soared to the lanternfish above. Spit flew from his mouth as he careened off his stool and roared, "The Mers will have no dealings with those traitors! After ignoring us when we begged for help?" He slammed his fists on the table. "We had *twelve years* of nuclear testing right over our heads, and the Surfecti did NOTHING! Sixty-seven bombs, Shaman! Do you think our cancers are only from plastic? I will never work with the Surfecti! NEVER!!!"

He hyperventilated, his eyes stricken wide and tortured. He appeared close to tears and fled the room. An uncomfortable silence followed his exit, and the other Trident members shuffling uneasily on their stools.

Tro spoke quietly. "I remember very well. I have suffered a significant loss to cancer. My daughter lost her mother. Jelly lost hers. None of us are strangers to tragedy at the hand of the humans."

Lady Salmy looked down at her lap. Lady Amphi wiped her face, and Lord Manta reached over to lay a comforting hand on the shoulder of Lord Synanceia, the Stonefish. True to his name, he had watched the proceedings without emotion, remaining impassive while everyone else fractured. The older merman dropped his face into his hand, nursing the creases in his forehead. He lifted his eyes and nodded to me. "Was your glamor an accurate representation of the world beyond the bubble?"

My voice was soft. "Yes, sir. It was not an exaggeration."

He lifted his chin to Synchi. "Thus, I will assume it is a challenge to keep us protected, and only becoming more difficult as the pollution progresses. Is that true, Shaman?"

She frowned before nodding, her sleek hair swirling from the motion as she replied. "Despite the magical donations from the Mers, it is not enough." She choked. "The bubble is vulnerable. The shark tore through the protection zone and bit through the main shield. It was a young shark. An adult would have obliterated it."

He sighed heavily. "The pearl activates when the ocean is in peril. We must follow its direction, especially if prompted by Goddess Kelbazi. Warrior Jelly should go to the surface. She must work with the Surfecti to stop this menace."

Lady Sphyraena, named for a barracuda, stared at me with a critical eye, her voice slurred as her lips caught on her sharp teeth. "Are you prepared for such a perilous mission?"

My chin lifted as I spoke with all the confidence I could muster. "I am not afraid of the surface. The pearl will destroy our enemies."

She flashed a smile that made me shudder. "I like your gumption. I hope that our faith in you is well-placed. It's a yes from me."

Lord Manta looked at the Shaman with narrowed eyes. "You truly believe she should go to the surface?"

Synchi touched her heart and stated, "I do. I see no alternative."

"All in favor?" asked Lady Amphi.

Lady Salmy scowled so profoundly I thought she'd never recover. With obvious reluctance, she nodded in agreement. The remaining Trident members raised their hands one by one. Six yesses and one most definite no. I was going back up.

Tro nodded to me. "My office, Warrior."

"Sir, yes, Sir."

Synchi spoke in my mind. *I will arrange transportation.*

NINE

SIMMI

I looked through the square in the stone walls. No glass protected me from the chilly breeze, heavy with sea spray and humidity. The sky, a crisp, cyan blue, streaked with pink and orange, the end of another endless day. The ocean rolled in the background; the waves providing the soundtrack to my captivity.

Outside, a bird made a terrible screeching noise. Nature had been unkind to it when handing out songs. He yelled again, more urgently. My forehead wrinkled. I heard him vacate his branch, and the sweet scent of falling blossoms drifted toward me. I sensed my captor was near.

He pulled off my hood and paced at the foot of the bed, his hand running through his thick hair in frustration. Tugging on the straps around my body, he caused them to cinch tighter as he unbuckled them. I winced. My ankles ached as he released the metal cuffs, pain surging as blood massaged through my bruises. I tried to move my feet, but they were listless and unable to respond to my command.

I hated he was so achingly gorgeous. It didn't seem fair. Someone with such fine bone structure, such thick, shiny hair, who moved like a dream in a sleek, graceful body shouldn't be a monster. He should be a rock star, a movie star, or at least an underwear model. Something fabulous and famous.

He snarled, "Twice my possessions have failed. Twice! I was certain the shark would be strong enough. Bad news for you, sweetness. I will need more blood if I want a stronger ocean pet."

My shoulders ached as he lashed my wrists above my head, the metal cutting into raw skin. I croaked, "What are you doing with it? What ocean pet? Are you trying to adopt a whale?"

He ignored my question. Too weak to sit by myself, he hauled me up under my armpits, rattling my skull against the metal frame headboard. Bits of rust flaked off and settled on my thin cotton shirt. He held my jaw open, pouring a dark liquid down my throat, the only sustenance he offered.

I fisted my hands helplessly, shackled to the bed frame. Distracted, he poured faster than I could swallow, and I choked, some of it dripping off my chin. It smelled and tasted wonderful, like chocolate and honeysuckle. It was potent, and vital strength returned with each gulp. I reached my tongue beyond my lower lip to chase the spilled drops.

There was a rushing through my blood like someone swept away my fatigue with a vigorous broom. My brain was electric, sharp, and cunning. I needed him to talk. I drew on my Mers power and whispered huskily, seductively, "What should I call you? My Beautiful Nightmare? The Stunning Son of Sin? What's your name, gorgeous?"

He leaned in close, scouring my eyes, his hand snatching out to my face. "How did you call her?" I shook my head through the solid grip he held on my jaw. His rich voice dropped to a snarl. "I asked you a question, sweet Simmi. You would be wise to answer me."

"I didn't," I said in a stronger voice. "I swear." It was true. The woman had just appeared. I'd been staring out the window when the bird started hopping up and down as he looked past me. The fabric of my hood was a loose linen weave, sheer enough to let me make out silhouettes and shadows. I'd turned my head, and there she was.

She was clearly a woman because of her curves. But I'd smelled her more than anything. The air in the room had turned sweet and salty, like my favorite taffy. There was something oddly familiar about the scent, but I couldn't grasp it. I should have told her my name, but I was too desperate to warn her.

My handsome captor released my chin with a shove, and the back of my head smacked painfully. He unchained my wrist cuffs from the headboard and yanked my body down, the thin shirt gathering around my waist. He tugged it somewhat into place and lashed my hands to the side of the bedframe, uncaring when I cried with pain. I groaned as he cuffed my ankles to the footboard. He held up the hood. I balked. "Can you leave it off? I can't breathe through it."

He bundled it into a ball, throwing it across the room as he shouted, "She shouldn't be able to do that!" He paced back and forth and muttered under his breath. The strange chocolate drink heightened my senses. I caught his whisper. "If I force the bubble, they will all die. That's not the plan. Think, Terrun!"

Terrun.

"Is that your name? Terrun? Where are we? Why are you doing this?"

I tried to get him to stay and talk, but after he thrust the needle into my arm, all my strength, smarts, and courage drained away with my blood. The world faded to a pinprick of light. When I came around, the needle was gone, replaced by a slice of gauze and tape. Distracted, he'd left off the hood.

It was dark outside, and the air was damp and cold. There was an orchestra of small voices: tree frogs. Slowly, as if cotton pulled from my ears, the little chirps and whistles formed words I could understand.

"Wake up!!"

"Si-mi!!"

They looped over themselves, calling me. I blinked my eyes and whispered, "I'm here. I'm awake." They returned to their weaving chorus of frog song.

"He took a lot," said a trilling masculine voice at the window. The bird perched in the square opening in the stone wall. He had a brilliant yellow chest, and his wings and back were brown, as if he were wearing a wool coat. With a black stripe over his eyes, he resembled either a highway robber or Zorro.

I sighed and mumbled, "Well, that's just perfect. I'm losing my freaking mind."

The bird chuckled. "You're far from delirious or delusional. You can understand us because he's heightened your Fae blood with the drink."

I perked up. "Where are we? The last thing I remember is swimming in the ocean in Mexico."

The bird fluffed his wings against the cool night air. "You're in Bermuda. On Castle Island. In the fortress. Strapped to a bed. In the cellar."

I smiled and winced as it hurt my chapped lips. "Thank you for the precision. Can you tell me why I'm here? And who is the man, or whatever he is?"

"We've all been scrambling to find out information. Both of you simply popped into existence. I overheard him muttering about the lead content in Bermuda Rock and that it would be impossible to find you with magic. It pleased him. I've been watching from the oleander tree. He gives you the drink, then he bleeds you. About an hour later, he paints your blood on the ceiling. You're usually unconscious when he does it."

Above me was a vast array of rust-colored symbols. I'd studied them when awake, but didn't recognize them. The man had refreshed some, making them more red than brown. I turned my head to the bird. "Do you have a name?"

"Call me Kindee," he said with a bow. "I am your knight in yellow feathers. Now, you must be hungry. When he drains you, he draws from your muscles. You're wasting away."

"I was always on the thin side. This is alarming."

"He's sucking you dry. He was more aggressive tonight and took a lot. We brought you something."

"We?"

I watched weakly, stunned, as a lizard stalked up my chest before jumping onto my cheek with clammy toes. He cradled a half-eaten cherry to my lips, resembling a small red pumpkin. It was sweet, a little tart, and my mouth watered as I chewed. It must be real. I wouldn't hallucinate the taste.

Kindee said, "They pitted them, but watch for stones just in case."

One by one, a dozen eight-inch lizards brought me gnawed cherries. Their bodies were green with blue hind legs and purple tails. After delivering their prize, a couple of them puffed out a bright orange dewlap, an expandable flap of skin under their throats. The last lizard shrugged and said, "I hope the cherries make you stronger."

The bird, Kindee, hopped onto my chest, his little talons holding on for purchase. "I saw the woman."

My eyes flew wide. "You did? I thought I made it up!"

Kindee said, "Quite a beauty. But she lay there like a lump. I thought she'd at least speak, if not free you."

"I don't think she could. You're certain we're in Bermuda?"

He cocked his head to the side. Ignoring my question, he said, "The man will return when the sun rises. At dawn and dusk, he bleeds you. We will keep feeding you as best we can. Esmerelda will give you some cover for the night. She'll have to tear it down every morning, but it will keep out some of the cold. Good night, Miss Simmi."

He spread his brown coat and flew away, pausing at the window to screech a god-awful sound. A beast of a spider skittered across the stone. She got to work immediately, quickly weaving a thick, golden web. It was highly complex, and she danced deftly back and forth along her strands.

I watched with fascination. She was a master. Her back was reddish, and her belly was white and plump. Her web muffled the ocean breeze, a gauzy curtain to keep out the chill. When she finished, she paused in the middle of the net. In an ancient voice, she said, "I will keep watch. Hopefully, I will catch my breakfast before he comes."

I smiled faintly as the goosebumps on my skin settled. "Thank you, Esmerelda. How did you do that so fast?"

She chuckled, the sound like a two-pack-a-day smoker. She waved three of her striped legs in the air. "I'm a Hurricane Spider. We have adapted the tips of our legs for weaving. They point inward rather than outward, as in most other spiders. Sleep, Simmi. Try your best to dream. Dream of the mermaid so she can come and rescue you."

I whispered, "How do you know she's a mermaid?"

Esmerelda tapped a striped leg to her face. "I can smell things. She was salty, like fresh seaweed."

I slept well. Not exactly warm, but less frigid than before. However, frustration consumed me when I woke. My mermaid hadn't come back. I shuddered at the smooth, honeyed voice of the beautiful man as he silently entered the room. "Good morning, sweet Simmi. It's time for your bleeding, darling." I glanced at the window as he fussed with the needle and tubing. Esmerelda and her web were gone, and outside, on the branch of the oleander tree, a bird with a yellow chest nodded to me, singing his terrible song.

TEN

JELLY

Fillian was on guard outside Tro's office. When he saw me, his face contorted. I couldn't tell if it was a smile of pleasure or a grimace of worry. "Are you really going back up?"

"Word travels fast," I mumbled.

He shrugged. "Gorn is furious you broke his nose. He contacted me to report what my 'psycho ex' had done, and that you were on your way here. It's probably good that you're leaving." He looked at the other merman on duty and leaned closer. "See if you can get pregnant while you're there. Remember, get someone with blue eyes." He drew back with a wink and a nod.

I looked at him incredulously. He just couldn't take no for an answer.

I banged on the door. Tro called me in, and I bowed deeply, respectfully. "Lord Pterois, Commander, thank you for what you said to the Trident." I used his full title to express my gratitude. Fillian and the other guard shifted, listening in. Tro waved me in and crossed the room, closing the door. His stern face softened when he turned.

I cleared my throat. "That was, um, quite the meeting." I stared at the walls, scrutinizing the crossed swordfish bills instead of looking him in the eye. I'd lost my temper outrageously, and despite the agreement to send me to the surface, the Trident could still punish me for terrorizing them. If reprisals were coming, Tro would determine them.

He chuckled. "Sit, Jelly." He exhaled loudly. "Your fury has always been your driving force. As much as you nearly gave me heart failure, that was the most entertaining Trident session to date. Relax. There are no repercussions for your actions. I've been trying to get the Trident to venture outside for years. They always waved me off. They've neglected their duties to the Mers, and it was high time they see the truth." I gave him a lopsided grin, relieved I wasn't in trouble.

He moved behind his large stone desk and pulled open a drawer. His eyes shadowed briefly, and he hummed in his throat, his eyes vulnerable when they met mine. He said, "I have something for you. I probably should have given them to you years ago, and Goddess knows you've earned them, but I was reluctant to let them go." He handed me a bundle of supple pale gray leather, the straps carefully looped and tied together.

"What is this?"

"Open it and see."

I wrestled with the frozen knot, and when I unrolled the leather, my breath caught, and tears sprang to my eyes. I whispered, "Da's knives." My hesitant fingers caressed the hilts. "I thought they were lost."

Tro swam to my side. "Traditionally, the blades of fallen Warriors go back into service. I couldn't..." he choked on the words. "Your father was my best friend, Jelly. I couldn't bear to see his blades in someone else's hands. You're so like him, so outspoken and opinionated. He and the Trident also butted heads. He hated the Procreation Missions."

His voice dropped, heavy with sadness. "I wish I'd recognized how distraught he was after your mother's death, but my own grief made me oblivious. Both of us lost the loves of our lives within five months of each other. I was blind to his pain." His eyes rimmed with silver tears as he whispered, "But he gave me you, Jelly. He gave me a second daughter."

Mori's mother died before mine did. Mori had handled her grief, wallowing in it and feeling its full extent. I'd taken the opposite stance, burying it deep inside to fester. She and I had already been friends, but our mutual and tragic loss cemented it.

I blinked back my tears, stroking the knives I'd seen strapped to my father each time he'd gone to work. One had a hilt of heavy white bone, crafted with four holes for knuckles, perfect for close-quarter combat. The other knife's hilt was black stone, the inset contrasting in a wave of mother-of-pearl. I felt a strum of energy. "They're vibrating," I whispered.

Tro nodded. "That's another reason I didn't put them back into service. His magic still infuses them. I didn't want anyone else to touch them." He drew away and swam behind his desk. "I so often think of you as my little girl. It's difficult to remember that you're not. Go ahead. Slip your fingers into the handle of the knuckle one first. It will change in shape to fit your fingers. You'll sense his essence as the knives shift to your energy."

I tore my eyes away from the knives to look at Tro. He was the merman who had taught me to navigate the world with a strong spine. "You're the best Da I could have asked for, Tro, after…after mine died. Are you sure you don't want them for yourself?"

Tro swallowed thickly. "I had many years with him, Jelly. Years that were stolen from you." He nodded to the knives. "They belong to you now."

Sorrow pierced my heart at his words. Tentatively, I picked up the bone knife and a brace of familiar energy ran through my blood, as if my father stood at my side, smiling with approval. Stunned delight ripped through me as the handle shimmered and shrank around my grip. I held it tight in my right fist and slashed the five-inch blade through the water. I inspected it closer, and noticed the spine had reverse serrations, allowing it to slice through thick flesh.

Tro grinned at my captivated expression as I admired the wicked blade. I asked, "What do you call this kind of knife? One with this kind of grip?"

"It's called a knuck. It's useful in combat because you won't drop it. The bone will protect your hand when you punch someone with it."

I cackled. "I like you said when and not if." I punched aggressively through the water, immediately dragging the blade sideways.

Tro snorted with approval at my technique. "Just like your father."

I lifted the other knife and pressed the button on the handle. A stiletto blade sprang free, and I inhaled as I twisted it back and forth, the metal glimmering in the light. My voice was reverent. "They are beautiful, Tro. He never let me look at them up close. Probably scared I'd slice my fingers off." I set down the knuck and thumbed the stiletto carefully. It was deathly sharp.

Tro said softly. "If he hadn't died so young, your life would be so different."

I shrugged. "I wouldn't have studied environmentalism. After Mom died of cancer and Da drowned in the net, I was so enraged." I frowned as my pleasure at the gift soured. I said bitterly, "You and Synchi mapped out my life. She made me an expert in pollution, and you made me a ruthless Warrior."

His voice was gentle. "I wanted to adopt you so badly. You were so lost, so angry. You'd only talk to Mori. The Shaman and I... We argued viciously over who should take you in. I was the better choice for your emotional health, especially because of Mori. But then she told me about the pearl and its visions. I couldn't fight that. But I didn't want you defenseless if it activated during your lifetime. I pushed you hard. I had to."

He rubbed at his eyes as his voice dropped into a croak. "And now it has. Goddess, help me, Jelly. I am terrified for you." My jaw went slack. Nothing scared Tro. I slowly snapped the blade back in its handle and placed it on his desk beside the knuck. Thoughtful, I smoothed out the pale gray leather. It was a holster. The long straps bent at the ends from being knotted for so long.

I said in a soft voice, "You have been my father, Tro. I am so grateful for you and everything you have given me. But I *cannot* have you be frightened for me. I need you to believe in me." I whispered, "So many Mers look at me and think I'm all wrong. Too vicious, too loud, too smart, too opinionated, too cold. No one understands me like you do. Whatever small team I have? Well, they *must* believe I will succeed. I need to lean on that faith."

Bubbles swarmed him as he exhaled harshly, disappointed with himself. He rounded the desk and gripped me. "Jelly, I believe in you. Of course I do. Besides Mori, you are my greatest accomplishment." He pulled back, his eyes lined with furious tears. "You will find our enemy and rip them to pieces, just like you did that shark. It is who you are. But you cannot go alone. Fillian will accompany you. He's strong and adores you. He will be your guard."

I said firmly, "No. He will not. He does not adore me at all. He will not come with me." I took a deep breath and said with a tiny tremble, "Sir...Tro...I want to take Mori with me. I haven't spoken to her about it yet." He drew back, his breath tight in his throat. He squeezed his eyes shut, but I glimpsed stark terror before he did. I whispered, "I don't trust anyone else by my side, Tro. It has to be her. I'm sorry—"

"No," he barked. My heart sank. He was going to refuse my request. His jaw clenched. "No, you will not apologize. I trained Mori myself. The Shaman warned me twenty years ago that the pearl might call you. I knew you would want Mori if it did." He pinched at his eyes as if warding off tears, tears that broke through his voice. "But to have both my girls in danger..." He gave himself a sharp shake.

I almost choked on the lump in my throat, overwhelmed by his emotion. I'd never realized just how deeply he cared for me.

He swam back and forth across his office, mumbling under his breath. His face spun through mixed emotions until it settled into steady determination. He smacked his fists on his hips and said, "You shouldn't trust anyone else. If she agrees, she will go with you. My two female Warriors will take the surface by storm. They'll never see you coming." Relief swam through me. "But Jelly?" His eyes flared with anxiety. I raised my eyebrows in anticipation. His voice faltered. "Take care of my little fish."

"With my life, Tro. I swear it." I crossed both fists against my heart and bowed, giving him my solemn vow.

He nodded sharply and returned behind his desk, unnecessarily shuffling pieces of algae paper until they formed a neat pile. He settled them with a heavy bone paperweight. With a deep breath, he asked, "When do you leave?"

I said, "Synchi is making arrangements as we speak."

He frowned and ran his meaty hand through his thick hair,

unwrapping some braids. "The pearl amplifies what you already have, who you are." He cocked his head and studied me. A wicked smile crept across his face. "Use your rage, Jelly. Find the bastard that's controlling our creatures and scream until his brain explodes."

"With pleasure, sir."

I left his office soon after, calling Mori telepathically. I had my fingers crossed, hoping she would receive my request with enthusiasm. She agreed to meet me at our secret place. Ever efficient, she arrived before me, and I smiled at the row of intricate sandcastles she'd built with her magic, complete with turrets and flags. She brightened as I entered the dim cave. "Hey, girlfish, what's up? Whoa! What are those? When did you get them?"

I flopped onto the sand beside her, accidentally destroying half her castles with the tip of my tail. "Oops. Sorry." She waved away my concern and turned her mischievous hazel eyes on me, staring greedily at the holster on my hips. I steadied my breath. "I need to tell you something, Mori. Things I only just discovered myself. And they eventually all concern you."

Her freckles scrunched together as she frowned. "Well, that sounds serious. Can I ask questions as we go along?"

"I think I need to dump."

"All right. Do you want to start with me and how I'm involved?"

I said, "It will make more sense if I give the background first."

She frowned but listened silently as I explained the pearl's ancestry and my orchestrated upbringing. When I stopped for breath, she held up her hand. She blinked a few times, her voice raw. "I love knowing Toto fought to have you. I would have loved for you to live with us." Her lips twisted into a grin. "Do you remember when we were nine, and I *accidentally* stabbed you, and you broke my nose in response?"

My shoulder twitched. "I didn't mean to hit you that hard. We've been over it a hundred times."

She chuckled. "And we didn't speak for two days." She moved closer and rested her forehead on mine. "Yeah, well, those were the longest two days of my life." She sat back. "Toto told me that family forgives, and he made me go talk to you. You've always been my sister."

I blinked heavily as my heart swelled. "I was a menace. Synchi got the full force of my temper as I swung between tears and tantrums. And then you knocked on the door and apologized. Then you asked if I wanted to play with swords."

Mori laughed. "Poor Toto. It's all his fault, though. The only toys we had were weapons." She squeezed my arm. "Okay, so you're wearing a magical pearl, gifted to the Mers by the Fae, and it heightens your abilities. I knew something was up after you exploded the shark. What else does it do?"

"It gives me visions. Well, one so far. It's different from the murky nightmares I've always had." I told her about the emaciated girl.

"What did you say to her?"

I flicked my tail irritably. "Nothing. I was desperate to ask her where she was, but I had no voice."

She frowned. "That sounds like a binding of sorts."

"What do you mean?"

"I've been studying the darker side of magic, the manipulations. Given enough power, you can bind another person's magic, even without their knowledge. Or you can bind people together or fix people to objects. I don't fully understand it."

"Do you think that's what's happening to me?"

She shrugged, "Not sure. But it's strange that you couldn't talk. Did you notice anything in the dream that suggested magic?"

I shook my head. "Kind of preoccupied with the tortured girl strapped to a bed."

Mori chewed on her lip, her forehead crumpled. "Who is this girl? Why did she reach out to you?"

"I have no idea. Earlier, Synchi contacted a powerful witch named Anna—"

Mori's eyes flew wide. "Anna Smith of the New Forest Coven? Oh, my Goddess! She's like the shining star of the Surfecti! And the Shaman knows her?" She clapped her hands together in glee. "I would *die* to meet her. She did a Cone of Power during World War Two!"

I frowned. "No clue what that is." Mori was about to launch into an explanation. She slapped her hand over her mouth and waved at me to keep speaking. I grinned at her excitement, and then my face fell. "So, this Anna isn't friendly. I don't think she likes me much."

"You were there? You met Anna Smith, and didn't tell me?" Her face was fiery with outrage.

"I haven't talked to you since all this went down! I'm telling you now! Synchi contacted her through a mirror."

"Telemirr," Mori interrupted.

"Telemirr, to tell Anna about the lingcod attack, and that the Goddess said we needed Surfecti help."

Mori paled, causing her freckles to stand out in stark relief. She tore at her thumbnail with her teeth. "Go back to the vision, Jelly. What did you see? It's important."

I closed my eyes. "I saw the girl strapped to a bed and her skin was raw from struggling. She had a needle in her arm, dripping blood into a bowl."

"Crap, crap, crap, that's bad. That's so bad. Blood magic is really dark. I wonder what he's doing with it." She released her nail from its torture and cocked her head, her eyes gleaming with rage. "He's using it to possess the sea creatures! That means she's at least part Mers. So, maybe a Walker's daughter? And the voice said it would kill you?"

I shivered and nodded.

She swept her hands through her long red hair, clamping her palms to her head. "This is a lot to take in. Are you done? Anything else?"

"I lost it during a Trident meeting. They wanted to punish me for the shark. But it turns out that none of them have been outside the bubble to see what it's like."

"Seriously?"

"Truth. So…the pearl dropped a fierce glamor and showed them." She shrieked with laughter as I gave her the gory details.

She clapped her hands. "I would have loved to have been a crab on the wall! I can just picture it. Lord Thunni stormed out?"

I nodded. "He hates the Surfecti because they didn't help during the nuclear testing at the Bikini Atoll."

She frowned and flicked at the sand with her fingers, creating a tiny mushroom cloud that settled back on the ocean floor. She mumbled, "He's not wrong."

I took a nervous breath. "Mori, there's one more thing." She lifted her eyebrows expectantly, hearing the tremor in my voice. "I told Tro I wanted you to come with me to the surface. He said he supported it, but it's your choice."

After a thousand seconds of silence, she asked, "Can I hold your knives?" Her face showed no emotion.

My forehead wrinkled with confusion. "Uh…what about what I just said?"

She scowled. "I'm still processing. Give me a hot minute and let me see your blades."

"They were my Da's." I slipped the knives from the holster and handed them to her handle-first. She took them with greedy fingers.

"So sharp," she muttered, testing the blades with her thumb. She made a thrusting motion with the stiletto. She swooped through the water with the knuck. After she gave them back, she crossed her arms and with a straight face, shook her head. "I don't think I should go."

"What? Why not? You're getting a doctorate in the Surfecti. You could meet Anna. Since we were little, you've wanted to repair the rift with the Surfecti. This is your chance!"

She shrugged and said, "Yeah, no. I don't think it's a good idea."

I slumped back, utterly deflated. My throat was thick, and a black hole settled where my heart lived. Mori bowled me over into the sand and wrestling me in a ferocious hug, laughing like a lunatic.

She shrieked, "Are you crazy? Of course, I'm coming with you! This is the chance of a lifetime! When do you think we'll meet the Witch? I wonder if she's friends with other Surfecti, like Shifters. I've always wanted to meet a Shifter. Ah, hell, who am I kidding? I want to sleep with a Shifter!"

She lowered her voice unnecessarily, her eyes darting around the cave as she rolled off of me. I sat up and watched her face contort. "I can't openly date anyone here. Word among the guards is that Toto threatened to decapitate anyone who dared to touch his precious daughter." She flung her arms out to the side. "I can go wild!"

I cocked my head at her. "Our lives will be in danger. I'm not sure shagging should be your primary aim."

She bumped her shoulder against mine playfully. "Come on, Jelly. It will be a blast! Two mermaids on the surface flexing their seductive powers."

I muttered, "More like hunting down an evil source of magic who wants to kill us all and will torture a girl to find my pearl. Sure, real sexy."

She sucked on her lip, pouting. "I plan on having fun while we hunt down this monster."

I softened. "Deal. Just don't get caught with your pants down."

"Pants!" she squealed as she spun in a circle of joy before throwing her arms around me. "I get to wear pants! I've never even seen pants. They only gave me dresses last time. Well, one dress. I didn't stick around long enough to wear anything else." She pulled back with stars in her eyes.

I giggled at her dizzying pleasure and pressed my fingers to my temple. *Synchi? Mori agreed to go. We need to call the Witch.*

ELEVEN

JELLY

here are you? Are you with Tro?
I replied to Synchi. *Mori and I are at the cave on the North side of the bubble, behind the fire corals.*

Synchi stepped out of a whirlpool right beside us. Mori screamed. "Shaman! Don't sneak up on me like that! I could have stabbed you!" She held up her hands, her fingers tight on her throwing stars.

I noticed Synchi was in her true form, without glamor. "Are you okay?" I asked, worried she was weak.

Synchi threw her hand up. "Mori saw me after the shark attack. There's no point in wearing that tight, young skin. It makes my spine ache."

Mori darted her eyes to me and confessed, "Jelly told me ages ago that you weren't as young as you appeared. But... Shaman...you're gorgeous just as you are. And you've earned every wrinkle on your face through laughing, crying, or scowling."

Synchi chuckled and dipped her chin, the shell swaying below it. "Thank you, Mori, that's sweet." She tugged at her braid as she eyed my best friend. "Are you ready to return to the surface? Your first trip was a disaster."

Mori beamed and nodded her head vigorously. "It's my dream, Shaman. Not the whole kill a demon thing, but working with Surfecti. It's all I've ever wanted. Will I get to meet Anna Smith?"

Synchi grinned at her enthusiasm. "That is a definite yes. She's the only Surfecti I've kept as an ally, or whatever you want to call her. I'm not sure ally is the right word." Her smile dropped when she looked at me. "You went too far. Was it you or the pearl?"

"It took over, Synchi. It was…excited."

Her eyebrows furrowed deeply. "It latched onto your emotions. You cannot terrorize the Surfecti with your temper. We need to work *with* them. Possibly for a long time. You *can* play well with others, can't you?" Her sarcasm raked nails down my spine.

I snorted and crossed my arms. "Sure, Synchi. I'll do my best to submit to people we've alienated for decades. Something you struggle to do yourself. I don't want to be here, anyway. I'm getting dirty looks everywhere I turn because of the shark."

Synchi sighed. "It's not like the Trident can announce your situation."

Mori swept the sand with her tail, her eyebrows tight together. "The gossip mill is going wild. It's ridiculous. It hasn't even been a day. The rumor is that Jelly is being forced out of the clan, banished to live alone in the ocean. Down at The Dive, they're taking bets on how long it takes to find her skeleton."

Synchi's face was pensive. "That benefits us. If they think Jelly's excommunicated, she'll be yesterday's news and take the focus off the bubble and my flagging magic."

I said, "Fine, whatever, but how do we explain Mori disappearing?"

The Shaman grinned wickedly. "Which do you prefer, Mori? Salacious or studious?"

Mori barked a laugh. "For my dad's sake, let's go with studious."

"Very well. You're going to the surface to do advanced studies on the Surfecti. Done."

Mori nodded approvingly, but then her lips turned down. Her eyes were wary. "What happens to our magic on the surface? I can manipulate sand here, so I'd assume I can do the same with dirt, but obviously, I've never tried."

Synchi slowly swam to the entrance of the cave, her voice soft. "Without a steady submersion in salt, your magic will gradually deplete. Salt is the key to life. Without it, all creatures weaken. So, to answer your question, your magic would eventually fade if you remained on the surface without recharging."

"For how long?" Mori asked.

Synchi shrugged. "I'm not sure. If you find your power diminished, you need to get back into the ocean. If you use an inordinate amount of magic, use sex to recharge and heal."

Mori squealed with joy. "See, Jelly! The Shaman gets it!"

I rolled my eyes. "Really, Synchi? Use sex?"

She looked at me with puckered lips, the wrinkles of her cheeks gathering toward her mouth. "Are you not Mers? And do you not recharge like Mers?" She narrowed her eyes slyly. "Dear Goddess, are you a *prude*, Jelly?"

"No!" I shouted. "I…I've only been with Fillian. And it's been a while." Mori snorted and rolled her eyes. "Fine, it's been a long while," I muttered. "I'll go to the ocean when I need a boost."

Synchi's bushy caterpillars crept toward her hairline. "And if you're not near the ocean? What if you're blasting and screaming across the vast, green countryside? What then, Jelly? You'll drain yourself? You'll let evil win because you're embarrassed?"

I grumbled, "I don't like using people."

Synchi chortled, "For Goddess's sake, that's absurd. You're Mers. I thought I raised you smarter."

Mori nodded enthusiastically. "Sex is natural. It's like breathing. We *need* it, Jelly. I plan on seducing everything that has two legs: male, female, human, Surfecti, Shifter, whatever. I wonder if Shifters can do it half-changed. How hot would that be?"

I muttered under my breath. Synchi, sharp as ever, caught it. "What was that, Jelly?"

I cleared my throat. "I don't trust men and want nothing to do with them. They're nothing but disappointing."

Synchi pulled on her braid. "You'll do it if necessary. If you feel weak, you will resort to using sex. Tell me you understand." I nodded complacently, secretly vowing otherwise.

Synchi turned from me and said, "Mori, while on the surface, rely on your physical strength and fighting skills. See what you can do with earth manipulation. But do not be disappointed if it's not as strong as your sand work." She faced me with a scowl. "And you must learn how to control the pearl. What happens in your body when it takes over?"

Relieved with the change in topic, I brightened. "First, it vibrates and gets hot. Then it pulses and slides along the chain, and then it yanks and strains toward to whatever is offending or upsetting it. There's a noise, but it isn't like singing that reaches my ears, more of a sensation inside me. It's difficult to explain." I looked down at my fingernails. "It went too far with the Trident, but I *needed* to make them suffer. I *wanted* them to be hysterical with fear." I couldn't help it as my lips curled up into a smile. "So, as much as the power came from the pearl, or it amplified my emotions…we both enjoyed it."

What I didn't admit aloud was that I finally had power, and I wanted to use it on anyone who tried to belittle me. I could appreciate how easy it would be to abuse it. It was seduction at its finest.

Synchi tapped her nails on her crossed arms. "You must run if you get the slightest inkling the pearl is taking command. If you hurt one of the Surfecti, they will put you down. They are ruthless, and I cannot help you. Do you understand?" I nodded.

She created a whirlpool and motioned for us to follow her. "Where are we going?" Mori asked.

"A secret space. Only your father knows of it, but even he's never visited. I'm very protective of it. Come. Don't waste time."

I frowned and looked at Mori. We'd explored every square inch of the bubble. I swam into the whirlpool, my hair tumbling around me as I spun before being spat out in an open space. It was glorious, the water crystal clear, the reef thriving, flush with vast schools of fish darting back and forth. Purple and deep brown sea fans waved in the current amidst the orange, yellow, green, and pink coral. There wasn't a scrap of plastic anywhere. This must be how the ocean looked before humans and their pollution.

"Where is this Synchi?" I asked, quickly launching myself from the edge of the swirling water to avoid getting struck by Mori coming through behind me. "It's gorgeous!"

"The Goddesses created it for me. I come here to recharge." Synchi's old shoulders relaxed as she took a deep breath. She winked. "I'm too old for sex. My spine couldn't take it." I could see a faint shield shimmering around us.

"A bubble within the bubble?" Mori asked, recoiling from the magical barrier that hummed when she drew near. She turned in a slow circle, flicking her tail. A wide smile broke up her freckles as she said, "Is this what it used to look like?"

Synchi nodded. "I call it Pūrus from the Latin word for pure. This is a replica of my favorite place as a child before the humans wrecked the ocean. The sea creatures can come and go as they please, but no Mers may enter without my permission."

I stared with a slack jaw. I'd never seen such beauty. Synchi took a deep breath and released a strong sonar blast, making my hair blow back.

"Who are you calling?" I asked, pulling blue strands from my face.

"Hannah."

Mori clapped her hands together. "The Surface Emissary? I only met her once, well, twice. We didn't speak much. I found her a little…salty."

I smiled. Mori was so excited. I said, "Hannah will take us to the agreed rendezvous spot to meet Nell and Jack."

Mori said, "My Walkers were Jessica and Samantha. Will we see them?"

I looked at Synchi. "I haven't met them. How many Walkers are up top?"

Synchi said, "We have several now. Nell was the first, and she was lucky she found Jack. Samantha and Jessica are lovers. The humans welcome them, unlike here. It wasn't always like that. When we lived under our queen, she said to love who you love and be done with it. It was nobody's business who you slept with. But then we had trouble conceiving, and mermaids went into service for the larger good. Samantha and Jessica went up together, plotting to remain on the surface. I suggested they become Walkers and appealed to the Trident. The chauvinists and homophobes were happy to see them go. They're lovely women and loyal to the Mers."

Mori sighed. "Well, they're great. Maybe we can see them while we're there. How did Nell communicate with the Mers and petition to stay up top? She wouldn't have risked returning and getting thrown into the hole, so someone worked on her behalf."

Synchi said, "Hannah and I worked as Nell's intermediaries. Ah, she's here."

A Bottlenose dolphin burst past the shield, pulling to a screeching halt before us. She dipped her head. "Shaman." She looked at me and winked. "Jelly."

I said, "Hi, Hannah. It's good to see you."

Synchi smiled. "Hannah, do you remember Mori, Commander Tro's daughter?"

Hannah looked her up and down. "Sure. You're the one who pulled a knife on a freak. You were lucky I was visiting a friend and was still in the area. I got you out toot sweet."

Mori, an expert in human languages, softly corrected her pronunciation, "It's tout suite. Let it roll off your tongue more."

Hannah rolled her eyes. "Sure, sure. Yeah, well, your exit was better than this one's," she said, jerking her beak at me. "Did she tell you what happened after the explosion?"

Mori laughed, "She did, but I'd love your version."

Hannah, a natural storyteller, chuckled. "So, Jelly goes bustin' into Nell's brain, screamin' and hollerin' and sure enough, Nell turns on the news, and there's Miss Jelly, blue from head to toe, spittin' soap bubbles. Nell tells Jelly to get to the beach and goes flyin' outta her house, screamin' for me in my head. Well, I'm nowhere near her house, am I? I wasn't expecting this one back for another couple of weeks. I tell her I'm down at the docks, watching the humans do stupid things."

Hannah blew bubbles out of her blowhole as she laughed. "Nell comes tearin' down the public dock, squealin' and shrillin' like a crazy lady, tryin' to get me to come in up close. She's so freaked out she starts talkin' dolphin, and she's tellin' me, 'We gotta go, Hannah! Now!' I swim up and start talkin' back, tellin' her to slow the heck down."

She winked at Mori, "To humans, my voice sounds like clicks and whirs. And here's this big ol' lady, hoppin' up and down, wavin' her arms makin' dolphin noises, explainin' that Jelly's blown shit up, and the girl's gotta go. I'm playin' the crowd, chattin' right back to her, and all their phones are out, and they're callin' Nell a dolphin whisperer. Nell screams at me to quit messin' around, so I got my friends, about five of them, to start doin' tandem jumps to distract the crowd, and Nell slips me the transformation potion for Jelly."

She cackled and waved her flipper at me. "And then I pick her tail up on a deserted beach saturated with soap. She's pacin' back and forth, got blood on her lips from chewin' up her mouth, and she's freakin' out. Can't get her tail and swim away without the potion. Don't know where the boat is." She tossed her head at me. "You were disgustin' covered in that stuff."

"Hey," I protested, "I rinsed the soap off before I got into the ocean. I dove into that guy's pool." I smiled as I remembered the look on his face as the water changed from clear to scummy.

She snorted. "You were head to toe slime."

I frowned. "Laundry soap doesn't wash off that easily."

Hannah chuckled, "And this girl swallows the transformation potion like it's tasty and turns back to Mers so fast she blurs. You didn't even scream."

My lips twitched into a smile. "I wanted to escape as fast as possible. I didn't want them to catch me and risk getting locked up on land."

Hannah's tone abruptly switched from amused to angry in less than a second. "No. You do not want *that*." She snarled, "Dirty humans, makin' money off our captivity."

I touched my temple to explain to Mori, her eyes wide from the fast transition. *Hannah lost her pod when a human water park captured them. Watching dolphins do tricks is entertaining for humans.*

Mori cleared her throat nervously, worried about further upsetting Hannah, but needing to speak her mind. "They're trying to ban it. Many humans are against dolphin incarceration."

Hannah yelled, "Tryin' and doin' are two different things!" She changed the subject again and spun to me. "Did you read the research on the long-term effects of *Deepwater Horizon* I brought you?"

I froze, my eyes downcast. "I did, and I'm so sorry, Hannah."

Mori murmured, "Was that the 2010 explosion that spilled two hundred million gallons of oil into the ocean?" I grimaced and nodded in reply.

Hannah turned to Synchi with incensed eyes. "It happened over in the Gulf of Mexico, but we dolphins talk, share our stories and pass them along. They lost over half their population. Got strange diseases. Can't carry babies to term. Only one in five babies makes it to bein' born. If the humans were dyin' like that, they'd be on it like a crab findin' bare naked shrimp. Don't get me started on water integrity and red tides."

Her eyes swung to me. "But I don't need to tell you about the bullshit pollution. You're gonna put all them smarts in your head to use this time. Blow up something bigger, something huge. Make 'em pay. You can do better than laundry soap."

I opened and closed my mouth, finding I had nothing to

say. Hannah snorted repulsively at my silence. She picked up a sponge to dust at the reef and uncovered fat fish hiding deep in the coral. She snacked greedily, refueling and growling as she did.

Mori hedged carefully, "I read they did attempt to clean up the spill, Hannah. The company paid big fines, and many humans joined the rescue effort. They're still researching the impact of the accident. That's good, isn't it?"

I muttered, "Eleven humans died and seventeen went to the hospital with injuries."

She spun on me. "Are you defendin' them? It's their fault it happened! You're upset over twenty-eight humans? The dolphins were breathin' oil for years! What do you think that did to their lungs?" She snapped her beak in frustration, swallowing. She shook her head. "Doesn't matter."

I crossed my arms, irritated she'd suggested such a thing. "I am not defending humans. Just pointing out that they also suffered. But no, definitely not defending them."

She grumbled, "Sure sounds like it to me." She swam away to the reef, brushing aggressively with her sponge. I stirred the sand with my tail, chewing on my lip, my eyes downcast. It was always difficult to hear the impact on the animals.

Mori sculpted a small sand dolphin, twisting and turning, letting the figure slowly disintegrate and drift back to the ocean floor. She murmured, "It's not right to lump the humans all together. They can't all be bad. Humans are trying to make a difference. Some of them have to be." I snorted, but said nothing.

Hannah returned and tipped her head at me. "You're different. Somethin's changed. I can sense it. What happened?"

I pursed my lips and said, "The Vetula pearl activated." I held it up on the chain.

Hannah came close and nudged it. She whispered, "Well,

som' bitch. That's not good news. You be careful with that thing, Jelly. It often predicts the end of days, and it's up to the Mers wearin' it to hold off Armageddon."

Mori nodded solemnly. "The ultimate battle between good and evil. Although it's never final, is it? Evil keeps coming back."

Hannah said, "I'll spread the word that the pearl is back in action. We're all on alert for sharks with black eyes. There may be more things comin' for you."

I dug my tailfin in the sand. "That's the point of us leaving. We want to draw it away from the ocean."

Hannah snorted through her blowhole. "You sure that's a good plan? You're stronger down here."

I shrugged. I didn't have a choice. Hannah faced Synchi again and asked, "So since this isn't a Prostitution Mission, oh, ha, slip of the tongue, Procreation Mission, how soon do we leave?"

Synchi pulled at her braid. "I have to contact the Surfecti and arrange it. Don't go too far."

"Fine," replied Hannah. "I'll be on the reef. I'll have an escort ready. Nell and Jack are on standby, out deep-sea fishin'. Say the word, and we go." She nodded to us. "Jelly, Mori. I'll see you soon."

She left, and Synchi said, "Well. Let's go call Anna. But before we do, here, drink these." She handed us two small bottles of yellow goo.

"What is it?" Mori asked, sucking it down trustingly. I'd taken it regularly for years. I swallowed the acidic potion.

"Contraceptive," Synchi answered. "The last thing we need is for you to get knocked up." She eyed Mori. "Especially by a Shifter. Goddess only knows what those babies would look like."

TWELVE

JELLY

Mori could not be still. She was too excited. She swam across the room, twirling a thick throwing star in her nimble fingers. It was whalebone, and she'd crafted her set herself, spending hours whittling down the sharp points.

Synchi sat with the mirror resting on a cushion on her lap. We expected to have a long chat, and she didn't want the shells around the heavy mirror to leave indentations on her tail. She tapped the glass and muttered the spell, and Mori swam over, spinning her star as the cloudy surface shimmered and sharpened, showing the Witch's angular face.

"Shaman."

"Anna. You remember Jelly, and this is Mori, Commander Tro's daughter." Mori waved her fingers, her eyes blinking wide. Synchi cut right to the chase. "Jelly killed a possessed shark with the pearl's help. We believe it prompted a vision. Anna, we are decidedly up against dark magic."

Anna jumped toward the glass, her eyes wild. "Vision?"

"She saw a girl strapped to a bed."

Anna was almost frantic. "Where is she?"

Synchi frowned and said, "She didn't say."

"What did she say?" Anna asked with worried, ice-blue eyes. "Is she well?"

I moved a little closer to the mirror, shaking my head. "I'm sorry, Anna, she's not. Not at all. She's emaciated and tied down. There's a needle in her arm, draining her blood into a bowl."

Anna's face went paler than it already was, making the blue veins in her skin take command. "Tell me what she said."

"She said, 'He wants the pearl. Using my blood. Slaughter all of you, us. Stop him.' She could barely talk."

"Did she say who this he was?"

"No. But he spoke." I bit my cheek to center myself. I'd memorized his words. "His voice is melodious. It's beautiful, but horrifying at the same time. He said, 'Oh! You have a visitor. How wonderful! Your blood is useful. Shall I pop the kettle on? I adore fresh fish. It's lovely with those sweet local bananas.' Then he laughed and said, 'You got lucky tonight. Last chance, mermaid. Give me the pearl or die.' And then the Shaman woke me up because I was screaming and thrashing."

Anna paled further. Any more, and she'd disappear. She swallowed and leaned into the mirror. "What did you see around her? Anything at all, Jelly. Anything will help." I thought Anna was acting strange, so quickly invested, but shrugged. I didn't know her well.

I closed my eyes. "I saw her on the bed, an old metal bed, rusted, in a stone building of sorts. There were holes in the walls. But no windows. I mean, no glass or frames, just rectangular or square holes. They aren't a standard size. She's cuffed by the ankles and wrists to the ends of the bed, and leather straps are across her torso and legs. She...she's beat up, Anna. Her skin is raw from struggling."

"Any smells or sounds?"

"No. I…I wasn't able to hold the vision as long as I wanted because I was paralyzed and struck mute. I tried to talk to her, to get to her, but I was helpless."

Anna's eyes narrowed. "What do you mean you were mute?"

"Inside my head, I was screaming like a banshee, begging her to give me an idea of where she was and who she was, but I couldn't make my mouth work. I also tried to move toward her, but I couldn't."

Anna ignored me, turning sharp eyes on Synchi. "Shaman? What do you make of this? Are you familiar with paralytic visions? Are they common with the pearl?" Mori had been wiggling by my side like an eel, desperate to speak, and she couldn't hold her tongue one more second.

She blurted, "I think it's a binding spell because Jelly couldn't speak or move. Maybe Jelly could travel to her in a vision because of the pearl. Or maybe the girl had the power to reach out to a clairvoyant. Either way, they connected, but Jelly had no autonomy. So, I think someone's doing a binding spell, either on the pearl or the girl."

She exhaled with a great sigh, her eyelashes fluttering at Anna. I blinked at her rush of words and kept my snicker to myself. Mori had a serious girl crush on the Witch. Anna lifted her chin and studied Mori carefully. "Mori, how are you so informed?"

"I'm getting my doctorate in Land Magic, and I've been studying, um, blood magic and the… um, darker side."

Anna's eyebrows lifted fractionally before her face settled into a scowl. "Have you now?"

Mori shook her head explosively, "Oh, not to do anything nefarious! I'm simply curious. When Jelly said she couldn't speak in the vision, that's what first came to mind."

"Impressive, Mori. I shall take it into consideration."

"Thank you!" she gushed, reaching out with her hand to grab mine, squeezing hard enough to make me wince.

"Anna," Synchi said, "The Mers Trident held an emergency meeting, and decided that Jelly should go to the surface to track the source of our attacks. I fear I cannot hold the integrity of the bubble with that kind of magic assaulting it. The possessed shark almost broke through. If Jelly hadn't stopped it with her scream, well, I don't like to imagine it."

Anna's lips quirked. "I'll bet that went down well." Synchi grinned ruefully. Anna's voice turned colder, stiffer, as she returned to my vision. "Jelly, were there any identifying features of the girl? Did you see her face?"

I shook my head. "She had a hood over her head. Why?"

Anna's mouth twisted into a grimace. "My goddaughter, Simone, has gone missing. I went to find her, but she vanished without a trace, leaving all her belongings behind. Her blood carries deep magic from the Fae, from her father. I can't help but wonder if the girl in your vision is her."

Synchi pulled on her braid. "The father is Fae? Full Fae?" When Anna nodded, Synchi mused, "And he stayed? I thought all Fae had withdrawn from the Earth dimension, summoned to wait until the humans had finished with their mindless destruction."

Anna snorted. "Sebastian would not abandon his family. He's not that kind of man."

Mori shoved herself in front of the glass. "Does your goddaughter have Mers blood?" When Anna nodded, lifting a brow in curiosity, Mori kept talking. "That's what I suspected. I think our villain is using her Mers blood to access the ocean creatures and her Fae blood to control them. He's trying to flush Jelly out for the pearl." She slumped back, whispering, "He's insanely powerful if he can control a shark." We fell into desperate silence.

"Wait!" I shouted. "A tattoo! A wave on her upper arm. It was thin, barely there, but I noticed it because," I swallowed, "Because it was the arm being bled."

Anna shouted, "That's her! Bloody blazing hell, you found her! How did you reach her? Can you do it again?"

My shoulders sagged. "It happened spontaneously. I don't think I did anything specific to cause it."

Anna pinched the top of her nose. "We've exhausted our Seers and Visionaries. They can't find a trace of Simone anywhere. Well, we have ourselves a conundrum. On the one hand, the Goddess says Jelly must surface. However, by doing so, we risk him getting the pearl." She shook her head. "This is impossible. I wish we had a better idea of his greater plan."

Mori cleared her throat and said, "Based on Jelly's vision, he wants to kill everyone. Paraphrasing, but that's the gist of it." Anna's lips pursed. We stared at each other. I chewed my lip. Mori gnashed her thumbnail. Synchi pulled on her beard, while Anna scrubbed a hand across her eyes.

Anna broke it with a disappointed sigh. "I will arrange your accommodations. You will stay with Simone's family. Magic protects the compound, so you're safe there. You'll be staying with Sebastian Fields, the Fae, and his wife." Her eyes sharpened as she leaned forward. "She is a Mers. Simone's mother is Sophia Corallium."

"What?" Mori shrieked. "She! She! She has a daughter? She's alive?"

Anna narrowed her eyes. "Yes, she lives. When she went on one of your god-awful missions, she became pregnant and stayed. She is a dear friend, so be careful with your words, Mori. The Trident cannot discover her location. They have no claim on her or her family. Am I clear?"

Sophia Corallium was the mermaid who defied the Trident by staying on the surface. She did not return to the reef after her mission or appeal to become a Walker. She simply disappeared without a trace. Mori and I stared at each other in silent shock. We were about to meet the most famous rebel on the reef.

Anna continued briskly. "Your contact, Nell, knows where to go. I will arrive the day after tomorrow. I'm afraid I have Coven's business to see to first. I will come as quickly as I can." Her face took a sly expression. "Mori? I do hope you'll be joining Jelly. I'm curious to discover what they teach about the Surfecti."

Mori blinked and stammered, "Yes, of course, I'll be there. I can't wait to meet you, Lady Anna, Lady Witch. I've read so much about you and the Cone of Power, and all you've done... it's... you're... well... amazing."

A genuine smile spread across the Witch's face. She said, "Anna. Just Anna is fine." With a grim nod to Synchi, she said, "Shaman." Her image faded into the mottled glass with a pop. I almost jumped out of my skin when Mori shrieked with excitement. Oggie spurt out a frightened cloud of ink, and Synchi chuckled as I waved it away.

I made a quick and simple lunch, a Mers version of sashimi, with the soft bones still in the flesh. Mori babbled on about Sophia and her choices, and wondered whether she agreed with Sophia's decision. She fell silent as she started chewing. I said, "Anna is so frosty."

Mori was quick to defend her. "I didn't think she was that bad." Synchi snorted noncommittally.

I asked, "The Surfecti...are they still that upset at the Mers? What kind of reception will we get?"

Synchi shrugged a shoulder. "As you know, Anna and I did not part well. I am surprised she's been as civil as she has. But

Jelly, she may not trust you. And she might want to punish you simply for being a Mers. Be aware of that."

"That's not my fault," I said with a huff.

Synchi held up her hand, closed her eyes and exhaled a small gasp, nodding before tapping her index finger on her temple. I waited until she finished before I asked, "Who was that?"

"Hannah. It's time to go. Nell and Jack are heading into position."

Mori's eyes widened. She whispered, "So soon? Okay. Where shall I meet you?"

Synchi answered in a rough voice. "At the North Gate. One hour." She lifted her eyes to Mori. "I won't be seeing you off." She waved her hand through the water. "Too much to do." It was a blatant lie, and as Mori rushed to hug her, Synchi's eyes squeezed closed, her long white locs floating around her shoulders.

Mori whispered, "I'll take care of her, Shaman."

Synchi's arms tightened. "Be careful. Use that big brain of yours with the Surfecti. You are brilliant, Mori. Use it. But if anything goes wrong, get your tail in the ocean and come straight home, understood? And see that Jelly stays strong." Her eyes slid to me. "By any means necessary."

"Yes, Shaman. I promise." She left without a word to me, but her face showed everything: fear and excitement wrestling for dominance. She nodded and swam through the door.

I shivered as the weight of duty and responsibility pressed on my chest. I left Synchi in the living room and swam in a slow circle in my room, staring at the shelled artwork, and my staggering pile of already-read research filed carefully in algae folders. There wasn't anything to pack besides my weapons, and I would carry those on me. I slumped on my bed, fingering the kelp blanket fringe.

There was no one else to say goodbye to. No one would miss me. For a moment, I considered calling Fillian, but quickly shook my head. What would I say? I clicked the water for Oggie. "Come here, Oggie." He flew in immediately and chirruped, suspecting I had a snack for him.

I kissed his rubbery skin and relished the strong wrap of his arms around my torso. "Be good for Synchi. Don't eat the fire urchins. They upset your stomach. And don't leave your shells lying around on the floor where Synchi can trip on them. I'll be back as soon as I can. I love you." My breath hitched as I squeezed him closer, swallowing back tears.

He chittered and snuffled. With enormous eyes, he looked at me with severe concentration. His body swelled with effort. He said haltingly, "Love…You…" His voice was high-pitched and squeaky, like the toy Nell's dogs played with.

I gasped and squealed, "Oggie! You spoke! Those were your first words! We've waited so long to hear your voice! And now…" My heart plummeted to the tip of my tail. I hugged him harder. I whispered, "And now I'm leaving." A lump formed in my throat.

Oggie practiced his words, his confidence growing. "Loveyouloveyouloveyouloveyou!" I pressed my face into his skin, both of us clutching each other with entangled arms.

Synchi's voice was soft. *Jelly, it's time.*

Oggie chirped in my ear, nuzzling his head against me as I entered the living room. I looked around, claiming every insignificant item to memory. Reluctantly, I pulled off four of his arms and held him out to Synchi. He wrapped around her, gazing back at me with gigantic eyes.

I wiped my nose with my hand, beaming, "He said his first words."

Synchi nodded and kissed his head, stroking him with her gnarled knuckles. "I heard."

I pulled the chain mail over my tail, tugged on my chest plate, strapped my swordfish sword to my back, and wrapped the holster with the knives around my hips. Nervous, I quickly braided my hair away from my face, securing it with a strand of kelp. "Can I still talk to you with telepathy?"

Synchi nodded. "You can. It might be difficult, depending on how far apart we are." She swam closer and placed a wrinkled hand over my heart. "But I'm right here, Jelly. I always will be right here. Go live your destiny, my girl. And remember what Professor Penelope always says."

Penelope taught Seduction. I laughed to keep from crying. "Chin up, chest out."

"That's right." She tipped her head to the side, listening as she received a message. "Hannah is waiting. I'll see you soon, brave one." She reached for me and hugged me close, with Oggie squished between us. Without another word, she turned and swam into the kitchen. She sighed, and when I glanced back, she was wiping her eyes, Oggie trying to help with clumsy arms.

I sunk my teeth into my cheek, the taste of blood straightening my spine. I sped to the North Gate, ignoring the hostile looks from the crowds on the reef. Tro nipped back and forth at the edge of the bubble, tension in his jaw as he peered outside. Mori fiddled with the straps of weapons across her chest while Lady Amphi waited with two guards, thankfully, neither from the earlier meeting.

Tro stopped when he saw me approach. I bowed. "Lady Amphi. Sir."

Lady Amphi tipped down her chin. "Thank you for your service to the Mers, Jelly." Her serious countenance dropped with a small smile. "Try not to blow anything up." She finished with a louder, "Be well. Defend us bravely." I clapped my fist to my chest and bent at the waist. I turned to my commander with steel in my eyes.

Tro frowned and embraced me firmly, not caring if his guards saw his affection. It shattered my attempt at protocol as I flexed my arms to hold him tighter. His voice trembled. "Be safe, my daughter. Both of you." He cleared his throat and held me at arm's length by the shoulders. "Warrior Jelly. Do your duty and come right home. We need you here."

He did his best to sound stern, but under his words was a prayer for our quick return. I bowed again, staying longer to express my gratitude for his guidance and faith in me as a Warrior.

He lingered in his hug with Mori, his hand cradling her head. He whispered in a hoarse voice. "Your mother would be so proud. Take care of yourself. Be careful with the Surfecti and remember, go to the ocean if there's danger." He sighed, his voice wavering as he said, "I love you more than all the stars on the sand."

"More than all the fish in the sea," she replied, struggling against tears. "I'll be careful. We'll send reports through Hannah as often as we can. I love you, Toto." She squeezed him harder. With a broken sob, she let go. He kissed her cheek, holding her gaze until she turned her head and pressed through to the protection zone. We wrapped our faces without speaking. She held her fingers to her temple, likely telling her father she loved him one last time.

Hannah waited ahead, her eyes scanning the water as Mori and I donned our gear. She looked at our goggles with jealousy as she dodged a floating water bottle. She sang out her signature whistle, drawing the attention of her crew. We greeted the rest of the pod, fifteen in total.

"Ready?" she asked. "I've checked in with the whales

stationed along our swim path, and they say there's no sign of dark eyes. We're good to go, but just in case, hide yourselves. We'll be swimmin' in a group for cover."

I wove a Bottlenose dolphin glamor on Mori and myself, wiggling under the shimmering sensation as it dropped into place. The pearl's magic thrummed against my blood, excited for the mission. I stared over my shoulder at the reef, barely visible through the double shields and the thickness of the microplastics. A lump formed in my throat, and I faced forward, tears in my goggles as I swam hard, my Da's knives heavy and reassuring on my hips.

We swam for hours, breaking off in the middle for a snack as we cruised through a school of anchovies. If any dangerous creatures searched for us, our large pod had escaped their attention. Speeding in the depths, we made good time. Once close to the rendezvous point, we breached the surface.

"There's the boat," cried Hannah. "By the dark blue marker. See? It's the *Lucky Love*." The others swam ahead, but Hannah paused, holding Mori and me behind. She stared at us sternly. "Sophia is my friend. I don't adhere to the nonsense of ostracizin' her. She's one of us, and she adores her children. With one of her kids missing… Maybe wait for her or Sebastian to speak about it first. Let them broach the topic."

"Children, plural?" Mori spluttered. "Dear Goddess, the Trident would burst an artery knowing she'd had more than one child and kept them on the surface!"

Hannah nodded. "Yeah, and they can never find out." She stared hard at Mori. "She has two kids. Had three. The girl is the youngest. Middle child is a boy. Come. Let's hurry. I don't want to stay exposed for too long if somethin' evil is floatin' nearby. This would be the perfect time for an ambush."

I stalled her. "Wait, Hannah. You said she had three children. What happened to the third, the eldest?"

She shook her head. "Not my story on't ask about it, Jelly. I mean it. It's too painful." She turned and swam hard, leaving us open-mouthed. We slowed when we reached the cheerful green boat, the name contrasting in bright white on the stern. "Nell!" Hannah shouted, leaping above the water.

Nell shouted back, "Hello, gorgeous! Jack, they're here! So nice to see you, Hannah!"

Hannah called, "And you! Hello, Jack!" Nell relayed the message.

The grizzled man on the boat tipped his battered straw hat at Hannah. "Hello, Hannah!" He laughed as she executed a perfect front flip for him. He cheered and clapped enthusiastically. "Right, Nell, I'll get the platform ready." He clambered to the back of the boat.

Salt crusted Nell's rich black skin, and she wore cut-off trousers with frayed hems, a flannel shirt with holes in the elbows, and a large canvas hat to protect her head from the sun. I said, "Nell, this is my best friend, Mori."

"Hi Mori, nice to meet you. Jessica told me about your last mission. What a doozy! That poor bastard probably never recovered. Either he's sworn off sex, or he's very, very good about consent now." She snorted with laughter, and Mori and I joined in.

Nell grinned as Jack came up behind her and cupped her generous backside with both hands, kissing the side of her neck. Her large brown eyes twinkled as her husband openly loved on her. Jack said in a grizzled, sea-worn voice, "All set, treasure. Give these mermaids their legs."

Hannah and the dolphins swam in circles around the boat, keeping watch. Nell kissed Jack before turning to me, grinning. "So, you finally got a mission with no requisite shagging."

I laughed. "Yeah. I'm guessing Hannah told you why we're here?"

Nell put her hands on her hips, scanning the waves. "She did. So let's get a move on. You're vulnerable while shifting, so be quick. Hand me your armor and weapons." I passed her my chest plate, chain mail, sword, and knives.

She handed me a vial of viscous, purple liquid. I nodded to a pale-faced and nervous Mori. She whispered, "I can't remember what to do with my legs. I had them for, like, a second. It was so long ago that I blocked out the whole memory."

I uncorked it and said, "I'll go first." She observed, keeping a cautious distance from me. I drank to the last drop, sticking my tongue out and scrunching my eyes, shuddering from the sour taste. I tossed the empty bottle to Nell. The surrounding water trembled, and then the potion hit.

I thrashed as the scales on my tail disappeared and morphed into caramel-colored skin. From nose to tail, I was the same smooth color. My hips turned into a series of bowls and holes to hold leg bones, making me shriek. I swallowed it down, not wanting to attract attention. My back arched violently as my pale tail split into two pieces, leaving fins at the bottom. I grunted as my uterus shifted, sucking up higher with a jolt. A canal unfurled and tingled as it fell into place. My teeth gritted together.

My tail's thin, flexible bones thickened into heavier, denser ones, and balls formed at the top to slot into the caverns of my pelvic bones. Joints shaped and creaked to create knees, one part breaking off to form a patella. My smooth flesh became a network of unfamiliar tendons, ligaments, and muscles. My nervous system spun into place, electrocuting me and stealing my breath until it settled into position.

I panted as I paddled in the water with my hands to keep me afloat, my eyes staring wide with pain. I counted the seconds in my mind. Ankles and feet were the worst. Twenty-six bones, thirty-three joints, and I'd be done. I clenched my teeth as the intricate appendages formed. I sobbed with sweet relief as the last joints of my little toes clicked into place. Dazed, I flailed in the water—feet made for terrible fins. I latched onto the platform and croaked, "You can hold my hand."

Mori bravely tipped back the potion, and as her dark red tail morphed into pale and freckled legs, she swore so violently even Jack blushed. She gripped my fingers until I thought they'd break. Throughout her transformation, I coached her to breathe while she shot me murderous glares. When she finally had her feet, she sank. I yanked her up next to me to hold on.

Her eyes were wide with panic as she moved her legs awkwardly underneath her. I soothed, "You didn't train the last time you came up. We'll practice. I'll teach you how to kick. It'll be fine."

Her knuckles were bone white on the platform. She whispered, "I hope I don't live to regret this."

THIRTEEN

SIMMI

Terrun was vibrating with excitement. He sang, "They're coming, sweet Simmi! I just had a report, and they've reached the boat. Silly things, thinking they could hide themselves from me. Dolphins? Psssh. They must think I'm an amateur. Aren't you just thrilled, darling? This is wonderful news! It will be so much easier to get the pearl up here."

He yanked out the needle, and I hissed from the lingering burn. When my blood burbled to the surface in fat drops, he leaned down and licked my arm. He shivered and moaned, "You are simply delicious, my sweet, sweet girl. Your blood is thick and rich with Fae." His tongue darted out as he savored the taste, "but there's that touch of umami from the Mers. Despite being mixed blood, obviously inferior, you really are quite divine."

He picked up the bowl, humming, and stirred with a long, graceful finger before sucking it between his lush lips. I tried not to notice the way his tongue chased after every drop or how his cheeks hollowed as he sensuously dragged his finger from his mouth. He tipped his head up, exposing a prominent Adam's apple. It bobbed sexily as he swallowed my blood. Gods, I resented his attractiveness.

He smiled, and the joy of it blinded me. His smooth voice rolled over my skin. "Normally, I do this while you're sleeping." He jumped onto the bed, his lithe legs straddling my head. I had no choice but to look at what hovered above me, and I hated myself for admiring it. His tight trousers left little to the imagination, especially as his excitement strained the fabric. A stick materialized in his hand, the end bushy with fur from some animal. He dipped it into the bowl and continued humming an aimless tune as he refreshed the markings above me.

One looked like three waves sandwiched together; another a seven-pointed star. A third was a swirl of intersecting lines, looping to the taper at the ends. I silently cursed, wishing I knew what they meant. Not that I had anyone to tell.

The one directly over my head differed from the others. It was far more intricate, with thicker brush strokes, dots, and blood flicks that scattered around it like snow. He sang to himself while he refreshed it, then sprayed my blood with a snap of his wrist. He muttered an incantation in a language I didn't understand. The symbol sparkled with spots of purple light before fading to crimson red.

Satisfied, he sprang from the bed to the floor, landing without a sound. "There we go," he said with a proud smile. A drop of blood shimmered from the symbol before it fell, splashing on my cheek. He looked at my face and frowned. "Oh, no, darling, that will never do." He dragged his tongue across my cheek—slowly and voluptuously. He chuckled darkly as I winced and squeezed my eyes shut, hating the flare of lust that shot through my body like a cannonball. He whispered, "Don't want to waste a single drop."

He plunged a needle into my other arm, and I bit my

tongue. He crooned, "They'll be here soon, sweet, sweet Simmi. And then the fun will begin." He giggled as he placed the bowl under the tubing. He left the room on silent feet, whistling merrily.

I looked to the window. Kindee was hopping up and down on his branch. He fluttered to the window, tipping his head to peer at me. "Why is he bleeding you twice?" He turned on his sharp feet and cocked his head, letting out a three-syllable screech. A calling card, it seemed. Then he bellowed, "We need the fruit!"

To my amazement, an army of ants moved in a mass and carried a peeled, small banana on their backs. It slipped from their grasp as they tipped over the sill, falling to the floor with a soft thump. Their eyes collectively swung to Kindee, brimming with apology. He said, "Well done, lads. I'll take it from here."

He flew back and forth, breaking off small pieces and feeding them to me as if I were his fledgling. I swallowed over the grit of sand that stuck to the soft flesh. When the banana was gone, he frowned. "We'll get more. One isn't enough if he's doubled the bleeding."

"With me!" he cried, and together, the ants swung on their minuscule feet and marched single file back outside.

FOURTEEN

JELLY

"Come here, sweetheart, let me pull you in." Nell hauled Mori onto the platform, where she sprawled to catch her breath, staring wide-eyed at her new appendages. Nell and Jack carried her into the boat and sat her on a padded bench. I scrambled over, wobbling on unsteady legs.

Once secure, we waved goodbye to Hannah, who did a backflip and called out, "Remember! Somethin' big, Jelly! Make it count!" I grinned at her desire for anarchy.

Nell handed us bathing suits and shouted above the roar of the engine. "Can't believe the Trident finally agreed to coordinate with the Surfecti! About damned time! We've needed a Mers envoy up here for ages! Walkers can only do so much!"

I nodded, my eyes flashing as I shouted back, "Not the greatest circumstances, though! How friendly are you with Sophia? And why didn't you tell me about her?"

Nell stepped closer to save her vocal cords. "She's wonderful! She gave Jack and me this new boat last year." Her pretty brown eye winked at my open mouth. "She and her husband are crazy rich and like to give back. Sophia says it's her quiet way of atoning for leaving the Mers. She's made all the money. Total whiz with the internet. And I didn't tell you because I promised to keep her a secret. Rest up, girls. You might not get another chance if there's a monster chasing you."

She swayed to the cabin to be with Jack, her large body graceful as the boat lurched, leaving us gripping the green and white bench as we slammed against the waves. Mori's face turned sickly as Jack sped up, and I showed her a pressure point on her wrist to help with the nausea. Mori bounced in a forest-green bikini, gripping the back of the bench. She wiggled her toes and said, "These are ridiculous. I can't believe you can walk on them."

I nodded. "It's a miracle they work as well as they do. When I was here the first time, I tottered on four-inch heels." I rolled my eyes. "Nell's suggestion. Supposedly, it accentuates the lumbar curve of your spine, making you walk sexier. It was torture!" I frowned. "A sadist invented heels to hobble women."

Mori chewed on her thumbnail. "Probably so they couldn't escape predators. I can barely walk, let alone stagger around on spikes."

I laughed. "You'll remember. Did you ever run?" She shook her head. "It's hard to imagine, but believe me, you can go fast once you get the hang of it. When I ran from the store, the world went by in a blur. The hardest part is making a turn. Well, and stopping. Stopping is hard, too. But you'll get it. You're strong."

Mori frowned and stretched her shapely leg in the air, circling her ankle to test its range of motion. "If you say so," she said, dropping her foot to poke at her knee, trying to remember how it worked. She pulled out the fabric of her bikini bottom and looked down. "I forgot about that! Mine matches the color on my head. Is yours blue?" I laughed and nodded yes.

We rolled along the waves, dipping, plunging, and rising as the boat steamed through the water, the surface pollution thinning away. Eventually, Nell shouted she could see land. We kneeled, clinging to the back of the bench as the distant cliff face grew larger on our approach. Two people waited on a wooden dock and returned Nell's wave, preparing to receive the boat. Jack cut the engine and drifted in while Nell threw bumpers over the side. We nudged against the pier, and Nell tossed the ropes to an enormous man. Sebastian, I presumed.

He was tall and thick and dressed in ratty shorts, a faded shirt, and flip-flops, with his hair tucked under a baseball cap that sported a unicorn riding a carrot. He tied off the boat and slid an arm around the slim woman beside him. She held up her hand to shield her eyes from the sun, smiling as she took us in, her long linen dress floating around her ankles.

"Hello, Nell, Jack!" she chirped. "And hello, Mermaids. I'm Sophia, and this is my husband, Sebastian. Welcome to our home." Her long blond hair hung in a braid down her back. Like most Mers, she looked athletic. Given her magic, it was difficult to determine her age. Once I met her children, I'd have a better idea.

Nell pulled me into a hug. "We'll see you soon, Jelly. Try not to blow anything up on your first day." Her face turned serious. "I mean it. We had a hell of a time cleaning up."

I grinned and squeezed a grunt out of her while I laughed into her thick locs. "I'll do my best. Bye, Jack. Thanks for picking us up." He said a gruff goodbye and smiled, his deep wrinkles almost swallowing his eyes. Nell hugged Mori and wished her luck on her virgin mission.

Mori drew back and whispered with a wink, "Shh. Don't tell my dad, but I'm not a virgin."

Nell grinned. "You are up here. Jelly, too, from what she's told me. Have fun, Mori. Sex is different in human form."

I crept across the rocking boat, grateful for Sebastian's hand as he helped me onto the pier. I expected pointy ears and teeth, considering he was Fae. Disappointingly, Sebastian had neither. Thanking him, I turned to his wife. "Hello, Sophia. I'm Scyphozoa, but please, call me Jelly." Out of habit, I fisted my hand and brought it to my chest, bowing. She smiled, returning the gesture, and my eyes flew wide as I realized my mistake. "Oh. I should have done a handshake. Sorry. I totally forgot."

"It's lovely to be met with an old greeting," she said, smoothing over my embarrassment. Mori gingerly stepped onto the wooden planks, not releasing Jack's hand until she gripped Sebastian's arm, clinging to it like a life preserver. He chuckled when she didn't let go.

Her voice was soft and breathy. "Hello, I'm Mori. And I haven't been on feet in ages. You don't mind if I hang on, do you?" She blinked up at Sebastian with big doe eyes from beneath her lashes, causing him to laugh and tip his chin back.

"Not a problem, Mori." He patted her whitened knuckles. "Your seduction skill is admirable."

She blinked at him with surprise. "Is it that obvious?"

He winked at her. "Only to one who knows. Sophia seduced me without me even realizing it. I was head over heels in a heartbeat."

Sophia beamed at her husband before beckoning me. "Hi Mori, it's nice to meet you. Come, Jelly, take my arm. I see you're more sure of your feet, but it doesn't hurt to have support on the first few steps." Sophia smiled warmly, and I linked elbows with her as we ambled along the pier. "We'll have to cover some sand," she called over her shoulder. "That's challenging, sweetheart, so hold her tight."

"Will do, Soph," said Sebastian, firming his grip on my friend, who lurched and staggered beside him.

Sophia's fingers dug into my arm for a second. "Jelly, I can't help it. Anna told me word for word what you said about your vision. Are you sure there's nothing else?" She lifted grief-filled eyes to me.

I shook my head, wishing I could give her more. "I'm praying she will reach out to me again. I'm not sure how it happened the first time. But I promise, if she does, I will run straight to you." Sophia blinked in disappointment and straightened her face, nodding back her emotions.

We crossed a wide beach, struggling on the soft surface, only to find ourselves at the bottom of an endless set of stone steps, the centers dipped and weathered from traffic. "Oh, dear Goddess," muttered Mori, "you've got to be kidding me." She turned to Sebastian. "Okay, you have to help me with this."

"Hold on to the railing. Put your weight on one foot, use your thigh and butt to push up, and then swing the next foot forward and up." He showed her what to do and gently tapped the muscles he wanted her to use. The first few steps were shaky, but Mori quickly adapted, using the rail cemented into the stone wall to help drag herself up the climb.

I stopped halfway to catch my breath and smirked at her tortured expression. "It will get easier. You'll be running on these soon." Mori rudely flicked two fingers in my direction.

"Almost there!" sang Sophia, not at all winded. As I reached the top, what little breath I had escaped me. An elegant, modern building perched back from the cliff. Thick, pale concrete snugged gigantic glass windows and doors. Solar panels covered the singular slanted roof. The gardens were a riot of color, and the yard beyond an expanse of dandelions and wild purple clover. An enormous infinity pool seemed to pour into the ocean below.

"Sophia," I gasped, "It's beautiful!" She grinned and led me along the path while bees and butterflies flitted among the flowers, filling their tiny bellies. Behind us, Mori screamed in excitement when her toes touched the grass, and Sebastian's boom of laughter echoed against the house. Sophia crossed past the most prominent building, continuing to a smaller guest house in the same style.

She slid open the glass door and waited to speak until Sebastian and Mori entered. "This is yours while you're here. Now, a reminder. You need to hydrate. I can't stress that enough. You aren't used to drinking, but it's imperative to make your body work properly. There are stainless steel water bottles for you to use. No plastic," she said to me with a smile. "Add a pinch of sea salt, which you'll find in the kitchen. After your body adapts, you can skip the salt, but I still like the taste."

She led us into the sitting area, and we spun slowly, appreciating our new home. The view of the ocean was spectacular, providing a familiar comfort. I stared at the horizon, thinking of home and wondering when I might see it again. Turning back to the room, I admired the calm, neutral décor.

The floor was light wood, the ceilings high and dotted with skylights, and a giant lazy fan stirred a breeze. All around us were varying potted plants, the greenery lush and vibrant. I grazed my fingers over a glossy leaf, marveling at the energy coming off of it, like a magnetic pulse against my skin. Sophia noticed when I gasped in delight. "That's Sebastian's magic," she said. "The man can grow anything anywhere. Comes in handy when camping. No freeze-dried veggies for us." She threw an adoring smile at her husband.

"What did you study as a Mers, assuming you went to the University?" Mori asked, lifting her nose from a fragrant bloom.

Sophia replied, "Like you, I focused on Land Magic, fascinated by magic beyond the Mers. It was well before they identified the Great Pacific Garbage Patch. That was in 1997. Had I known, I would have studied the environment." She nodded to me.

Mori asked breathlessly, "When is Anna arriving?"

"Tomorrow. You have the evening to rest. She's bringing Roan and Richard, co-chairs of the Wizardry Council, as well as Gray, her son."

Mori gasped and fanned her face. "The co-chairs of the Wizards? Oh Goddess! This is almost too much!"

Sophia's eyes sparkled. "They are excited to meet you after the explosion." She grinned. "Best story ever."

I groaned. "Tell that to the Trident. They sent me to the hole when I returned."

Sophia's eyebrows shot up in surprise. "They put you in the hole? I would have given you a medal!"

I shrugged. "Yeah, well, they weren't happy. They said I threatened to expose the Mers. They wanted to make an example of me. Procreation Mission: what not to do."

Sophia shook her head. "I hate that they're still doing those missions to you girls." She briefly squeezed her eyes and then dropped whatever she was thinking. She grinned. "We saw it on the news. It was spectacular. I had to scramble to cover it up so the humans couldn't try to identify you."

I coughed. "You altered the video?"

She winked. "I'm a master of the internet. I made sure my copy was the only one anyone would see. We watched the original repeatedly and roared with laughter as the humans fussed over the destruction. Beautiful work. Very satisfying."

A dark chuckle escaped me before my face fell. "I wish I could say I meant to do it. I lost control of my scream."

Understanding filled Sophia's eyes. "Ah. That's why the Trident punished you."

I threw my hands in the air. I thought back to when I first started butting heads with them. "The Trident and I have been at odds for…for…"

"Ever," finished Mori.

Sophia crossed her arms, scowling. "Something we share in common."

Mori and I grinned. Sophia dropped her arms and smiled. "Well, you have enthusiastic cheerleaders here in this house. Nell called ahead to give me an idea of your clothing sizes. Everything is from the second-hand shop. No fast fashion. Except the underwear; they're new. And I had to guess for shoe size, but we have a vast array of flip-flops, so I'm sure you'll find something that fits."

She walked toward the door, pausing. "We'll let you get settled in. Use the pool to practice your legs, and we have a full workout room in the basement. My son, Mako, is likely in there, beating the stuffing out of the bags. Sebastian and I have to run to town for errands and buy dinner. The house is yours. Please, make yourselves at home."

"Thank you, Sophia," we said in unison.

As they slipped out the door, Mori flopped on the couch, rubbing her fists against her thighs. "She's really nice. I don't know what I expected. And no mention of high heels. What are flip-flops?" I filled the metal water bottles, and Mori drank deeply and tipped her head to the side. "It's easier to breathe than I remember."

I strolled into the bedroom Sophia had said was mine and looked in the full-length mirror, admiring my human reflection. My hair was the same. Wavy and blue, hanging down past the middle of my back. I had broad, sculpted shoulders and a tight waist from years of swimming hard and swinging a sword. Given that my tail was so strong, my transformed legs were thick with muscle, and I had a substantial booty. I was tall, probably close to five foot ten. I adjusted my breasts in the navy bikini. Mine weren't as full and lush as Mori's, but I couldn't walk around topless up here. Shame, that.

Passing by the bed, I wandered into the bathroom. There wasn't a single scrap of plastic. I noted the soap bars—one for skin and two for hair. On the white stone countertop, there was a bamboo toothbrush, plain cotton dental floss, and toothpaste powder in a glass jar. I dipped the wet brush in the powder and scrubbed my teeth before I flopped onto the bed, studying the pale green color of the walls, before rising again and pacing. I was restless.

I wanted to work out the knots in my back from my transformation. Not to mention the bouncing journey on the boat. A dip in the pool would set me right. I wandered into Mori's room to find her modeling everything in her closet, a heap of garments on her bed. Her eyes glittered with excitement. She twirled for me in wide white linen pants. "How do they look?"

I smiled. "Gorgeous."

She held up a bra and frowned. "Are these for my boobs? They look so restrictive. Last time, I had a dress with a shelf."

"Humans don't like to let their breasts bounce freely. They trap them in captivity."

"That is so weird. I hate my chest plate. It hurts when I wear it too long." She pressed the foam of the bra cup between her fingers. "Why are they so squishy?"

"Ah, yeah, they're also terrified of nipples. They pad everything. Goddess forbid someone sees a hard nipple."

"But nipples are beautiful." She tipped her head to the side, puzzled. "And critical to seduction. Not to mention pleasure. It's how a male knows he's doing it right. A happy nipple sits up and waves for more attention. Either that or it's telling you to put on a sweater."

She held up a sports bra. "This looks like a torture device. And what are these? Are they hats?" She flicked a thong in my direction. I caught it and laughed.

"Underwear."

"Under what?"

"Under your clothes. The bigger triangle goes in the front."

She blinked, not understanding. "Let me get this straight. You're in the middle of seducing a man, and you take off your clothes…only to have more clothes to take off? Jessica didn't give me any of these. They make no sense."

I shrugged. "It's how they do it."

"Wouldn't it be better to take off your clothes and already be naked? Why wear any of this at all? Just put a sheer dress over a naked body, and boom, hello, I'm ready. Let's go."

I laughed as she struggled with human protocols. "If you look too easy, as they call it, too ready for sex, then decent guys avoid you. And trust me, you don't want to end up with a sleazy guy. They don't take care of themselves. They certainly won't take care of you."

"Wait, wait, wait. So human males want their females to *be* easy, but they don't want them to *look* easy. Do I have it right?"

I nodded. "Yup. You got it. It makes little sense. I'm pretty sure they're all wildly confused. I'm going for a swim. Want to come?"

She looked at her closet longingly. "I have so much to try on." Her face split open in a wide smile. "I want to figure out how it all goes together before we meet the Surfecti. I want to make a good first impression. Once I've found my favorites, I'll join you."

"Practice wearing the thongs, so you get used to the feeling of a string in your crack. It's unsexy to pull at your ass."

I slid open the glass door with a towel around my neck,

snorting to myself. Mers were perpetually wet, and needing to dry off was foreign. Gingerly, I walked up the gravel path barefoot as the flip-flop strap slipped awkwardly between my toes. My footsteps crunched toward the pool. They paused at the sound of a great splash. I huffed in sharp annoyance. I'd hoped to be alone.

Sighing, I figured it was their son, Mako. My breath caught in my throat when he moved to stand at the shallow end and gaze at the ocean, fully exposing his back. I recognized the wave tattoo that ran across his tanned shoulders and down his arms. My jaw dropped open, and I hurried closer, throwing my towel on a chaise.

"You!" I shouted accusingly. "I saw you in the Patch!"

He whirled toward me, his face shocked. He said in a loud whisper, "Shh! Keep your voice down!" He swam to me and held on to the edge of the pool. I leaned over, looking more carefully at the ink on his arms, unable to avoid noticing how chiseled his chest muscles were. They flexed under a light dusting of hair. When wet, it looked silky.

I dropped my voice, hissing, "It was you! What were you doing out there alone? In the middle of the night? So far out? Do you *want* to die?" I thought of the possessed shark, just below where he'd been cutting nets.

He scowled. "I wasn't in danger. I've been going for years. But keep it to yourself. I don't want my parents to find out."

I frowned. "Why not?"

He rolled his eyes as if I were stupid. I narrowed mine in response. He bit his bottom lip, his white teeth playing over the plump flesh. I noticed a small chip in his front tooth, the only flaw I could find. This bothered me. Not the chip. I resented he was so attractive. I didn't need any distractions.

He beckoned me closer, so I crouched down with splayed

knees for balance. When his eyes went wide and dark, I realized my crotch was directly in front of his face. I sucked my teeth and dove over his head, swimming to the shallow part of the pool. He followed.

His eyes flickered over me as I surfaced, pushing my long, blue hair from my face. He cocked his head, slowly perusing my wet body. "I'm glad you got to keep your hair color. You can't see it in the video beneath all the blue soap." He winked. "Good camouflage."

I snorted. "Unintentional."

He stared at me, a slow grin creeping up his face. "I saw you too. What were *you* doing in the Patch in the dead of night?"

I crossed my arms over my chest defiantly. "You couldn't have seen me."

He threw his head back and laughed, a deep, rich sound that made my skin prickle. His cobalt blue eyes sparkled. "How many dolphins have turquoise eyes?"

My mouth opened and closed without comment. It hadn't occurred to me to glamor my eye color.

He bowed deeply, flourishing it with outstretched arms. "Greetings, Queen of the Goo Lagoon," he proclaimed. "Welcome to my castle."

"Queen of what?"

His eyes flashed before the corner of his mouth turned up. "That's your nickname. That's what people call you. What you did was outstanding. I've wanted to blow that place up for years. So, yeah, Queen of the Goo Lagoon."

I scoffed. "Oh, for Goddess's sake. That's ridiculous. I'm nobody's queen."

He chuckled, a low rumble of noise, and held out his hand. "I'm Mako. Huge fan of your fireworks."

I pursed my lips before I sighed and shook his hand. "Jelly." He looked at me curiously, but I turned away from him and pressed my fingers to my temple. *Mori. You will not believe it. Come to the pool right now.*

FIFTEEN

MAKO

She was in my pool. In. My. Pool.

The video hadn't done her justice. Not even close. The object of my infatuation stood before me in a tiny bikini, her full lips pressed together in a frown with her arms firmly crossed as if guarding against me.

I'd obsessively watched the YouTube video, grinning as she stood gloriously drenched in a thick lake of electric blue detergent, her fists vibrating with rage. The explosion had gone viral. Podcasters wanted to find her. There was excited talk of a new trend of naked soap wrestling. My oldest friend and I had discussed her at great length, both captivated by the violent woman. He would be here tomorrow. He was going to lose his shit.

Nell had to run interference and cover for her. She'd called my mom, who was a Dark Internet genius, and she'd done damage control, altering the video to stop speculation. I had an original version before Mom doctored it. I watched with fascination as the pearl around her neck jerked and tugged before hovering away from her neck, dragging her feet toward the jugs.

If you looked closely, you could see invisible footprints splashing in the liquid like a ghost running for its life. I wasn't the only one who noticed the soap's displacement. Mom could only do so much. Her priority had been to hide the levitating pearl and Jelly's identity. The conspirators said she was an alien. Come to Earth to kill us all.

She was undoubtedly a trained fighter. I could tell from the way she held herself, and the honed cut of her muscles. Her unblemished skin was a warmer gold than I expected, considering she lived deep in the ocean. She had a straight nose and a lush mouth she worried over and over with her teeth—gods above—those lips. Bright turquoise eyes narrowed on me. Seeing her in the flesh had my head in a spin. But I was more curious about the power in that pearl.

She sank under the water and pushed off, swimming twenty laps on one breath before surfacing. When she did, her head swung toward the walkway, relief clear on her face. Another mesmerizing woman staggered toward the pool, her unsteady gait reminding me of a baby giraffe. Her body was firm, and red hair hung to her waist. If I had to guess, another warrior.

Life just got a lot more interesting.

The redhead leaped into the pool, popped up next to me, and shouted, "You! We saw you cutting up nets!" Simultaneously, Jelly and I shushed her. Jelly's face flashed with annoyance when she realized it.

Jelly dropped her voice. "He's keeping it from his parents."

The beauty frowned, the freckles on her nose scrunching together. "Why? It's totally badass! And you're an adult. Why do you care what your parents think?" She eyed me like a snack and pressed two fingers to her temple.

Jelly snorted and huffed loudly, rolling her eyes while

touching her temple before jamming her fists on her hips. They were speaking telepathically. I used to do it with my siblings, but had fallen out of practice. The redhead teasingly splashed her. She turned to me and said in a breathy voice, "I'm Mori, Warrior, Land Magic expert."

I opened my mouth to introduce myself when she slid closer. The strings of her bikini top strained from the luscious weight they carried. She reached out her hand, and I shook it, not surprised to find her grip solid, perhaps too much if she was trying to seduce me. Her skin carried a galaxy of freckles, and her hazel eyes were warm with mirth.

"Mako, Surfecti, Fae-Mers." I added in a whisper, "Secret ghost net hunter."

She held onto my hand. "Mako? After Mako shark? They're so fast."

I grinned. "The fastest. And Mori? Moray eel?"

"That's right. They work in cooperatives, are adaptive, and give great hugs." She batted her lashes at me.

"Don't forget vicious if attacked," Jelly smirked.

Mori ignored her and cooed at me, "I can bite nicely."

I laughed when Mori let her middle finger drag across my palm as she slowly released the handshake. My voice dropped. "Let me guess. First time playing with seduction?"

"No. I came up once before. Barely made it twelve hours, though." She frowned. "If you're half Mers, why weren't you using your tail when cutting nets?"

I grinned. "It's easier to work the boat on legs."

She hummed and traced up my arm tattoo with her fingertips. Goosebumps broke out on my skin from her touch. When she got to my face, she booped me on the nose with her index finger while biting her lip, angling her body closer to mine. I stepped away and grinned. "You're being too obvious, Mori. It's best to be coy."

She dunked underwater, and on rising, she arched back, her ample breasts pushed toward me in the wet top. "We could have some fun," she offered suggestively. She slid her fingers down the thin straps of her top. "No strings attached, if you get what I mean." She stared at me from under her lashes and licked her lips before giggling, "Do you like garlic?"

"I love the stuff. Live for it. Grow it in the garden. Why?"

Her seduction ended abruptly as she scowled and glared at Jelly, who broke into untethered laughter, the sound contagious. I laughed with her as Mori rolled her eyes. "Long story."

Jelly splashed her and asked me, "So, what's with the secret? Regarding the nets?"

I ran a hand through my hair, slyly pleased as both mermaids eyed my flexing torso. "It's dangerous to be out there alone. I'm a skilled swimmer, but there's a chance I could get myself tangled while chopping nets."

My mind flung itself to familiar territory: guilt. My parents had already lost one son. I shrugged my shoulders, shaking off the unwelcome emotion. "I can't help it. Sleep…doesn't come easily, so I go to the reef. I need to make a difference. Even if it's as small as one net."

"It's reckless," said Mori. She and Jelly shared a loaded glance. "But it's admirable and one of the very stubborn qualities I love in my best friend here. She does the same thing; cuts up nets at night."

Jelly lifted her turquoise eyes to meet mine. The light caught her face as her voice softened. "Thank you, Mako, for your nighttime excursions. I appreciate it—more than you could ever understand."

My mother's voice interrupted the question I was about to ask, curious why cutting up nets so obviously touched her. But

Mom was singing for us to come inside. I jumped out first, rubbing a towel over my body before shaking my head and scooping my hair off my face. I grinned at the two sets of eyes glued to me. "Like what you see, ladies?" I dropped the towel and spread my arms, taking a slow turn to let them check me out.

Mori threw her head back and laughed from her belly, and when she dropped her face again, she looked at me like a starving animal. Jelly rolled her eyes to the sky before calling, "Don't get too full of yourself. Mori's unfamiliar with human males."

With a wink, I said, "I'm far from human." I wrapped the towel around my hips, heading for the house, chuckling at the heated whispers that broke out in the pool. I strolled into the kitchen where Dad tossed the salad while Mom laid out the sashimi, slapping my hand when I grabbed a piece from the platter.

She said, "You met the mermaids, I see. Set the table, please, love."

I grabbed forks and chopsticks. I called over my shoulder, "As expected, they're gorgeous. But they haven't mentioned the possessed sea animals, the shark attack, or anything about her vision."

"Mako, don't," warned Dad, waving his hands to create a gorgeous display of cut flowers. "They just got here. Don't poke the bear, son. If they don't mention it tonight, let it lie until Anna and the others come tomorrow." He set the arrangement on the table, turning to me. "It's a big deal that they're here."

"Only because something's threatened them," I grumbled.

"Mako, stop. Take it as a win." He ran a hand through his hair. "This isn't easy for anyone," his eyes darting toward my mother.

Pain washed Mom's face as she gripped the edge of the

counter with white knuckles. I kissed her cheek as she fought away tears. "Sorry, Mom. I won't say anything, I promise." Dad took my spot and wrapped her in one of his bear hugs.

"Soph," he said softly, "let's keep it light, okay?"

"I stayed," she whispered. "I abandoned the Mers. I came here to live after everything between the Mers and the Surfecti. The Trident branded me a traitor. Who knows what they've been told about me? And I hate I care." Her voice choked off.

I swallowed against the lump in my throat, hearing the sorrow and guilt in her voice. When I was younger, I'd been so frustrated at the Mers. I'd raged about how selfish they were and how much I hated them. I was about sixteen when Mom explained why it all fell apart between the magical races.

She'd been a child and seen the effects of the nuclear fallout on the sea creatures. Forced to live under the Trident's draconian law, when she got older, she saw an escape and took it. When sent to the surface on a mission, she never looked back. She chose a different life. In her eyes, when she fell in love with Dad and stayed up top, she relinquished the right to call herself a Mers. It haunted her.

The glass door slid in its tracks and the mermaids stepped through. With Dad's friendly wave, they sat at the table, their expressions guarded, their mannerisms jumpy and nervous. I sat beside Jelly, and her eyes darted to me apprehensively. Dad gently pulsed his Fae magic into the air, soothing our fraught nerves as it settled over us like a mild sedative. Mom sighed with relief, and my frustration with waiting faded. If either mermaid noticed the magic, they said nothing. As I placed my napkin in my lap, Dad gave me a look, reminding me to hold my tongue.

I passed Mori the plate of wasabi and pickled ginger. Her eyebrows raised. "This is the stuff?" she muttered to Jelly, whose eyes widened with warning as she nodded. Mori smiled at me politely and shook her head, declining.

Dinner was relaxed, and their skill with chopsticks and table etiquette impressed me, not to mention the sheer volume of knowledge they had about the human world. Mori especially, considering she'd only been on the surface once. It was honestly staggering. I swallowed my ego, content to listen to them share stories. They caught Mom up on the gossip and laughed uproariously at her stories of their professors' childhoods.

I noticed they never once mentioned Mom's choices or questioned why she'd stayed. I appreciated their diplomacy. At one point, Mom sobered and laid her hand on Jelly's, eying the pearl pendant nestled at her throat. "Jelly," she said, her voice coated in sorrow, "I'm so sorry. We grew up together. They were both wonderful."

Jelly swallowed a few times, her jaw tense before she closed her eyes and bobbed her head in silent thanks. When she opened them again, she looked vulnerable. Sensing her awkwardness, I swiftly changed the subject, blurting, "Is Jelly short for something? I meant to ask you that earlier."

Momentarily stunned, she nodded. "My full name is Scyphozoa."

"The scientific name for jellyfish," I smiled. "So, Jelly for short."

"Yeah," she breathed. "It's what my mother used to call me. She craved jellyfish while pregnant, and my father said she became snappy if he brought home anything else." She lowered her chin and eyes. Something shifted in my chest, catching that she spoke of her mother in the past tense.

"Scyphozoa," I repeated gently, feeling her name on my tongue. "It suits you. Beautiful and lethal." She blinked and looked away, missing the longing edge to my voice; or perhaps not.

Mori chuckled, breaking the spell, "Mako, speaking of

lethal, how do you fight with legs? I'm used to smacking things with my tail."

I tore my eyes away from Jelly, grinning at the freckled mermaid. "Wanna fight?"

Mori flashed a wicked smile and nodded. "Oh, hell yes." She stared down at her chest and frowned. "I'm going to need the torture device."

My forehead wrinkled with concern. Jelly laughed, "Sports bra. She needs to put on a sports bra."

I smiled and said, "Ah. Okay, I'll clean up while you change. I'll see you in the gym in fifteen." I pushed back my chair and stood. "Thanks for dinner, Mom."

Jelly's lips twitched as she appraised me. "Are you sure you want to take on two Mers Warriors?"

I scoffed, pushing my hair back. "I can handle it."

Her eyebrow quirked up as she snorted, "We'll see." She and Mori rose from the table and stacked the dishes, carrying them into the kitchen. I followed, bringing the salad bowl and cups. She set down the plates and looked at my parents, biting her lip nervously. My stomach did a backflip as I watched. She said softly, "Thank you for dinner and for hosting us. I wish I had more to give you, more information, another vision."

Mom opened her arms wide, and Jelly hesitated before stepping in. She gave Jelly one of her incredible hugs and whispered, "She'll find you again. Or you'll find her. You're powerful." She let go and eyed Jelly, a smile twitching her lips. "I heard your garbage glamor was outstandingly accurate."

Jelly bit back a laugh. "How did you find out so fast?"

"Hannah. She has spies everywhere. A lanternfish from the meeting told her, and she told Nell, who called me immediately, barely able to get the story out from laughing so hard."

I called over as I scraped our scraps into the compost

bucket. "You'll have to tell me everything. Mom didn't give me the full story, except to say you scared the crap out of the Trident. Nice one, Jelly."

Jelly blushed before she said, "We'll tell you while we fight."

SIXTEEN

JELLY

Mori stared at her whalebone stars, frowning when they didn't fly as she expected. They kept veering off course, at least five inches to the side of the target painted on the cork wall. Mako walked over and handed her some metal ones. "Here, try these. The ones you have are for throwing in water, not air. What are they, whalebone?"

She nodded. "I made them myself."

Mako grinned. "Nice. They're sturdy. Well, use these. If you like them, keep them. I have tons of sets."

Mori weighed the new stars in her hand, cocked back her arm, and with satisfying thwacks, the three of them stuck in the heart-shaped center of her target. She shouted, "That's better! I was worried for a second."

I grinned at her and clapped my hands overhead with wide, vigorous star jumps, warming up my legs. She watched me in horror. "Yeah, I'm going to practice these for now. I'll start learning *that* tomorrow," she said, twirling her fingers as I grunted.

Mako shook his head. "Come here. Let me teach you

something that's great for your legs. They're called split squats. They help with joint mobility, improve balance, and strengthen muscles like nothing else. If I could only do one leg exercise, I'd do these." I stopped to watch as he stepped forward on one foot, put his hands on his hips, and sank. His knee went past his toes, and he drew our attention to it. "It's normal for your knee to go this far ahead, so don't fear it. To get up, push into the heel of your front foot and rise." He lifted effortlessly.

Mori tried and got stuck, unable to determine which muscles should work. So many were engaged at once. Mako poked her in various places to help her feel it, eventually hauling her back up under her arms. She frowned and tried again, frustrated with her unruly legs. "These squid splots are awful! Who does these? Masochists?"

"Split squats, not squid splots," Mako corrected with a grin. "Hang on to something for balance, Mori. The more they hurt, the more you need them."

She rolled her eyes. "Sure, says the guy with the beautiful legs."

He winked at her. "How do you think I built them?"

Mako picked up the pads and jerked his chin at me. "Are you ready to spar? Hit me as hard as you can, Jelly. Let's see what you've got." His face was smug. He followed with a taunt that stalled my breath. Laughter edged his words as he said, "I'll bet you can't take me off my feet." He narrowed his pretty blue eyes, bent his legs into a crouch, and tucked in his chin.

"Hoo boy," Mori groaned under her breath, pushing her legs through her squid splots before abandoning them for stars.

Nothing, and I mean nothing, enraged me as much as a cocky male with a throw-down. I'd spent my entire damned life proving myself. The Mermen I worked with thought I couldn't hold my own because I was a female. I'd shown them wrong, and I'd do it again with this guy. Mew and I spent hours of training on my legs, but Mako didn't know that. I rolled my shoulders, nodded, and unleashed myself.

His eyes flew wide when my foot kicked high for his face, followed by a fist slamming toward his ribs. He adjusted his position at the last minute, more alert from my surprise attack. I punched hard, relishing the reverberation up my forearms. Mako growled, bracing himself deeper in his crouch as I pummeled the pads with my fists and feet, putting every ounce of frustration into my hits.

As I attacked, I fell into my familiar emotion. I thought of the Trident, my ex, the leering, groping guards, the possessed shark…so many angry thoughts spun through my head. Mako grunted from the impact of my hits, and it sounded like sweet music, complementing the background thwack-thwack-thwack of Mori's stars. I moved faster, varying my approach, but couldn't knock him back.

He badgered me, "That all you got, mermaid?"

Mori stilled and cautioned, "Mako…don't."

I used Mew's techniques, but Mako outmaneuvered or blocked me and laughed at my irritation. I took a step back to recover. He cocked his head and said, "I expected more. This is disappointing." I burned inside at his words. I was going to send him on his ass if it killed me.

Mori looked over again and said louder, "Did you hear me, Mako? Don't rile her."

I hit harder and faster, but he was a seasoned land fighter and expected my moves. Sweat soaked my shirt, and I gritted my teeth against the ache in my muscles. "Come on already!" he groaned. "Are you done warming up? Can we get to the fighting?"

I snarled, "Shut up, Mako. Your yapping is throwing me

off." I tore off my wet top with a scowl. He looked unruffled, whereas I fumed, red-faced with sweat streaming past my ears. I bent over, panting, with my hands bracing heavily on my knees. A small pool gathered on the floor as salty drops rolled off my nose.

He relaxed the pads and sighed. "I thought I was fighting a warrior. Not some... girl."

"MAKO! NO!" shouted Mori. Her warning came too late.

My outrage unfurled with brutal force. I lunged, moving so fast that he struggled to block my hits. I saw an opening and took it. He was slightly off balance from a punch and left his middle unprotected, only for a second. I roared as I sank my heel into his gut, putting all my power behind it. He didn't just stagger; he flew. With a harsh cry, he hit the far wall and slid down, dazed.

Mako's eyes were closed as he struggled for breath. He groaned as he shrugged off one pad, wrapping his arm around his stomach with a hiss. A trickle of blood ran from his nose to his mouth, and he licked it before smearing it away with the back of his hand. He touched his head and winced.

Mori rushed to his side and pulled off the other pad. She crouched beside him, her hands running over him to check for broken bones. "Mako, Mako? Are you okay? Thank the Goddess you have padding on the walls." She glared at me, horrified. "That was a kill strike, Jelly! What the hell were you thinking?"

I shook as the adrenaline left my body. I crept closer to see how much I'd hurt him, panicked by my loss of control. Mori was right; I could have killed him. If he'd been a human male, that kick would have burst his organs. That's if the slam against the wall hadn't split his skull like a ripe melon. I squatted on the other side of him. I lifted a hand to push the hair from his eyes, but dropped it. Ashamed, I whispered hoarsely, "I'm so sorry."

Mako coughed, weakly raising his hand to wave away my apology. When he opened his eyes, they overflowed with blue fire. He grinned through bloody teeth, snarling, "There she is. There's my savage queen. You're fucking perfect." Wild energy pumped from him and stroked across my skin like a rough caress.

Startled by his heated reaction, I turned and fled, racing across the gravel path to my room. The hunger in Mako's eyes burned in my mind. I threw myself on the bed, humiliated by my lack of control. Synchi had warned me about harming the Surfecti. I hadn't even been here a full day, and I'd drawn blood.

Later, a light knock on the door roused me from my troubled thoughts. "Come in," I called, assuming it was Mori.

I straightened on the bed when Sophia entered, holding a cup of tea. "Brought you something to help you sleep," she said softly, her eyes warm. "Hopefully, it will ward off any nightmares. I know your mom used to have them."

"Oh Sophia, you didn't have to do that." I couldn't meet her gaze, so ashamed of how I'd behaved in the gym. I whispered, "I'm sorry about Mako. Goddess, help me; I am so sorry."

She rested the tea on the small circular table and pulled out two chairs. She patted the seat next to her. I nodded and cautiously padded to her, sitting and sipping the tea. It tasted of sweet flowers, and I purred with pleasure as it soothed me from the first taste. Satisfied, she began speaking. "Mako is gushing about your strength and power. He's beside himself with excitement. I could barely get him to shut up and sit still so I could put an ice pack on his head."

"Sophia," I said, settling down my mug, "I'm sorry I hurt him."

She blew out a puff of air. "Nothing a little arnica won't take care of. He's a fast healer."

"But I made him bleed," I insisted, believing I warranted a punishment. "I kicked him across the room."

"He deserved it. He goaded you. Mori told us what he said to make you lose control. She warned him. Twice, I believe." Her lips were tight as she frowned. "He knows not to rile a female's anger. Especially not a Mers Warrior." She sighed. "He pushed you too far, hoping to make you snap so he could get a sense of your power. Sebastian said he deserved the broken ribs after what he said."

My face bloomed red with shame. "I broke his ribs? I should have kept it together better."

Sophia casually shrugged. "Like I said, nothing he can't handle, and he earned his pain with his stupid remark. If you hadn't smacked him for it, I would have." She noticed I hadn't picked up my tea again. "Drink, Jelly."

I obeyed, taking another soothing sip. She sat back in the chair, her eyes drifting to the pearl at my throat. "This isn't the first time there's been bloodshed between our families. I'm ashamed to say I hurt Scaridae when we were children." My breath hitched at hearing my mother's name. I set the tea down and folded my hands in my lap.

Sophia continued in a faraway voice, "I wanted her pearl. I was told it was sacred to her, a family heirloom from the Vetula Line, but I didn't care. I was jealous; it was pretty, and I wanted it something fierce." Sophia tilted her head. "You look just like her, the spitting image, but I figure you got your Da's personality and drive. Nell says you're a formidable warrior, just like he was. Your mother was quite different. She was so peaceful. But I made her lose her temper once."

She looked at me affectionately before her face clouded over. "One day, I tried to rip off her necklace, and she screamed, knocking the wind out of me as I fell back. I was so angry I straddled her, and I was much bigger, you see, and I punched her several times. I bloodied her nose until she screamed again. That time, she tossed me across the sand like a leaf in the wind. I rolled and rolled until I crashed into a rock." She chuckled. "Breaking my ribs. I never tried to grab her pearl again. Even when it's dormant, it's powerful, and from what I understand, it amplifies the emotions of the person wearing it."

She wiped a hand over her eyes. "Ever since we lost…" She didn't finish the sentence, her face pinching with pain. Hannah's warning about the third child flashed through my mind. I kept my lips pressed together. Sophia shook her head sadly. "Mako constantly seeks his next fix. The next adrenaline hit. He tested you and pushed you until you snapped. He forgets that not everyone enjoys it. Mako channels his frustration into dangerous activities." She looked at me calmly. "Like his nighttime trips to the Patch."

She grinned as I kept my face blank. "Ah, good. You're not a rat. I just wish he'd take one of us with him. It's too easy to get tangled." She added quietly, "As you know." Her eyes flashed with sympathy as I bit my cheek so hard I jolted.

She pointed at my cooling tea. "Drink up. Get some sleep. We have a big day ahead of us tomorrow with the Surfecti." She rose from her seat and patted me on the shoulder before she paused. "Mako thrives on chaos and violence. It's what he thinks he deserves."

The tea turned bitter on my tongue, and I pushed it away when my door clicked shut. Our sparring flashed through my mind, and I heatedly remembered how he'd become more excited the harder I fought, needling me until I blew. He meant for me to lose control. He craved it, and I'd fallen for it like a fish to a shiny lure.

I crossed to the bathroom and splashed my face with cold

water. I lifted my eyes and stared into the mirror. The Trident had punished me for my violence. Now, I was with a male who relished it. I wasn't sure what to think. There was another knock on the door. I thought it was Sophia, forgetting something, or Mori, coming to yell at me for losing my temper. "It's open," I called from the bathroom. I hissed in a breath when Mako entered, his eyes scanning for me.

I wiped my face with a towel and stood in the doorway, frozen. He inched across the room to sit at the table. He audibly winced as he lowered into the chair. I moved forward to help him but stopped several feet away, not sure if he'd come for payback. I cleared my throat. "Mako, I lost control. I'm sorry you're hurt." Squaring my shoulders and putting more accountability in my words, I corrected, "I should say, I'm sorry I hurt you."

He closed his eyes and took a shallow breath. On the exhale, he turned to look at me. "No, Jelly. I'm sorry. What I said was grossly disrespectful. I'm an idiot for taunting you like that." He shoved his hand through his hair, and a hiss of pain escaped him as he forgot about his head injury. He dropped his hands into his lap. "Will you sit with me? It hurts to twist my neck up to look at you."

I stood awkwardly, twisting the towel, unsure how to respond to his apology, considering I was expecting punishment. I asked, "Do you want some ice? I can get some from the kitchen."

He waved me off. "No. It's fine. Where did you train? You pulled out some moves I wouldn't expect from a mermaid." He shook his head, scowling at himself. "That didn't come out right. Moves that are obviously land-based."

I stepped to the chair across from him and sat stiffly, my teeth nibbling at my bottom lip. His eyes grew dark and wide as he watched my mouth, and I stopped, gathering up my restlessness and squashing it down, making my face blank. He winced. "I can understand why you don't trust me. I'm Surfecti. And I'm the asshole who suggested the Queen of the Goo Lagoon fights like a girl. You're formidable, Jelly. Gender has nothing to do with it, and I'm a jerk for suggesting it does."

My face remained vacant of emotion, but I sawed my cheek with my teeth as I eyed him. My chair tipped back as I pushed into my toes, as if to get further away from him. He leaned closer, staring. I crossed my arms and asked, "Are you reading my emotions? Mori said the Fae could do that."

He snorted a short laugh and met my stare. "Jelly, the air is thick with suspicion. Even a human could read the room. Come on. Talk to me. I'm trying to apologize. Where did you learn to kick like that?"

Dropping the chair back down, I softened. "My moves come from a man named Mew, tweaked with my special sauce of, what did you call it? Savageness?"

Mako laughed and flinched. "Savage is right. And Mew is no man."

I leaned forward, excited, my curiosity piqued. "I knew it! What is he?"

Mako cocked his head to the side. "He hasn't told you? Ah, well, not my place to say." I made a disappointed sucking sound with my teeth. We fell into silence. It stretched, not exactly uncomfortable, but I became fidgety.

I asked, "What's your take on the Mers? From a Surfecti point of view."

He inhaled as deeply as his ribs would allow, contemplating. His voice was soft when he spoke. "I am angry at them. I share their blood, but I am so angry, Jelly. They've let the ocean rot on their watch and don't lift a finger to stop it. I do what I can out of respect for the ocean, not the Mers."

I muttered, "We're not all like that."

"Really? Is that why you've been hiding for decades while the planet crumbles?"

I shook my head. "It's the Trident. They're too scared of discovery to let any of us out. They say the bubble is for our protection, and it is, but it feels like a prison. They stubbornly refuse to work with the Surfecti after the nuclear testing."

Mako snorted. "Still holding a grudge, huh?"

I scowled, "Like the Surfecti?"

The side of his mouth curled up. "Fair. So, what about you? What do you think of all this?"

I shrugged, "I'm here because the pearl woke up. Otherwise, I'd still be sucking it up in Seduction class."

Both of his eyebrows reached for the sky. "Do I even want to ask?"

I snorted and pursed my lips. "Procreation Missions?" He cocked his head like he wanted my version. "Mermaids seduce human males, thus, the lessons. We're taught to be pretty and docile; perfect specimens for human men. We're groomed and exploited and have no rights over our bodies."

His face stiffened. "That's awful, Jelly. The Trident should be ashamed. And to clarify, not all men want their women subservient." He chuckled darkly, his eyes flashing. "Some of us like the fighters."

"Well," sourness colored my voice, "I wouldn't know. I never sealed the deal with anyone. I spent all my time at the library or with Mew. The Trident thinks I've been up here working my way through the male population, but I'm not. I have no interest in human men or babies."

I blinked as the words tumbled from my tongue. What in the Oceans possessed me to confess that? Mako remained silent, his face a smooth mask. I met his eyes for a flash of a second, embarrassed. Then I stared at my hands on the table. Silence strummed between us. I reflected on the Trident's treatment of mermaids. On my lack of choice. My face betrayed no emotion, but inside, I burned.

He broke the quiet with a hoarse whisper. "You're right. The Fae can sense potent emotions. You've endured your rage for a long time. It's like… It's like my tongue hurts from biting it. Does that make sense?"

I swallowed thickly, not answering, overwhelmed by having my life summed up so succinctly. He waited until I found my voice. "I've been outspoken about the environment my entire life. And the Mers ignore or belittle me when I tell them about pollution. They don't go outside the bubble. The ones that do? The other Warriors? They don't care. Not like I do. It makes me so angry."

He reached over and laid his hand on mine. I jerked at the contact. "Look at me, Jelly." His cobalt blue eyes flashed with heated passion. "Own your wrath. No one here wants you to bite your tongue, especially not me." His eyes dropped to the pearl. "From what I understand, the pearl magnifies magic. Did the pearl send me flying across the room?"

I chuckled and gave him a lopsided grin. "That was all me. You pissed me off."

He turned my palm up, and his fingers swept across my earned callouses before pulling away. His voice was soft. "We're on the same side. I never considered life from a Mers perspective. Certainly not a mermaid's. I'll do better." All I could do was blink. He smiled, and my eyes snagged on his chipped tooth.

He cleared his throat. "Can I ask about your vision?" I nodded. "Anna said that my sister is…She's emaciated, hooded, strapped down, and being bled. Is that true? Is she really that bad?" His face twisted in agony.

I leaned forward, scanning his worried eyes, and reluctantly nodded, my lips pressed together tightly. In a broken voice, I said, "Yes. It's that bad, Mako. She…she looks terrible. When did your sister go missing?"

He frowned. "She was on a retreat for turtles in Mexico and missed her check-in calls. That's not like her."

Comprehension hit me like a speeding train, and my heart froze before beating faster. "Turtles in Mexico? Mako, what does she look like? Do you have a picture?" It couldn't be. It was too coincidental.

He pulled out his phone and showed me a photo of him and a vibrant young woman. "I use my favorite photo of us as my screensaver, like it will summon her home."

"That's Simmi!" He flinched as I leaped to my feet, my hands flat on my cheeks in horror. "Anna called her Simone, never by her nickname. None of you mentioned her nickname! Why are there no pictures in your house?"

I paced back and forth, rubbing my forehead. "She's always worn long sleeves! I've never seen her tattoo! Why didn't I recognize her voice?" I spun to Mako. "How is it Simmi!?!" My voice broke on her name.

Mako slumped back, his breath hitching as the chair knocked on his ribs. "She probably didn't sound like herself, considering the state she's in. How do you know her? Are you two friends?"

I nodded, biting back tears. "She asked for my help with her invention. Nell introduced us because I know about the chemicals. How is this happening?" My mind spun, anguish beating against my ribs.

He growled, "Why is he draining her blood?"

A deep line creased between my brows as I halted,

desperately worried for Simmi. "Mori thinks it might be a binding spell, but we need Anna to explain." I covered my mouth with my hand and bit hard on my cheek. I wanted to dissolve into tears, but I wouldn't show weakness; not with a stranger.

He read my emotions, or simply my face, and softened. He pushed back his chair and rose slowly, carefully holding his ribs before inclining his head to my lukewarm tea. "That dulls your senses and puts you in a deep sleep. Knocks out all your dreams." He gazed at me. A beat went by as I grasped the message behind his words.

"And it might knock out my visions. I won't drink it."

He leaned heavily on the back of the chair. "We'll get her back, Jelly. We have to." He moved to straighten and sucked in a breath, swaying. His jaw ticked from the pain. He stared into my eyes and said softly, "Thank you for accepting my apology."

I whispered, "Thank you for giving me one. I don't think I've ever received an apology from a male before."

"Well, it sounds like you've deserved one for a long time. I'm glad I'm the first."

He nodded and quietly slipped out the door. I chewed on my lip and paced, distraught about Simmi. It took precisely thirteen seconds until Mori entered without knocking. After banging it shut, she slouched against the door, her eyebrow raised accusingly.

I dismissed her look with a wave of my hand. "We're good. We apologized to each other. Him for his stupid remark and me for taking the bait. Sophia also came by. She brought me tea that makes you sleep. But I won't drink it. I need Simmi to reach out to my dreams."

"Who is Simmi?"

I hung my head in my hands. "Simmi is Simone. I worked

with Simmi during my last visit. She's amazing. Super smart like you. I can't believe it's her. I've never seen her tattoo, and I didn't recognize her voice."

Mori looked at me in shock. "Shit. This just got a lot more personal." She twirled the chair and sat, her arms draping over the back. She pointed a finger at me. "I understand you're freaking out. You're upset you didn't know it was her. And you're blaming yourself. But you couldn't move or speak in the vision, so stop doing this. Plus, there was a hood on her head. There was nothing you could do, and no way you could have possibly known."

I exhaled and stopped pacing.

She frowned. "But the main reason I came in here…that stunt in the gym was not the same as the shark. You were under no threat. Your ego made you throw him across the room, and Jelly, you can't do that. You cannot lose your temper. The Surfecti are brutal. If that had been Anna…"

"It was all me. The pearl wasn't involved. Hopefully, Anna is smart enough not to goad me."

"What if she does?" Her hazel eyes were wide with concern.

I blew out a breath. "I'll do better, Mor, I swear. But help me if it looks like I'm going to blow. Get me out of the situation. Run interference."

"Okay, girlfish. I got you." She downed the tea. "I hope you get another vision, something that will help us and help your friend."

"Me too." I curled up in the soft cotton sheets, missing Oggie, and prayed to the Goddess to send me to Simmi. She didn't.

SEVENTEEN

JELLY

"Jelly, wake up. Try this! It makes you invincible! It's amazing! Wake up, wake up, wake up!" Mori's voice screeched across my brain. She yanked up my blinds and bright sunshine streamed over my face. I winced and cracked an eye. Mori loomed over me, holding a mug. She set it on the wooden bedside table and bounced on my bed, jarring and jumbling me.

"It's espresso. I've had three, but they were doubles, so maybe six? I'm not sure how you count them. It's really, really, really good, Jelly. Sit up. Try it. Try it now," insisted Mori.

"Okay, okay, get out of my face first," I grumbled. I rested against the headboard, rubbing my eyes, and laughed at her. Her eyes darted back and forth, and she was jumpy, as if ants pranced disco in her thong. She sailed off the bed and paced the floor. The coffee was sweet and creamy with a touch of cinnamon. After the third sip, the caffeine raced through my blood. "Mm, that's good. Did you make it?"

"I did, I did, it's so good, right?" said Mori, doing calisthenics in her small, silk pajamas.

"You had three? I'm good with one, maybe two."

"Ya," she puffed as she did jumping jacks, her breasts swinging with the motion. "Mako told me last night to add cream and sugar, and I did, and Sophia added the cinnamon and it tasted like a dessert, and I wanted more, so I've had three, and it's so good I could die," she babbled in one breath. "Wait, you've had it before?"

I laughed. "Stay up here long enough, and you'll see coffee is their drug of choice." I took another sip and said with disappointment, "I didn't see Simmi."

I had dreamed, though—heatedly. Mako soaking wet in the pool, that stupid chipped tooth showing as he came close and stroked his rough fingers down my arm. My head falling back as he whispered in my ear. Stupid brain. I set the coffee on the table and rubbed my face.

She stopped flapping her arms and dropped to the floor, stretching this way and that. "That sucks." She snickered. "You should have seen Mako's face when I told him about Toto. His jaw dropped to the floor."

She mimicked him in a deep voice, "You're Commander Tro's daughter? The Head of the Mers Army? For real?" She opened her mouth as wide as it would go and crossed her eyes. She added, "You might have some competition for his attention. I think I have a new admirer. I really like his eyes, but my favorite so far are his legs. He has fantastic legs. You like his legs, right? You saw them. They're hot. So hot. Like me. I'm hot. Like, dear Goddess, I'm boiling! Does caffeine ramp up your temperature?"

I chuckled, finished my coffee, and rose from the bed. "It can. You're also not used to it. Build up a tolerance. I'm going to get cleaned up and head to the house. The others should be here soon. I wish I had time for a swim in the pool."

Her eyes flew open, and she squealed, "The pool! Why didn't you tell me about the power dot?" I shook my head, having no clue what she was talking about. She pushed her face close to mine. "You don't know? You've been up here a gazillion times and you don't know? The thing between your legs, at the top of your hoo-hah. The Mers are totally missing out because we don't have one. I found it last night. Your fight with Mako rattled me, so I went for a swim. I was in the water, against the wall, up against some jet thing, which was amazing on my back, and I spun around to get my towel, landing my chest on the pool deck like a fish, and the jet thing hit me in the…" She whistled a looping noise. "And I almost screamed and passed out at the same time! It's this little bump and holy scrod's balls; it's sensitive! I had an incredible magical rush after that. You've got to check yours out."

She sat back, panting from her story, her eyes twitching from too much caffeine. "Look for it when you have your shower! It's phenomenal! I'll see you at the house. Sophia said the Witch and three Mages will be here soon, so I'm going to drink a gallon of water to dilute the coffee, so I don't embarrass myself in front of Anna by not being able to shut up, because the way it's going right now is so so so not good. Okay. Bye." She slammed the door behind her.

A short time later, when I entered the kitchen in the main house, having specifically not searched for my power dot, Sophia smiled. "Morning, Jelly. How did you sleep?" She was chopping a cabbage for a salad.

"Good, thanks."

"It's the tea. It's one of Sebastian's. Fae blend."

I swiped at my face. She lay down the knife and asked in a soft lilt, edged with hope, "Any visions?"

I shook my head. "Unfortunately, no."

She pursed her lips and muttered, "Shouldn't have given you the tea."

I swallowed against my sudden tears. "Did Mako tell you I know Simmi?"

She nodded and swept trembling fingers over her forehead, flecking it with cabbage pieces. "I knew she was consulting someone for her marketing, but I don't remember her saying your name. Or if she did, I'd forgotten. Jelly, knowing it's Simmi…It might make things worse. There's an emotional edge that wasn't there before. If you lose control…"

"I won't." I spoke with as much confidence as I could, but she was right. Anxiety had a clutch on my heart.

Her lips tightened. She returned to the brassica with renewed vigor, dropping the subject. Sensing she wasn't up for company, I grabbed a bowl of fruit, sat in a chaise by the pool, and stared at the ocean. As I chewed on green grapes, I slid the pearl along the chain, listening to its rasp above the distant sound of waves crashing on the beach below.

I pressed my fingers to my temple. *Synchi? Are you there?*

Jelly! Yes, yes, I am! How is it?

Fine, fine. I didn't tell her about cracking Mako's ribs. She'd only scold me for losing my temper on the first damned day. *How's Oggie?*

He's wrapped around me like a scarf. Have you met the Wizards yet? The Witch?

Not yet. They should be here soon. And I think they're called Mages, not Wizards.

She grunted. *Jelly. Be careful with them. There's a chance—*

A rush of energy poured across the property, stealing the air from my lungs and causing my skin to break out in goosebumps.

Synchi? Synchi, you cut off. Synchi?

I perked up, assuming it was the Surfecti. My heart was nervous as I stood and smoothed down the dark blue maxi dress with a halter top, exposing my back. I liked how it showed off my muscles.

The pale gray leather containing my knives wrapped around my hips, the long ends of the straps rolled and tucked away. Mako's voice carried with excitement. "Mom said she's out by the pool. I can't wait for you to meet her!"

Mako burst through the door, his face lit with a massive smile. He dragged someone by the arm. The world tilted when the stranger stepped out from behind Mako. A tremor skittered through my body as I gaped at a tall man with broad shoulders, carrying himself with the grace of a dancer. His hair was sandy, curly, and roguishly shaggy, the ends hovering just above his casual linen shirt collar. He wore slacks, cut to perfection, and they snugged his legs in a way that made my throat tight.

I whipped my dress into my fist to ease my movements as I strode across the clover lawn to meet him, drawn to him like metal filings toward a magnet. His face was perfection, with a strong nose, a sparkling smile, and a dimple that sat squarely in his chin. I wanted to lick it.

I stuck out my hand immediately, drawing my head back to meet his eyes, and breathed, "I'm Jelly."

The handsome man took my fingers and squeezed lightly. I gasped. Then he bowed, kissing the back of my hand. "Gray Smith. Charmed to meet you… Queen Jelly." The words rolled off his tongue like liquid, coating me and making me dizzy. He didn't let go of my hand when he straightened, and my breath caught again as he looked at me. I snapped my jaw shut, suddenly aware I was staring as if seeing stars for the first time.

His eyes danced with laughter. They were deep brown, the color of dark chocolate with sparkling gold flecks, and they twinkled with promise. I smiled, instantly comfortable in his company, utterly hypnotized by his charm. "Come, let me introduce you to my parents," he said smoothly, leading me to the house.

"I'd love that," I sighed, happy to follow him anywhere. I saw Mako's face as we passed him. His eyebrows pulled tight together, and a scowl stained his full lips. I glanced at him with vacant eyes. Mako? Mako who? He trailed behind us silently as I studied the beauty of Gray Smith.

"Please, after you," said Gray, sliding his hand on my lower back as he guided me toward the small group inside. I shivered from his touch as we approached the only female. "Mum, I'd like you to meet Jelly. Jelly, this is my mother, Anna Smith." I smiled at her, my caution lazy after meeting Gray.

I blinked out of my stupor when our hands met, as a sharp spark flashed across my palm. I snarled, pulling it back, and clenched it into a fist. The temptation to take that fist and run it through her face was overwhelming. Surfecti bitch.

Anna said coldly, "Hmm. Fireworks. This will be most entertaining."

She looked me up and down before her eyes flicked to Mori, who strode toward us with a wide smile. Anna's voice was icy with mistrust. "Why are you both armed?" Mori, confused, patted her thighs where she'd strapped her new metal stars over her flared linen pants.

I snapped, "We're always armed. We're Warriors. This is Mori. You met in the mirror."

"I'm a huge fan, Anna," she gushed. Anna's magic did not zap her when they shook hands.

Anna turned to the slim man beside her. "My husband, Richard."

"Hello, Jelly," he said with a nod, wrapping my throbbing

hand in both of his. The sting from his wife's touch faded in a flow of warmth, calming my irritation. "Do forgive Anna. She likes to test people on first contact. The shock you felt was your body repelling her magic, so in a way, you caused it. You're powerful."

His dark eyes glimmered as I swallowed my thoughts about his wife. He called over my head. "Roan, come meet Jelly and Mori, the Warrior Mermaids."

An enormous man strode across the room. I cricked my neck back to look up at him. He shaved his dark hair tight on the sides and left it longer on the top, braiding it back like a thick mohawk. He sported a beard that covered a broad chin.

He had ink everywhere. Tattoos climbed from his shirt collar up the back of his neck, making patterns and swirls on his skull. He'd pushed up his sleeves, displaying more tattoos on his arms, with dots, lines, and zags on various fingers. His energy was as impressive as his body, which was immense.

He pumped my hand enthusiastically, speaking all the while. "Aye, lass, a pleasure, an absolute pleasure to meet ye. Been waitin' on the Mers to come up top for bloody ages. About fookin' time, aye. Right mess this world is, right mess." I blinked a few times, my brain adjusting to his thick dialect.

He let go of my hand and turned to Mori. His emerald-green eyes flared with keen interest. He held her hand for longer, squeezing as she spoke. Without missing a beat, Mori replied. "I'm Mori, and, aye, been far too fookin' long. Da Mers is tardy. I canna believe we be da ones dey sent ta meet ye. We'll sort out da shambles between us, eh?"

He looked at her, puzzled. He burst into a roar of laughter, throwing his head back. Roan's green eyes twinkled under thick eyebrows as he dropped his chin. "Ah, lassie, ye don't need to copy me speech. I can understand ye perfectly as is. But ye got an ear on ye, don't ye? And with yer red hair, I'd guess ye came from near the Emerald Isle?" He released her hand to stroke his tight beard.

Mori cocked her head to the side, thoroughly enjoying the view. "I've studied languages. Yours is unique. Rough and mixed, but definitely Celtic." She smiled. "My family originated in the waters near Ireland. We migrated to the Pacific ages ago. And you?"

"Scottish and Irish mix. Probably some English bastard in there, too. Bit of a mutt, me." He stroked a giant mitt across his beard, eying us with warm curiosity. He yelled across the room to Sophia. "Sophie, love, it's wee early here, but I'm gasping for a whiskey!"

She called back, "Help yourself, Roan. Does anyone else want something besides coffee?"

Gray winked at Roan. "I'll have a dram with you." Before he moved away, he stroked two fingers down my bare arm, hardly touching, and I gasped at the sensation of my thong catching fire. He chuckled, and it rolled over me like flames. The tip of his tongue traced the corner of his lip, and I chomped on my cheek to stop myself from climbing him like a rabid monkey.

He and Roan walked away, leaving Mori and me with Anna and Richard. The four of us stood together in awkward silence. I tucked my hair behind my ear, yelling at Mori. *Is it just me, or is he sex personified?* I nodded to Gray at the bar.

She frowned. *I think it's just you. Why?*

I'll tell you later. So, Anna zapped me when she shook my hand. And now she's staring at me.

Because your hand is frozen to your head, drop it.

Sebastian joined us, affectionately slinging an arm around Anna, breaking her from her hostile glare. He sighed happily and said, "This is the best part about old friends. They walk into your home and take over." He kissed the side of her head. "It's good to see you again, Anna. Let's have refreshments, and then we'll settle down to talk. Sound good?"

Richard piped up, "Tea would be lovely. Come help me, darling," he said to Anna, breaking her steely gaze, honed in on me. I didn't think we'd be best friends, but I didn't expect such a frosty first greeting.

"Of course. Excuse us," Anna said, nodding at us curtly. I returned the gesture, exhaling as Anna followed Richard to the kitchen.

Sebastian patted my shoulder, and relief flooded my bloodstream. He murmured, "It's bound to be overwhelming. It's a lot of magic under one roof. Thought I'd head them off for drinks to give you some space from the pressure of meeting everyone." He shoved his hands in his shorts, his voice dropping low. "Just remember, no matter what happens today, we invited you. We need you, Jelly. We need your help."

I nodded. "Thank you, Sebastian. That's kind of you. I don't think Anna likes me much."

Mori snorted. "That's an understatement. That old expression of if looks could kill...well...look."

We casually scanned to the kitchen, where Anna was throwing daggers at us with her eyes. Sebastian dropped his voice with a sigh. "Honestly, she's miffed that she needs a Mers to get to Simmi. You're the first one who's caught even a glimpse of her. Anna exhausted all her people. They tried to get a location or a small sniff of Simmi, but came up with nothing. Anna is the most powerful witch in the world. Her nose is out of joint over this."

He frowned. "Even I can't find Simmi with my Fae blood, and she's my daughter." He raised his eyebrows to stress his point. "The pearl is important. You're important. You and Mori both. Don't forget it, no matter how many glares she gives you."

I grinned and softly bumped my shoulder against his arm. "Thanks, Sebastian." He nodded and strolled away, Mako taking his place at my side. He was about to ask me something, drawing my attention, but stalled as I almost jumped out of my skin. Gray's warm fingers brushed the back of my neck, and a flurry of tingles rushed between my legs. Mori looked at me in puzzlement.

She asked, "Why are you blushing so hard?" Mako scowled, his blue eyes accusatory as he glowered at Gray.

Gray leaned down, his lips near my ear, to murmur, "We're almost ready, Jelly. Are you? We can take more time if you need." I shivered as he stroked his fingers down my naked spine. The gesture was quick and light, yet possessive. I leaned into it, almost stumbling backward. A small, involuntary sigh slipped from my lips.

Mako's eyes darkened as he saw my response to Gray. His hands fisted by his side, and he faced Gray and snarled, "Jelly's fine. She's a Warrior. She doesn't need you to coddle her."

Gray tipped his head with graceful acquiescence, and Mako took a slow and intentional sidestep to widen his feet. It was a fighting stance. Puzzled, I turned from them and walked toward the living room's seating area, leaving them growling in whispers at each other. Mori wove her arm through mine and tossed her chin over her shoulder.

"Men," she muttered, "I got you, girlfish." She led us to a small loveseat for two. Her hazel eyes scanned mine, worried. "Seriously, though. Why do you look like you're about to catch fire?"

"Later," I hissed, annoyed with myself for letting Gray

distract me. I couldn't figure out why, but I was uncomfortable with this entire situation.

When everyone sat, our eyes gravitated to Anna, who had remained standing to head the meeting. She said, "Let's not waste time with pleasantries."

I swept my hair back, touching my temple to speak privately to Mori. *Of course not. Why would we do that?*

Anna said, "Jelly's vision. What remains unknown is if Simone initiated it, if the Vetula pearl prompted it, or, as Mori, the Land Magic *aficionado* suggested, it's a binding spell." Anna exaggerated the word, making both Mori and I bristle.

Mori casually cradled her head in her hand, her elbow resting on the arm of the loveseat. She said, *I'm not crushing so much anymore.* I humphed and scanned the room, seeing Roan staring at us with laughter in his eyes.

Anna continued, "But before we jump to any conclusions, Jelly, did you manage to remember anything else about the vision? Perhaps something useful?"

Well, that's just rude, Mori huffed indignantly. Roan's dark chuckle caught my ear before he wiped it away with his hand over his beard.

I said, "I told you everything I saw, Anna. Why don't you explain the ins and outs of a binding spell for us? After all, Mori had the idea before you did."

Anna sniffed and looked down her nose at me. "Fine, I shall enlighten the ignorant in the room." She stared pointedly at me and said, "I'll keep it very simple so you can understand. A binding spell uses blood to tie two things together."

"People or objects?" I asked.

Anna said, "Depends. Sometimes both. My assumption is that Simone's blood is being used as a locater. That makes the most logical sense. Whoever is bleeding her must have some history with the pearl."

"But why her?"

"Because of who she is." Anna's voice was sharp with impatience.

"I still don't understand why someone targeted her specifically."

Anna snapped, "She's a powerful blend of Mers and Fae. Fae-Mers. Simone's magic is phenomenally strong, making her the most obvious target for siphoning magic."

"He can get her magic through her blood?" I asked, attempting to piece it together.

"It would explain the damned needle thrust in her arm!" Sophia choked on her coffee, and Anna's tone softened. "I'm sorry, Sophia. That was unnecessary. My emotions are quite fraught. But Simone went missing after Jelly blew up the store."

"I'm not responsible for the kidnapping, Anna."

"Are you not?" Anna smoothed down her white dress, taking a moment for a deep breath before continuing. Her eyes were on Sebastian's. "Simone is a Fae-Mers, and she's powerful. Unfortunately, that means she can be bled repeatedly without dying too fast, especially if he's replenishing her, which again, I assume he is." Anna turned her icy stare back at me. "Can you control the pearl?"

I dipped my eyes and shrugged. "I only just learned about it. I was in prison for three days after the soap explosion. Then the shark happened, which prompted the vision of Simmi. And Anna, in case no one told you, Simmi is my friend, so don't think you're the only one suffering here." The look of shock on her face pleased me. "After that, the Shaman had me flex my increased powers, which are still undirected. I'm playing catch-up. The past couple of days have been a lot."

"Yes," she sneered. "Your Shaman should have told you years ago. You could have trained."

I inhaled and pulled at my dress, smoothing down the non-existent creases. "She didn't want to burden me if the pearl stayed quiet during my life. But don't worry, Anna. I'm a quick study."

Anna's lip curled up, prepared to drop something sarcastic. Richard interjected. "Anna, darling, we are all upset about Simone. There's no need to take it out on Jelly."

She ignored him and said in a haughty tone, "Regardless, we're working with a child with a new toy, completely unaware of its power."

Mori snorted her outrage on my behalf. *Bitch! What is her problem?*

I ignored Mori and snapped through tight teeth. "And yet, you need me! It's driving you crazy that you can't do this alone. Typical Surfecti. You're exactly what I expected."

Anna sneered, "Is that so? And what was that?"

"The pearl showed me its memories of the bombs on an endless loop for three days. The Surfecti could have helped us! You could have stopped the humans, but no, you had better things to do. It's no wonder we haven't worked with you since."

Anna trembled with anger. My hands curled into fists in my dress. Mako scooted forward in his seat, his eyes cautious. Roan frowned into his whiskey, and Sebastian reached for Sophia's hand. Gray and Richard sat as still as stone.

Anna spat disdainfully, "You Mers. You have no idea what we dealt with on the surface. You scurried away like crabs. You think you're better than us because you could hide. We didn't have that option! And you have the audacity to question our decisions? Wonderful! Just what we need! A child to enlighten us all."

"I can handle myself just fine, Anna. And I'm far from a child. I'm twenty-seven." I bit into my cheek as the pearl pulsed at my throat, reacting to my simmering anger. Blood coated my tongue as I bit the other side, the sting of it distracting me. I controlled my breathing and kept my voice level. "For whatever reason, I bear the pearl, and I have a duty to protect the Mers."

Anna sneered, "Oh, it's the Mers first? Of course, it is. It always is! You're worried about fish while my goddaughter is being bled by a monster! Think beyond yourself, girl!"

I clenched my jaw. "I will always put them first, but I'm certain I can handle this man, or whatever—"

Anna shouted, "You daft bint! You are completely ignorant of what you're dealing with!" Her voice dropped into a mutter as her anger scathed the air. "Our best Seers…outdone by a freshman bloody fishgirl. Preposterous!"

I was unaware of what a daft bint was, but her derogatory tone was clear. The pearl trembled, sensing my desire to blast a hole in Anna's white dress, preferably straight through the middle. Hot magic thrummed through my blood, muddling my vision and clamping my lungs. As Anna continued to rant, I could see her mouth moving, but my mind blanked out what she said.

Voices flew up to mock me. There were too many too fast, and I fought to keep control. My head rang with a cacophony of jeering. I bit on my cheek hard enough to electrify me. It jerked me back to the present just as Anna threw her hands over her head, yelling, "Bloody useless! She isn't even paying attention. Where did you just go, *girl?*"

My lip curled back as I snarled, lost in my mind, especially when Anna called me 'girl.' Mori saw the pearl flick on the chain under its own volition and shrieked, "What the hell is wrong with you, Anna? We're on the same side!"

Mori was shouting back and pointing fingers, but her voice muted into static, drowned out by previous mocking. 'So irresponsible,' 'murdered in cold blood,' 'useless,' 'exaggerating,' 'I'll visit your hole.' The slurs looped and swirled, stealing my breath, dragging me deeper into chaos.

Blood stained my lips as I ravaged my cheeks to anchor myself. I started shaking, desperately trying to reclaim my mind. Mori's eyes flew wide as the pearl levitated on its chain. She bellowed. "Mako! Get us out of here! NOW!"

EIGHTEEN

MAKO

The floating pearl and the terror in Mori's voice spurred me across the room in a heartbeat. Jelly had entered a trance, taken under by some force, glazed as she stared at Anna with venomous intent. I wrapped my arms around Jelly's waist, dragging her through the open glass door. She was shaking so hard her teeth clacked. Mori followed, fearful of an attack, although nothing had happened…yet. I'd never seen Anna so angry.

I gritted my teeth, my rib not fully healed, and bore her dead weight away from the house. I shouted, "Get it out, Jelly!" She moaned something unintelligible, her head lolling like her spine had turned to soft noodles. "You're vibrating, Jelly! Let it out! Shoot it in the water where I can help you!" I swung her around and aimed her at the infinity pool. I bent at the knees and braced one arm around her torso, holding her up.

She raised her trembling hands and flung her magic at the water, causing it to swirl and burst up in a turgent column above our heads, threatening to engulf the house. I lifted a hand and used my magic to still it in its pillar form. She ripped her hands back down, and I released my hold so as not to fight against her.

The water crashed into the pool and slammed over the sides, soaking us up to our knees.

Hissing, she shot her right hand toward a potted palm. She annihilated it, dirt and shattered pottery flying in a wide arc, while shredded leaves fluttered down like confetti. With a blast from her left hand, she demolished a cement statue of a mermaid, the irony not escaping me. She thrust her hands at the pool again, creating whirlpools and waves that tumbled, fractured, and smashed together, causing a spray to drop like dense rain.

Her body went limp as she panted and moaned, her whole body quaking. She hadn't dispersed enough magic. The pearl wasn't pulling at her neck anymore, but it still jumped and slid on its chain, looking for release. Her voice was raw as she gasped, "Salt."

Mori grabbed my arm. "Take us to the ocean, the quickest way possible." Her eyes were frantic as they darted down the stairs to the beach. "She'll never manage the steps. She'll detonate the cliff. Get us away from the house! Hurry!"

I yanked Jelly's hand to get her moving, and Mori pulled at her other side. She stumbled, almost falling to her knees. I hoisted her over my shoulder in a firefighter's carry, stifling a groan from the strain on my ribcage, and ran around the house to the front. Mori yelled, "Hang on, Jelly, we're going to the ocean! Don't lose your shit, girlfish!"

I wrestled open the sliding door to my battered VW van parked in the driveway and pushed Mori inside, tossing Jelly in her lap. I slammed the door, started the engine and gunned it. A thick press of magic snapped around us as we left the compound, the magical ward biting against my skin. Jelly stuck her head between her knees, taking deep breaths to diffuse the rage. She moaned.

Mori's voice was scathing. "Why would Anna do that? Is she an idiot?"

I shook my head, watching in the rearview mirror as Mori rubbed slow circles on Jelly's back. We eased onto a bumpy dirt road down to the ocean and the van wheezed to a halt, shuddering twice before shutting off. When I yanked the door and helped Jelly out, her knees gave way.

"What's wrong with you?" I asked. "You ran from the store."

"Too much," she said through clenched teeth. "Holding back…too much. Get me to the water." When she stumbled, I lifted her into my arms and ran into the waves, both of us fully dressed. She exhaled as the salt water touched her skin. "Deeper," she croaked, and I walked in until she submerged, drinking in the salt water. The pearl hissed and then settled, halting its jerky movements to lie still against her throat. She tapped my arm, and I took a few steps back, hoisting her higher so she could breathe.

Mori stroked her friend's cheek and whispered, "Jelly, what was that? Anna's a bitch, but whatever just happened was more than that."

Overwhelmed, Jelly started crying. She wrapped her hand around my neck, nails digging in, and pressed her face to my chest, her body heaving with tears. My throat closed from her distress, and I adjusted my hold, bringing her body closer to my mine. Her dress was heavy and pulled in the waves, wrapping around my calves. I spread my feet for balance and controlled the water using my magic, creating an eddy, the waves passing around us.

"I've got you," I murmured against her wet head. They were the words that always calmed Simmi. I hoped they'd do the same for Jelly.

She sobbed in frustration. She spoke through hot tears, muffled against my shirt. "All the voices came back, all the shitty things people have said to me over the years. They just layered all over each other, taunting me. Anna triggered it, and it was all I could hear. The pearl reacted. I can't..." Jelly shook her head and pressed the heel of her free hand to her forehead. With a shuddering breath, she said, "If I don't free Simmi, this monster will keep attacking the Mers, and the bubble will fall. But I can't get to Simmi without Anna, and Anna despises the Mers, and particularly me. I don't...I can't do this."

Mori lifted her fingers to her temple, her other hand on Jelly's shoulder. She said, "Mako, I'm calling the Shaman, and as we're all touching, you'll be in on it." She frowned. "But maybe keep quiet." I nodded.

Shaman, come in! This is Mori. It's an emergency!

An elderly voice replied immediately. *Mori? What happened? Where's Jelly?*

Jelly mumbled, *I'm here.* Her voice splintered into tears.

The old lady snapped, *Why are you crying?* When that made Jelly sob louder, she barked, *Mori, why is Jelly crying?*

Mori's face hardened, throwing me a tight look. *Anna attacked Jelly, saying she was untrained and a stupid child. She's pissed that she needs the Mers and took her jealousy out on Jelly. Then they argued about the rift between the races. It was her tone. She was derisive. And Jelly got pulled under by past voices. The pearl jumped on its chain and levitated. Mako, Sophia's son, dragged her outside, and she shot pool water in the sky and blew some shit up. Not people, thank Goddess, but it wasn't enough, so Mako drove us to the beach. We're standing in the ocean in our clothes, looking like idiots, but it was the only thing I could think of to do.*

There was a beat of silence. The Shaman's voice was sharp.

Jelly, talk to me. Jelly didn't respond. The Shaman shouted. *WARRIOR Jelly!*

Jelly let her scowl shine through her voice. *I know what you're saying in your tone. It's no use trying to intimidate me, Synchi. We have to find another way. I can't work with Anna.*

The Shaman sighed as though the world had climbed onto her shoulders. *Mori, thank you. You did the right thing, but I must speak to Jelly alone.*

Jelly froze up and shook her head, panic on her face. As she was in my arms, our skin touching, I could hear everything. Mori said, *Okay, Shaman, I'm stepping away.* She kept her hand on Jelly's shoulder and shuffled back an inch. I grinned. She hadn't lied.

Jelly lifted her fingers to her temple. *I'm here, Synchi.*

Synchi said, *Can you see why I fell out with her? She's the worst sort of witch: arrogant, pretentious, and bloated with self-importance. She's a damned fool for tangling with a Warrior mermaid—especially one with a temper. And she knew this about you! But as much as she has sand for brains, she's my only Surfecti contact. You must work with her. Jelly, I'm sorry. There is no one else.*

I pressed my lips together, biting back my laugh. Sand for brains. I liked this Synchi. Jelly snickered, buoyed by the Shaman's words. *Now, come on, Synchi, don't hold back. Tell me what you really feel.* Then she sighed. *But what do I do? Don't you dare tell me to go back and apologize. I'll tell Sophia and Sebastian I'm sorry about their pool, but not Anna.* She paused and asked, *Are you sure there's no one else?*

Jelly, we're out of time. I wasn't going to tell you this. I didn't want to distract you. But we've had another attack. Not a shark, but moray eels. Tro took heavy damage to his arm. I've mended it, but he's out of service for a bit. Don't tell Mori. It isn't bad enough that she needs to worry.

Mori's eyes widened, and Jelly stiffened. I held her tighter, hoping it was reassuring.

The Shaman said, *He's recovering, but it was a nasty bite, as several eels attacked him together. The dark magic is getting bolder and more assertive. Work with Anna and find the girl. Otherwise, the bubble will fail. I'm using everything I have, Jelly, but it's flagging. I don't have enough magic to hold out for much longer. You have no other choice. I am sorry about that. That's on me for not bolstering an alliance with the Surfecti.*

I swallowed, unaware the Mers Shaman was so weakened. Jelly said, *I understand. Will you keep me posted about Tro?*

Of course. Don't worry. He'll be fine soon. There was a pause, and the Shaman spoke sternly. *Jelly, you must manage your rage without blowing things up. You know what to do.*

Jelly shot Mori a look, and Mori bit her lip, her worry turning to mischief. Her freckled face scrunched up in a wicked grin. Jelly's eyes darted to mine for a second before she looked down. Her brow creased and her voice was furtive. *We went through this, Synchi. You don't have to say it again. I swear, really, you don't.*

It appears that I do, Jelly. Have sex with one of them. All of them. Have hot, angry sex with every damned Surfecti you meet over every Goddess-damned surface of the planet. You're a danger to yourself and the mission if you explode every time you get upset. Just fuck it out.

I almost dropped her. Mori clapped her hand over her mouth so hard it brought tears to her eyes. Jelly spluttered, *Synchi!!!*

Suddenly, I was painfully cognizant of every place our skin touched: my hand on her bare back, the other under her knees, her arm wrapped around my neck.

The old voice scolded. *Until you control yourself, and*

Goddess only knows when that will happen, use sex. I can't believe the fate of the world depends on you having a damned orgasm!

Mori's face twisted as she tried not to laugh, pinching her nose. Her shoulders shook violently, and she clutched onto Jelly to avoid missing a word. Jelly screamed at the Shaman, making me wince as her voice scored through my mind. *How is it different from the Procreation Missions?*

The Shaman yelled right back, giving as good as she got. *Diffuse your anger by any means necessary! Salt or sex, that's what I told you, and sex is more potent and faster! I shouldn't have to remind you! Goddess, give me strength. Do better, Jelly!*

Jelly was rigid and barely breathing. She slowly slid her arm from my neck and leaned away from me, as much as she could, while still in my arms, shooting Mori a dirty look. She sucked her teeth. *I hate this pearl.*

The Shaman's voice softened. *Go back and deal with Anna.*

Jelly's voice was sulky. *I hate you, too, Synchi.*

No, you don't. Hurry, Jelly. We're out of time.

Jelly dropped her fingers from her temple and scowled as Mori buckled over, positively howling with laughter. A wave caught her off guard, and she choked on the water, still guffawing. She stepped closer to where I held the water still. She bumped me with her elbow. "Cool magic, Mako. Water manipulation? It's cool, right, Jelly? Mako is so totally cool." She winked at her salaciously and sniggered. Jelly scowled.

I lowered Jelly to her feet, holding her lightly around her waist until she was steady. She closed her eyes, her jaw clenching and releasing repeatedly. She inhaled through her nose, trying to regain some composure. She ran her tongue over her lips before biting the bottom one, sucking it into her mouth. When she opened her eyes, she stared at me hard. She stammered, "That…she…you…" She pinched the bridge of her nose and groaned.

My lips turned up in a grin, just a tiny smile. I couldn't help it. She was so flustered. I wanted to joke about what the Shaman said, saying I was available for service, but I wasn't a stupid man. I cleared my throat. "I'll give you two some space." I strode from the water, leaving them talking in low, tight voices. I caught the name Fillian and wondered if he was her Mers lover.

I squashed the flare of jealousy in my chest and yanked off my wet shirt with a frown. The last thing she needed was to get tangled with me. Twisting aggressively, I wrung out the fabric. A massive raven flew over my head and turned, back-flapping its wings to hover before me. I had strong Fae magic and could understand birds and animals in short bursts. It looked me in the eye and cawed, "HOME! NOW!"

I spun to the mermaids and shouted. "We have to go!" Jelly's legs got tangled in her long dress, but she bunched it in her hands, scowling at my offer to carry her. They jumped in the front seat, and the van sputtered and whined to life. I hit the gas hard. The drive to the house was silent and tense, Synchi's caution of the faltering bubble rolling beside the raven's warning.

I turned into the driveway. Something was wrong. The magical barrier was down. There wasn't even a fizzle as we crossed. I dropped into a lower gear so we could stealthily approach the house down the long driveway. Pulling into the circle, I whispered, "What the hell…" Something or someone had ripped the door off its hinges, and we heard screaming when I cut the motor. We sprinted for the house, Jelly's wet dress hampering her movements.

I held up a fist to stop us from barreling in. Mori yanked a handful of Jelly's dress, tying it into a swift knot at her hip. Jelly did the other side, freeing her legs. She breathed out, "What is that stench? It's like asphalt in the sun." She wrinkled her nose. "Like tar or something." She silently drew her blades, and Mori pulled her stars from the straps on her thighs.

The stained glass sidelights lay in colored pieces on the floor of the destroyed foyer. We crept in, staying close to the walls to avoid our feet crunching on glass. A shriek and a boom echoed, coming from the next room. Crouching, we looked around the corner and gasped.

The furniture was in shambles, splintered and shattered. Feathers floated from torn cushions, and glass and china lay in fragments on the floor. The few surviving pieces of art lurched crookedly on their nails, chunks of the walls dug out. Dad shielded Mom in the corner, his large body covering hers while his hands shot defensive magic.

A shadow, no, a beast, flew across the room into the wall. Mori screamed when she saw it, and its awful face swung in our direction, its eyes narrowing on Jelly's throat. It lurched forward. A blast of blue magic struck it, Dad's from the looks of it, and the beast screeched, exploding into a jellied pulp, leaving thick blood and an oily smudge dripping down the white wall. Roan roared, "Too fookin' many! Where are the mermaids? We can't leave without them!"

Before I could stop her, Jelly cried, "We're here!" and stepped forward. Another monster sprang toward her from the far side. It snapped its fangs and swiped for her throat with sharp nails, its eyes bright red and glassy. She instinctively ducked and raised her knives, slashing across the belly with the knuck while plunging the stiletto blade into its throat. It snarled as it dropped to the floor, the red of its eyes going blank. It shimmered, changing shape, and I yanked on Jelly and Mori to get away.

To our left, a creature froze mid-leap, suspended in the air, aiming straight for Jelly. It struggled and gnashed against the cocoon of purple magic. A crackling bolt of green obliterated it, spraying black goo across the ceiling, dimming the room as it coated the light fixture. Anna careened around the corner, eyes and hair wild. "We have to go. Now!" Mori was in shock; her throwing stars gripped so tightly that blood trickled down her wrists. "NOW!" Anna roared.

"Where are we going?" Jelly asked. Anna gaped at her incredulously, a hairsbreadth away from imploding, stunned by a question in the middle of the raging madness. I grabbed Mori and Jelly by the hands and tugged them across the demolished room, my flip-flops slapping as I skirted them around the worst.

Mori slipped in the black liquid on the floor, and my shoulder jerked as I kept her from falling. My voice was tight. "Hurry, there could be more coming."

Anna's face was ashen as she ran with us. Her voice was shaky from fear. "This will be disorienting."

"What will?" breathed Jelly, her dress still wet and cumbersome. If we had a minute to stop, I would have pulled it right off her to give her the freedom to move faster.

Mori's face contorted as she yelled, "Are those what I think they are? That's impossible!" She stumbled over the step, and I grunted, struggling to keep us all upright. My head injury throbbed, and my ribs wailed, but terror kept my feet moving. Roan swept in from the side and took Mori around the waist, freeing me of half my burden.

He dragged Mori with him. "Keep yer voice down," he hushed. His head was on a swivel, constantly monitoring the grounds as we escaped. Dad waved his hands in a pattern in front of the hedge bordering the far side of the pool, and Jelly sucked in a breath as it parted like a door, revealing a circle of enormous trees, their tall tops previously invisible. Her running stalled, and she fumbled before regaining her stride.

I whispered, "We're teleporting. We have to get out of here. More might come. It's no longer safe."

Roan pushed Mori through the hedge, waiting outside until everyone was in. He thrust against my back to make me and Jelly move faster. I looped my arm around a disoriented Mori, pulling Jelly and rushing us inside the circle of trees. Gray and Anna came next, followed by Roan and Richard, their faces pale. Once inside the enclosure, Dad wove the hedges together, not a single leaf shaking to give us away. Anna's voice was tight. "Grab hands, and don't let go."

The hairs on my neck rose, and I saw the pearl jerk on its chain around Jelly's neck. Jelly and Mori each clutched my hands. The pearl beat and pulsed and rattled a warning. "Anna, something's coming!" Jelly warned. "It's getting closer!" A scrabbling sound and hiss came from the bushes. Waiting for Anna's spell, we couldn't drop our hands to use magic. Jelly leaned into me, her body beginning to tremble.

"Mum..." Gray yelled, "Hurry!"

She screamed through panic, "I'm trying, damn it!"

I threaded my fingers through Jelly's and gripped to the point of pain, and she winced from my strength or the dread that clawed at our nerves. The smell of hot tar filled the space, and a creature exploded through the hedge and roared through a jaw of serrated teeth.

I'd swum with great whites, fought schools of barracuda, and encountered packs of Shifters mid-battle, but nothing frightened me like the face of this creature. Blood-red eyes sparked with delight as they focused on Jelly's throat. It snarled through long fangs and clacked them together as if already tasting her veins. My heart turned to ice as it roared and sprung from its thick haunches, claws ready.

A wind funnel encircled us, followed by a flash of light, and

I fell into pieces like every cell in my body had abandoned its casing. The circle, the monster, and the blue sky blurred. I clenched Jelly's hand so I wouldn't lose her.

NINETEEN

JELLY

It was dark, the thick of night, and the ground was cold and damp, unforgiving in my sodden dress. A heavy weight pressed me down, and I grunted. Was I dead? The pressure released, and groans and moans sounded around me. I was dizzy when I sat up.

Anna was already on her feet, pacing back and forth as we reoriented. Roan and Sebastian scanned the area on the outskirts of our group. I noticed Sophia sitting as I was, elbows propped on her knees, with her head in her hands. She offered me a weak smile. "Awful, isn't it?"

"Magnificent!" shouted Mori, rubbing Sophia's back. She didn't seem at all affected, and she sprang up and rushed to me, sliding to a stop and dropping to her knees. She squealed too loudly in my ear. "That was incredible! Wasn't that incredible, Jelly! We teleported!"

"It was something," I moaned. "Help me up." Mori stood and hauled me to my feet, steadying me until my equilibrium balanced. She left me to help Sophia. My eyes adjusted to the darkness, and I saw we were in a circular grove surrounded by massive old trees. I staggered to lean against one as I worked out the knots in my dress, hoping it would dry faster. I patted my hips for my knives and sighed with relief. "Where are we?" I croaked like an old frog.

Anna replied, "England. Coven headquarters."

"What were those things?"

Her voice was chilly as she snapped, "Eators. And we would have left sooner if you'd been at the bloody house!" She stormed away without another word.

I turned my head and pressed my cheek against the tree, shivering as it seemed to kiss my skin. Mako spoke heatedly with his father, his eyes on me as he gesticulated. Sophia and Mori were with them, Mori throwing out her index finger in Anna's direction. My ears couldn't decipher what they were saying, but I was confident I was the subject.

Suddenly, Gray's breath was hot on my neck, whispering, "Jelly, are you all right? Are you hurt?" I turned, and his eyes burned into me with concern. He exhaled loudly and hugged me, whispering, "Where did you go? They attacked, and I couldn't find you. I thought they'd taken you."

The safety of his arms relaxed me, and I swooned, loosely wrapping my arms around his waist and resting my cheek on his warm chest. He exhaled heavily, his chin grazing the top of my head. "What are Eators?" I mumbled into the soft fabric of his shirt.

He stiffened and said, "We'll explain once we get inside."

I nodded numbly, not really caring about his lack of explanation. "What are these trees? They have such a presence."

"Oaks. They have a strong sense of duty and can absorb and endure all sorts of trauma. You probably find them comforting. They're taking your fear from you." His arms tightened, and his face nuzzled into my hair. He softly kissed my head. A burning tickle raced from my head to my feet. "Jelly, you're freezing. You're dressed for the beach, not the English countryside. And why are you soaking wet?" When he pulled back, the cold fully hit me, and I shivered, my teeth clenching together.

Gray frowned and, in one quick move, swept off his shirt, leaving his torso bare. My mind blanked, and I couldn't find my tongue to speak, staring at the thick wall of muscle before me. He told me to hold my arms up, and I complied without question. He slid the warm linen shirt over my shaking body, his lime and sage scent surrounding me.

"Won't…you be…cold?" I chattered, my mind going into spasms as I stared at Gray's chest, smelled his scent, felt his warmth, and heard his deep growl…

"You're what matters, Jelly."

All I needed was taste and Gray would completely overwhelm my senses. My body vibrated with anticipation. We needed to get inside and find a bedroom—or a broom closet. I reached out and grasped his hand. He tugged me close before frowning at my flip-flops, squelching in the damp grass and mud. "Those won't do. Shall I carry you?" The pearl buzzed at my throat, shaking me from my haze.

"Carry me? What? No. I… I…" My heart flipped like a dolphin and I squinted in the dark to find Mori. I couldn't see her. I rubbed my face, trying to clear the cobwebs in my brain. His eyes twinkled in the dark as if lit from behind, watching my inner struggle.

Mako blazed up beside us and dropped into a crouch at my feet. "Get on, Jelly. Hurry. It's freezing out here." Gray stepped back and released his hand, his lips turned down.

"Get on?" I asked, staring at Mako's broad back in a daze. He was also shirtless, having left his wet top in the van. His tattoos rolled under his bunched muscles as he waved an arm behind him, encouraging me. The cold of the night swallowed me. "Um," I started. "I've never…um."

"Had a piggyback ride? I suppose not. Press yourself against my back and wrap your legs around my waist. Hang on around my neck. It's the quickest way to get you inside." He looked over his shoulder, his smile gleaming mischievously as his voice dropped. "Come on, Jelly. Let me take you for a ride."

I giggled at his silly insinuation. Gray snorted, and the noise startled me. He nodded to me once and walked away. As soon as he'd put distance between us, common sense returned along with the bracing wind.

Mako urged, "Jelly, come on."

I was so cold that my toes had gone numb. Hesitantly, I placed my hands on Mako's shoulders. His voice deepened. "Closer, Jelly. Right against me." I swallowed the heartbeat in my throat and leaned against his warm skin. He stood quickly and effortlessly, his fingers digging into the meat of my thighs. I yelped and wrapped my legs around him instinctively, clinging to his shoulders, my body swaying backward.

He sounded husky. "Grab up your dress so I don't trip on it, and wrap your arms tight around my neck. Don't be shy."

I did as instructed and he took off in a trot, bouncing me against his back. I gripped him tighter with my arms and legs and moaned in his ear, "Your skin is so hot. You feel so good."

He inhaled sharply and softly warned, "Careful, Queen. That kind of talk can get you into trouble." I chuckled in his ear, snuggling as close as possible, my skin greedily soaking in his heat. A smile plastered my face, almost drunk with relief. We overtook Gray, reaching Mori, who jogged slowly to keep warm.

She turned as she heard our approach. I lifted my eyes, catching the smirk on her face. She called, "Can I hang on to the front?"

I tapped Mako's shoulder. "I'm good. You warmed me up. I want to walk."

"Are you sure? You're still cold."

I pointed to Mori. "So is she." He lowered me to the ground. I crossed my arms as he stood. "Now, tell me what those things were."

He ran his fingers through his long hair, taming it back. "Eators."

I rolled my eyes. "Anna said the same thing, but it doesn't help me."

Mori's face turned sickly. "From what I've read, they are possessed humans who have been under someone else's control for too long. I didn't think they were real."

Mako nodded. "They suck the joy out of you. They take your love for life."

My stomach rolled over. "What?"

Mori grimaced. "I learned about them in a history of dark magic class. I seriously thought they were a myth." She looked at me with giant, worried eyes. "Don't ever let one break your skin. Ever. Understand?"

I swallowed, thinking of the close claws of the one I stabbed. "Okay."

We started walking. Mori snickered, "So, we haven't talked about what the Shaman said. I'm going to make T-shirts with the slogan Just Fu–ow!"

I punched her in the arm and glanced at Mako. He kept his face straight, but his cobalt-blue eyes burned. His steps hesitated, and he said, "You two go ahead. I need to talk to Gray about something."

Not far in the distance, along a flat dirt path, a stone mansion loomed out of the rolling hills, lights brightening the windows. I shivered violently, and Mori pushed her arm in front of me, blocking my path and taking off into a sprint. With a whoop, I bunched my wet dress in my fists, along with the flip-flops, and laughed at Mori as I caught up to her. "You got the hang of your legs quickly!"

"Yeah, terror will do that."

We stopped when we reached the courtyard, bending over to catch our breath. I glanced over my shoulder to see Mako arguing with Gray, his hands flying around as he spoke.

Mori stated bluntly, "They both like you."

"I don't want to be in the middle of that."

Mori grinned as she licked her lips. "Are you kidding? I'd get in the middle of that in a *heartbeat*. You could be the tuna in their sandwich."

I swatted her. "So not the time, Mori."

She lifted a shoulder and shrugged, eying the two men. "You heard what the Shaman said. I almost want you to get angry to see who you choose." She thrummed her fingers on her lips. "But then again, why choose?" She sighed dramatically. "It's such a shame he likes garlic."

I chuckled. "I think you're part vampire."

She cackled and bared her teeth, lifting her hands above her head. "I vant to suck your…" She wrinkled her nose. "Well, not blood," she glanced back at the arguing friends, "but I'd suck something else."

I shoved her forward and climbed the staircase to the impressive front door. The dark wood was heavy, ancient, and intricately carved with roses and swords. I pushed it open by the weathered brass handle, sighing with relief as warmth surrounded me.

We stood in the vast foyer, our eyes wide. Antique brass lights graced the space, complemented by fat candles burning on tables and various shelves, the flames safely sheltered behind hurricane shades. Along the left side, a staircase rose elegantly, covered in a dark red carpet. The stairs reached up to a landing above. Portraits lined the walls, all women. Anna's strict face glared at me in thick paint.

Shadows flickered across the floor, drawing my attention down, where I saw my dress dripping on the intricately knotted rug. I dropped my filthy flip-flops at the door and called, "Hello?"

"In here, Jelly." Sophia poked her head around a door and waved. "Sebastian has the fire going. We'll get cleaned up later. Come and get warm." We followed her into what appeared to be a library. "The study is smaller than the sitting room. Not enough chairs for everyone, but it will warm up faster." Roan and Sebastian sat in wingback chairs, sipping golden liquid from heavy crystal glasses. When they saw us, their deep voices halted, dropping us into an uncomfortable silence.

Sophia said, "Stand by the fire. I'll get you some blankets." She pulled two heavy wool throws from a shelf in the corner and handed them to us. She left us, making excuses that she needed to go to the kitchen. Sebastian nodded to us and followed Sophia through a swinging door, leaving us alone with Roan.

The firelight danced across the dark wood paneling, the room cozy with gentle lamplight throwing shadows. One wall was floor-to-ceiling books, the cracked spines showing how many hands had cherished them. Heavy drapes blocked the frosty night, and a grandfather clock ticked, the only sound except the popping of the fire. Massive oil paintings of serene landscapes filled the walls.

Wrapped in our blankets, we held our hands silently by the fire. Once warm again, I collapsed into a chair, the fabric old and soft. Mori sat in a burgundy velvet wingback, the arms worn bare from the years. It would have been lovely if it weren't for the company. Roan set down his glass and stared at his hands, scowling.

He pulled a thick knife from his belt and slid the tip under his fingernails. Snick. Snick. Snick. He broke the heavy silence, his voice soft and menacing as he concentrated on his task. "Haven't seen an Eator in a long time. Haven't bothered us in years, even. Strange they show up when ye did. Don't ye think?"

He lifted his eyes to mine, and I shuddered inside. His green eyes were as cold as the bottom of the ocean. Ice slid through my blood. I fought the urge to tremble, furrowing my brow as I cautiously asked, "Are you accusing us of bringing those creatures? The Eators? Of calling them somehow?" He dropped his gaze to his fingers. Snick. Snick.

He carried on with his thread. "Suspicious, aye. Strange indeed. Two little fishes come to the land. Within a day, hours even, we're hunted. And then, just before they attack, ye disappear. Poof." He stared at his handiwork. He grumbled aloud, "Can't get their slime from under me nails."

Roan leveled his gaze on Mori. "Yer Da leads the Mers army, yes?" She nodded. "Hmm," mused Roan. Snick. Snick. Snick. He held the blade up to his face, examining its shape in the firelight before resting his hand on his knee, still clutching the knife. "The head of the Mers's military sends his daughter up top to guard the keeper of a powerful artifact…"

I cleared my throat nervously, not liking where this was heading. "Commander Tro didn't send her. I picked her. She's my oldest friend, a Land Magic expert, as well as a formidable Warrior."

He ran his thumb over the sharp edge, stroking it gently. "Land Magic expert. Warrior. How handy. And ye sussed out the Eators, too, didn't ye, Mori?" The hairs on my arms rose from the threat in his voice. Mori looked at me sideways, her fingers drifting to the throwing stars on her thighs. Roan shook his head, still staring at the edge of his knife. "Ye'll be moving yer hands away from yer stars. Nice and slow."

I tucked my hair behind my ear and pressed my temple. *Do as he says. But pull them when he's not looking.*

Roan's eyes snapped to me, and my stomach turned to stone. Could he pick up our telepathy? I calmly asked, "What do you mean Mori sussed what they were? How could she possibly know?"

Roan snorted. "She studied Land Magic. She knows the wickedness up here. Aye. I saw ye staring as we killed them. Saw yer eyes flashing with understanding. Bet ye didn't expect them to pop like that, eh? Like an overripe berry?" Mori's expression stayed blank, but the blood drained from her cheeks. He tapped the knife against his chin and crooned, "Curious indeed." His lip turned up with a sneer. "Fishy, even."

My heart beat faster. We were miles from home, an entire ocean and continent away. I couldn't communicate with Synchi, and teleporting wasn't in my arsenal. We were at Anna's mercy, and it seemed, in the company of a madman. I scanned the pearl. It remained silent, not seeing Roan as a threat. Roan harrumphed, returning to his nails. Snick. Snick. Snick. He paused and studied me, jerking up his chin. "Yer a Warrior. What would ye do in me shoes?"

I straightened, staring him dead in the eye, making my voice as cold as I could muster. "As you are. Hold the suspects isolated and see if they'll slip. Guard them with a casual but obvious threat, like a wickedly intimidating knife. Wait while others gather more information. I assume that's what Anna's doing. Richard, too." I snorted derisively. "Where we differ, though, is I wouldn't pick my nails in company."

He blinked at me, chuckled, and slid his knife back into its sheath. "Aye, 'tis uncouth." He looked me up and down, and I held his gaze. I would not show my fear despite shaking on the inside. He tilted his head. "I can sense yer worry, lass. That's a good thing. If ye sat there with them brass balls and I couldn't smell yer fear, well, then ye'd surely have something to fret about."

He lifted his chin, eying the massive mahogany door of the library. "Let's see what the verdict is for our wee fishy friends."

The door swung open. Anna stood stiffly inside the doorway with Richard, Sebastian, and Sophia. Richard looked at our faces and sniffed the air. "Good Lord, Roan. What have you been saying to them? The fear is so thick I could bite it."

"Only what I needed to," he scowled. "Well?" They entered the room and took a group position against the bookcase. Roan stood, standing with his legs wide and arms crossed, his back close to the fire.

Anna's voice was ice. "The Eators came because of the mermaids."

"What?" exclaimed Mori, "How dare you! First, you berate Jelly to the point of her losing control, then we're attacked by those, those things, then you whip us away to a remote castle in the middle of nowhere, miles from home, to be guarded by this brute, who's all but accused of summoning those vile creatures! Maybe you've kidnapped us! Maybe you want the pearl! You've got some damned nerve accusing us of duplicity!"

Her hands slid down her legs, despite Roan's previous warning. Roan dropped his arms and snarled in a low voice, "Keep them stars fixed tight to your pretty thighs, mermaid." Indeed, you could see her legs clearly as damp white linen clung to her tense muscles. I had a ridiculous moment of pride. She hadn't pulled on her thong once, despite it being obviously clenched up too tight.

Mori curled her lip as she stared him down, inching forward on her seat, readjusting her feet to put weight on her toes. Every movement was an intentional taunt. She gripped her shuriken, edging them from the straps. Roan's hands closed into thick fists. He remained still, but his voice thundered as he bellowed, "Leave yer weapons be!"

The windows rattled in their frames, and the fire gasped before burning brighter. Mori jumped up, and I moved in an instant, the blanket falling from my shoulders. I was ready to take them all on, the odds of surviving be damned. My fingertips skittered to the hilts of my knives as I slid into position beside her, my knees bent and thighs tense. My eyes darted briefly to the door as Mako and Gray burst in, alarmed by Roan's shout. "What in blazes is happening in here?" cried Gray, his eyes absorbing the tension in the room.

Mako crossed to me without hesitation and tapped the wrist I had hovered over the knuck. He said tersely, "Mori, holster your stars. Stand down, Jelly. No one here is threatening you."

I snarled at the Surfecti at the bookcase, ignoring him. "Our Shaman sent us here to work with you. She said we could trust you. Is this how you treat your allies?"

Roan sneered, "Unless the old fookin' sea-hag is in on it."

Sophia shot over, grabbed Roan's ear, and twisted hard, his body following her grip. Her voice was low and filled with fury. "You will show my Shaman respect. I may have left them, but I am always a Mers. I will not have you speak of her like that. Nor will you threaten my clans-women like a feral animal. Do you understand me?"

He muttered under his breath and then yelped as she yanked down hard. Her growl prickled the hair on my neck. "I can't hear you, Roan."

"Aye! Aye! Leggo ye mad hen!" He rubbed his earlobe furiously when she stepped back.

"Okaaaay," soothed Sebastian, blasting the room with calming Fae energy. "Let's all take a nice, deep breath. No one is accusing anyone of anything. No need for violence." He crossed to kiss Sophia's scowl and set a heavy hand on Roan's shoulder, whispering in his sore ear. Roan grumbled and reached for his glass, tossing back its contents.

Anna's face pinched as she addressed Mori and me, her tone scolding. "I said the Eators came because of you, not that you summoned them. Temper your assumptions! You put words in my mouth before I could finish!"

I spat at Anna. "I've had enough of your attitude, Anna. You're used to being in charge, but guess what? You're not. The pearl is. I want to speak to the Shaman now. And I want Mako there to witness the conversation. I trust him." My eyes flicked to his shocked face. I growled at him, "And I better not be wrong." I looked back at Anna. "Now show Mori and me your mirror." Mako spread his feet and crossed his arms, solidly confirming who he stood with. Sophia's chin jerked up, approving.

"Mori, ye stay with me," Roan snapped, still rubbing his ear. He leered at me. "For security. Make sure ye come back. Not that ye'd get too far if ye ran off. Yer a long way from home, ye are."

Anna stared at my expression. She frowned. "Roan? What the bloody hell happened in here while we were gone? Everyone's as fraught as an over-wound violin! I told you to watch them, not terrorize them!"

He scowled, his accent thickening. "I don't like it, Anna. Not a wee bit. Ye'll forgive me fer not trusting blindly. She blows up the pool, leaves the house fer fook knows where, and suddenly, we're flooded with Eators? Too much of a coincidence for me. Nah. Mori stays here for collateral. End of story."

Mori slowly secured the throwing stars in their holsters and perched lightly in the wingback chair, rubbing her palms down the worn arms. "Fine. I'll stay here and keep *him* company." She shot Roan a filthy look.

His eyebrows lifted, and he snorted at her expression. He reclaimed the chair on the opposite side of the fire, crossing heavily inked arms over his chest. "Aye. That's right. Ye'll stay right here with me, little fishy. Right here where I can keep me eyes on ye."

TWENTY

SIMMI

"She wasn't there! I sent six Eators, a veritable army! The Surfecti slaughtered them before she even entered the door! Useless! Only one stayed alive, and he still failed!" He paced the room barefoot. It was as if a shadow swept the floor. I stayed quiet as he shouted. "What's the point of having monsters if they can't follow through? One job! No, no. They go in and get decimated by the Surfecti!"

He made a sucking noise with his tongue when he saw the hope in my eyes and yanked against the cuffs on my ankles, making me moan in pain. He snapped, "Don't look so pleased, darling. It only means more torment for you."

He spun in a circle, throwing his hands up. "Uh! Now I'll have to make more! Do you appreciate how difficult it is to find greedy humans?" Then he laughed uproariously before collapsing into tiny giggles. "Far too easy, sweet Simmi; almost boring. That's the problem with the humans; they are too dim to resist the simplest temptation."

His smooth forehead wrinkled when he inspected me. "Darling, you look terrible. That won't do. I need you now more than ever." Flustered, he made the chocolate and honeysuckle concoction in front of me, pulling the chain from his neck and opening the vial of dark liquid. He added precisely one drop to a glass of water. He guarded the vial vigilantly. I'd seen one of the Eators bump against him, accidentally touching it, and he'd evaporated the creature on the spot.

I waited to speak until he'd poured the drink down my throat, listless until he did. "What's the blood in your vial?" I whispered, praying the direct question would catch him off guard and hoping my assumption was accurate.

Distracted, he answered. "Fae."

"Fae? Is it yours? Why not give it to me directly?" The wheels turned in my rapidly perking mind. There was a reason he diluted it. Considering one drop electrified me…Maybe I would become too powerful if I drank directly from his vein.

"Never you mind," he grumbled, irritated with himself.

Undeterred, I mused, "It must drive you insane that the all-powerful Fae can't locate a little trinket. You need my inferior magic, my touch of Mers, to make it work. You're not strong enough without me." I laughed, a raspy noise that caught in my throat as I choked, coughed, and snickered. His high cheekbones bloomed with a vibrant shade of fuchsia.

He slammed the empty glass down with force, shattering it, and slapped me so hard I saw stars. I cried out in shock. My cheek stung before burning from the impact, but seeing him lose his composure made me smile. I felt reckless. I jerked my chin toward the ceiling. "And what are all these? Special drawings to help you locate the pearl? What do you want it for, anyway? What does it give you?"

He roared, "It's mine! My father had no right to give her away. The pearl belongs to me!"

"Her? Is the pearl a person?"

Terrun fumed when he realized his slip. "It's none of your concern."

"Do you love her? It? Is that what this is? Or does she give you power? Are you just another male siphoning something that doesn't belong to you? Gods, it happens everywhere, doesn't it? Just can't escape you damned bullies."

His lips drew back in a hiss as he held up a glass fragment. "You need to mind your sweet tongue, Simmi Fields, lest I be tempted to slice it clear off." He stormed from the room, the lack of pounding footsteps making it less dramatic.

It didn't take long for my knight in yellow feathers to appear at the window. As he perched on the bed, he tutted, "He's in a mood today." He tipped his masked face to the sky outside. "Look. Up in the air."

Five birds, as white as untouched snow, floated gracefully on the wind. Kindee sighed. "Aren't they beautiful? They're called Longtails because, well, look at their gorgeous plumage. Two extraordinarily long tail feathers. Simply marvelous." If my brown-coated friend had hands, he'd be clasping them reverently in front of his yellow breast.

"They nest here each summer. It's the only time they set foot on land. Otherwise, they're out at sea. Their numbers are dwindling fast. So sad. But half of their North Atlantic population returns to our tiny island every season. They'll have one egg and one egg only." He turned to me and blinked. "Such peril. Life is so fragile."

He blinked again, his philosophizing abandoned. "It turns out that it's a ladies' night. The lads are home on the eggs, taking their turn with the nest. The girls have caught you fish, which is good because you desperately need protein."

He flew to my chest and gently pecked at my clavicle, which lurched from my skin like a shipwreck. "Too thin. Much too thin. Well, we've done our best to gut the fish. Sorry if you find any bones."

The team of lizards arrived, all puffing out their orange sacks, terribly pleased with their bounty. They carefully balanced a small heap of raw fish on a shiny bay grape leaf. Each hobbled on three legs as the fourth gripped the treasure.

"Leave it there," grumped Kindee. "Don't want the banana event to reoccur. I will feed Miss Simmi myself." He flew back and forth with great importance. He thought these few mouthfuls of fish would change my destiny for the better.

"Kindee, please, have the last bite. As a thank you. You're working so hard to keep me alive."

A small tear shone in his eye. "You are very kind, Miss Simmi. I do hope your family arrives soon."

I swallowed the taste of desperation in my mouth, feeling so weak. My lunatic captor was bleeding me faster than I could recover, even with his chocolate Fae blood. Fear was in my throat, and I bit back tears, unwilling to show Kindee my resignation. I turned my face from him as I whispered, "So do I, Kindee. So do I."

TWENTY-ONE

JELLY

Anna led us up the wide staircase to the upper floor. Mako whispered, "Jelly, I'm sorry about Roan. He's a good man. He's rough around the edges, but he didn't mean you any harm."

I drew to a stop. "He insinuated we'd summoned the monsters and then left! Intentionally abandoned them!" Mako squeezed my shoulder; his lips pressed tightly as he gave me space to be upset. My throat burned with indignation. "Has he ever met a Mers warrior? We'd never do that!"

Anna barked from the top of the stairs. "Keep up, you two!" We hurried after her. She entered a room at the end of the hall. The interior contrasted with the rest of the ancient mansion, far more contemporary in its furnishings. It had the same pale gray stone floor but modern lighting. The LED lights dimmed low, reflecting gently off the tranquil teal walls.

My eyes drifted to a wide shelving filled with assorted magical artifacts. I studied the statues, cups, knives, crystals, gemstones, and silver trays bearing pressed flowers and dried berries. Multi-colored candles graced every shelf, next to wands of tied sage and lavender, some of them burned to short stumps.

Anna selected a sea foam candle and reached for an old mirror; the circular, silver frame darkened from a lack of polishing. She pointed to a pile of large cushions in the corner. "Grab a few of those, please, Mako."

As he and I settled in the middle of the floor, Anna drew a circle around us in blue chalk, murmuring words I didn't recognize. She sat inside the chalk, lit the candle with a long wooden match she dragged against the stone floor, and propped the mirror between us, setting it against a metal frame. Mako was silent on my right.

After more strange language, the mirror's surface shimmered, and tears of relief filled my eyes when the familiar wizened face of the Shaman stared back at us. She squinted. "Well, if I'd known I was having company, I would have put on my face!" When I didn't laugh, she sobered immediately. "Right, no time for jokes. You both look very serious. And Jelly, what on earth is stuck to your arms? You're covered in filth!"

I blurted, "Eators attacked us!"

Synchi blinked. "When? I just spoke to you a minute ago! Where are you?"

"We left the ocean and went back to Mako's house, and everyone was fighting these beasts with fangs and claws called Eators, and they suck the joy out of you if they cut you."

Synchi's cheeks reddened with anger as she stared at Anna. "You didn't protect her? You let Eators get past your magic?"

Anna sniffed. "She's here, isn't she? If she hadn't run off for the ocean—"

Synchi roared, "I sent her with your assurances you would protect her!"

"If she could control her pearl, it wouldn't have happened!"

Synchi's braid shook as she trembled, "And if you had half

a brain cell at your disposal, you would have expected her anger and avoided provoking the pearl!"

Anna's eyes turned to slits as she hissed, "If you had prepared her properly, we wouldn't be in this mess."

I shouted, "Stop it! Both of you, stop!"

The Shaman and the Witch shared glares. Synchi capitulated first. She settled and tsked. "But you're safe? Are you in England, in Coven headquarters?"

Anna confirmed, "We are."

I ran a hand through my hair, frustrated. "He knows where I am. We have less time than I thought. We need to circle back. To what the Goddess said. She said to use my blood to find Simmi. What do we have to do?"

Synchi nodded, pulling on her braid. "I'll leave Anna to explain it, Jelly, as you'll use Surfecti blood and magic. You'd better get a move on. But before you go, someone wants to say hello."

Oggie swam into the frame, distractedly munching on a minnow gripped in one arm, three others securing more snacks. One stroked Synchi's wrinkled skin, and the final three curiously sucked on the glass.

"Oggie!" I cried.

He flinched at my voice, dropped his fish, and reached for my face with all eight arms. He chittered and squeaked, "Jebby!"

I gasped over a broad smile. "You said my name!" Mako leaned in for a closer look, wonder lighting his face as the little octopus latched onto the mirror. Oggie balked at Mako and shot away with a squeal, leaving a cloud of black ink behind.

Synchi's voice was distant beyond Oggie's murk. She sucked her teeth. "Well, that's that, then. So far, he knows the names of oysters, clams, mussels, and yours. I'll let you go. Keep your anger in check. And Jelly? Don't forget what I said earlier."

She gave a lusty chuckle. "That one next to you will do. He'll do nicely." My cheeks heated.

The image faded and swirled and ended with a pop. I sat back while Anna scuffed the chalk circle to break it and stood, pacing in a tight path while she thought. Mako gently asked, "You okay?" I shook my head, unable to meet his eyes, mortified by what Synchi had said at the end. She didn't know Mako had heard every word on the beach.

He stared at me quietly, then said, "Oggie's cute."

I smiled at the subject change. "Oggie's my companion, like a dog. But with eight arms and suckers, a ridiculous food drive, and an overly enthusiastic fear response. He only just started speaking. That's the first time he's said my name."

"Sorry, I scared him. Must be my ugly mug," he said jokingly.

I met his eyes and mumbled without thought, "You're hardly ugly." As the words escaped my lips, I internally groaned. I didn't want to lead him on. His lips parted with a small breath, and cobalt blue eyes searched mine as he looked for more behind my statement. I dropped my face and shook my head, annoyed with myself.

He stood and held out his hands, helping me to my feet. Mako tossed the cushions back in the corner while Anna extinguished the candle and placed it on the shelf beside the mirror. She turned to me, her hands on her hips. I jutted out my chin defensively, bracing for an argument.

She exhaled a sigh and said, "I owe you an apology, Jelly. I am holding you accountable for the sins of those before you. It is not your fault the Mers have been reclusive and stubbornly stuck in their ways, hiding away in a bubble, avoiding all responsibility to the planet for decades and—"

"Anna," Mako interrupted gently, holding back a laugh.

"Yes, quite. Well, I apologize, Jelly. I shall do my best to be more congenial."

In my head, I said, *Don't strain yourself, lady.* But instead of being catty, I replied, "Thank you, Anna. I want to start fresh."

She gave me a sharp nod. "Excellent."

"Are we going to talk about blood magic?"

"We will, but I want everyone's input."

We returned to the cozy library without another word, and Mako and I claimed the couch, sharing it with Sophia. Mori was still in the burgundy chair, stroking the worn, velvety arms with her fingertips while bouncing her knee, glowering silently at Roan. Gray lowered the music and leaned against the stone that lined the edge of the fireplace.

I warily studied Roan, who stood across the room at the bookshelf, his face half-hidden in shadows. His thick arms still guarded his chest, and one hand pulled at his beard as he stared back at Mori. Anna took the unoccupied chair at the fire. She spoke to Roan directly without turning around to look at him.

"Roan, the Eators came for the pearl when Jelly's anger triggered it. And I goaded her to the point of losing control. It is now our responsibility to assist her with the pearl. She should have been training for years, but… It is what it is." She nodded to Mori and said, "I apologize for what I said. I am flustered and upset about Simone.. I expressed my frustrated history with the Mers by turning it on Jelly. Forgive me."

Mori looked at me, her eyebrows raised, lips tight. I inclined my head, letting her take the lead. First, she addressed Anna. "Thank you, Anna. I appreciate your apology." She slid her fingers through her hair. *She's pretty good at saying sorry, isn't she? I'm surprised.* I snorted.

She looked over Anna's chair to Roan. "But you," she

snarled, gracefully lifting and stalking toward the giant man. "Your behavior was unnecessary." Her red curls caught the light, dancing against the backdrop of the fire. She narrowed her eyes and pointed a finger at him. Her voice was icy. "You terrorized us. You owe us an apology as well."

He growled, "I owe ye nothing, mermaid." He jerked his chin at me. "And yer a fookin' liability if ye can't hold yer temper." He turned from her, grumbling under his breath. I looked at my hands, embarrassed. But Mori wouldn't let it lie. She sprung at him and spun him around, shock coloring his face.

"On the reef, if someone doesn't want to apologize, that's fine, but they have to take a hit. So which will it be, big man? Say sorry or get punched?" Roan's lips curled up. She met his cool gaze with fire in her eyes.

He cocked his head. "Fine, little fish. Ye can have yer hit." He anchored his feet and put his hands behind his back. He looked down at her with a smirk on his lips. She stared up. He was huge.

I touched my temple. *Take your time. Make it good.* Roan's eyes flashed to mine with amusement.

Mori shook her hands, flexed them, and slowly curled them tight. She crouched low and twisted her hips, her weight distributed for maximum power. She took two deep breaths, gathering her strength. With an exhaled roar, she sprang up, swinging her entire body. At first, I thought she would go for an uppercut given their height difference. But she struck him with a hard right hook, her strongest punch.

Roan's head ratcheted to the side, his eyes squeezing shut. His leg muscles tensed to absorb the shock, and he rocked on his heels. The room groaned, "Oooh!" and I laughed out loud, clapping. Mori could hit.

When he slowly turned his face back to center, he touched his split lip tentatively, his tongue flicking out to taste blood. He stared at Mori, humor and respect in his eyes. His voice was deep and measured. "Feel better, little fish?"

She leisurely looked at his feet, her eyes traveling up his body. When she reached his face, his eyes expressed something to make her breath snag. It was subtle, barely there, but I noticed the hitch. So did Roan. Heat simmered in his eyes. She slowly and intentionally blinked at him. She lifted one shoulder casually in a shrug and purred, "For now." He growled through a smirk, nodded to her, and left.

After the drama, Anna sighed heavily, drawing our attention. She slumped in her chair, her pale face waxen. "We need to discuss blood magic, and we will do so in the morning. We need Roan for the discussion, and I need to rest. I cannot bear one more moment of this day." She waved a hand at her son. "Gray, please show Jelly and Mori to their rooms."

Gray crossed the room with purpose and held out his hand. As soon as I touched his fingers, I gave him a brilliant smile and exhaled a small giggle. Gray would show me upstairs to my room, where there was a bed. I fluttered my eyelashes with anticipation.

Mako jumped up quickly. "I'll take Jelly. I need to speak with her in private." Gray's chocolate and golden eyes fractionally narrowed around the edges, but he nodded curtly and kissed my hand before releasing it. He escorted Mori, offering his elbow, and left without a backward glance. I shook my head, confused, and rubbed my eyes with my hands, suddenly desperately drained. I looked up as Mako waited patiently, his face unreadable.

"Did you want to talk about something?" I asked.

He gave me a tight smile. "We'll talk in your room." I took

his outstretched hand, letting him help me from the chair. He led me upstairs and guided me down a dim, unfamiliar hallway.

"Do you know where we're going?"

"Gray and I grew up together. I've been here a lot." He twisted a brass doorknob and flicked on the lights, stepping back so I could enter first.

"This is beautiful!" I exclaimed, my eyes casting around the room. An intricately embroidered blue quilt covered the queen-sized four-poster bed, and fluffy, inviting pillows butted against the carved wooden headboard. Fat roses sat in a vase on the bureau, the dark pink petals perfuming the air. A fire puttered happily in the stone hearth, and Mako drew the heavy curtains, blocking out the stars. I switched on the lamp on the bedside table and turned to Mako. He closed the door to give us privacy.

He said with a slight shake of his head, "This has been the day from hell with Anna pushing you, Mori's dad being hurt, then the Eators, teleporting, and Roan's attitude. I'm amazed you're still standing. You're stronger than I gave you credit for." He stepped into my space, his long fingers reaching to tuck my bedraggled hair behind my ear.

I stared at him, finding his eyes filled with concern. And something more. His male scent surrounded me, woody and lush, like the forest drenched with morning dew. His voice was husky as he said, "You need to recharge, Jelly. You're exhausted. That quick dip in the ocean isn't enough."

I swallowed and whispered, "Mako... what the Shaman said. I'm not... I'm not looking for a hookup. It's too distracting. I can't."

"You used a lot of magic today. You need to recharge...in case..." he left the rest of his thoughts hanging.

"In case Simmi reaches out. Or we're attacked again. Or any number of things," I grumbled.

He nodded. "You can't let yourself get depleted here. The ocean is too far away." His fingers whispered on my skin, the tips sliding behind my ear, his thumb softly tracing my cheekbone. "I can help you. It doesn't have to mean anything." He looked at me kindly, knowing a simple kiss would make me feel better.

I held his gaze for a beat, deciding. He shrugged, "I'm half-Mers, but the other part is Fae. It might make it more powerful. I'm honestly not sure what it will do for you, but at least the Mers part of me will help you replenish your magic. Think of it as just business."

"Just business?" I whispered, licking my lips and leaning toward him. I honestly was exhausted. I wouldn't withstand an attack right now. And it was just a kiss. I hadn't invited him into my bed. A simple, restorative kiss.

His mouth inched toward mine as he murmured, "Just business."

Every nerve in my body sprang to attention when his lips brushed mine, fatigue swiftly forgotten. He didn't kiss like Fillian, who was sloppy and impatient. Mako kissed like he was tasting fine wine or leisurely savoring a decadent, rich dessert. His lips were reverent.

My pulse jumped up, banging faster, and the hairs on my arms prickled from the rush of magic he gave me. I gasped. He groaned and tenuously traced my lips with his tongue, letting me lead. Mine flicked against his chipped tooth. I came undone. Any hesitancy dissolved like sugar in coffee as I plunged my tongue into his mouth, moaning from the magic that flew through me.

He ended it too soon by nipping at my bottom lip and spiking more heat in my blood. He rested his forehead on mine. "Better?" he whispered hoarsely.

The pearl vibrated at my throat as if greedily soaking in his magic. I tugged him closer. "Not nearly enough." The pearl was hungry for more. So was I.

One of his hands tangled in my hair, urgent, his strength barely restrained. He tightened his fingers, and when I groaned, he angled my head to take command of the kiss. His other hand snaked around my body and under my shirt to spread heavily, hotly, against the bare skin of my back. His tongue teased against mine, promising so much.

The pearl luxuriated in his Fae power, throbbing and pulsing, consuming as much magic as possible. He kept giving, pouring it into me. The flow only moved in one direction. Softly gasping with dismay, I pulled back. "I'm sorry. I didn't mean to use you like that. The pearl…it's ravenous. I took a lot of power from you." I hid my embarrassment by dropping my face.

He tipped up my chin. "You didn't use me. I'm willingly giving it to you. There's a difference." His warm breath brushed my skin as he confessed, "I've wanted to kiss you from the moment I saw you in the video." He chuckled. "Believe me, I don't feel used."

Through a grin, I fluttered my eyelashes coquettishly. "You like dangerous things. Do I live up to the fantasy?"

His eyes flashed. "And then some. When you blew up the pool, the plant, the statue…" He didn't finish the sentence, but I could see the desire in his eyes, yearning to hear my voice break as I gasped his name in raw pleasure. His jaw ticked as he controlled himself.

He forced a small smile. "But we should get some sleep. And take a shower to wash off this gunk." I looked down at myself, noticing the dried black slime on my arms under my sleeves…Gray's shirt. I was wearing another man's shirt while kissing Mako. As if reading my mind, he stole my disgrace, pressing his lips against mine for so long that we gulped for breath when we broke apart.

His Fae magic was like none I'd ever experienced: spicy, alluring, dynamic, and terribly, terribly seductive. It frolicked in my blood, teasing and tempting. I wanted him. All of him. Any prudishness flew out the window as my heart beat faster. My voice was breathy as I looked up at him. I felt exposed, but I trusted him. "Mako, will you sleep with me?"

His blue eyes throbbed with power. He swallowed thickly. "Jelly, it would be your first time with legs. You deserve more than something transactional."

I choked on my breath. He had no idea how powerful his statement was. He was the polar opposite of Fillian, who would have taken the slightest inkling of interest as permission to go all the way. My heart melted hopefully as his magic continued to flicker around me.

The pearl roared for him, wanting everything, driving me to wantonness. I leaned in, sure I could coax him to surrender to me. He was clearly interested; I just had to push him over the edge. But before I could try, he sighed heavily. "But I'm not the right guy for you, so, no, I won't sleep with you."

Indignation flared through my chest, slapping the softness away. His rejection mortified me. I shoved myself from his arms. "So typical!"

"What?" he sputtered, throwing up his hands, incredulous that I was so angry. "What's typical?"

Humiliation clung like a curse. "Men deciding what's best for me! Never letting me choose! Just when I thought you were different, you say something stupid like that!"

He shook his head impatiently and stepped back. His magic entirely retreated, leaving me chilled. I huffed out a breath, so stung from his refusal that I was deaf to his words. His voice was low, almost sorrowful. "I'm looking out for your best interests, trust me." I rolled my eyes. He looked broken and struggled with my anger. He whispered, "Do you feel better? Are you recharged?"

"Yes." My voice was surly. Kissing Mako had topped me up better than any potion Synchi had in her arsenal. I wanted more, but he didn't. Or wouldn't allow it for some stupid reason.

He cleared his throat. "Good. Mission accomplished." He took another step back and rubbed his hand across his chin. Silence hung the air. The day's events flooded me, and I felt profoundly alone in a strange room in a foreign land, standing in a different body, so far from everything familiar. My pulse raced.

I blurted, "Mako, will you please stay? As in actually sleep, nothing else. The bed is big enough. I swear I won't touch you."

He said regretfully, "I don't think I should." He said tenderly, "Good night, Jelly. Sweet dreams."

He retreated slowly, walking backward as if through cold molasses. The blue of his eyes flashed, clear he was second-guessing himself. I watched him, knowing he would stay if I asked again. But maybe not, and I couldn't bear another refusal. I steadied my voice as he reached the door. "Thank you, Mako. For having my back earlier, when the pearl reacted. Thank you for helping me."

"Always," was his soft reply. "Get some rest. I'll see you in the morning."

"And Mako? I appreciate the top up." I tried to sound sincere; I meant to, but the words rolled with a touch of sarcasm I couldn't hide. It seemed my seduction skills sucked, and I pushed my embarrassment on him.

He nodded his head and pulled the door gently closed behind him.

I threw Gray's shirt in the corner with my dirty, stiff dress, the navy fabric crusted white with salt and black with guts, and sighed, hoping a hot shower would help me sleep. Washing off the grime, I sourly watched it swirl away, still stinging from his rebuke. So out of my comfort zone, I'd offered myself on a silver platter and he'd declined a taste.

I changed into the cream-colored silk nightie I'd found in the drawer and nestled under the thick quilt. Too wired to sleep, I thought of Mori finding her own recharge at the pool. Goddess, that felt like forever ago. What a long day.

I'd never touched myself before, the purpose of the missions destroying any curiosity. I refused out of stubbornness, feeling that no one on the surface should enjoy my sexuality. I snorted to myself. I was ridiculous. I'd allowed the Trident to manipulate me to such a degree I didn't even know this body.

I slipped my fingers between my legs, shocked to find such slickness. Tremors rocked through my body from the light touch. With a yelp, I discovered my power dot, my spine arching immediately from the sensation. A few circles and some strokes…I swiftly detonated, biting my cheek to stop from shouting out loud. I lay stunned and sweaty, energy racing through every cell. It was delicious, but it wasn't like Mako's magic. Not even close.

TWENTY-TWO

JELLY

A seductive voice slid through my mind. I shifted in the bed, rolling over as it crooned to me in my sleep.

Silly girl, you left one of my pets alive. I'll have to punish you for escaping me, darling. You seemed quite smitten with the man. I saw how tightly he held your hand, how you whimpered for comfort. Maybe I'll eat him for supper. Or perhaps I'll unleash my rage on sweet Simmi. But I did like the breasts on your red-headed friend. She's luscious. Then, there's always her burly father. His tail alone would make quite a meal. Or that old shaman you love. Not much meat on her bones, but she's proving quite good with her magic, and that just simply won't do. I just can't decide who to hurt first to motivate you.

Searing pain drove through my chest, squeezing, pinching, poking at the edges as if trying to dislodge my heart. The pearl pulsed and fought back, causing the probing, hot fingers to retreat. The voice sang out in surprise. *Well, well. You're quite strong, aren't you, darling?*

I moaned, caught in the depths of the dream as it changed. Images flashed through my mind. Mori snarled and threw her stars. Roan shouted. A crimson Mako lay still. Stone wings, bared fangs, dead fish washed onto pretty pink sand. Rainbow magic, missing yellow. Then, rows upon rows of red, demented eyes and sharp teeth lashed and gnashed, acid drooling from their jaws as they went for my throat.

I thrashed, trying to move, to escape, but I couldn't. Paralyzed, I screamed in terror, and in another world, glass shattered, startling me. My mind went as white as new snow.

JELLY!!! FOOKIN' WAKE UP, LASS!!!

Roan's mental shout cut through, and I gasped, my throat raw and bone-dry. Mako pushed my sweaty hair away from my forehead, murmuring, "Come on, Jelly, come back," while Mori hovered beside him, chewing on her thumbnail.

Relief flooded their faces as I blinked at them. My head painfully twisted to the right, and I tried to speak, but my tongue wouldn't cooperate. I strained in a panic as I couldn't move. My eyes flicked to Anna standing beside Mori, her bathrobe unbound as if she'd grabbed it quickly, grimly weaving patterns in the air. She dropped her hands, and the magical restraints eased.

Mako leaned down to my ear and whispered. "I should have stayed with you. I'm so sorry I wasn't here."

"You would have stopped it from happening." I groaned. "Dear Goddess, my neck is killing me."

Mori's face pressed near. "Jelly? Are you okay?"

Anna asked, "Was it Simmi? Did you see her?"

"No. Not her." My brain struggled to wake fully, still halfway caught in the nightmare. I clenched my eyes shut from the pain. To my left, there was a steady dripping noise. I slowly turned my head and saw flushed pink petals littering the floor, scattered next to a set of tattooed feet, surrounded by broken glass. I closed my eyes against the brightness of the room.

Roan cleared his throat. I squinted as he said, "No one could reach ye." He tapped the side of his head. "I had to go inside. Might be why yer neck is so tight. Yer body was thrashin' while I held yer head still."

I bolted upright as the vision came back to me, almost slamming my head into Mako's face. My voice shook as I squawked. "He knows I'm here! He's going to hurt someone!"

"Did you see a location?" Anna pressed hopefully, her eyes scanning mine. Her shoulders slumped when I shook my head slowly, trying to remember all the details.

Richard entered the room, muscling past Mako to hand me a mug of hot tea. So perfectly British. He waited until I sipped it and groaned in delight. Richard's lips perked into a smile. "Extra sugar and condensed milk. There's nothing as medicinal as a strong cup of tea. Now, tell us what you saw and heard."

I opened my mouth to speak, and people started filtering into my room. Sebastian stepped through first and lay his hand on my feet, grounding me with his calming touch. His eyes flicked to the broken glass, and with a spin of his fingers, the vase reassembled, empty of its fragrant treasure, wobbling gently on the dresser until it stilled.

Sophia bustled straight for the bed and leaned over to kiss my cheek, stroking back my hair. "We were so worried. You were screaming and screaming."

Gray entered last and stood beside Anna, who had moved to the foot of the bed. When Mako slipped off the bed to hug his mom, Gray squeezed my ankle. A rush of yearning flowed through me, and I gasped over my tea. I lifted my face to smile at him, and he winked and moved to the window, leaning against it heavily, his hands in his pockets.

The pearl buzzed at my throat, clearing my head. My bedroom was very crowded. I pulled the blankets up in one fist like a shield, subtly pushing my hair back as I covered myself. *Mori, there are way too many people in here.*

She gave a quick nod and turned to the assembled crowd. "So, can we give Jelly a moment? We can meet you downstairs in a minute." She acted as if rubbing her ear innocently, but she bellowed in my head. *Look at Roan. He's built like a Stellar sea lion. He's so…thick.*

Roan thumped his large hands on his hips and cocked his head, studying Mori with a raised eyebrow. His face was stoic, but his eyes skipped with laughter as she tried not to stare, her eyes flicking to his body repeatedly. Only then did I notice he was in a pair of black boxers, quite small, and nothing else. My brain hadn't registered it earlier.

Ink covered his entire body. The tattoos swirled in dark patterns, the elaborate artwork dancing across his cut muscles, primarily in black with shades of gray. There were faces and feathers, sharp lines and soft clouds, mandalas and dragons, a skull and a snake… there was too much to look at once. My brain stalled on the barbell piercings through his nipples. I stared at the center of his broad chest to the only colored ink on his body.

A raised, thick scar ran from his throat to his groin, covered in scarlet roses, replete with twisting, dark green vines and leaves, punctured with wicked white thorns that looked like they'd draw blood if caressed. I tried not to ogle the bumps and ridges of his abdomen in my slow perusal of the tattoo, but their impressive definition mesmerized me.

As I sipped my tea, I observed the deep grooves on the sides of his hips that sloped into a v-shape, pointing south. I couldn't help but follow the lines, noting just how well he filled his shorts. Mori purred. *Am I right or amiright?*

Roan growled. "Eyes up, lass." I choked with mortification

and snapped up my eyes to meet his. His gaze skimmed to Mori before settling back on me. "Ye sprung me from a pleasant dream, wee jellyfish. Ye woke the whole bloody house. We all want to know what ye saw."

Sophia soothed, "We're family, Jelly. We're here for you." Sebastian wrapped his arm around her, hugging her tight. Gray nodded, his father copying the gesture. Anna's expression was worried but eager, and Mako...Mako looked at me with affectionate, deep concern. The pearl delicately sipped the tendril of magic he let slip as he stroked back my hair.

I believed them. It heartened me. I set my mug on the bedside table, and with a deep breath, I told them what happened in the vision, goosebumps breaking out on my skin.

Mori whispered, "So, he's threatened my father, the Shaman, Mako, Simmi, and me. Dear Goddess." She'd shuddered when I said he'd noticed her breasts. Roan had growled.

Roan asked hesitantly, "Did ye have a physical sensation with the vision?"

I nodded, frightened. "Like my heart was being ripped from my chest. I think the pearl protected me. It fought back."

Roan said grimly, "He will shatter yer brain, lass. He'll pick it apart like a crab." He pinched his fingers together for emphasis. "Ye don't have the wherewithal to withstand him."

"What do you mean, pick it apart?" I swallowed, finding his visual disturbing. "Do you mean his voice or the second part? You were all screaming or hurt. It was a premonition, not a memory." I thought of the drooling fangs and claws and Mako soaked in blood. My body trembled from shock as the color drained from my face. I squeaked loudly as my black mug rose from the bedside table and floated toward me on a purple thread of magic.

Richard spoke crisply. "Cold tea is a travesty. Drink it while it's hot." Dumbfounded, I did as instructed.

Roan ran a hand over his beard and scratched at his chin roughly. "Ye said yerself; it was like something was digging at yer heart." He shook his head and looked at Richard. "He could speak to her clear as day, yet she couldna move. I don't like this. He can trap her down, hurt her. If it weren't for the pearl…"

Richard's face dropped deep in a scowl. "No, I don't like it either."

Anna agreed, "You must go in, Roan. I don't see another way."

The tea soured in my belly. I balked at the looks on their faces. "Do what now?"

Roan grunted, "I have to go in."

"Go in where?"

Roan tapped his head with a meaty finger. "Yer mind. In a vision walk. With blood magic."

"My mind? But you just said—"

Roan interrupted. "*He* will shatter ye. Not me. I'm as delicate as a ballerina. I'll do a wee twirl and see what I can find. But we need to do it soon, before he comes back."

Mori snarled from my side. "I don't trust you to march through Jelly's brain, no matter how delicate you promise to be. Just last night, you were certain we'd called the Eators." She held up her fingers, spinning them in the air. "And now you want to go inside? Do a wee twirl? I don't think so." I hid my grin behind my mug. Mori ran hot and cold. One minute, she was drooling over Roan, and the next, swinging a verbal sword.

He barked, "Ye couldn't wake her, now could ye?" She paled. "Ye almost burst yer brain trying, but ye aren't strong enough. I did! Last night, I said things…" He inhaled sharply, cutting himself off from finishing the sentence. He glowered at me. "I've already been in there, lass, and I won't hurt ye. I swear it."

I frowned. "Did you rustle through my thoughts when you woke me up?" I had a brief flash of my mighty orgasm, imagining Mako's body hovering above me, tight and hot as he groaned filthy words while thrusting with powerful strokes. My cheeks heated. Roan lifted an eyebrow and then shook his head.

"Nah. I just yelled at ye to wake up. Jelly, yer brain stores yer visions like a video. When ye saw Simmi, it was yer first one. Ye didn't pick out the details. In a vision walk, I'll be with ye, looking around to see what's what, like I'm peeking over yer shoulder." He put his wide hand over the roses on his chest. "I swear it won't hurt."

Anna's lips fought to stay dispassionate and lost themselves in a downturn. "You haven't had another vision of Simmi since the first one. This voice is getting brasher. It *attacked* you. Roan can gather information and get clues. Jelly, I'm afraid you don't have a choice."

Mako interjected swiftly. "Jelly always has a choice."

Anna scowled at him and turned back to me, hands on her hips. "Jelly, you must let Roan go in your mind. We have to find Simmi. If we can cut the monster off from her blood, he won't be able to reach you or the pearl." She added an afterthought, "Or the Mers."

I glanced at Sebastian and Sophia, who remained silent but begged with their eyes.

Mori's voice rattled. *He will kill someone if we don't stop him. Simmi is the most vulnerable, but you're a close second. And what if he sends more sharks to the bubble? I hate to admit it, but Roan's right.*

Responsibility drooped my shoulders. I turned to Anna. "What does blood magic entail? What are the repercussions?" She opened her mouth to explain when my eyes rolled back in my head and my heartbeat stalled. Mori shrieked as I collapsed against the pillows.

The room turned dark green; all sounds sucking away. A familiar and terrifying voice slithered through my head. *Sssssscyphozoa! Make hassssste!*

The room spun back into focus, and I slammed my hands to my ears. Roan's thick eyebrows flew up in shock. "Da fook? She's got a Sea Goddess in there chatting like a school chum!"

Mori shouted, "Get out of her mind, Roan!" She threw herself between us as though she could block his powers. She leaned over the bed, shielding me from him with her body. He took a heavy step back as her silk-encased bottom pushed out and brushed his black shorts. She whispered furtively, "Did the Goddess just talk to you? Which one?"

I squeaked, "Kelbazi."

Anna shouted, "Well? What did she say?"

I shivered, "Make haste."

Again, something took me under. My vision went stormy as my body fell into convulsions. Another voice, not the Goddess, but smooth as dark honey. It wriggled, squirmed, and wormed across my brain, making my stomach roil. My heart thumped in terror. *Tick Tock, little fish. Tick Tock.* In the background, Simmi screamed in agony.

I leaped to a crouch on the bed, tangled in the sheets, and slammed heavily against the headboard. My hands grasped for knives that weren't there. Voices shouted in my direction. I blinked wildly against the fog until Mako's worried face swam into focus, his hands firm on my cheeks, his magic boosting the pearl, steadying me.

Roan raged and spun in a circle as if expecting an attack. "Remember, I said he'll shatter yer mind? He's doing it, lass! Right now! He'll drive ye mad and break ye, Jelly! He's torturing Simmi to break ye!"

Anna begged. "Jelly, please. Only you can do this."

Roan lay a heavy hand on my shoulder. I stared at his wild green eyes, fear strangling my throat. I licked my lips nervously and croaked, "Do it."

Anna sprinted from the room, dragging Mori, yelling that she needed supplies. I shook so hard my teeth clacked together. Mako climbed on the bed behind me, wrapping me in his arms. I melted into his warm silence, scouring my soul for my courage. I whispered, "Why are you being nice to me?" I'd expected the cold shoulder after I'd pushed him away last night.

He squeezed gently, his woody smell comforting. "I'll only ever support you."

Sebastian, Richard, and Gray murmured to each other in deep voices near the window, casting worried glances in my direction. Someone had drawn back the curtains. It was still dark outside. Roan stood impassively at the foot of my bed in his small boxers, one hand on his hip, the other pulling his beard. The motion reminded me of Synchi. My fingers trembled as I held them to my temple, my eyes on Roan as he watched with new curiosity.

Synchi? Synchi, are you there?

Nothing. Roan grunted, "Yer too far away, lass." I thought of Amira and my ability to speak with her from such a great distance and doubled my efforts, trying again, the blood vessels in my forehead pulsing from the strain. I whimpered, holding my breath as I concentrated.

Mako carefully folded his fingers over mine. "Jelly, are you trying to contact your shaman? You're over five thousand miles away." A sob left my throat, and I dropped my hand, letting Mako weave his fingers through mine. He soothed, "We'll call her through the mirror as soon as we're done."

Done. Like we were washing the dishes or taking a stroll. My voice came out so small. "Roan, what can I expect?"

He frowned. "Ye'll revisit the vision. I'll be watching for clues, things ye missed. We can speak to each other, but no one else will hear ye. It's like I'm straddling both places. Make sense?"

I whispered, "You promise it won't hurt?"

He spoke confidently. "Nah, lass. It's like watching a movie. Except ye can stroll around and look at things. I'll guide ye. Nothing to worry about. Just a wee twirl, remember?"

TWENTY-THREE

JELLY

In a burst, Anna and Mori returned to the room. Mori balanced a pink bowl and two candles while gripping a tiny brass statue of a fish. Anna brandished a long knife, the handle encrusted with precious gems. Her other hand clenched around a square bottle of amber liquid. She passed it to Roan silently. It must be a ceremonial nectar, allowing him to trip through my brain on light feet. He pulled out the cork and gulped deeply. "What is that?" I asked.

He shook himself like a wet dog. "Scottish whiskey." He slammed the bottle on the dresser. "I'm ready."

Anna motioned to Mako. "You can't touch her while we do this. Off." He grumbled under his breath, kissed my temple, and moved away, pacing with his hands on his hips. Anna's voice was brisk. "Set the white candle on the left table. Put the blue one on the right. Give Jelly the figurine. Roan, on the bed. Jelly, hold that in your left hand." I took the small metal fish, warm from Mori's touch, watching as she rushed to place the candles. "Gray, fire."

The wicks blazed to life when Gray snapped his fingers. My

throat closed from nerves, and beads of sweat balanced on my upper lip. Roan's sharp eyes noticed, and he said in a low voice, "Lass, keep yerself steady. I can't go in there if yer pearl sees me as a threat. Calm yerself. Clear?"

"Okay," I whispered. "Okay." I breathed in through my nose and out of my mouth, nibbling on the tip of my tongue. I bit too hard and jumped with a start.

Roan looked over his shoulder. "Sebastian?"

Sebastian moved to my side. I lifted my hand. "No! Look, I have to learn how to control my emotions. Sebastian, I appreciate you can numb me, but I have to do this. So, let's make a deal, Roan. You don't hurt me, and I won't hurt you."

Roan snorted before he chuckled, diffusing my nerves. "Fine. I'll trust ye to keep yer peace."

I squared my shoulders as Roan climbed on the bed; the mattress dipping under his bulk. He faced me and crossed his thick, tattooed legs with an unsuspected grace. He said, "I'll speak out loud so the others can take notes. We enter and exit from the same spot. It's the anchor point in the vision walk. If ye get spooked, go back to where ye came in. But don't be frightened, lass. It can't hurt ye."

Anna placed the bowl between us. "Jelly, put the fish in the bowl. It's the centering for the magic. Open your right hand. I have to cut along your heart line." She slashed my palm with an incantation, and I hissed. She instructed, "Squeeze your fist." A trickle of blood stained the bowl's bottom.

Roan held out his left hand and did not flinch from the slice of the blade, his eyes gripping mine spellbound. Anna used the knife tip to blend the bowl's crimson contents. "Here we go," she whispered.

She dipped her left thumb in the blood and smeared it on my forehead. There was no expected sizzle of magic or flying sparks. I didn't feel a thing except her smooth pressure. The symbol she painted on Roan was like an upside-down question mark with a line at the top. She removed the bowl and stepped back. Roan gave me a steadying look. "Give me yer hands. Deep breath." I mirrored him, lifting my palms to touch his, the difference in size almost comical. My palm burned when the blood from our cuts met, and a smell like warm musk hit the air. "Close yer eyes and don't let go."

He curled his fingers around mine and dropped them between us. My lashes slipped down and solidified. In an instant, we fell through time and space, like traveling through one of Synchi's whirlpools, with no idea which way was up. The blur behind my eyes sped up and narrowed into a tunnel, lights flashing, voices calling, all a cacophony in my mind. With an abrupt jolt, we landed.

"We're here," muttered Roan, his voice sounding like he was underwater. I stared at a wall, the cracks and holes in the stones vaguely familiar. There was a gasp behind me. I spun.

Simmi. She lay as she did before; only this time I could move. I ran to her. "Simmi? Simmi, can you hear me?" I could have cried with joy. I could speak. Her face turned to the wall at where I'd just been. I wanted to rip off that hood.

She said roughly, "Over here."

I waved my hand in front of her eyes. "Simmi! I'm here!"

Roan's disembodied voice floated around me. "It's a memory. Look for clues. Go to the window."

I reluctantly left her and crossed the cold floor. I leaned out of the square hole in the wall to look around. Roan noted what I saw. "Pink sand, turquoise water, oleander tree. Hibiscus, heavy air, thick salt." A bird screeched.

Roan's voice called, "Birdsong, three syllables, staccato, sharp. Can ye go outside, lass?" As there was no obvious door, I ran for the largest opening, but it repelled me and threw me back. I lost my footing and slammed into the bed. Roan growled. "Protective barrier. Look around the room more."

Simmi stammered, fighting to spit out the words. "He. Wants the pearl. Using my blood. Slaughter. All of you. Us." I turned around to look at her.

Roan said, "Already happened, lass. Stay focused."

Ignoring Simmi, I spun and scanned the walls. There was nothing but cold, weeping stone, wet with humidity. I looked up and yelped. Above Simmi, rust-colored symbols covered the ceiling. Roan's voice shouted, "Get closer!"

I climbed on the frame at the foot of the bed and stared up. Roan's voice was urgent and garbled, "Archaic symbols. Power, possession, ocean, shark, fish of sorts… That one! I can't see it clear enough! What's above her head?"

I jumped down and scrambled around, hoisting myself high on the rusty headboard, teetering as I got closer to the marking on the ceiling. My face pressed against thicker air, heavy and dense, and the symbol blazed in bright purple, sending sparks flying across the ceiling. Roan's voice recoiled in horror. "Jelly! Get back to where ye came in! The far wall! Now! I'm pulling ye out!"

Simmi used the last of her breath and shouted. "Stop him! Find me!"

There was a moment of pressure, as if the world took a deep breath, and I winced and swayed as it pushed down on me.

"Too late," came a sultry voice. I recognized it immediately and crashed from the frame, jarring my heel painfully. Skittering to the foot of the bed, about to dash for the wall, a figure blurred, blocking my escape and causing me to retreat. I pressed my back to the wet stone, trapped. The smell came first, like hot tar. Then there was a snarl, and a black shadow materialized with claws and fiery-red eyes, forming behind the most stunningly gorgeous man I'd ever laid eyes on. I lost my breath.

His long hair glimmered with the iridescence of a raven's wing, so dark and shiny it held every color of the rainbow. It fell in waves around a face sculpted by a masterful artist, perfectly symmetrical, with high cheeks, a strong nose, and a devastatingly sensual mouth, tweaked up in a devastating grin. His eyes were luminescent, a strange color I couldn't place, maybe close to the vibrant, neon green of a deep-sea glowworm, but even that seemed flat in comparison.

He wore a black top, the buttons open to show an expanse of smooth skin over finely sculpted muscle. He'd rolled the sleeves, exposing veins that crawled like thin ropes on his forearms. Dark leather, tight and soft, molded to his slinky, long thighs. A heavy chain hung around his neck, and a half-full vial containing a dark liquid swung from it. He was barefoot and silent as he strolled closer.

With a casual flick of his graceful hand, my eyes following the movement, he motioned over his shoulder to the monster behind him. "I believe you've met my pets," he purred in a voice like thick syrup. "I was hoping you'd come sniffing for clues." He laughed, and the sound was like discordant wind chimes. "So predictable."

"How are you here? This is my memory."

He pulled his hair over his ears, the tips arching into high points. I blinked hard, staring with parted lips. I blinked again as if it would change the shape of his ears. He said, "Darling, I'm Fae. We travel through all sorts of dimensions. Oh, look at your face. You look positively aghast. Am I your first? The way you're staring suggests I am. Stunning, aren't I?" He swept his fingers down his body. "But truly, darling, you are quite the specimen yourself."

His eyes roamed my body hungrily, and I looked down. I was naked. My brain spun. Of course, I was. I'd had the vision in my Mers form, and we didn't wear clothes. I pulled my hair around to cover my breasts, but I had nothing to hide my lower half.

The stranger stepped toward me, and I pressed harder into the stone, my mind clawing for an escape. He read my expression and tutted, disappointed. "Now, Scyphozoa, or shall I say, Vetula Heir, don't get any grand ideas."

"How do you…?" My breath came in rapid pants.

"Darling, I told you. I've been waiting for you. Now, shall we chat about the pearl?" I raised my hand and screamed. Nothing happened. The beautiful man's eyebrows rose in amusement. "Oh, dear girl, your power won't work here." He tipped his head to study me.

I kept my eyes on the Fae. My voice came out in a shriek. "Roan, get me out of here!"

"Ye need to be back at the wall!" Panic seared through his voice. He sounded so far away.

The gorgeous man giggled with delight. "Well, *hello,* Roan. It's been an absolute age since I last saw you. How is your dear mother? Oh, that's right. She's dead." He looked at me and fluttered his eyelashes. "One of my pets ripped out her throat. Right. In. Front of him. He was just a child then, but I recognize his energy pattern in the ether."

Even the scowl on his face was attractive as he spoke to the air, knowing Roan was watching and listening. He folded his arms in irritation. "I thought I killed you, Mage. I left you as cold as stone on top of your pretty mummy. How *did* you repair that great gash in your chest?"

He nonchalantly waved his long fingers through the air as his eyes swung back to me. "No matter. Let's get down to business, shall we? I want the pearl." His eyes flicked to my throat, and I automatically covered it with my hand. "Hmm. Shame it's not the real one. It would make all of this so much simpler." Menace rolled off of him like a thick fog, choking me.

"Why do you want it?" I whispered hoarsely.

"Have they not told you its power?" He tsked. "Truly, your shaman has done you a disservice." He slowly slunk toward me, stopping at the foot of the bed. I scanned around for a weapon but found none. "It never should have gone to the Mers. It belongs to the Fae. The pearl belongs to me."

I whispered, "You didn't answer my question. What do you plan to do with it? Besides terrorizing the ocean?"

The beautiful Fae shrugged and sighed dramatically, flipping his iridescent hair behind his pointed ear. "Scyphozoa, my experiment is sadly out of hand. At first, it was mild entertainment, turning humans into mindless consumers. It was fascinating, as they found more creative ways to manipulate the world. I wanted to see how far they would go. But they bred uncontrollably, spreading their filth across the planet and living longer than they should, devouring finite resources."

He crept forward an inch, and I pressed more of my skin to the wall. He stopped, fluttering his ridiculously lush eyelashes. "The world is dying, Scyphozoa. You've seen it. Pollution clogs the oceans. Whales beach themselves in desperation, their stomachs full of plastic. The chemicals mutate fish in the water. The air tastes like poison, and the animals are dying. No one's having babies anymore."

I frowned. Everything he said was true. His honeyed voice oozed, "Darling, can't you see? I am the solution. The humans don't deserve this planet. They are a disgusting parasite and need to be washed away...permanently. With the pearl, I can eliminate the humans and leave the magical creatures to rule again." He cocked his head to the side, his green eyes flashing. "Can't you see, sweet girl? We're on the same side." He winked at me saucily. "Lovely work with the soap, by the way. I truly adore a good bang."

My eyes darted around. Maybe I could fling myself from the window. But then I'd be even further from the wall, and the Eator was licking its chops behind the Fae. On seeing my distress, the beautiful man stilled, gently caressing the tips of Simmi's toes.

I stalled. "So, with the pearl, you can kill the humans. And what? Leave the Mers and Surfecti to live in peace? That's your plan?"

He stared, his eyes hovering over my breasts. A sharp canine tugged on his full lip. He took another step closer. "Isn't this what you want, Scyphozoa? To destroy the humans and let the planet heal?"

I thought of the superstore, of my blinding rage. "I want...I want..." I wanted clear water to swim in, to have the sea creatures live free lives without fear of poison or dying from plastic waste. As horrifying as his plan was, reluctantly, I could see its merits. Far away, there was a rumbling noise, like distant thunder. Roan must be losing his mind, watching me waver.

I reflected on the Fae's words and said brokenly, "Part of me agrees. I hate the humans for what they've done to the planet." Mori came to mind, and I recalled her steadfast belief that humans were worth redemption. "But I have to believe that some of them are innocent. They're victims of circumstance. They can do better if we help them."

His lush lips pulled back, exposing dazzling, perfect teeth, the canines delicately elongated. "But, darling, there are no innocents. Not anymore. Every human uses plastic. Besides, they'll all be dead soon enough, poisoned by their stupidity, but at least I can save the plants and animals. Can't you see? I'm doing something good."

I choked on a bitter laugh. "By wiping out an entire species?" He was utterly insane, and my heart and brain raced together in panic. I had to get away from here.

He dropped his charming facade and snarled. "The humans do it daily! Their greed is destroying the planet! Hundreds of species are gone, thanks to them. Thousands are on the brink! The Earth is in her sixth mass extinction because they raze down the forests for cheap fuel and food, destroying yet-undiscovered lifeforms! They know more about the stars than the creatures who roam their planet!"

Again, I had no counterargument. "Why do you need the pearl? It's mine, after all. I'm the one who wears it." I played a dangerous game by taunting him, but I wanted as much information as I could about the mysterious pearl, and he seemed to have answers.

He hissed through his teeth. "The pearl heightens your power. You know this. You've felt it. And every time you draw on it…it's like a slap in my face. That power is *mine* to use." He waved at me in a once-over, sneering. "Not a mermaid."

Slowly, as if inspecting something stuck in my foot, I lifted it and set it on the bed frame, fiddling between my toes. He didn't seem to notice, or if he did, he didn't care. His eyes fell on my upper thighs and slowly traced higher. I shifted my weight, cocking a hip, internally dying as I exposed myself to him. My Seduction lessons kicked into high gear. Pretend, pretend, pretend. I kept my face neutral.

He took another step toward me, licking his beautiful lips. His voice dropped to lusty, dark honey again. "Nature has done her best with plagues and cataclysmic storms, but even she can't eradicate them. The pearl is my only choice. So darling, we can do this one of two ways. You give me the pearl willingly and stay as you are…" He looked me over, ravenous. "Or I kill you."

"Not crazy about either option," I muttered.

He tipped his head from side to side, staring at me greedily. He ran two long fingers across his lush lower lip before whispering, "Perhaps there's another way. I've never had an Eator mermaid. I could turn you and make you work for me." He shuddered with pleasure. "Now, isn't that a beautiful thought? I've been so busy possessing the sharks and whatnot. I really must focus on the Mers."

"We have a pact with the Fae! You can't do that!"

He purred, "Can't I? Sweet girl, I am not bound to Fae laws."

"The King will never allow it!" I gambled on his fear of retribution. My heart sank as he threw his head back and laughed, the sound of jangled wind chimes filling the air.

"The King, *my father*, doesn't know where I am or what I'm doing. I'm afraid you'll have to find a better threat."

My blood froze in terror. He was a Fae Prince? He was one of the most powerful creature on the planet. I had to escape. He waved graceful fingers through the air. "No, the Fae just wait and wait for the humans to kill each other off. Not me. I'm tired of waiting. I'm taking action."

He was almost within touching distance. My heart pounded, and I'd never wished harder for the power of the pearl. There was a faraway pulse, as though it were active in another place. He moaned, "I am so bored with the humans. They have become so unremarkable. But you…you are quite delicious, darling. I could have great fun with you."

His long fingers swept up his jaw to clasp against his high cheekbones, and he gasped from his vision, crooning, "I can just see it. You and your army of EatorMers terrorizing the humans in the ocean, destroying the fishing fleets and oil rigs. What a fascinating idea. After we've played with them for a while, like a cat with a weak little mouse, I'll wipe them out permanently. But it will be delightful to beleaguer them first." Enamored and purring with his twisted fantasy, he closed his eyes.

That was my moment. I thrust my weight onto my raised foot and catapulted across Simmi's frail body with every ounce of strength I had. The screech of the bed jerked him out of his reverie. I rolled across the floor and slammed into the far wall, screaming for Roan. My body shimmered and disintegrated. Glowing green eyes flared and sparked as he shrieked ominously, "I offered you a chance!"

Roan ripped me from the vision and hurled me through the blurred tunnel of voices and flashing lights. It stopped abruptly, giving me atrocious vertigo as I mentally landed, clenching hands with a relative stranger. The room was empty and destroyed. I yanked away from Roan and keeled to the side, vomiting sweet tea so violently it came out of my nose. My body seized as I gasped and spat, desperately trying to inhale.

I wiped my face on a shred of the quilt and twisted around. Torn curtains whimpered on a crooked rail, shattered glass salted the floor, and large chunks of the stone walls were missing. A stiff breeze came through the broken window, lifting the remains of my bed, now feathers and stuffing, twirling them off to spin in the corner.

"Roan?" I bleated. "Roan, did I hurt you?"

The giant man shook. Shards of glass lurched out of his muscles, blood dripping onto the ruined, pale bedding. Unable to speak, he looked at me with such agony I wanted to close my eyes to escape it. His hands clenched and unclenched, nostrils flaring with quick breaths, his emotions frenzied and raw. He wasn't upset with me. Grief speared through his eyes rather than anger. I choked, "Did I do this? What happened?" He didn't reply, unable to speak. I whispered, "He killed your mother in front of you…Roan…"

Roan jumped from the bed, causing me to roll as if riding a wave as he stormed from the broken room, his footsteps heavy as he thundered downstairs. Out the smashed window, I saw the trees bend under his anguished roar. I followed and ran into the rain, chasing the sound.

I found him huddled under a massive oak tree, over one hundred feet tall, making him appear tiny and fragile. He had picked the glass from his body, leaving smears of rust over black and gray tattoos. His body tucked tight, his knees at his chest, one arm wrapped around them, the other holding his face. A fat squirrel skittered high above his bowed head with an acorn in its teeth. It bristled its tail as I slowly approached. "Roan? Roan, I'm so sorry."

He shook his head, his voice thick. "Go away, lass." I pressed my lips together, thinking of all the times I'd been so alone, so lost. When my parents died, grief clung to my heart like a feasting tick. It still fed. I sat beside Roan, leaning against the sturdy trunk, letting its presence enfold and soothe me. A woodpecker hammered methodically overhead, searching for breakfast.

"Where did everyone go?" I asked softly.

"Yer pearl chased them off."

"Was anyone hurt?"

"Aye."

I swallowed my fear. "Badly?" I barely squeaked out the word. He sighed roughly.

"Anna transported them in time." He lifted his eyes to mine. "She wanted to pull ye out, lass, yank ye from the vision walk. Would've fried yer brain. We stopped her, but she's furious."

I dropped my chin, shame and despair washing through me.

Mori found us minutes later. Without a word, she sat facing us, her long legs crossed, reaching to take one of my hands. I raised my face and gave her a sad smile. Gently, she stroked the fingers of Roan's hand, pulling it away from his face. He bowed his head deeper and sighed so heavily it chilled my wet skin. She rearranged herself to sit more comfortably, her hands quietly occupied with ours.

A little while later, her trembling and chattering teeth stirred us. Maybe it was the booming thunder that shook and rattled the sky. I blinked my eyes open. Her red hair had plastered to her skull from the drenching, sideways rain, water dripping off the long ends onto her pebbled thighs.

Roan lifted his head, disoriented. He looked at his hand as if it belonged to someone else, lying firmly in the grasp of a shivering, silent mermaid. "Lass," his voice rough, "yer half froze."

"Mmm hmm," she quivered. "Maybe fully. Storm blew in." She lifted her face, squinting as the rain hit her eyes.

He looked over at me. In a torn voice, barely discernible above the drumming of the rain and the howl of the wind, I said, "He wants to turn me and use me to slaughter the humans."

"Aye."

"He's going to hunt the Mers. I have to stop him before he kills anyone I love. I don't have many left."

Roan's whisper cracked with emotion. "Aye. But lass, ye let us help ye. I know yer used to fending for yerself, but we're here now. Ye need to trust us. Both of ye do."

I dipped my chin, nodding as I looked at my muddy feet. "Okay."

"Okay," echoed Mori, squeezing our hands before gently letting go.

TWENTY-FOUR

JELLY

Someone had prepared breakfast. We came in from the storm through a side door, and went straight to the kitchen, Roan insisting we eat before seeing anyone. After eyeing our wet, translucent night clothes, Roan provided throw blankets and retreated without a word. Neither Mori nor I had eaten since yesterday, and we groaned over warm croissants and fluffy eggs dotted with smoked salmon.

"What magic is this?" Mori sighed happily as she pulled apart the flaky pastry.

I frowned, unable to be jovial. My mind spun, knowing once again I'd hurt the people around me. I just didn't know who. I answered, "Butter. What happened while I was under?"

She chewed silently, swallowed, and said, "Roan was yelling a mile a minute. His dialect was so thick that I could barely understand. Jelly, he *raged*. There were so many fooks. His face was alternately terrified and furious. And then, somehow, you triggered the pearl."

"I was grasping for it."

"Well, you called it. It was up on its chain, spinning and

spitting with noise. As soon as it lifted, I screamed to Anna, and she raised her hands, and Roan shouted, 'No!' then Mako jumped up. Then something exploded. The window, I think. Then she spat out some words and whipped us all to the study. There was crashing and smashing above us, and Anna cursed and swore and threatened to send you to the ocean as fish food. Richard and Sebastian were calming her down, so I took off, hiding outside in case she turned on me."

I set down my fork as my stomach soured. "Who did I hurt?"

Mori shrugged. "I'm not really sure. It happened so fast. I ran straight outside. She was livid. I was on the front porch, and then Roan sprinted past, blasting the air with his magic. I waited, figuring you'd come, and sure enough, you chased after him. Jelly? What happened to him? What happened in there?"

I answered quietly. "A Fae entered the vision. He's the one making the Eators. The Fae…he was seconds away from touching me. I think…I think if he had, he'd have consumed me." I frowned. "Roan didn't say?"

"Say what?"

My face fell. "The Fae killed his mother." She recoiled and carefully placed her napkin on her unfinished breakfast, sagging back in her chair.

She combed her fingers through her sodden hair. "He was yelling about the Prince. He's the Prince?" She looked at me, her face ashen. "He's stronger than any of us, Jelly."

I nodded. We sat in silence, staring at our half-empty plates.

We crept upstairs via the back steps and found Sophia waiting in Mori's room. She looked up as we entered. "You need warm clothes," she said kindly. "I brought some. Come downstairs when you're dressed. You're not in danger, I swear.

Anna is fine. Sebastian's been doing his magic. Everyone is okay."

Apprehensively, I asked, "Mako? He was right next to me."

Her lips pulled into a line. "He'll be fine." She paused as she walked for the door. "Mako threw himself in front of you, Jelly. When Anna raised her hands to yank you from the vision, he defended you and stopped her, knowing she wouldn't risk hurting him. He saved your sanity."

Mori and I blinked wordlessly as she pulled the door shut. I turned to my best friend. "Why is he so invested? Do you think he's just another male wanting my power?"

She shook her head. "I don't get that vibe from him. I think he cares for you."

"He does. He told me. He told me a lot of things." I bit my lip to hide my grin. "His magic is extraordinary."

She tipped her head, her mouth dropping open. "And exactly how do you know what his magic is like?"

I glanced up and chuckled at her expression. "He gave me healing last night. We kissed. It was incredible. I've never felt anything like it. Mori...I would have gone the distance. I wanted to. I was almost pathetic with my wanting and made it crystal clear that I was up for it. But then he stopped, saying he's not the one I need. I was furious."

She rolled her eyes, her voice dripping with sarcasm. "Gods. A man who only wants the best for you. At his own sacrifice. Against his base desires. Whatever shall we do?"

I pinched her thigh, making her yelp. I said, "Then, me being me, I got angry and yelled at him for not having sex with me, telling him he was another stupid man trying to control my choices. And then he throws himself in front of the most powerful witch alive to defend me? Talk about mixed messages."

Mori said soberly, "Jelly, regardless of his confused feelings, you're worth defending."

I groaned. "On top of that, every damned time Gray touches me, it's like I burst into flames. I get all ditzy and giggly." I steadied my eyes at her. "Mori. I am *not* giggly."

She laughed. "No. You are not." Her forehead scrunched up as if she were thinking hard.

I sighed heavily. "It doesn't matter. It doesn't. I'm not here for a lover. So, I'm going to put all thoughts of men to the side. That's it. Finished. I can't get distracted, not now."

We dressed quickly and followed the voices downstairs. We skulked into the living room on the other side of the foyer. The room was grander than the study, more imposing, but I didn't see any of it. I only had eyes for Mako. He curled into a vast wingback chair with his eyes closed, one arm around his middle. He looked like he was sleeping.

Every eye in the room swung at us. Roan cleared his throat, nodding with a grin. "I was just finishing up. Like a fookin' ninja, she was. Cartwheeling right over Simmi. Come here, lass. Ye got us a tremendous amount of information by keeping yer head and getting him to talk."

I stepped across the room nervously and squawked when he gripped me in a hug. He said loudly, "We're all right, wee fish. We're in a magical castle with magical witches who are putting yer room right as we speak. No one will hurt ye. Isn't that right, Anna?"

I pulled back from Roan and stared at the witch, tense as I waited for her wrath. She glanced up from her notes, waved her hand dismissively, and grumbled, "Yes, yes, we're fine." Her eyes darted to Mako and worry creased her forehead. Mori settled into a chair beside him, grabbing a blank notebook and a pencil from the table as she walked past.

Anna returned to her papers, reading out loud. "Here's what we have. Pink sand, turquoise water, oleander, hibiscus. In Jelly's first vision, he said he likes fresh fish with local bananas. Unfortunately, bananas grow in too many places. We're still trying to narrow it down to a custom, native dish. You said the air was heavy. Jelly, do you remember the temperature?"

"That's it?" I said in disbelief. "You want to talk about bananas and ignore that I lost it again? I blew up your room!"

Sebastian and Sophia swallowed their smiles, grinning at my confusion.

Anna looked down her nose, which was quite a feat considering she sat and I stood. She said haughtily, "What do you want? A trial? Fifty lashes? Banishment from the kingdom?" She sniffed, "We are not Mers, Jelly. You are not the first to lose control of your power. I may have overreacted in the moment, but that quilt was a fine antique, and, frankly, irreplaceable." She scowled, "Now, the air temperature?"

Stunned, I replied. "There was a chilly breeze. A damp cold. The walls were wet."

Mori's voice rang in my head. *You'd be in the hole back home. Synchi told us the Surfecti would snuff us out. You demolished a room and hurt her people, and she's pissed about a quilt?*

I answered. *Seriously? No punishment? That's twice I've put them in direct danger. The Trident was ready to behead me for the shark! I am so confused right now.*

I sat opposite Mako, my fingertips worrying the arms of the chair, wanting to be the first thing he saw when he woke. Hopefully, he wouldn't be upset. All I did was harm him.

Richard frowned. "A chill in the air in late April. That doesn't sound like the Caribbean. It's already hot there by then." He mumbled and tapped his tablet, most likely searching for weather reports.

Anna continued. "Then, birdsong, three syllables, staccato, sharp. The blood symbols on the ceiling are from the ancient language. There's power, possession, ocean, shark, some fish, and then—"

Roan snarled, "And then *his*." Mori looked up from her notebook. Concern marred her smooth forehead as she watched him pace in front of the fire. He turned to me and said, "He's Terrun, the Prince. That flashing symbol ye saw? That was a tripwire. When ye got close, as the bastard figured ye would, it activated." Roan gulped his whiskey and seethed through his teeth. "He suspected we'd be coming to look around. I fookin' walked right into it."

Abruptly, Sebastian stood and stormed from the room, the air crackling with energy as he did. Sophia curled deeper into her chair, watching him leave with shadowed eyes. Gray leaned his back against the stone jamb of the fireplace, one ankle over the other. It was a casual stance, considering the topic at hand. He looked at me silently for a long while, his eyes sliding to the pearl. They stopped and hovered. His jaw tightened as his teeth pressed together.

Richard broke the silence and turned to his son. "Gray, you've studied the Darker Arts. How do we handle the Fae Prince? There must be a ritual of sorts."

Mori startled and dropped her notebook. She gulped before gasping, "Darker Arts? Are you a practitioner?"

Gray smothered a laugh at her expression. "It's not like I do them all the time, Mori. More like…research. I understand you've peeked into Pandora's Box. Don't pretend it's not fascinating."

She leaned down to retrieve her fallen doodles and slipped

her hair behind her ear. *Jelly, I don't like this one bit. Whatever he's about to say? It is NOT GOOD.* Her eyes flitted over to ensure I'd received her message. I subtly nodded my head once.

Gray exhaled, as if full of regret. "As far as I can see, there is only one option." He ran tense fingers through his sandy curls before sliding them over his mouth, shaking his head almost imperceptibly. He dropped his hand by his side and shoved it in his pocket. "We are dealing with an unhinged Fae Prince with the power to destroy the humans if he has the pearl as his weapon." He pushed off from the stone and faced me. "He's also threatened to possess the Mers. That would be catastrophic. Therefore, we need to increase your power so you are equal to him. We can do a ritual to make it happen."

"Whoa!" yelled Mori. "What ritual, Gray?"

He looked at Mori with narrowed eyes. "Are you familiar with the *Coactus Fusionem*?"

She sprang from her seat and was at his throat in a second, bunching his shirt in her fists as she hissed, "We will NOT be doing a *Coactus Fusionem*! Are you insane?" She slammed him against the stone. He kept his hands in his pockets and let her.

"Why?" I asked, confused and alarmed by her response. "What is it?"

She released her grip and whirled to face me. "It's Latin for Forced Fusion, and it's dangerous, absolute insanity. It requires a ritual that is so painful it…It is so painful that you pray for death so it will end. Jelly…Not everyone survives it." She cut her eyes at Gray. "I can't believe it's even being suggested."

"What does it entail?" I asked Gray. To Mori, I whispered. *Let him speak.*

Gray frowned. "We would infuse you with our magic. It's uncertain how the pearl will respond. It may resist and see us as a threat. There's a chance it might retaliate and hurt us."

"What? Well, then, no. That's a hard no from me," I said. "Think of something else."

Roan gave me a piercing glare before passing his hands over his head. He said through clenched teeth, "He'll not quit unless we make him. We have to stop him."

Sophia softly cleared her throat. "Roan, tell them what happened to you. It will help them understand what we're up against."

His face shadowed and darkened, sucking the light from the fire. He nodded his head. "I was seven years old. I had me back to Mum. We were trying to protect a crowd of peaceful protesters, marching against the bombs, the ones they were dropping on ye Mers. I saw the red eyes in counter-protesters. They were well-hid to look like humans. Except for someone with magic, their pupils glowed. It scared me, but I was wee, too young to use magic. It hadn't manifested yet. I turned to warn her when one of the Eators came up behind her…"

He swallowed a few times. "Came up behind her and tore out her throat. Just…" his voice broke, "dropped her. Then it slit me up the center and left me fer dead. One of ours found us and took me to be healed. It was too late for Mum."

He drained his glass. I expected him to do something violent, like smash it into the fire, but he set it intentionally and gently on the mantle. "The ones who fixed me did a healing version of the *Coactus Fusionem*. Four of them hit me with their magic to chase out the rot from the Eator. It hurts like a bastard, lass. I won't lie. And any form of forced magic will leave a permanent mark."

Mori asked softly, "You were helping the humans who wanted to stop the bombing?" Her voice cracked. "We were told the Surfecti didn't try. That they ignored what was happening to us."

He rubbed his fingers across his forehead. "We were trying desperately, lass. We had little impact, being in Europe and all, and heavily drained of our magic. It was the Americans blasting up the ocean." He looked up as Sebastian entered, silently crossing to his wife. Without a word, she rose from the chair, let him sit, and curled into his massive body. Roan nodded to Mori. "Aye, we did what we could. Weren't enough, though. Not nearly enough."

I mulled over Roan's words. "What do you mean, it will leave a mark?" To answer, he lifted his shirt, causing Mori to hum softly, and pointed to a thick, forked lightning mark around the left side of his ribs.

He said, "Mine is bigger than most. I was almost dead. Lost most me blood. Ye'll probably only have a wee dot, hardly a thing, as we'll do it to ye while yer strong and healthy." He glanced at me, then Gray, and then back at me. "Now, if we do it, and lass, I think we should, we need two more male Surfecti. Personally, I'm thinking Shifters."

I squinted at him. "Why Shifters and why men? We're here with powerful witches. Why not ask them?"

Gray answered. "It's the magic that our group lacks. We have Fae and Mage representation, with a touch of Mers in Mako. Shifters have different energy patterns that would better cover the magic available to the Surfecti. We need male energy for balance, to counter the tremendous feminine you carry. Jelly, you're a Mermaid Warrior, amplified by the Vetula Pearl."

He chuckled as he looked at me. "You're already too much for us, as you've shown. We need seven to have any chance of success. Despite being formidable together, the five of us won't have enough power for the ritual. If we don't give you enough magic in one go, the ritual will fail, and we risk losing you and ourselves." He looked at Mori cautiously before sliding his eyes back to me. "It's forced magic, Jelly. It's perilous."

"Why seven?" asked Mori, her eyes narrowed on Gray.

Richard answered. "Seven is a mystical number. It is eager and ardent, and magic loves enthusiasm and responds to it well. Seven male Surfecti together will suffice to protect Jelly, as well as protect us from her."

I asked quietly, "Is it painful for everyone?"

Gray crossed to where I sat in the dark leather wingback, the texture supple under my worried fingers. He took my hands in his, and warmth rushed through my blood to stain my cheeks pink. His voice was gentle. "I won't lie. It is excruciating, Jelly, for everyone involved." He looked at our hands, stroking my skin. "And it may cause death if we don't do it right."

My jaw dropped open. I had no words. I looked at Mori; her eyes were as large as dinner plates. No one spoke. "I have someone I can call," muttered Roan. "He's between assignments." He pulled out his phone and crossed the room with determined steps.

Mako woke up without my noticing. I was too busy being horrified, staring at Gray as he gently suggested I might kill him. Mako's voice was bleary as he murmured, "What about Jacob? He might be free."

"Good idea. He's strong," agreed Gray. "I'll call him." He released my hands, took out his phone, and walked across the room, taking the warmth with him.

I stared after him. "Wait! We have to talk about this! Death? I'll take the risk, but I'm not willing for anyone else to!"

Gray's voice faded as he said, "Jacob, it's Gray Smith. Look, we have a situation. You came to mind." I stared at him before drawing my gaze back to Mako. My heart did a flip. He was staring at me. My pulse pattered at the intensity of his eyes, and my power dot woke up and pulsed. Damn it.

"Jelly..." Mori whispered and stopped. She pulled me from

the room, bypassing Gray and Roan, who paced in the foyer on their phones, and shoved me out the front door. She yelled, "Jelly, what they're talking about is incredibly dangerous! Seven Surfecti are going to force their magic into your body. Seven! It might change you. No, scrap that. It will definitely change you! You can't do this!"

I shouted back. "He hurt Toto, Mori! He's threatened to kill him and Synchi, and Mako, and Simmi! What about you? What if he came after you? If I don't do this, we won't be able to stop him!" My voice caught.

We were quiet for a beat, and then she threw herself at me, squeezing so tight my spine popped. "I don't want anything to happen to you, Jelly. You're my best friend."

I gasped at her iron grip. "You're my only friend."

She tossed her chin up as she released me. "You have more friends than you realize, Jelly. Each person in the room is ready to fight for you."

"I'm not sure I want them to," I whispered. "What if it gets them killed? That's on me."

"If they don't try, then Terrun will kill them. Maybe not immediately, but eventually. He's psychotic. You're their only shot. I don't like it, not at all. But if anyone was going to do this ritual, these are the people you want. Do you trust them?"

"Do I have a choice?" We stared at each other silently.

A soft cough disturbed us. It was Mako. He limped toward us slowly. "Jelly, you always have a choice. We aren't the Trident."

"Mako!" I swallowed my guilt, watching him stagger. "I always seem to hurt you."

He grinned. "Only because I'm right next to you." He stepped in close and gently tucked my hair behind my ear. "I've heard of this ritual. But never with a Mers and never with someone who wears a power amulet. These are uncharted waters. You can say no." He gazed at me, waiting for me to nod in understanding. His voice was gruff. "No one would hold it against you if you refused."

He turned to leave, his face flinching from the pain. I grabbed the front of his sweater and dragged him to me. I stared into his eyes, saying, "This is a contract kiss, a business deal. You only take. Do not give me a single spark. It's the least I can do." I snared his face in my hands and slammed my lips to his, pouring gratitude into my kiss.

Mako's soft moan caused Mori to chuckle. I kissed him until I felt his magic grow and strengthen, power surging through him. I fisted his silky locks, whispering, "Thank you, Mako, for saving me—again."

His fingers tangled my hair as he tilted my head roughly and kissed me back, sending me a rush of magic so potent it curled my toes. I arched into him, pressing my body against his before I recovered myself and pulled away.

Mori's mouth twisted into a smirk as I struggled to catch my breath. Mako's magic was that powerful. I sputtered, "Mako! I told you to take, not give!"

"Can't do that, Jelly. Not with you. You deserve even more." He stepped back and cleared his throat. "You can say no to the ritual. I need you to understand…You aren't being forced into this." He turned and strode from us, chin high, chest out, his body robustly recovered, leaving me speechless.

I threw up my hands. "What does that mean? I deserve even more."

Mori shrugged as we watched him go. "Maybe he thinks he's not good enough for you. Although, from the look on your face after that kiss, I can't imagine why. He's made for you. Gorgeous, powerful, violent." I stared after Mako with a slack jaw, the pearl purring happily at my throat. Mori pulled my attention back by physically turning my chin to her. "Well? What are you going to do?"

I pressed my hands to my forehead, blocking visions of a naked Mako from my mind. "We have to stop the Fae before he attacks the Mers again or hurts Simmi further. Despite what Mako said, I don't have a choice. I have to do this."

She blinked back tears and nodded ferociously, always my staunched support. She wove her fingers through mine, and we sprinted back into the library. I stalked to the fireplace, staring at the popping logs, twisting a strand of blue hair through my fingers. When I turned and scanned the tight faces around me, Roan and Gray were still absent.

I slapped my hands on my hips. "I don't get you people. You're in danger because of the pearl, but you're calling Shifters to ask them to join us for a dangerous ritual, like asking them over for tea."

Anna looked up from her notes. "If he has the pearl, he will go further than killing the humans. You and your pearl need to defeat him, but you can't do it alone. This is how we help you win."

I paced. "What we need to do is find Simmi. Terrun was so angry, and I'm worried he'll take it out on her. She's already so damaged. I'm not sure she can handle more abuse."

Sophia stood on shaky feet, her hand to her mouth as if she would be sick. She ran for the kitchen, Sebastian hurrying after her. Mako's eyes shut tight, his lips pulled into a deep frown before he followed his parents. I slapped my hand to my forehead. "Should I go apologize?"

Richard sat forward, setting his mug on the table. "No. Leave them be. Now, Jelly, the ritual will be…" He chose his word carefully. "Difficult."

I swallowed over the lump in my throat. "Yes, the death part suggested that."

He smiled kindly. "We will be with you every step of the way."

I cleared my throat roughly. Emotions were tangling my voice box. "Thank you, Richard."

Anna glanced anxiously at her husband, saw me see it, and sobered. "Based on what Roan saw, we can safely assume Simmi is somewhere tropical. I'm still running the birdsong through identification software." She smirked. "I made Roan mimic its call. If he did it correctly, the sound is nearly intolerable, like claws on a chalkboard. Poor bird."

The room fell into silence again. The fire provided the only noise. A loud pop caused Mori's eyes to fly open. "Anna? What if Jelly tried to contact Simmi telepathically? Jelly can throw her mind at great distances." She looked at me with excitement. "Remember? You said you spoke to Amira when she was in San Francisco. You couldn't reach the Shaman from here, but maybe you can reach Simmi."

I shrugged and looked at Anna, saying, "I think it depends on how far away she is, but if she's somewhere tropical, let's assume the Caribbean or Central America, then that's closer than my trying to call Synchi in the Pacific. It's worth a shot."

Anna tapped her fingers on her lips and met her husband's intelligent stare. I could see the wheels turning in their minds. After a beat, she sighed. "You might open your mind to the Fae Prince. But then again, perhaps you won't. If you're willing to take the risk, I would say to try."

I sat in the leather chair, tucking my legs underneath me. I murmured, "Well, be ready to yell for Roan if my eyes roll up in my head or the pearl goes berserk. Here goes nothing." I pressed my middle finger and thumb of both hands to my temples, hoping it would give me more power. I pulled on the magic from the pearl, waiting until I could sense the vibration in my blood.

I visualized Simmi's pale face and saw her strapped to the rusty bed in the cold stone room. In my mind, I pictured the red hibiscus blooms, smelled the rich perfume of the oleander and tasted the heavy salt air. Turquoise waves crashed onto a pink beach as I reached out with my mind.

Simmi? It's Jelly. I don't know if you can communicate telepathically, but if you hear this, I want you to picture my pearl. It's a black teardrop and hangs at my throat on a chain. Imagine tapping on it three times if you get this message. We are desperately trying to find you. We're coming. As soon as we see where you are, we're coming.

TWENTY-FIVE

MAKO

I scrubbed my hands against my cheeks, watching helplessly as my mother fell to pieces in my father's arms. I hadn't seen her this bad in years, and it was my fault. He stroked her back, whispering into her ear. But even his soothing Fae magic couldn't calm her down.

Her body shook as she wept. "I can't do it again, Sebby. I can't lose another. This is the Goddess punishing me. I left the Mers, and she's taken two of my children from me."

My father's voice broke. "You can't say that, sweetheart. Maybe I'm the one being punished. I disobeyed the Fae."

"To stay with me," she wailed.

"And I would choose you every time."

My throat was thick and hot with guilt and remembering. Dad lifted his eyes to mine, and sorrow seared across the room, my father unable to hold in his feelings. It hit me like a truck, making me stagger. I steadied myself on the white granite countertop and pressed my palms against it, my head hanging heavy.

It was like it happened yesterday, an hour ago, a second. The memory of losing my brother flooded over me like a wave, tearing at my lungs and heart. It was challenging to breathe. Dad reined in his emotions, and the grief that remained was my own.

My brother had been sixteen, his powers already full and lush, ripening into something incredible. Everyone marveled at his strength. As the eldest son, his Fae blood strummed through him heavily, demanding he push the boundaries of his magic. One day, he pushed too hard.

We'd been playing on the beach unsupervised. We were old enough to be alone. I was twelve, and Simmi was a year younger. We were poking around in a cave, the one our parents warned us to avoid. The tides came in quickly, and it would be easy to become trapped inside. None of us listened, of course. We had the arrogance of youth and too much confidence in our Mers blood. The ocean didn't frighten us. It should have.

The tide was low, and in the back of the cave, going in further than ever before, I'd found a deep vertical chasm. It was a well of sorts. I peered over the edge, throwing in sand and small rocks to see how far it went down. It was wide, and I lay down on my belly, the black depth of it giving me vertigo.

My brother, Leif, lay next to me and said he wanted to go in. Simmi begged him not to. I did the opposite and egged him on, daring him to see if he could touch the bottom. He hesitated. I said if he brought me a handful of sand, I'd give him my treasured necklace, my Hai Matau, knowing he'd always coveted it. Leif eyed the pendant that hung from my neck on a leather cord. A friend of our father's had gifted it to me at birth. So far, I'd never taken it off.

My Hai Matau was a protective talisman representing strength, prosperity, and good luck, especially ensuring safe travel over water. It ensured I'd be strong-willed and determined, always enjoying vitality and abundance. Carvers shaped the dark green jade into a whale's tail, an orca, which gave it the additional power of the intelligent, graceful creatures who roamed the oceans.

Leif's face flashed with naked want as he weighed the dare. He was otherworldly to me in the way only big brothers could be, an insurmountable force of nature, invincible, incredible. He grinned at me, his blue eyes excited and mischievous. We shook on it—a handful of sand for my necklace. Simmi had wailed that Dad was going to kill him if he went down there, and I'd hushed her, telling her to keep her mouth shut.

I wanted to see if he could do it. Simmi, whimpering, lay beside me, the sharp coral poking our tender bellies as Leif slowly descended, his arms and legs splayed wide like a starfish. He'd looked up at one point, winking at Simmi, telling her not to cry. He went down and down and down until we couldn't see him anymore. We called for him, our voices bouncing back to us unanswered. The tide tickled our feet. We screamed for him. The water found our mouths, making us cough and gasp. So much time had passed. We couldn't wait any longer.

I grabbed Simmi, pulling her through the surge, timing our race to the entrance with the push of the waves. When I glanced back, terror gripped my heart as water rushed into the well. I urged Simmi to hurry, saying she needed to stop crying, swim, run, and keep up with me. She'd yelled that I was stupid, it was my fault, and that Leif was going to drown.

I remember shaking my head and laughing at her worry. It's Leif, I said with such confidence. He won't drown. She broke away from me when we finally reached the mouth of the cave, sprinting up the stone steps as fast as her spry legs could take her, screaming for our parents. I sat on the beach, waiting for Leif to appear with sand dripping from his fingers and smugly demand my necklace.

He never did.

Every day for weeks, my parents would return to the cave. Mom changed to her Mers form at high tide, using a transformation potion that caused excruciating pain, swimming to the bottom of the well. She would return exhausted, cut from the sharp walls, her eyes red from crying, her voice gone from calling.

They told me never to return to that cave, but I didn't listen. I had to get him back. My Fae blood allowed me to change to my tail at will. I swam down in that cursed hole, grabbing fistfuls of sand at the bottom. I screamed for Leif, begging him to come back, thinking he would miraculously appear, scruff up my hair, and tell me to stop being such a baby. I pleaded to every God and Goddess as I yelled his name. It was all I did for months. I went back long after my parents had resigned themselves to the loss.

It broke me.

When he'd disappeared, I'd put the Hai Matau in a box and hidden it in my closet, vowing never to wear it again. I didn't deserve its gifts; not worthy of a rich life with love and light and ease. I withdrew from the world and isolated myself, my hobbies turning hazardous. I punched holes in the hulls of commercial fishing vessels under the cover of night, knowing if they caught me, they'd kill me. I wrestled sharks, swam too deep to cut nets, and alienated myself from all reason. Some said I had a death wish. It terrified my parents, but I couldn't stop. In my mind, I was trying to make amends.

"Mako, have you told her about Leif?" my father asked softly, shaking me from my grim thoughts.

"Jelly? No. I haven't said anything."

"Why not? It might help her understand why we're so desperate."

My heart pinched painfully. I was already in love with her, with everything she was, but I wasn't worthy of her. We'd gone too far with the healing kisses, the power of them electrifying me. I couldn't stop myself from craving her, wanting her so badly I'd sell my soul. I shook my head. If I told her my dark shame, she'd see a murderer. I killed my brother over a bet. For sand. After everything she'd been through, she deserved someone better than me.

Dad looked down at my mother's ash-blonde head, stroking the top of it with his big hand. His deep voice was tender. "Have you been intimate with her? Does she trust you?"

I murmured, "A couple of restorative kisses. That's all. Dad, it hasn't exactly come up. It's not like I can say, hey, there's this tragedy in my family; lemme juice up that power of yours so you can find my lost sister faster."

Mom sobbed at my words.

"Don't be an asshole, Mako," he growled. I hung my head.

Mom wiped her nose on Dad's shirt and whispered, "You should be with her, Mako. She'll be stronger."

"Use her, you mean." I scowled. "Just like everyone else in her life."

Dad's following words slayed me. "Well, if you won't boost her power, maybe a Shifter will. Or maybe Gray. He seems quite taken with her, and she responds to him." He kissed Mom's hair softly and held her tighter while steadying his gaze on me. His eyes overflowed with grief. He said brokenly, "We have to get your sister back, Mako. We have to. By whatever means necessary."

"So you're saying I should seduce her for personal gain, or someone else will?"

Mom shook her head. "It's not like that. You'd be helping her. You two have a connection. Just…just build on it. But do it quickly."

Dad kissed my mother's cheek and settled her on a stool. He crossed to me and pulled me into his arms. Initially, I was stiff, his words still stinging. He sighed, "Son, forgive yourself for what happened to Leif." He drew back, holding me by the shoulders so I would meet his eyes. "It. Is. Not. Your. Fault." He tugged me in again. "You are a good man, Mako Fields. You are honorable, kind, and loyal. What happened so many years ago has no bearing on your worth. Have we ever given you a reason to think we hold you responsible?"

I shook my head, biting back tears. My voice was soft and shaky. "No. If anything, you've given me too much leeway. I've been reckless with my life."

Dad cupped my face with his massive hand. I leaned into it like a child. He said through tears, "Mako, you care for Jelly. We all see it. Tell her what happened. She'll understand. She might even surprise you."

He patted my cheek softly. "Mako, you are worthy of love. Even if you don't believe it."

TWENTY-SIX

JELLY

I opened my eyes and waited, then waited some more, pacing, willing the pearl to react or hum or indicate that Simmi had received my message. "I don't think it worked," I said desolately.

"It was worth a try," Mori whispered. Her face turned as Roan entered the room, stepping across the dark red rug, embroidered with birds and trees, in gold and cream-white threads. He settled into a forest green chair, large enough to accommodate his thick body. He closed his eyes, appearing to meditate. I couldn't quite read Mori's expression as she watched him.

I rested my head on my fingers. *Why are you looking at him like that?*

Like what? I'm not looking.

You are. You're staring. Like you're hungry. Do you have the hots for him?

She tipped her head to the side. *I'm sorry, did you not see him? He's covered in tattoos, has pierced nipples and scars, and from what I could gather from those tiny shorts, he's seriously packing.*

I huffed a laugh. *What about his personality?*

What about it?

He's growly.

Oh, he's not that bad. He was sweet with you. Out by the tree.

I snorted. *That was a one-off. He's like a hungry bear just waking up after winter. He's all anger and snarl and grrrrr.*

She shrugged. *I like it. I think it's hot. But it doesn't matter, anyway. Now that I've found my power dot, I can take care of myself.*

I giggled. *I'll bet it's not the same as being with someone. There's no power share. If Mako touched mine, my head would pop off. His kisses almost take me to my knees as it is.*

She grinned at me excitedly. *Did you find it?*

I coughed. *Did I ever. It was insane.*

Mori purred in her throat. *I think you're right about the power share. Now I have to sleep with one of these guys. Maybe a witch would be game… Goddess… His hands are huge. You know what that means, right?* She waggled her eyebrows at me. I shook my head with a smile.

Mori snickered and jerked her chin toward Roan. *Look at him. You're not looking! Look! He's snarling to himself and flexing his muscles and twitching like a wound-up spring. His arms are so thick. His legs too. I wonder how sensitive those barbells are, like, do they give him an electric shock or something? I'd tug them with my teeth. Then I'd lick them… Seriously, look at his body. He's massive. He would throw me around like a rag doll. I would let him.* She moaned softly under her breath. *I would beg him.*

Roan's head snapped toward us, green eyes blazing as though he were about to shoot lasers. I cringed and bit my lip, glancing at Mori with a scrunched face, my cheeks heating ferociously. I projected across the room. *Yeah, um, Roan, you didn't catch any of that, did you?*

His lip curled up, and he tipped his head to the side, his eyes blindingly bright as he stared at Mori. She squeaked, "SHIT! I forgot he could do that!" She glanced around the room, looking anywhere else but at him. Roan chuckled from his chair and closed his eyes again.

Mori sank into her wingback as deeply as she could, glaring at me for starting the conversation. Her eyes burned into me before she jerked her head for me to follow her. She curled onto the sofa, far away from Roan. Her eyes flashed as she looked at him.

Roan cleared his throat, eyes still closed, and said loudly and gruffly across the room, "Shouldn't tangle with bears, lass. They're unpredictable and surly."

Anna turned to Roan. "Sorry? What was that?" She gestured to her husband, "Richard, darling, will you pass me that highlighter, please?"

Richard levitated the pen toward Anna and piped, "Did you know that an adult grizzly bear weighs seven hundred pounds? Massive beasts." He tapped his fingers on his lips. "I read about a rotund bear named Fat Otis…was he a black bear or a brown bear? Anyway, he ate forty-two salmon in one day, thus earning his nickname. Forty-two! Can you imagine eating that much fish?"

Roan cracked open his eyes and stared at Mori, his tongue stroking his lower lip before he said in a slow, deep voice, "Aye. Bears love to eat fish." She wiggled in her seat, her eyes intense and staring back.

Richard, oblivious, continued. "Indeed. They're omnivores, but prefer fish if given the choice. They could eat it all day. Brown bear! Yes, I'm quite sure Otis is a brown bear."

Roan's eyes narrowed on Mori as he slowly rubbed a hand across his chin. "All day, ye say?"

"Oh, quite," quipped Richard. "Fat Otis ate roughly a hundred and fifty *thousand* calories' worth of salmon. That's a gluttonous amount of fish. He must have been positively *gorging* on it!"

Roan leaned forward, elbows on his knees, his eyes burning holes into Mori. She squirmed and gasped and groaned under the heat of his stare. She fanned her face when Roan growled softly in his throat, his eyes never leaving hers. I watched breathlessly, dying with laughter inside.

Richard frowned and shook his head. "They're remarkable creatures, bears, but quite terrifying if found in a mood."

"Aye," Roan agreed with a short laugh. "That'd be a truth."

Anna looked up from her papers. "Why are we talking about bears?"

Mori exhaled loudly beside me and covered her face with her hands.

Richard looked at her and blinked. "I'm not quite sure how it came up."

Roan's phone pinged, and he went from flirtatious to serious in a heartbeat. His voice was gruff and all business. "Branko is on his way. He'll be here soon. Flyin' in from London."

"Is there an airport near here?" I asked, grateful for the distraction, as Mori's body was hot and sticky with sweat. She couldn't take much more. "I thought we were in the woods."

He grinned. "He's not flying like that."

Roan continued to steal sneaky glances at Mori. She was just as wily with her eyes. When their furtive gazes connected, they either held them too long or coughed and turned away. She lifted her fingers to her temples several times and dropped her hand in frustration.

Gray returned and reported. "Jacob is unavailable, but he put me in touch with Simon, the Wolf Shifter."

Roan's eyebrows shot up. "The Drifter? That'd be a score."

Gray nodded, smiling smugly. "The very one." He turned to Anna. "Mum, he's currently in Russia. He's at the Mushaner Lake in the Mariy Chodra National Park. Can you collect him? He's ready whenever you are. We caught him on a rare break, and he has no immediate plans."

Anna shuffled her papers and stood. "Of course. What does he look like?"

"Like an endurance runner. Rangy, a little over six feet, scruffy, long blond hair. Last time I saw him, he had a goatee. He'll be waiting for you. I told him to watch for an attractive woman who emerges from thin air."

She laughed and kissed his cheek. "I'll be back shortly." With a flash of light, she disappeared.

Gray sat down in the chair beside the sofa and reached out his hand toward me. I steadied myself, ready to see if I lost my senses. He stroked his thumb across the back of my hand, melting me. "So, Jelly, we have our Shifters." I clenched my jaw, fighting his allure.

He slid closer and kissed my hand, watching my reaction. His lips caused a burn to travel up my arm. Dark chocolate eyes, with a splash of gold, danced as he held his lips in place, breathing warmly over my skin. The burn moved toward my chest, making my heart patter. I was breathless, inflamed, and the pearl shuddered in my throat, snapping me out of my stupor. I drew back, but he squeezed tighter, the gold in his eyes flaring. Flames licked at my will, daring me to succumb.

Anna's sudden arrival shattered the moment. Startled, I yanked my hand from Gray's and leaped to my feet, my heart pounding as I grabbed for my knives. The stranger beside her crouched down to catch his balance, his fingertips splayed on the carpet. He stood, and, like a dog from a swim, shook himself hard. He raised his hand to the room, waggling it. "Wow, that's a trip! Hi everyone," he said cheerfully, "I'm Simon."

His long, light hair tied up in a bun, strands falling around his face as if windswept. Given he'd just transported, he looked remarkably unruffled. He dressed in olive green, both his jacket and his pants, and his sturdy boots were thick with mud. Burrs were stuck in the laces. Light blue eyes swiftly scanned the room as he set down a massive backpack. He toed off his boots and laughed. "Roan! I haven't seen you in years!"

Roan met Simon halfway, and they hugged, thumping each other like men do. Roan growled, "Thank ye for coming, Drifter. I can't believe our luck that you were free. Not to mention willing."

Simon grinned. "Gray said we're doing a mermaid. That's a first for me. And we need seven Surfecti? That's a hell of a lot of thrusting."

"What?" Mori screeched.

I yelled, "Excuse me?"

"With magic, lass," Roan chuckled. "The correct term is thrusting magic at ye." He grinned at Simon and jerked his head in our direction. "They're a wee touchy with the word thrusting. These are the mermaids, Jelly and Mori." His eyes lingered on Mori as he rolled her name in a rich baritone.

Simon shook our hands firmly. "I'm Simon. Good to meet you. So there's a story if a single word sets you off. Care to share? But before you do, can I have one of those?" He eyed Mori's cappuccino with envy. "I've been straining my coffee grounds for weeks." He grinned. "You shouldn't have to chew your coffee."

I smiled at his friendly ease and volunteered. "I'll get you one. I could use another after the morning I've had. Do you want a cappuccino or something else?"

"Black coffee is fine. Thanks, Jelly. Appreciate it." He and

Roan strolled to the fire to catch up, and I turned for the kitchen. Gray stroked my back as he passed me, heading for the foyer. My spine arched at his light touch and a soft moan escaped my throat. Mori shot me a worried look, waving me back to the sofa.

She hauled me down to whisper right in my ear. "Gray is definitely using magic on you."

"You saw that?" I hissed. "See what I'm saying?"

"What he's doing is past giggly. That was downright jiggy." Her eyes darted over my head to watch Gray. I turned, seeing him pacing, phone to his ear while he shoved his fingers through his hair.

"Why would he do that?"

She frowned. "Not sure. But I don't like it. Avoid him."

I nodded. "Copy that. Run interference."

"That's turning into a common theme with you, girlfish."

I waved a hand down my body with a grin. "What can I say? I'm special. Okay, let me get Simon his coffee. Want one?"

"No," she laughed. "I learned my lesson. Two is my limit." She returned to her sketching, the outline of one of Roan's roses perfectly drawn from memory.

I mindlessly pushed through the kitchen door and stopped dead as the eyes of the Fields family swung to me. Sophia's were bloodshot and bleary. She wiped her nose with the heel of her hand and looked at Sebastian silently. He stepped back from his son, awkwardly sliding his hands in his pockets. Mako glanced at me and dropped his eyes to stare at his hands, the knuckles white as he gripped the countertop.

I stammered, "Oh, I'm sorry. Didn't mean to interrupt. I was just getting more coffee."

Sebastian's voice was smooth, the antithesis of the energy in the room. "We were just leaving." He looked pointedly at

Mako and guided Sophia away into the dining room to avoid me. The wooden door moved on its double-action hinges, swinging slowly until it stopped.

"I didn't think when I said that about Simmi," I rushed. I clutched my mug to my chest defensively, as if needing a shield.

"Can you sit for a minute? I have something I need to tell you."

"Can I ask questions along the way? Or do you need to get it all out in one go?" Mako lifted eyes so full of tortuous sorrow that I nodded and whispered, "Oh. One go then." I pulled out a stool, facing him with my full attention. He dropped onto the one opposite me.

He took a deep breath and exhaled. "I'm worried this will change how you feel about me. How you treat me."

"Mako, you've been so supportive. You deserve the same. I'm ready. Tell me what's troubling you." Despite my vow to avoid men and their complications, Mako had been a friend to me. A friend whose kisses curled my toes.

He spoke in a soft voice, staring at his hands, as if he couldn't bear to see my reaction as he unburdened his heart. It was worse than I could have imagined. My heart raced and thumped, and I ached for his family. I stayed quiet, biting my cheek, blood turning my mouth metallic. I swallowed the tears I saw in his eyes, the torment he carried in his soul.

I wanted to tell him it wasn't his fault, that he'd been a child. It was an accident, and Leif had been reckless. I held the platitudes on my tongue, firmly clutched behind my teeth.

"My parents told me to seduce you." He whispered brokenly, shaking his head. "I said I wouldn't manipulate you like that."

Fleetingly, betrayal lashed my heart, but understanding took its place. It made sense to increase my power by any means.

He met my eyes and said, "Do you see why they're so desperate? My mother won't survive if Simmi dies."

I slid from my stool and stepped close to his body. He stayed like a stone until I nudged his legs apart to step in and wrap him in a hug. His arms rose to hang limply around my hips. I held him silently, absorbing the shudders that wracked his body. His breath shortened as he struggled to master his emotions.

The door swung open, and I protectively crushed Mako to my chest, sheltering him from the intruder. Gray paused before murmuring, "Simon said you were fetching him a coffee." When I didn't move, he muttered, "Right, I'll make him one. Did he say how he takes it?"

"Black," I said hoarsely, my larynx strained from holding unspoken words and tears. Gray looked at us and frowned.

"Everything all right, mate?" Gray asked lightly. I shot him an incredulous look. His eyebrows raised at my expression, and his lips mashed into a tight line as he pushed the espresso machine button, flicking on the kettle to make an Americano.

Mako's voice muffled in my sweater. "I told her about Leif." Mako squeezed my waist and let go. I reluctantly returned to my stool, waiting for him to remove his hands from his face.

"Oh," Gray said quietly, his face pained. "Won't be a moment." He stared at the kettle as if willing it to boil. Finally, when it chimed with a ding, Mako exhaled. Gray made the coffee and moved toward us. I tensed, waiting for his touch, but Gray passed me by, pausing behind his friend and squeezing his shoulder firmly. Mako nodded. The door whomped on its hinges, slowly settling.

Mako cleared his throat. "Simon's here?" He blinked his lashes and opened his eyes, his breath hitching at my concerned expression. "Then you're doing it. You're doing the ritual."

"Don't change the subject. What can I do to help you?"

He shook his head sadly. "Nothing. I have to live with what I've done. I wanted you to understand why my parents are so terrified." He looked up at the ceiling.

I chewed on my lip, deciding. "Then we'll have sex. Transactional. Business."

Mako let out a strangled noise and shook his head. "No. I'm not doing that to you. Not forced, never coerced."

I snorted. "It's not forced if I agree. Just last night, you told me there was a difference between being used versus someone offering it. You can increase my power, Mako, so let's do it. Come on. We can go now and get it done."

His cobalt eyes fixed on mine. "The Trident used you as a tool. I won't manipulate you like that. I will always give you a choice."

My jaw clenched as my heart beat heavily, overwhelmed by his respect and concern. "I'm making my choice. Mako, strengthen me. It's a good idea. We should do it."

He took a deep breath. "That's the thing, Jelly. We already need seven Surfecti to match your power. Increasing it now could backfire." He studied my face, watching me gnaw my lips. He gently tugged my lip from my teeth. "You're scared. I can sense it. I hate to say it, but you should be." He stood and held out his hand. "Come on. Let's go back in. We need to hear what they're saying."

"Mako." My voice was stern, giving him the opportunity to change his mind. I would do it. It was hardly a burden.

"Jelly," he replied in an equally austere voice. I sighed and relented, taking his fingers in mine. He squeezed, brushing his lips softly against mine. "Let's go, savage queen."

Simon whistled when we entered the room. "*You're* the Queen of the Goo Lagoon? Yeah, I can see it now. Beautiful turquoise eyes." He shook his head and laughed. "That was some crazy magic! What made you lose your shit?"

"Plastic."

He nodded as if the word explained everything. He turned to Roan and asked, "So, who else is coming?"

Mako and I sat on the sofa, sharing it with Mori. Just then, a great thump rattled the ancient windows in their casings. I stiffened from a deep shout outside, the voice thick with scorn and frustration. "Zmrd! Blasted English rain! I'm drenched!"

"And that," Roan chuckled, "Will be Branko. He's our seventh."

He strode for the front door to greet the newcomer. I grinned at hearing more slapping and pounding of backs. Roan entered with another enormous man. He was over six and a half feet tall, without a fleck of hair on his body. His head was as smooth as his chin, no eyebrows or lashes. He yanked off his sodden jacket and shirt, hanging them on the bench by the fire. He was sleek on his chest and arms.

He unbuttoned his pants, and Mori sucked in her breath as he slid them down his tree-trunk thighs. Her hand flew to her temple. *I like this one. I like this one very much. He looks like stiff silk, with emphasis on the stiff. He's like marble.*

Roan's head whipped toward her. "Ooh," I giggled. "You poked the bear."

She followed my eyes and threw her head back with laughter. She snickered, "I keep forgetting he can hear us! Ah well. It was fun while it lasted."

"Nah. Look at that face. He still wants to eat fish," I whispered. Roan looked up at the ceiling, pinching the bridge of his nose.

I set my mug on the table to meet the stranger standing in his shorts by the fire. He looked at my outstretched hand, frowning. I stood my ground, my eyes flashing impatiently. His fingers grazed mine after a rude amount of hesitation. He dropped his hand briskly as if burned. If anyone burned, it was me. His skin was glacial and stung. I fisted my hand, keeping my face composed. He noticed, and his lips contorted into a frame of a smile.

He said thickly, "My skin hurts, but you're stubborn. Open your hand." He scrutinized my palm, the chill of his skin skating over me. "There is no frostbite." I re-clamped my hand for the warmth. He tipped his head at me. "So, you're the mermaid we're thrusting."

"I really wish you all would stop saying that," I scowled. "Find a different word."

Simon cocked his head at me. "You were going to explain why the word so repulses you. It's not like we're having group sex."

Mori's voice breathed huskily through my mind. *For the official record, I'm not opposed to that. Not even a little.*

I bit my lip to stop my laugh when Roan muttered, "Fer fookin' fook's sake."

Simon waited expectantly, unaware of our silent drama. I said, "Thrusting. Right. Well. How familiar are you with the Mers?"

Simon shrugged a shoulder. "Not much."

I explained the Procreation Missions succinctly; that the Trident forced mermaids to sleep with strangers in order for us to survive. Simon drew back, horrified, and told me as much with his reaction. Branko's face became increasingly stern, and I thought I'd offended him somehow. He leaned in close, the coldness of his skin grazing my cheek like frost. His breath was like ice. "My mother had a similar experience. I am sorry for your burden."

"Branko…" I started.

He cut me off. "No, there is no more to say about that." He looked at me with compassion. Then his face hardened and his eyes went stony. He turned to Gray. "Tell us your plans for the saturation ritual."

I deeply appreciated his new word selection and reclaimed my seat by Mori. Richard held up a finger. "Before you start, son, the storm outside will be at its height at half-past one this afternoon."

Anna nodded, looking at her watch. "We have a few hours. Gray, tell us what to expect. Leave nothing out."

Mori and I held hands while Gray spoke. Mako had the other firmly in his grip, and he stroked slowly back and forth across the top, as one does when soothing a frightened animal. My stomach clenched in knots, my throat parched, and my heart pounded with panic. I could die. If I reacted badly, I could kill one of these men. I might kill them all.

Painfully clearing my throat, I whispered, "I need to talk to Synchi." I wanted to see her face again, in case it was the last time I would.

TWENTY-SEVEN

I must have moaned in my sleep or pulled at my restraints. I was dreaming. Someone was contacting me. I couldn't see them or make out the words. Like an energy, I could sense the desperation urging me to understand.

A cantankerous voice woke me. "Girl, snap out of it! You're upsetting the flies!" I blinked awake, and Esmerelda scowled at me. "You're wiggling around so much they've all taken to the ceiling. They were heading my way, and now you've upset their flight paths." I looked up and saw dark spots clinging to the symbols.

She sucked against her jaw and sighed. "Win some, lose some. What's got you in such a lather? What were you dreaming about?"

"Sorry about ruining your breakfast. I'm not sure. Someone just rampaged through my mind like a bulldozer, but I couldn't get the message."

The spider crept down her web and waved a striped arm at her head. "Like a psychic message?"

"I guess. I'm not sure."

Esmerelda strummed two legs against her chin. "I can help you access it. It hurts, though."

"How much?"

She shrugged. "Given that you're so depleted, it might not hurt at all. Or it could burn like the devil. I can't say, but my venom can open up your mind. The message still hangs in the ether. If we hurry, we can get it." My eyebrows drew down. She said nonchalantly, "All spiders can do it. We are mythical creatures, terribly misunderstood. It won't kill you, even as weak as you are. It will help you receive the message."

She raced to the bottom of her golden web, blinking her eight eyes simultaneously, waiting for my decision. I nodded. She was on me before I saw her move, sitting on my chest. Although she approached slowly, and I couldn't help but flinch. She whispered in her smoker's voice, "Don't be frightened, Simmi. I'm going to bite you on your temple," she skittered closer, "and then your mind will open."

I swallowed nervously. My bucket list didn't include a five-inch spider injecting her venom into my head. Her feet were delicate and tickled as she traipsed to my ear and hovered. "Just a little pinch," she rasped. There was a sting, then a burn that rapidly spread across my face. My breath quickened. "Close your eyes and see," she whispered.

I saw flashes of light, intense pulses of white mixed with gold. A noise like static filled my head. "Breathe and accept it," the spider called, sounding a hundred miles away. The fuzziness slowly cleared into an urgent voice.

Simmi? It's Jelly. I don't know if you can communicate telepathically, but if you hear this, I want you to picture my pearl. It's a black teardrop and hangs at my throat on a chain. Imagine tapping on it three times if you get this message. We are desperately trying to find you. We're coming. As soon as we see where you are, we're coming.

My eyes flew open. I looked over at Esmerelda and gasped,

"You did it! She told me to imagine her pearl and tap it three times!" My elation sagged. "How am I supposed to do that?" I hadn't worked on my Mers telepathy skills in years. After Leif died, Mako and I stopped doing it.

Esmerelda said, "Tell me what the pearl looks like." I described the pearl that Jelly always wore with as much detail as I could remember. The spider sat back on two legs, the other six working with furious speed. She crawled onto my cheek and held up a replica of the pearl. "This shape?"

"It needs more bulk at the bottom. And it's black."

Seconds later, Esmerelda held up her modification. She said, "I can't do anything about the color, but you can use your imagination. Is this better?"

"Yes, that looks good."

"Where does she wear it?"

"Her throat. It lies at the hollow of her throat."

The spider skittered across my skin, ignoring my grimace, and set it carefully into position. "Now, Simmi, focus. Can you feel the weight of this? I know it's light." I nodded. "Good. Picture it as black."

"Okay," I whispered, "I've got it."

"Don't be frightened," she murmured. She slammed a foot down on the replica three times. Light smashed through my mind, blinding me and searing my senses. I yelped and quickly bit my lip to stay quiet, tears squeezing from my eyes. She paused momentarily and said, "I'll do it once more for good measure."

Kindee screeched from the window a few seconds later. "Esmerelda! What are you doing? Clear this web immediately! Agh! Damn it! I can't get through! Miss Simmi! Miss Simmi! Is she eating you? Oh, dear God! Esmerelda!"

"Calm your feathers, Kindee. I'm helping her contact the

mermaid!" Esmerelda blew a breath across my throat, soothing the lingering stinging. "That will tell her you received her message. Be right back." She chuckled and looked at my straps. "Don't go anywhere." I rolled my eyes at her lame joke. She grumbled at the window. "All that work and not a single fly or a cockroach."

She cleared her web in a fraction of the time it had taken to build it. Kindee glared at her and flew to my chest, swaying as he landed with a bump. "Are you hurt? What did she do?" He looked over his shoulder and yelled. "Why is there a lump of webbing at her throat, and why is her temple red and swollen?"

Esmerelda ran back over, sitting on my chest with two legs under her. Two others bent and pressed against the lower half of her body as if she had her hands on her hips. Three more waved aimlessly, while the last one jabbed in the bird's direction. "The mermaid sent a psychic message, which Simmi couldn't quite grasp. I merely helped her recover it and let the mermaid know she received it."

She looked at me and winked with five of her eyes. The other three remained on Kindee. She grinned through a husky cough. "Hate to say it, but the Fae is right. Your blood is delicious." Kindee squawked indignantly, and the spider chuckled darkly. "You're far too easy to ruffle, bird. Now, the question is. How do we get a message back to her?"

I wracked my brain before my eyes lit up. "Kindee, come closer, right on my throat. I need you to tap the fake pearl. I'll talk you through it."

He peered at me through worried black beads. "Are you sure? It hurt when Esmerelda hit it with her hollow little leg. My beak is far more robust."

"Do it before I have time to reconsider."

Under my instruction, he struck at the webbed pearl, and I hissed and clenched my fists through the pain and flashing lights. Esmerelda stayed near, gruffly telling me to be strong, five of her whiskered legs stroking my cheek, clearing away my tears.

TWENTY-EIGHT

JELLY

Anna, Mako, Mori, and I scrunched together around the mirror. When Synchi's face peered through, Mori's voice was anxious. "Shaman, how is Toto?"

Synchi frowned. "Jelly wasn't supposed to trouble you. He is recovering well, Mori. He told me that if I spoke to you, I was to instruct you not to worry. That is a command."

She sighed with relief. "Okay, thank you. Please give him a hug for me when you next see him."

Synchi's milky-blue eyes homed in on Mako. "I glimpsed you before. Who are you? I can tell you have Mers blood from the color of your eyes. They're like dark water."

"Mako Fields, Madam Shaman. My mother is Sophia. She sends her regards. My sister Simmi is the missing person."

"Mako! What a delight. Please say hello to Sophia. And I have every faith that Jelly will find your sister." She smiled. "She's tenacious." He tipped his head at her respectfully, glancing at me with a grin.

I said, "That's why we're calling Synchi. We have to do a... what do you call it?'

Mori and Anna answered simultaneously in blank tones, "A *Coactus Fusionem*."

Synchi spluttered, "A *Coactus Fusionem*! Are you insane?"

Mori shouted, "That's exactly what I said!"

Synchi peered into the mirror, lips turned down. "Jelly, what did you do to lead to this terrible suggestion?"

I made a noise of exasperation. "I had another vision. It was the voice again. He told me he was coming for the Mers. He threatened you and Tro, and Mori and Mako, and then Simmi. I saw things that are probably premonitions, and then he tried to tear out my heart."

Synchi paled. "But the pearl protected you?"

I nodded. "That's right. We were going to call you, and I tried telepathy, but we're too far apart. Then Goddess Kelbazi told me to hurry. Then the voice came back again, telling me 'tick tock' and I heard Simmi scream, so we did blood magic, a vision walk. Roan could see my first vision and tried to place Simmi… And he was there. The voice manifested into a body. But inside the vision."

Synchi asked, "In human form?"

I paused for breath, then dropped the bomb. "Synchi, he's Fae."

"FAE?" Synchi shrieked. "I knew it!"

I rushed, "He's using Simmi's blood to track the pearl and possess the sea creatures, and he wants to turn the Mers. He almost touched me… Goddess, there's so much to cover! Where do I start?"

"Shaman," Anna interrupted, "The Fae is Terrun."

Synchi drew back, aghast. "The Prince is on Earth?"

Anna nodded. "Yes. He plans to use the pearl to annihilate the humans."

Synchi was stunned silent. She pulled on her braid, her eyes moving back and forth as she weighed Anna's words. I read her like a book, and held in my chuckle, softly chiding, "Synchi, I can see what you're thinking. I thought it, too. It would solve all our problems if they were gone. I'll admit it; it's tempting."

Mori growled, "It doesn't make it right! We can't annihilate our way to peace or let him exterminate them. We'll be just like the humans if we take that approach. We're better than that." Synchi and I shared a wistful look. I snarled when Mori pinched my arm and snapped me out of it.

Anna chimed in, "Shaman, that's not all. He got the idea of possessing the Mers. Jelly and Roan said he skulked toward her in the vision walk, hoping to touch her. She flipped herself across the room to escape."

Synchi's eyes crinkled with pride. Then her wrinkles dropped. "Do you have at least seven men for the ritual? Are they strong enough?"

"Shaman, you surprise me," Anna quipped. "Yes, we have five Mages and two Shifters. There will be a storm overhead at thirteen-thirty Greenwich Mean Time."

"I will be ready," Synchi stated confidently. "Jelly, you must prepare. You must sit in silence and communicate with the pearl. Connect with it. As it stands, when you lose control, it takes over. You need to be in charge. I suggest you call Goddess Kelbazi and ask for her guidance."

She pushed her face close to the mirror, her voice steady. "Scyphozoa Vetula, you are the bravest Warrior mermaid to swim the seas. This ritual is painful, but you have survived pain before, and you have not let it harden your heart. That is your greatest strength. Do not lash back. I will be with you in spirit."

Without another word, the mirror glassed over. I reached for it, upset that I hadn't said a proper goodbye. I hadn't thanked her for my life or told her I loved her. What if I never had the chance? Anna said quietly, "Use this room. It holds great power. Mori? Mako? I appreciate you want to stay and help her, but you must leave Jelly alone. This is between her and the pearl."

I asked nervously, "What is?"

She looked at me with a tight mouth. She scuffed the chalk and put the mirror on the shelf. She hesitated before speaking. "Your life and the lives of the men. Their lives depend on you overpowering the pearl. You must wrangle control of it."

I bristled. The pearl only ever activated from anger and injustice. It was a champion of female wrath. I considered the pearl a friend, an ally of sorts. A violent and unpredictable one, but still.

Mori hugged me, said nothing, and followed Anna out of the room. Mako was at the door. I stopped him. "Mako, wait."

He dropped his hand from the doorknob and turned to me. He did his best to hide his apprehension but failed miserably as he crossed the room, worry in his eyes, his hands in fists at his sides. He said, "I'm trying to be strong, telling myself you can do this. I believe you'll be fine, but I'm not sure about the rest of us."

Scanning his eyes, I whispered, "I can take the pain, but I'm petrified I'll hurt someone. Especially you. I'm terrified I'll hurt you again." I choked. "Or worse."

He stroked my cheek with his thumb. "So brave. My savage, beautiful queen." Seconds later, his mouth was on mine, hungry and urgent. Both power and aching burned in my belly before sensuously sliding lower, demanding friction. I pulled his leg between mine, groaning at the spark that shot through me. The unfamiliar sensation of having entangled limbs made my lungs spasm. I couldn't catch my breath.

I arched my back, chasing the pulsing pressure, and my

fingers slid to his hips, pulling and grasping him closer. "Mako," I moaned, my desire loaded into the breathy sigh. He kissed me harder, driving into my mouth as the electricity between us became a frenzied storm. He poured in Fae magic, sizzling my nerves and popping my ears. I sent a wave of Mers back, the two of us desperate together.

I was a second away from tearing off our clothes. His kiss morphed, tender as he gently retrieved his energy. The fist in my hair slowly released, gliding reverently down my curves. He reached behind him, gathered my roaming, clutching fingers, and brought them to his lips, kissing the tips. The thick muscles of his thigh tensed as he reluctantly removed it from between my taut thighs.

I panted. The pearl thrummed.

He held my face in his warm hands and said firmly, "I believe in you." He turned and strode to the door, pausing briefly as he put his hand on the knob. When he looked back, I had my fingertips to my mouth, memorizing the feel of his lips. His eyes glowed as he spoke. "Find the magic of the pearl. It's Fae. It's there when we kiss. It wants to talk to you, Jelly. Open yourself to it. Find common ground." He bit his lip and said, "I disagree with Anna. I don't think it's about control at all. I think it's cooperation." With a nod, he pulled the door behind him.

The latch clicked shut. I yanked at the pieces of my scattered heart. Mako's kisses were addictive. I couldn't stop once we started. I shook myself roughly. I didn't have time to think about that. I lay down with no pillows, wanting the hard floor against my bones. I tuned into the pearl, seeking it in my blood. I closed my eyes and whispered, "Is there a way for you to talk to me? How about one pulse for yes and two for no? Does that work? We need to work together. We'll do better if we can communicate."

Nothing happened.

I sighed. In my mind, I called to the Goddess, asking for her guidance. Within seconds, her voice sounded, echoing around the room. "Open your eyessssss, Vetula Heir."

She hovered over my face, so close her snakes could have snatched my eye with a tongue. I rolled over so I could kneel. "Goddess Kelbazi, you honor me. Thank you for coming. We're doing a dark ritual where seven Surfecti will saturate me with their magic, heightening mine. The Shaman told me to consult you."

"Forced Fusssion, yessss. It will be painful. You will want to die."

I chewed on my lip. "So I've been told. Is there anything I can do? This is being done *to* me, and that makes me uncomfortable. I'm likely to fight back. Or the pearl will react. I don't want to hurt them. I told them my worries, but the Mages said to relax and just take it."

She hissed with laughter. "Jusssst take it. Sssso male. Yessss, I can help."

Her snakes swirled and snapped around her head. When I met her before, I recoiled. This time, I leaned in. Forked tongues lashed, and sharp teeth nipped, all over my face and neck, licking and tasting the pearl. They were in my hair and on my arms, their cool skin sliding on mine.

Kelbazi hissed, "It will take sssseven men to match your power. They will not hold back. Sssso, take it, yesss, take it all. Absssorb their magic. Make it your own."

Without warning, one of her snakes sank its fangs into my bottom lip. A fever sped through my body and I fell backward, banging my head on the unforgiving floor. The Goddess came with me, hovering over me, the snake's fangs still embedded.

"My venom will protect you on your journey."

"Journey? Where am I —" The words died in my mouth.

My pulse loosened and flooded my veins, throbbing painfully. It was as if I had too much blood and my body could barely contain it. Pulled through a riptide, a narrow rush dragged me under and away in a vision.

I woke to a strangely beautiful land. I held my breath in wonder. I watched an entire year pass through their seasons on fast forward; the trees bursting before retreating into themselves, the leaves swiftly falling, budding, and glistening before they crisped and fell again silently. Flowers bloomed and died as if sped up, and my skin was damp with rain, then snow, then dew.

Creatures walked past me, no, through me, and I realized I was a guest, a ghost, a visitor for a brief time. Within an inhale, I traveled to the ocean and plunged deep beneath. Monster whales with horns and wings swooped and dove through the dark blue water. Shimmering, pulsing fish swam in large schools, the colors otherworldly. I'd never seen such sea life, and my heart cried out to befriend them.

I settled on the sandy bottom next to a decorative reef, vibrant with glowing corals. The pearl hummed at my throat. I peered closer, seeing mussels, barnacles, and sea anemones. Baby blue crab, shrimp, and silver perch. Fish I recognized from home, yet different. I gravitated toward a particular shell, beckoning me like a favorite song.

It whispered through its gills. I saw its three-chambered heart pump colorless blood. *You have come home.*

A knowing pulsed in my blood. There were no words as an ache shattered my soul. The pearl sang through my tears. *Mother.*

I lay down on the sand, letting the pearl rest near the midnight black shell. It flew open, welcoming. I moved closer, my face pressed up against the reef, the sharp coral cutting into my cheek. I didn't mind. The pearl gently pulled on the chain and settled on its dark mother's breast, the shell settling closed around it.

I slipped to the back of my mind, giving them time together. Although I heard no words, their feelings thrummed through the water. Humbled to be a witness to their exchange, I knew the deep, pounding ache of missing someone so much it was like an unhealed gash, stinging and stretching every time you moved. They loved each other. Someone had stolen the pearl from its home.

Minutes or years passed until I stirred with Kelbazi's soft hiss. "It issss time. Wake, Sssscyphozoa."

I stretched. I glanced at the clock on the wall. Two hours had passed. I *felt* the pearl as if part of me. Curious, I whispered, "Can we talk to each other?" It gave a single strong pulse. My eyes flew wide. "One for yes, two for no?" Another single pulse, along with a tremor, as though it laughed. I sat up. In my mind, I asked, *Can you still hear me?* A single pulse.

I jumped to my feet, elated, invigorated, and ready for anything. *Have you ever done this ritual before?* Two beats at my throat. I leaned with my back to the wall. I lifted the pearl and whispered, "I'm sorry someone kidnapped you. I'll find a way to take you home." A wave of her gratitude washed over me.

The pearl gave three distinctive pulses, strong and intentional. I shook my head and said, "Three? We have a yes and a no. We haven't figured out three beats yet." Again, three clear, strong pulses. My heart fell to my toes, disappointed we were already failing in our communication.

Then I remembered and screamed. "Simmi!"

The pearl responded with one pulse. It heated with urgency. I ripped open the door, finding Mako with a lifted fist, about to knock. I grabbed him and kissed him hard and fast. He staggered back from the power that flooded him. I scrambled, sprinting for the stairs. He yelled, "Jelly! That's Fae magic! That vibration isn't Mers! Are you bonded to the pearl?"

"Hurry, come on! Simmi contacted me!" I flew down the steps two at a time and blasted into the living room at full speed. Sebastian and Sophia jumped in alarm. "Simmi got my message! It pulsed three times, which was my code for her and…Holy fuck, that hurts!"

I hissed as the pearl scorched me, yanking and jumping on the chain, spasming in some sort of pattern. Sebastian pounced on me. "Sit, Jelly. I'm going to hold the pearl." I perched on the edge of the seat, my knees bouncing, heart thumping. His large hand slipped around the pearl, his warm knuckles on my skin.

The pearl twitched and juddered. He shouted, "Mako, Morse Code!" He closed his eyes to concentrate, calling out a series of dots and dashes and spaces. There was a lengthy pause. Mako hastily scribbled on the back of Anna's notes, his eyes huge and hopeful. The pearl repeated the sequence once more, Mako nodding and confirming each beat.

Together, they yelled, "Bermuda!" The pearl trembled and fell silent. Thunder boomed overhead, reminding us the storm was almost upon us. Laughing with delight, Sebastian lifted me from my seat like a feather and twirled me, releasing me into Mako's excited embrace. He pulled his wife into his arms and kissed her soundly before making a whooping noise. Sophia laughed through her tears. Mako kissed me hard enough to make my heart stop, bending me back in a dip so deep I threw my arms around his neck.

Anna burst into the room. "You found Simmi?" I nodded, smiling. She shrieked joyfully and spun to slam her lips on Richard's. He responded with unrestrained surprise, his hands messing up her tidy bun. They broke apart, and Anna's face shone with relief and excitement. She pulled me in for a hug, startling me with its ferocity.

She whispered, "Thank you, Jelly. Thank you so much."

The others came running with our shrieks, elated by the news. There was so much thumping and slapping and hugging and laughing that I thought my soul would split open. Gray reached for me and I rotated, spinning away. I looked over my shoulder to catch his smirk. I pressed my fingers to my temples. *Simmi! We're coming!* Maybe she'd get the message, maybe not, but I wanted to share our joy.

Mori flung herself at me and cried, "I knew you could do it!"

I beamed at them all. "It was the pearl. I'm just here for the ride."

Anna's smile fell as her brow furrowed. "Does the pearl control you or…?" Her tone was hesitant, almost mistrustful.

There were two throbs at my throat. I grinned. "We're working together."

Lightning flashed, hitting the distant ground with an electric snap. Anna and Richard silently communicated, and Roan whispered to Branko, piling blankets in his arms. Anna's voice was sharp. "We still need to do the ritual. We can't defeat the Prince without it. We have to go. Right now. Hold hands."

I looked around the living room at the Surfecti. They stepped forward as one, fingers reaching for each other. A roaring growl of thunder swallowed my whisper as light flashed around us. The words faded from the air as we vanished. "Dear Goddess, protect us."

We landed on wet sand, and I fell forward on my hands and knees. The sky was black with thick clouds, and the air brutal with rain and wind, working together to steal our breath.

Anna took command. She nodded to her husband, her voice straining against the weather. She pointed to a stretch of the beach. "Richard, set up over there."

Anna turned and helped me to my feet. She tried to hide the fear in her eyes, but I read her expression and squeezed her trembling hands. I vowed, "No one dies today, Anna."

"Good," she said, looking at her husband's back. "Because I am terribly fond of them all, particularly him. Remember, your instinct will be to defend yourself. You must resist striking back."

I promised, "I won't hurt them. I swear I will turn it on myself if I lose control." She opened her mouth to say something, but bit it back with a sharp nod of her head. She spun away, barking orders at the men. I scanned for Mako, seeing him already watching me. He nodded, blew me a kiss, and turned away. I swallowed.

Mori, Sophia, and I waited near the water, huddled against the wind that lifted our hair and entwined it in tangles of red, ash, and blue. Every one of us had stripped down to our underwear except for Simon and Branko, who were fully and gloriously naked. They'd explained earlier that they would lose their clothes if they shifted, and didn't see the point in ruining their pants. Mori squeezed my hand, staring at the men. "If I weren't so damned scared, I'd be dragging my tongue off the sand."

Sophia snickered and wrapped her arm around the two of us for warmth. Being who she was, she tried to diffuse our nerves. She said, "I've been to Bermuda. With your mother, Jelly, when we were young. We did an exchange program with the Atlantic Mers."

Surprised, I turned to her. "She never told me that!"

Sophia nodded. "It's beautiful. The ocean is crystal clear.

There was no pollution at all. I wonder what it's like now. I hope the locals have maintained its beauty. Your mom particularly loved it, saying the water matched her coloring. She met a local by accident. He'd fallen off his boat and hit his head. I can't remember how she explained away her tail."

Anna called for our attention. It was time to begin. Mori grabbed me by the shoulders, her hazel eyes fierce, as was her voice. She gave me her battle cry. "Warrior Jelly! No one dies today!"

I slammed my fists to my chest, giving her the Warrior salute, and replied steadfastly. "I will not die, and I will not kill. Understood, Warrior Mori. Understood, loud and clear." We nodded to each other solemnly, forbidding our fear from shadowing our faces.

TWENTY-NINE

JELLY

Richard and Gray paced forward in measured steps. Branko and Simon repeated the movement, walking in the opposite direction. They shouted when they reached the edge, and Roan, Sebastian, and Mako filled the spaces between them.

With a twirl of her fingers, Mori gathered wet sand into a low wall around the men, her hands making sweeping, cupping motions. Thrilled to use her magic and take part, she squeezed the sand into a fifteen inch wall, nodding to Anna before returning to the water.

I shivered from a combination of nerves and cold. I whispered to the pearl. *Are you ready?* One solid pulse. The men gathered close to the circle's center, and the storm swept closer, the sky dark and menacing. Anna began chanting.

Mori said resolutely, "We're up. Let's go in."

We hissed as the icy waves hit our legs. Sophia kissed my cheek and took her position up to her knees in the water. Mori hovered at her side, refusing to show me anything but complete faith. I strode in far deeper, needing the pearl submerged.

I turned and stared at the men within the sand wall. I bit my cheek out of habit, the pain and taste of blood soothing. Anna pointed at me from the beach. I lifted my arms, raising my hands to the sky. I watched the Surfecti coax forward their power, the air around them shivering.

A ghost of a whisper floated through my head.

Be brave, Jelly.

Synchi.

My only task was to not retaliate. Kelbazi's words slid through my head. Take it all.

The rain came in freezing sheets. Lightning flashed, followed by a boom from the sky several seconds later. The hairs on my neck and arms pricked as electricity regathered overhead. The men chanted in a foreign language, their voices becoming louder, harsher, tumbling together in a resounding chorus, the deep sound battling the storm.

Anna threw her head back, calling to the tempest overhead. A shimmering ward dropped over the men, and seconds later, lightning struck Anna's dome and crackled with splintering flashes, racing over it to find Mori's wall. The bolt blasted the sand at fifty thousand degrees, melting it, and solidifying into a thick ring of dark glass. It would anchor and ground the shield, protecting the men…from me.

Magic from the dome charged the atmosphere and rushed me in a blast of heat under Anna's direction. Cold air hissed and steamed against my sweaty forehead, and the pearl jumped, convulsing on the chain. I panted, my muscles quivering. This was just the preparation. Magic connected me to the men, allowing them access to my body.

Mori and Sophia stepped deeper into the water, up to their hips, watching me. The wind howled, plastering their wet hair to their faces, but they stayed steady in the waves, waiting. I dug my toes deeper into the cold sand, savagely biting my cheek as my heart raced. The waves were up to my chin, periodically washing over my lips and churning with the storm's fury.

The Surfecti lined up beside each other, fierce determination on their faces. As one, they dropped into low crouches, thighs bracing as they raised their hands in my direction. Together, they repeated a word—MOKSHA. Their voices collided, challenging the thunder for dominance. Gray explained that 'moksha' forced the bare bones of one's self, the essence of the magic within each of them. They would weave their individual strands into a singular energy to thrust into me, exponentially increasing my power. The Surfecti would persevere until they collapsed or until my body received all it could. It was our only hope of facing the Fae Prince.

Their eyes glowed as they called forth their magic. Streams of colored light poured from their palms, dancing on the inside of the shield. Sebastian's Fae magic was an electric blue roar, zipping and darting and testing the space. Branko fired fiery red in thick pulses, while Simon's shot smooth, dark maroon, almost like a shadow that wandered around the shield. Gray's hands lit with wild orange flame, and Richard's magic was purple, thinner in consistency from the others, but no less potent as it slid into all the open spaces. Roan expelled rays of brilliant emerald green, sparking when it met the others.

My eyes settled and stayed on Mako. His magic was cobalt-blue, as deep and mesmerizing as his eyes. It flowed, moving like water as it twisted and skirted along the shield, flirting with the others. I studied his face, a vision of concentration.

They forced their magic into one mass, snarling as they dragged each strand together on the inside of the shield. Their muscles shook from holding the pressure, their faces pictures of pain, giving everything they had to the ritual. 'Moksha' warped and became a living thing as they snarled it. It twisted on their tongues, becoming more than a sound. It became a command. Their magic weaved into a spitting, writhing rainbow.

My arms trembled over my head, anticipation coursing through my blood. I whispered to the pearl. *Don't kill anyone.* To my dismay, it did not respond.

With a bellow of force, they shot it toward me like lightning. It struck my body, and the pearl responded with a retaliatory sonic boom, ripping a wave of sand against the shield. I keened in agony, screaming an unholy sound. My body shook from the pressure of taking their magic, which churned inside me, needing release. I struggled to direct it away from the men, blasting turquoise fire from my palms, igniting the clouds overhead.

The driving rain cleared the shield, and I forced myself to look, fear making my heart bleat. Three had fallen to their knees, their hands still outstretched and chanting the word, forcing the crazed rainbow further into my body. Their focused power targeted my throat, aiming for the pearl, and the pain of it choked me, wringing the life from me. Tears streamed from my eyes as I fought for breath, my fire still scorching the sky.

In my head, I screamed, *Hold on, hold on, hold on.* The pearl pulsed, waited, pulsed, waited. Yes, yes. My instinct was to grab my throat and pry away the invisible fingers, or attack the ones who wielded them. My vision blurred from the lack of oxygen and I wrestled with my compulsion to make my tormentors suffer.

The agony spread, blazing through my chest, causing my heart to clutch and stutter. My arms faltered and lashes of turquoise slammed into the shield. Strangled shouting and screams came from the beach. I forced myself to look, terrified of what I might see. Simon, Gray, and Richard were down. I couldn't see if they breathed.

Waves smashed against my face and my shoulders shook and burned. A strange creature roared. Branko had shifted. Red energy pulsed from his clawed hands in rapid bursts, as if he were giving me the last of what he had. Stuttering blasts of green came from Roan. The two blues remained steady. Sebastian and Mako.

Faces flashed through my mind. They were Fae, the memories of the pearl. The images slowed, and slowed, then stopped, hovering on a terrifying visage. Terrun. He screamed, his sharp fangs exposed, and venomous hatred dripped from simmering red eyes. The pearl howled at him through me, loathing thick in my throat, ripping the soft flesh of my larynx. Fire exploded from my hands, and the rigid muscles of my arms spasmed, sending unruly and wild turquoise magic across the sky. The pearl forced Terrun's face away, shaking and hissing in the water.

The energy beating inside me shifted. I sobbed and peeled my eyes open to see the creature and Roan on their hands and knees, heaving for breath. Only Mako and Sebastian remained standing. But it wasn't Sebastian, not precisely. He'd become a monstrous man with sharp ears. Mako was taller and broader, his lips drawn back in a grimace as both hands shook with cobalt-blue waves. His eyes flashed like a signal from across the water, telling me he was still with me.

Their magic evolved, weaving in sapphires and aquamarines, drawing blue from every corner of Nature's palette. Aszure, cerulean, and cornflower joined with navy, royal, and indigo, braiding and twisting together as father and son coordinated. Their magic felt different, peaceful almost, certainly more soothing as it swam through my body like music. The pearl yanked and vibrated, soaking and swimming in ecstasy. The rain eased, pattering on my face instead of slicing it.

My vision blanked out, turning iridescent black with shimmering turquoise and cream, like the delicate swirl of an oyster shell. I recognized it. It was the pearl's mother. Surely this meant it was over. I lowered my trembling arms, tears flowing down my cheeks as the blue magic still spun through my body. I tilted my chin up to the gentle rain and inhaled fully, expanding my aching ribs. Sweet Goddess, it was finally over.

I was wrong.

My exhale left with a tortured scream.

Turquoise fire burst from my eye sockets, shredding the clouds above me. Unable to raise my arms, I fisted my hands at my sides. My magic sizzled the surrounding water, the ocean reacting and roiling chaotically. Relentless pain spanned my back, like a whipping from a fever of stingrays, their barbs razing and cutting in slices. I shrieked as my skin blistered and split, the salt water biting as it met open flesh.

I clenched my teeth hard, popping my jaw. My nervous system jolted and seized. My legs slammed together, morphing themselves into a tail. It split back out, then together again, rapidly alternating, never completing one form. My magic was haywire. I swallowed water, alarmed, as I looked down at a caramel tail, then turquoise legs. Toes stuck out at odd angles, and knees formed backwards. My hips cracked and broke and fused again repeatedly.

I screamed and screamed and screamed. I withstood it for as long as I could, allowing myself to drown in the magic. My heart stuttered, my breath left. I shrilled to the pearl. *Make it stop!*

The pearl pulled away from my neck and stretched toward Mako and Sebastian. It vibrated and shuddered, threatening to split itself open as it boiled the surrounding water, collecting its energy. It thrust out a singular pulse of turquoise light, which struck the remains of the shield, shattering it. The noise of it drew my gaze to the men.

Their blue magic stopped immediately, as if the pearl had called a truce. They dropped heavily to their knees, Sebastian holding his face in his hands. I whimpered as Mako swooned and collapsed in a pile. My vision turned blurry. The pearl drifted down and settled at my throat, hissing and cooling in the water.

A wave washed over my face, and I choked on the sea, unable to keep my chin up. Although my back wailed from being shredded and raw, fatigue stole the pain. I looked down and saw four soft brown legs, the knees bending and plummeting me down. The last of my air escaped me as I hit the sand, vaguely wondering if I might drown in this form. I opened my eyes, wanting to see the ocean as I breathed in and ended my life. Instead, I found Sophia and Mori, worry etching their faces.

Mori's voice echoed through my battered mind. *We've got you.*

They hauled me to the surface, and I gasped and coughed as they wrapped their arms around me to drag me from the water. My back throbbed and shrilled with unyielding distress, as if the magic had flayed me alive. I lifted heavy eyes to the beach, but everything was foggy. I closed them again, my head rolling on a loose neck.

The rain and wind had moved on, the storm rumbling in the distance. My legs were utterly useless. My feet slid through cold sand into the waiting arms of Roan, who wrapped me gently in a blanket and dropped to his knees, cradling me. The soft fabric scraped like sandpaper on my skin, and I moaned weakly in protest.

His voice cracked as he growled, "Ye brave lass, och, ye did fookin' brilliant." He rocked me against his thick chest, careful to keep his arms around my shoulders and thighs, avoiding the mess of my back.

"Dead?" I croaked roughly. My throat would take days to heal from the screaming. I couldn't open my eyes.

"All alive, lass. Anna's transporting the ones ye knocked out. She'll be back to get us."

Rich magic flowed from a heavy hand on my neck, winding through my body and numbing me. Sebastian whispered in a rasp, "Well done, Jelly. That was extraordinary control." I shivered with relief as another hand fell on my bare thigh. It rubbed up and down to chase away the goosebumps. I recognized the magic.

Mako.

I forced my eyelids to crack open a slit, struggling to find focus. All I could see were his eyes, vibrant and sparking with shots of turquoise, scattering like stars against a cobalt sky. He held my face in shaking hands and kissed me softly, too quickly, before resting his forehead on mine. "You're the bravest person I know," he whispered, his throat hoarse. "That was phenomenal."

"We have to get her out of the cold," Sebastian murmured, his voice sounding distant in my head.

I shrieked as Roan gathered me close. "Sorry, lass. I know it hurts," he said tenderly. "Ye'll catch yer death out here." His voice dropped. "And that'll no do."

Mori spoke to me gently. *We're about to teleport to the house. Almost home.*

Home.

I'd only ever considered the reef my home. But now? Home was with these people, where I felt seen and trusted. When I hurt them, they quickly forgave me for my failings and moved on. Home. It was a feeling, not a place. As if in reply, the pearl throbbed once, a long, heavy beat.

I tried to speak, but my throat was too thick and ravaged for words, and I couldn't lift my fingers to my temple. My head lolled back, and I peeled open an eye to see an Anna-shaped blur. "No," I mumbled, but no one listened, and as light flashed around us, I howled with pain and passed out.

Lost in a fog, voices reached for me, pulling me out. I tried opening my eyes, but they refused. I went to move, and only a finger twitched from the effort. My mouth was dry, my lips cracked, and my throat too tight to swallow. I grunted, and even that seemed a spectacular feat. I drew my awareness into my body. Chilly air stroked my bare back, and a sheet gathered around my hips, covering my legs. Someone had tied my hair into a bundle, keeping it away from my sore skin.

"She's waking up." It was Gray who saw my trembling finger.

I winced as a clear and relieved voice rang through my head. *Jelly, don't move.*

"Mor?" I croaked.

Seriously, Jelly. Don't move. Lay still. Anna's healing your back.

I willed my eyes to open, and the gentle light by the bed was blinding. The pain in my back burst forward, and I gasped, my body seizing. I squeezed my eyes shut and coughed rawly. Mori held a stainless steel straw to my lips. "Drink, Jelly. Baby sips. It's a healing tonic."

I wet my mouth, swallowing painfully. Each sip eased the pain. I ran my trembling tongue over my lips so I could speak. "What happened?" I whispered. I tried to open my eyes but couldn't. "My eyes hurt."

Anna's soft voice grated against my ears. "You received an uncommon marking. I'm doing my best to remove the pain and heal your skin. It's not like Roan's. It's different. Very different." She called to her son, "Gray, wet a washcloth with cold water for her eyes."

Mori whispered in my head. *Your mark is circular, with two halves, like the yin-yang shape. They look like Mers tails, with fins flicking just outside the circle. On one side, the tail has multiple scales in dark navy, maybe black, with a silver new moon. The other tail has clouds on a blue background with a brilliant yellow sun. Jelly, it's stunning. But it's huge. It must have hurt like a bitch.*

I groaned, trying to move and make sense of what Mori had just said. Roan told me I'd get a small mark, a dot, smaller than his fork of lightning; not an elaborate symbol with individual scales and clouds and celestial bodies.

"A bit more. Be still," Anna said. Mori held the straw to my lips again. I drank more deeply, the liquid reviving me. Anna smoothed a balm over my skin, and I flinched from her light touch. A cool mist settled over my back, sinking in, and I shivered with relief. With a satisfied tone, she said, "That's good for now. It will keep working without me. And I have a healing tea for you, stronger than the elixir you've just had. Do you want to sit up? We'll help and keep your back from touching anything."

"Yeah," I said, my voice slightly stronger. I yelped when hands coordinated to shift me, but they carefully rolled me, moving me to perch hunched over. Someone bundled the sheet around my stomach, leaving my back uncovered. I crossed my legs and hissed as the skin on my back stretched. My eyes were too heavy to open, so bruised and sore.

Both Mako and Gray cleared their throats awkwardly, and Anna tsked and placed a pillow in front of me to cover my bare breasts. I rested against it while Mori pressed a freezing cloth against my closed eyes, tying a sash to hold it in place. Goddess, that felt good.

"What does it mean?" I asked, shivering. Gray grunted and snapped his fingers at the fireplace, causing the flames to rise higher. I assumed it was Gray, given his power over fire. I snuggled the pillow. Anna carefully sat at the foot of the bed so as not to jostle me. She led my hand to a mug, and I adjusted my pillow with a hitched breath. The tea immediately began repairing my vocal cords, warm and sweet with honey and lemon.

Anna said, "Your mark suggests balance and harmony of the land and sea, collected and centered into one being. It is unexpected, fantastical even. Usually, as you saw with Roan, it's a small, lashing tattoo. But yours…yours suggests much more. Your mark is a representation of all."

"All what?" I croaked.

"Just…all," she answered, awe in her voice. "I'm not entirely sure." She cleared her throat once and said solemnly, "You did well today, Jelly, far better than expected. I was ready for you, but you contained yourself and controlled the pearl admirably." I wanted to correct her assumption I'd wrangled the pearl, but didn't.

She patted my ankle and rose; her steps fading from the room. Mori gently pressed the cloth against my burning eyes while Mako combed his fingers through my tangles at my ears. She must have had her back to Gray, because she missed his approach as he drew near. He slowly stroked through the sheet from my knee up my thigh. I braced for the rush of sensual excitement that usually accompanied his touch, expecting it to be overwhelming. It did not come. Instead, the pearl hummed softly at my throat as if chuckling.

Gray suddenly burst out laughing, startling me with its deep resonance. "Finally!" he shouted. "Thank the Gods. I was so worried, Jelly. I can't tell you how relieved I am! You didn't feel a thing just now. Not even the smallest spark. No reaction at all, even though my hand's on your thigh."

I heard a slap, and the hand disappeared. I scowled and held out my drained mug. Someone took it. I untwisted the knot at the back of my head and rapidly blinked as my blurry vision focused on a euphoric Gray. He beamed like I'd hung the sun. I cleared my throat without pain. That tea was miraculous. Still, my voice came out in a growl. "What have you been doing to me?"

Mori shrieked and dropped the mug but stopped it from shattering with a shift of her foot. "Your eyes! Your eyes are different!"

She grabbed an antique silver mirror from the table and thrust it into my hand. I peered closely and saw a thin black ring around the outside of my eye. I gawked. "What does it mean? Is it evil?" The pearl pulsed twice, almost irritably, as if offended. I asked, *Did you do this? Is this you?*

It replied with a single pulse, solid and steady.

Gray rocked back on his heels, his head tipped to the sky as he grinned. Mako slipped his fingers into my knot of my hair, gently turning my face and peering into my eyes with wonder. He said, "It's Fae magic, Jelly. Black, like the pearl. She marked your eyes and your skin." He snickered at Gray over his shoulder. "She's stronger than you now. I knew she wouldn't break!"

I snarled, "What. Did. You. Do?"

Gray bowed deeply, almost piously, as he said, "Jelly, I have been testing you. Mers are exemplary with seduction, and yours is ridiculously strong. You're not even trying, yet every time you scowl, frown, or bite your lips in irritation…Every man in the room wants to take you to the floor."

I made a ridiculous noise with my lips, pursing them out.

Mako's eyes darkened, as did Gray's. Gray growled, "See, even that, when you're being a brat, it makes me want to…want to…"

Mori giggled beside me. "Screw the smirk off her face?" she finished helpfully.

Gray's eyebrows shot up before he laughed again. He said, "My Gods, you are refreshing. Yes, exactly that, Mori. Jelly, I needed to see how far I could push you. Your body thrummed for me as I expected, but…" his eyes slid over to Mako. "I wasn't the one you wanted."

Mako blinked, a faint blush on his cheeks as he avoided my eyes. He moved behind me to look at my back. His breath left with a rush. "Jelly…It's so beautiful…Now that Anna's healed it… It's so nuanced, so detailed." He pulled up a chair and leaned on the bed, resting his head on his folded arms. His eyes closed immediately. He'd fought his exhaustion until I woke up.

I kept my voice low, hissing at Gray, "You played me?"

His face grew serious. "Jelly, the Fae are masters at persuasion. I suspected that's who we'd be fighting, so I needed to ensure you could withstand their seduction. I used my magic to draw you to me, curious how strong you were and if you could resist me. But, in fact, you figured me out, didn't you? I noticed you avoiding my hug."

Mori and I nodded together, my eyes still narrowed with discontent. I tipped my chin toward Mako. "And his part?"

Gray's face shadowed as he shoved his hands in his pockets. "He hated the idea. We argued about it several times. After you saw the Fae in the blood magic and didn't succumb, I should have stopped. I didn't. I'm sorry, Jelly. It was manipulative and underhanded, and I apologize."

I looked at Gray, at his gorgeous brown eyes, no longer

sparkling with gold, to his smooth skin and sandy curls. He was wickedly handsome, but he was right. He wasn't the one I wanted. But I was furious at Mako for keeping this from me.

Gray saw the emotion in my face and said, "Jelly, I've never seen him like he is with you. I want to stress again. *He hated it.* He ran interference as much as he could, blocking me. But he also understood that we needed to flush out any cracks in your armor." I nodded to get him to drop the subject. But I was far from done with it.

Mori sat on the bed. She frowned. "At the end, there…It wasn't clear if you would be stuck with half a tail. Or blue legs or toes on your ass. Scared me to death."

I reached for her hand. "When my head went under, I was done. I was ready to go to the Goddess."

Mori nodded. "I swear your first boom shattered the stars. And your screams while you were marked… Sophia and I, we withstood your power because the Shaman protected us with her magic. We were there to fish you out when you went under. She figured you would. But the guys, even with that shield… your screams got through it and dropped them."

I gasped, "Synchi shouldn't have done that! She needs her magic for the bubble."

Mori said, "Anna said you wouldn't have survived without her. She had to do it."

Gray whispered, "We all gave you everything we had." I lifted my eyes to him as Mako breathed softly beside me. Gray said, "It hurt like nothing I've ever experienced. It was like getting an electrical burn. My whole body seized up, and I passed out."

"I'm sorry," I offered, but a slight grin escaped me at the twisted memory on his face. "But not really. Consider it payback."

He snorted, "And then some. At least my seduction felt good. I'm sorry I missed the best part: Sebastian and Mako's blue fire."

"It was...I can't describe it," I whispered. "It was... exquisite."

Mori's voice was reverent. "It was all the blues of the ocean, land, and sky together. It was everything together at once. Sebastian said the pearl drew on their Fae blood. He said it was like a deep bass sensation. Like it reverberated in his bones, and the pearl summoned it, demanded it."

"That's exactly it," murmured Mako. "It was...incredible. Like being plugged into the universe itself. I was the conduit, feeding you the higher magic. Dad's Fae form came out. I also experienced a shift. I didn't go full Fae, but I certainly changed during the ritual." He rubbed his round ear distractedly.

I whispered, "It felt good. The pearl loved it. And then came the pain from the marking." I stretched my arms around the pillow, testing my skin, finding myself healing faster than usual. "Can one of you check my back? I want to take a shower."

Mori hovered behind me, gently stroking my skin. "Totally healed up. Jelly, that's nuts. It was raw flesh an hour ago." Mako and Gray stayed rooted, staring at me in awe. "Guys, that's your cue to leave," laughed Mori.

I said, "Mako, can you stay a minute?"

Mori whispered, "Uh oh," as she dragged Gray out the door.

I cleared my throat. "I hate being played, Mako. I told you that. Gray was manipulating me, yet you said nothing."

He dragged his hand through his hair, looking exhausted. "We wanted to see how strong you were. We had to make sure you could withstand a Fae's seduction. Just in case."

"Again, not trusting me. Again, playing with me. Damn it,

Mako! I was like a lump of clay for him! He could have done anything to me!"

Mako cleared his throat. "Um. You're not really his type."

Now I was just outraged. "What is that supposed to mean?"

"Well, he'd rather kiss Simon than you."

I blinked and paused before shaking my head. "And us? Were our kisses real? Or maybe you were messing around and orchestrating my emotions with your Fae magic."

"Our kisses were real, Jelly. I swear it." His eyes closed as his shoulders sagged. "Gray did it to protect us, everyone, in case you needed extra support. It wouldn't have been a genuine test if you'd known what he was doing." He reached for me and I recoiled. His jaw clenched. "What? You forgive Gray so easily, but not me?"

I swallowed, my throat rough with emotion. "The night after the Eators, Gray was going to take me to my room. You interfered and stepped in. That was our first kiss. I grabbed at you and pulled you close when you offered to recharge me. I wanted to sleep with you. Was that supposed to be Gray?" I cocked my head, anger heating my chest. "What magic would Gray have given me? Should I stick my tongue down his throat and find out?"

Jealousy flashed in his eyes. "No."

"I feel like a chew toy! You played me!"

"Jelly, don't do this."

I barked, "I didn't!"

He reached out with his hands and took mine. I struggled at first, but his voice broke, stilling me. "I'm sorry. It was underhanded, and I hated it. I hated how you responded to his magic. You looked like he hung the moon when he touched you, and it drove me out of my mind. I wanted to give you something real. Jelly, what I feel for you is real. I swear it."

I swallowed and yanked my hands away, hating how his vulnerability made me feel soft. "I need some time alone to process all this."

Mako breathed heavily, his fists tight. He let them slowly relax as I studied him. He nodded curtly. "I'll give you some space." He turned for the door, wearing his regret as armor. I waited to move until the latch clicked behind him.

The pearl hummed gently at my neck, as though soothing me. I asked, *Does he speak the truth? He truly cares?*

One pulse.

I stood under the hot water and pushed Mako and Gray from my mind, trying to sense any changes from the ritual. There were whispers of new magic twirling within me. I reached for them, but they slipped away. Someday, I might wield these new powers if I could figure out how to control them. I wasn't Surfecti, but their magic was inside me.

I wiped the fog from the mirror and stared at the ring around my eyes. Then I turned and looked over my shoulder. The marking spanned my whole back. I flexed my muscles, watching the design ripple and shimmer. The pearl purred in approval at my throat—Land and Sea, sealed by Fae, or Fate.

THIRTY

JELLY

I climbed back on the bed in my bathrobe, nestling under the covers. The view from the window showed a freshly washed countryside, and oaks dotted the grounds, standing as sentinels. I closed my eyes to rest. Not long after, a sound by the door made me look.

Mori's face poked through. She nudged the door with her shoulder, carrying a small wooden tray. "I brought more tea. And a witch made oatmeal cookies." I fluffed my pillows and settled against the elegantly carved wood headboard. Ruefully, I noticed my quilt was plain, cream-colored, likely made by a machine. I patted the space next to me.

Mori settled the tray, careful not to spill the two mugs, and propped up against the headboard, handing me the plate before taking a cookie for herself. Crumbs dropped on her chest. She glanced at me, frowned, sipped her tea, chewed her cookie, drank more tea, and glanced at me until I couldn't bear it. I grinned. "Spit it out."

She went electric. "Everyone's speculating about what happened, why the magic marked you the way it did, and what it means. Seriously, they're tripping out. Everyone wants to see it. Do you still have that halter dress?" I nodded. "Good. Wear that because otherwise, you're going to be walking around topless. Everyone wants to study it. The Shifters included."

"Speaking of, what is Branko? I looked at the shield and saw a monster shooting red at me. It wasn't Simon because he passed out."

She took a big bite of cookie and chewed quickly to swallow it. "Branko is a gargoyle."

"A gargoyle? I thought they were stone statues that guarded churches."

"They are. But apparently, they're real, like flesh and blood real. Remember when you shook his hand? And you pulled it back as though you had an ice burn? He'd been flying in the rain in his stone form, so he hadn't warmed up when you touched him. Just now, I made the mistake of patting his bare shoulder, and my fingers got stuck. He's still defrosting. Gray had to throw heat on my hand to pry it off."

"But everyone is okay? The ones I knocked out?"

"You saw Gray and Mako already. Simon and Richard are fine. Anna brought them back as soon as you sank under the water. The witches tended to them straight away."

"Where are the witches? I haven't seen any of them."

Mori shrugged. "They only gather when needed or if it's a ceremonial day like Solstice."

I devoured the cookies, suddenly starving. "So, with all that magic…What am I? Am I more than just Mers?"

Mori shrugged. "That's what they're debating downstairs. They're all wondering if you can wield their magic." She tipped her head and studied me. "You seem off. Are you okay? Is it the aftereffects?"

I shook my head. "Betrayal."

Mori frowned. "What? Over what Gray did?" She dusted crumbs off her lap. The penny dropped when I stayed quiet. "Oh. It's that Mako went along with it. I get why that would upset you. But Jelly, he's been there for you. Truly. He's had your back."

I didn't respond, wanting to hold on to my hurt. Then I grumbled and scowled, sucking my teeth. She was right. After I'd thrown him against the wall, he'd been supportive. And if I had been aware of what Gray was doing, it would have muddied the test. I teased through my reaction, identifying if it was Mako who'd upset me or my history of feeling helpless and used.

Mori smiled, knowing me too well. "It's obvious you care for each other. He's always at your side when you're injured. You scan the room to find him. The way he kisses you…I'm not even involved, and my breath catches. Just enjoy what time you have with him. You won't have to see him again when this is done. We'll go home and he'll be a hot, steamy memory."

I swallowed thickly at the thought, bit my cheek, and snarled at the tears welling in my eyes. I guess that was my answer. I cared. I cared a lot. Maybe too much. Mori squeezed my arm. "Oh, shit. That was the wrong thing to say." She nibbled on a cookie. "Subject change?" I nodded silently. She smiled. "Have you met Icy yet? She came in with the storm."

"Who's Icy?" I asked.

"I am," lilted a trilling voice. I looked at the door and then the window. But I couldn't see a person to go with the pretty sound. "Down here." I peeked over the side of the bed. There sat a chubby, fluffy white cat. She blinked her eyes, like blue glass, and twitched her small pink nose. She said, "That's a high bed. No matter."

I skittered backward against the headboard. "It…it…talks?" I spluttered.

"Yeah…meowmeow is cat language," Mori replied, reaching up to check my forehead for heat. I swatted her away.

The small cat twitched her tail determinedly and jumped up, her nails ripping holes in the quilt as she hauled her girth up the side. When she reached the top, I stared as though she were a demon in disguise. She blinked at me, aloof.

I stammered, "No, Mori. She talk talked, like talk talked."

Mori scrunched up her freckles. "What? Yeah, she said meow, meow, meow. Are you sure you don't have a fever?"

Icy rolled her glass eyes and sat, twisting to lick her side. She flicked her tail before she stared at me, slowly closed and opened her eyes, as though collecting thin strips of patience. She said, "Two days ago, I left my luxurious home, where I am fed three meals daily, plus treats, to find you. I have been shivering and huddling under bushes. In the mud and the rain, *starving…*"

This cat did not look starving. I didn't say as much, but it must have shown on my face. She scowled and wrinkled her delicate pink nose. "But when the Goddess Sekhmet sends you on a mission, you leave your cozy home and go. Now, tell me why I'm here." Her tail twitched in irritation, as though thinking of her warm bed.

I whispered, "Tell you? I have no idea what you're talking about." Mori watched us wide-eyed, staring at me as if I'd lost my mind.

"Sekhmet instructed me to locate the girl with a delicate fishlike scent among the Witches." She looked at Mori. "I followed that one around for ages. All she said was that I was a pretty kitty, so she obviously wasn't the one. When she poured two mugs, I thought it wise to join her upstairs to see if she had a fishy friend."

I listened with rapt attention, so stunned by the cat that I barely noticed when Mori slipped out the door, worry on her face. She returned a moment later with Mako. Icy looked over her shoulder, flopped on the bed, and rolled on her back. "Hello, handsome," she purred.

Mako gave her one of the sexiest smiles I'd ever seen. He tickled his fingers across her ample pink belly, avoiding my eyes, probably waiting for me to take the lead. She squirmed and wiggled, flirting with him. Then she bit him. Not enough to break the skin, but still.

"Vicious little thing." He grinned and finally looked at me. "I see you've met Icy. Can you fully understand her? Mori was worried you'd cracked up when you said she was speaking."

He scratched Icy under her chin, making her turn on her motor and fill the room with a soft rumble. "That's…oh yeah…to the left…mmrph…"

Mori blinked as if waking up. "Jelly, you absorbed Fae magic! I am so jealous! Talking animals?"

I rubbed my face and unwrapped my towel, letting my damp hair fall free. Icy looked up and hummed through her purring, "Blue hair. Yes. You're the one I'm looking for." She rubbed her cheek against Mako's hand. "That was divine, Mako, but I need to get to work." She looked at him coyly. "Perhaps we can pick this up later?"

He bowed his chin to her. "As you wish."

Mori was awestruck. "Hang on Mako, you said you could only understand a little animal language when we were on the beach. Now you're hearing full sentences?"

Mako laughed, the sound making my heart swell. "The ritual opened my Fae magic beyond where it's ever been. So, yes, I can understand her."

Icy stalked across the bed with feline grace, swaying slightly as her belly unbalanced her. She sat directly in front of my crossed legs. "Your sea-snake, Goddess Kel-something, contacted Goddess Sekhmet, who contacted me. Kel…Kel…"

"Kelbazi," I finished. Icy nodded.

"I assume you're in trouble. She said, and I quote, 'Sssssshe needssss asssssissssstancccce.' Here I am."

Mori whispered, "Why is she hissing?"

Mako chuckled. "She's mimicking Goddess Kelbazi."

"Oh."

Icy blinked at me. "I need to be on your lap. Get comfortable, Scyphozoa. And that is too much of a mouthful. Do you have a nickname?"

"Call me Jelly." I turned to Mori and said, "Goddess Kelbazi contacted her Goddess, Sekhmet, and sent her here to help."

Mori exclaimed, "Sekhmet? She's the Egyptian Goddess of war!"

Icy said, "And also of healing and medicine. Two sides, one coin." I relayed this to Mori.

Mori watched with a mixture of envy and awe as I set my tea aside and rearranged myself to sit against the headboard. Icy paraded back and forth until I was still. She stepped into the space between my crossed legs and curled into a ball. She murmured, "Stroke my fur. The magic is in the purr. Tell them not to interrupt us."

I did as instructed, and as soon as she rumbled, I left my body, swiftly falling through a white tunnel, like Roan's, but cold, and without faces and voices. I landed, jolted to sharp consciousness, and saw Simmi asleep. With no sign of Terrun, I ran to her. A voice shrieked, "Don't touch her! She's resting!"

I spun toward the voice, and my eyes lit onto a puffed-up bird with a yellow chest and brown wings, clutching a massive bunch of delicate greens in one fisted claw. He tipped his head and said, "I'm waiting for her to wake up. I brought her fennel. It's high in iron."

He blinked his beady black eyes. "The Fae is bleeding her twice as often. He has something planned for you. Something not good."

I asked him, "Where are we in Bermuda? Simmi told me that much, but where?"

"On Castle Island. In the fortress. In the cellar." His head whipped to the side, and he screeched as he flew for the oleander tree. "He's coming! Go!"

Power ripped me from the stone room and thrust back to my bed, blinking awake with a pounding heart. Icy's back arched high, her fur sticking out as she hissed and spat. I had four thin streaks of blood on my thigh that stung like deep paper cuts. She jumped from my lap and turned in a circle. "That was too close. Did you get any useful information?"

"How did you pull me out so fast?" I asked, disoriented. I rubbed the beads of blood into my skin. Mako and Mori were right at my side, hovering.

"I see," she replied, smoothing her fur with a raspy pink tongue.

"Yes, I know your name is Icy. How did you move me so quickly?"

She blinked and repeated herself slowly, as if I were thick in the head, "I. See."

Mako smiled. "She's a visionary, a prophet. She knew precisely how much time you had. What did you see?" He asked hopefully. "Simmi?" He was close to me, about to stroke my hair, and on realizing it drew back, his face falling, assuming I was still angry.

I rubbed my temples, warding off a headache. "I did. She was sleeping. A bird is helping her. Come on. We need to talk to the others." I looked at the chubby cat. "Do you want a lift downstairs? I can carry you."

"I need to rest," she replied, drawing herself into a white snowball of fluff. Mako waited outside as I hastily put on the dress with the open back. Mori rushed to her room to change. I was about to leave when Icy whispered, "You cannot help but disappoint some of them." When I pressed for more details, she was already asleep.

They joined me outside my room, and I stalled, momentarily holding Mako at the landing and motioning Mori to go ahead. He searched my face, wondering why I'd stopped. I started, "Mako…" He stiffened, clasping his hands behind his back. I groaned. "Mako, I don't want it to be like this between us. Can we go back to what we were before I found out you were grossly manipulating my feelings?"

He raised an eyebrow at my words. I laughed. "Fine, when Gray manipulated me, and you were complicit. You said you were sorry. I accept your apology. I'm sorry for my knee-jerk reaction. I don't like what you did, but I understand the reasoning behind it. And I want to forget about it and move on. It doesn't feel right to be at odds with you."

His eyes crinkled warmly as he leaned in closer and slid his arm lightly around my waist, whispering, "No one knows you're up and awake yet. Want to slip away? We can go back to your room. Kick Icy off the bed. Finish the cookies." He said all the right things, but his eyes were tight with tension. He was desperate to find his sister.

I softened. "I'm good. And the cookies are gone. I wanted to clear the air between us before we saw everyone else." Relief flooded his face as he grabbed my hand, briskly leading me down the stairs.

As we entered the living room, I was immediately tugged

away from Mako, passed from person to person for hugs, kisses, squeezes, and tears, everyone so pleased and proud. I looked hesitantly at Mako, wondering if I should break it up and talk about Simmi, but he winked and mouthed, 'Enjoy it.' So, I did.

Their words tumbled over each other as they spoke excitedly, replaying their favorite parts of the ritual. They gasped and cooed over my eyes and my mark, and I laughed, somewhat embarrassed by the attention. I'd never been in the center of something so positive.

Eventually, Richard settled everyone down, taking seats, and I pulled on a fuzzy sweater. He said, "All right, you lot. Simmer down. The three of us who got knocked out are fine. How are you, dear Jelly? Noticed any changes yet?" A few low voices chuckled in the background.

I grinned. "Besides serious mystical ink on my back, and rings around my eyes? I can communicate with animals."

Sebastian laughed, "You met Icy, then. She's quite something. She stormed into the kitchen while we were making dinner. There's stew on the stove if you're hungry. Anyway, Icy marched up to us and demanded to be fed. Everyone thought she just had a bossy meow, but she was yelling, NOW! Mako fed her, and I suppose he's her person now."

I giggled as I sat with Mako, happy we were at peace again. "Yes, that sounds about right." I looked at Sophia and Sebastian excitedly. "Icy is a Seer. She took me to Simmi." Sophia bolted upright. All the background chattering stilled. I bit my lip. "Do you want the good or bad news first?"

A round of voices said, "Bad."

"He's bleeding her twice as often, and her friend, a bird, told me that Terrun is planning something bad for me and the Mers." People started grumbling, and Sophia and Sebastian paled. I said quickly, "Now the good. He's keeping her in the lower level of a fortress on Castle Island. We have her exact location!"

Sophia shouted, "Call the Shaman! See who the contact is for the Atlantic Mers! We'll need their help." She gripped Sebastian's hand and danced with excitement. "We can go immediately!" She spun to me. "If you're ready?"

I opened my mouth to answer yes when the pearl started bouncing on the chain, catching everyone's gaze. It rapped out a pattern. Three dots, three dashes, three dots. That one, I knew. I yelled, "SOS! Who?" I suddenly heard static in my head. I tapped against my ear. It sounded like a swarm of bees, then a faint cry. *Jel! Mir!*

I jumped up, my fingers to my temple. *Synchi? Is that you?*

Mir! Mir! The buzzing noise grew stronger. I looked at Anna in alarm. "Synchi's trying to contact me! She keeps shouting mir!"

She cried, "Mirror! Jelly, quickly now!" Anna shot out of her chair, but I shouted for her to stop.

"Wait, Anna! I can do this. I'm different, I can feel it. Mori, Mako, make a chain so you can listen." I focused all my attention on distance telepathy and asked the pearl to help as I pressed my fingers to my temples. Mori slipped her chilly hand on my back under the sweater, and Mako touched my neck. I didn't see who else connected.

Synchi! Are you there?

Synchi's voice snapped in my head. *Jelly? Thank the Goddess! I almost gave myself an aneurysm trying to reach you! Something is wrong with the bubble!*

My eyes flew wide. *Has it fallen? Is anyone hurt?*

We're being circled by swordfish! Masses of them!

I sucked in a breath. *That's impossible. We're allies. There's no way they'd betray us!*

Synchi's voice was hushed and frightened. *Their eyes are black. Guards await Tro's command. Jelly, you must come.*

I gasped. *You can't hurt them! Synchi, if you kill them, it will break the alliance. It will break our hearts!*

Anna cut into the call. *Shaman, when did this happen?*

Right at the end of the ritual. As soon as I sensed the mermaids had left the water. Tro called me to the bubble less than a minute later. I spent too much energy and magic. I can't hold the shield much longer.

Mori shouted, *Toto is fighting? But his arm… Synchi, he's not strong enough to fight a swordfish if he's still injured! Jelly and I are coming right now! Anna, get us back to Nell! Shaman, tell Nell to get my whalebone stars from the guest house at the Fields. Hold fast, we're on our way.*

I shook my head. *Synchi? Have they attacked?*

Sophia cried, *We're so close to getting Simmi! We have to free her!*

Richard said, *Darling, can you loan her your magic through the ocean?*

I shouted, *Stop it! Stop talking over each other! I can't keep this straight!*

My head pounded as everyone in the room ignored me. They all chipped in, their voices shouting to be heard. Somehow, my telepathy allowed them all to speak.

Synchi said, *Tro ordered emergency lockdown, but Jelly, swordfish? They'll kill us all.*

Sebastian roared, *Free Simmi, and you will cut him off from the Mers!*

I yelled, *The bubble is failing! They're all about to lose their lives!*

Branko's voice broke through. *Sebastian, I concur. That's the best solution to blocking his magic.*

Simon murmured, *I agree.*

Sophia sobbed, her tears coming out in gulps.

Mako shouted, *Everyone, one at a time! She's getting overwhelmed!*

Anna spoke. *Shaman, are you certain you can't hold it a little longer? We're so close.*

Sophia cried, *We know where she is!*

Sebastian, Branko, Simon, and Richard all spoke simultaneously, their words fusing into a mangled, deep hum. Sophia hiccupped and Anna questioned the Shaman, who tried to answer back. The call was chaotic, causing a sharp pain in my brain. I didn't dare relinquish the connection in case I couldn't get it back. I threw a terrified glance at Roan. He was the only one who had stayed quiet. He saw the panic in my expression and shouted in our minds. *RIGHT! The lot of ye, leggo! It's too many voices! Mori, Jelly, and Anna, ye stay on. Everyone else, leggo!*

I could have kissed him. The pressure in my head slipped away. It was difficult holding that many people on the call, especially as she was in the Pacific, and we were on the far side of the Atlantic.

Synchi's voice was awe-stricken. *Jelly??? How many people were just connected?*

Eleven.

What???

No time to gawk at my power, Synchi. Anna, we have to go. Take us to Nell. Synchi, tell her to get ready.

Anna looked close to tears. Frustration fought a battle on her face until, eventually, she nodded. She let her hand slide from my arm and walked away. I said, *Okay, Synchi. Stay strong. We're on our way.*

I dropped my fingers and studied the faces around me. This was an impossible decision. I heard muttering, some low arguing, and crying. My throat seized. This is what Icy had meant about disappointing them. I walked to the Fields family, huddled together, speaking in soft, urgent voices. They clammed up as I approached. I blew out a breath. "The bird did not say Simmi was in immediate danger."

"Except that she's getting bled more often!" cried Sophia. "How long will she last? Another day? Another hour? If he's using her to attack the Mers, and you don't get to them in time, we'll all lose! You should free Simmi, then go back home."

I looked at her incredulously. "A flotilla of swordfish is threatening the bubble as we speak! The Shaman can't hold them back. Sophia, if they fall, we all do! I'm sorry, but Simmi will have to wait. I have to help the Mers first. They take priority."

"But…" Sophia started, then, seeing the determination my face, turned abruptly and walked away. I'd made my decision. Sebastian shook his head, his eyes hollow as he glanced at me and followed her.

"Mako…" I faltered. I reached for him, but he pulled back and held up his hands.

"Just…just give me a second, Jelly. I need to think." He turned the other way from his parents and ran outside. I wanted to kick something, punch someone. As soon as I felt welcomed, celebrated even, the damned universe yanked out the rug. I ran out the door for air and planted my back against an oak tree to gather myself. The wind caused a rustling of leaves, whispering the word 'home.'

But where was that? Here? With Mako and the Fields? With the Surfecti? Nell and Mew? Or on the reef, where people sneered at me but needed me? Icy was right. I couldn't satisfy everyone. As if summoned, she walked around the tree, making a slight chirrup sound. She nodded to me once and said, "I'm ready. Let's go."

I shook my head and sighed. I just wanted a damned minute alone. "Where are we going?"

She jumped into my lap. "Back to the bird. Quickly, now. Simmi needs every second you can give her."

THIRTY-ONE

I was so weak, so tired. Despite the fish, bananas, cherries, spinach, tomatoes, fennel, and unidentifiable meat that I didn't question, I was drained. Literally. Terrun had become increasingly unstable, drawing as much blood as I could bear without dying. The symbols on the ceiling were thicker, often not drying between coats, the drops shimmering before plunking onto my filthy gown. He didn't lick them off me anymore.

He muttered to himself as he painted above my head. "Thinks she can use the pearl like a Fae; I don't think so, little mermaid, I don't think so."

I cleared my throat painfully and asked, "What is she doing, Terrun? You seem upset."

He looked down at me and spat, "They did a *Coactus Fusionem!* She had Surfecti thrust their magic into her! She thinks she's as powerful as me, but oh, no, sweet Simmi, she's not even close. I will ruin her world and kill everyone she loves, every blasted one!" He angrily dabbed at the symbol. "I warned her! I gave her a chance!"

Closing my eyes, I groaned inside. I had to tell her. But

how? I didn't dare even think of it. Not with him hovering over me, maniacally retracing the symbols. "What is that one?" I asked innocently. "You spend a lot of time on it."

He looked at me suspiciously. Then he shrugged and jumped from the bed, barely jarring me as he landed silently. "Fine, I shall tell you. No offense, sweet girl, but you'll be dead soon. Actually, I'm thrilled you lasted as long as you did. Although, it is puzzling. I didn't expect you to still be alive by now." I exhaled a breath of relief. My animal friends had remained a secret.

He waved the brush toward the symbol he'd reinforced. "That one is for possession. I'm controlling several ocean beasts at the moment. Still trying to possess a Mers, but it's proving quite difficult." He put his hands on his hips and tipped his head. "Try not to die just yet." He sprinted from the room like a ghost.

The symbol looked like a house with interior lines of various lengths, with one small swirl atop a triangle. I stared at it silently. Was there a way to erase it? Would that work? Could Esmerelda do something? She seemed a witchy sort of spider. I called for her. Within minutes, she scuttled through the window and ran up my chest.

"Do you know of any spiders or creatures who liked the taste of blood?"

She cocked her head this way and that before nodding vigorously. "They're rare, now. We used to have tons of them. Wonderful creatures. They're lightning-fast and as big as a man's hand, but don't worry. They won't harm you." With that shaky endorsement, she zipped away out the window.

The air shifted, like a change in pressure. I turned to see Jelly pressed against the wall. She patted herself down and giggled with excitement. "I have legs and clothes and knives!" She spun and gasped at me in horror. I must look awful.

I croaked, "Jelly! You shouldn't be here! It's not safe!"

She ran to me and laid her hands gently on my ankles. A sensation of cool water rushed over me, coating the inflammation that burned me from within. She whispered, "I am so sorry I didn't recognize you when I first saw you! I can't believe it's you, that you're here. We're going to get you out, Simmi. I have to stop Terrun from killing the Mers before we can come for you, but I want to keep you strong…" She chewed on her lip, apparently thinking. It was subtle, but I noticed her pearl do a small skip before she nodded.

"Okay, Simmi, these are weird days, and I have new magic. I have a hunch. Just roll with it, okay?"

"What are you going to do?" I watched her jaw clench, and she squeezed her eyes tight, inhaling sharply through her nose. I cautioned, "Hey, that looks painful. What are you doing?"

She smiled, and her teeth were coated red. "I heal fast, crazy fast. Your godmother's been hopping me up with her magic and tea." She scanned my face, peering closely at my mouth. "Okay, your lips are a mess, broken open. That'll do." Without further comment, my friend pressed her lips to mine.

A nuclear blast of power rushed through me when her blood touched mine, so intense it arched my spine, my body straining against the straps. Jelly pulled back, worried. "Too much?" she asked nervously.

"Give me tongue. Push it deeper," I answered hoarsely. It was strange, being kissed by my friend. But I couldn't deny the power in her blood.

"That's my girl," she growled, and then she kissed me as though my life depended on it, which, considering the state I was in, it did.

Her magic had an extra zip, like a spice that made my feet flex, cramping my toes and calves. She drew back to bite the inside of her cheek again. I gasped at the feisty mermaid, "Terrun said the Surfecti filled you with magic. I've been with a Mage and obviously recognize the Fae and Mers, but there's something else in your blood. What is it?"

She grinned through crimson lips. "Shifter. Gargoyle and Wolf specifically. It hasn't manifested in hair growth or wings, but here's hoping. Is that better?"

"So much better." I tipped my chin. "Look, the symbol above you is possession. He's coating it over and over. He says he's trying to control a Mers, but he can't manage it yet. But he has some creatures in his possession."

Jelly frowned and said, "He has swordfish." She looked up. "I could wash it down with water or something." She eyed the bucket of urine in the corner, the edges of her lips turning down before she shrugged. Bless her.

I shook my head. "No. He'll notice. It has to be discreet. I'll work on that part. A Hurricane Spider said she could weaken the magic. Just keep him from killing the Mers."

"Okay. I was hoping to get you out of here first. I'm sorry, but I have to go to the reef. Your parents are so upset. And Mako…" Her eyes stormed, tormented, like she hated she was disappointing him. She turned her face from mine.

"Hey, Jelly, hey, look at me. Don't worry about my family. Go to the Mers. Understand? Save the Mers. They come first. Tell my family I said that. Tell them…tell them it's what Leif would do."

Jelly rapidly blinked as her eyes filled with tears. "You're a good friend, Simmi. Thank you for understanding." She slammed her cheek with her teeth, hissing with pain, and kissed me fervently, blood dripping from her lips. This time, I chased every drop with my tongue. She pulled back and smeared the blood across her cheek. "I'll be back. I swear to the Goddess, I will come back for you." With a nod, Jelly disappeared.

I delicately flexed my ankles and wrists. The raw skin was rapidly healing, and the bone-deep ache was gone. I chuckled to myself, then stopped. I'd have to pretend to be out of it when Terrun returned. He'd kill me if I was stronger, or do something worse like make me his monster.

I swallowed a scream as five Herculean brown spiders jumped up from the window to the wall, springing in jerky movements. They had thick accents as they spoke to each other. One of them turned to me and said, "Esmerelda says you gotta blood sitch on de ceiling. Which a deese here tings you want us to lick?"

"That one, the one that looks like a house with a triangle. Don't erase it. Just dilute it, take it down a few layers."

He nodded his furry head. "You got it, gurl. Leave it to us."

Kindee arrived at the window. His eyes widened greedily as he looked at the ceiling, but he shook himself and cleared his throat. "Tonight's supper is a feast of heavily salted slugs. A human just did it about an hour ago. It's quite tragic for the slugs, but good news for you. We won't let them go to waste."

I almost told him no. I nearly turned him down or made a face. But my small friend was so pleased. There was no way I would refuse him. And so, I spent my evening gagging on rubbery slugs while flexing my muscles, watching spiders lick my blood off the ceiling.

THIRTY-TWO

MAKO

I was such an asshole. She was under so much pressure; in an impossible position. I should have supported her immediately, but selfishly, I wanted my mother to stop crying. I wanted my guilt over Leif to go away. If Simmi died… I aggressively ran my hands through my hair, grabbing and pulling in frustration.

An annoyed voice hissed. "I am not built for this. I am a pampered creature! Made for a life of worship! This is outrageous!" Icy came around the edge of the garden wall. She huffed and rolled her clear blue eyes. "Finally! Can't you all scatter in the same direction? She went one way. You went the other."

Icy sat and licked one paw, swiping it over her eyes in exasperation. She growled, "Let's cut to the chase, Mako. Do you want to stay here and snatch yourself bald? Or do you want to support the woman you love?"

"Love?" I mean, I knew it, but to have it spoken so plainly…

Her whiskers twitched. Her words were heavy and measured. "She represents all that is brave and wild in the world. She sets your heart on fire. Please tell me you're not too dim to see it."

I blinked at the cat, stunned. I stuttered, "Go on."

"Jelly did not come here to serve you or your family's needs. She serves a higher purpose, rallying to save the Mers and the sea creatures. She has fought her entire life to defend the ocean, and Fate thrust this Fae upon her. If she fails in this mission and the Fae succeeds, the Surfecti will fall next. She is under phenomenal strain."

"Have you seen the outcome?"

"I have seen many outcomes. And as much as I am supposed to stay out of Fate's way, I will give you a hint. We always do better when we fight for love. Jelly burns with her love for the ocean. What do you fight for?"

My throat bobbed as I swallowed, thinking of my stupid, dangerous activities. I painted my actions with guilt. I behaved selfishly, attempting to assuage my demons through chaos. My face must have reflected the clarity that swept over me.

Icy flicked her tail impatiently. "Exactly!" She licked a paw, pausing as she said, "Your sister told her to go to the Mers first. She said it's what Leif would do."

I flinched.

Small, ice-blue eyes narrowed on me. She growled, "Sekhmet will have my tail for this...." Her teeth chattered before she said in a rush, "Go with her. Support her. Help her defend her people, technically your people, as well. She faces the horror of slaughtering the creatures she has sworn to protect, the ones she has given her love, life, and soul to, through no fault of theirs or hers. You can't imagine the terror she's experiencing. And she thinks she's letting you down, which is ripping her apart. Open your heart, Mako. You've kept it closed for far too long."

She sat back on her haunches. Her pink nose lifted as she said, "So, Mako Fields, you can ask me one question. Make it a good one, and make it quick, or you'll miss the boat." She looked at me hard. "The literal boat, Mako."

I scanned my brain. Was Terrun strong enough to possess the Shaman? Commander Tro? Would we have time to help the Mers *and* save Simmi? What would my parents say? Then, the foremost question hit me. Would I be able to live with myself if Jelly died there without me? I swallowed all the uncertainty, my heart thundering. In a rush, I gasped, "Where's Jelly?"

Icy sighed heavily and purred. "That is the right question. In the living room. Run."

I sprinted for the house, bursting through the door. Jelly and Mori held hands, their spines straight and their jaws tight as Anna tossed back a healing potion and set down the vial. "I'm coming with you," I panted. Jelly's eyes widened, and she looked at me with such relief that my heart swelled. Then, I heard my mother.

"Mako, no! You can't!" Her face was a twist of fear.

I rushed to her and held her tightly, pouring in my love. Through swallowed tears, I said, "I have to, Mom. It's the right thing. It's what Leif would do. Simmi said so."

Jelly choked, biting her lip so hard it would bruise.

Anna said tersely, "Mako, if you're coming…"

I reached out for Dad and drew him into the hug with us. "I love you both so much. When we get back, we're getting Simmi. I swear it." I let go of them and grabbed Jelly's hand. Staring into her black-ringed eyes, I knew the cat spoke the truth. I loved her.

THIRTY-THREE

SIMMI

Jelly's blood had done remarkable things. Atrophied muscles woke, collapsed blood vessels plumped, and a fire returned to my belly. I'd feigned weakness when Terrun blazed into the room, excited for his ocean battle. I barely fluttered my eyelids, making my breath shallow and panting, the final throes of someone about to die. He bought it.

"Ugh," he'd tsked, "Such a shame. I hoped to get more blood from you. No matter. I've been painting the possession sign so often that I'll have plenty of strength for my flotilla. Swordfish, dear girl! A swarm of them! They're so violent with all that slashing and gashing." He rubbed his hands together in glee.

I watched him through cracked eyelids. He looked disheveled, like he'd slipped into deeper madness and forgotten to keep up appearances. His shirt was unbuttoned and wrinkled, his tight trousers were dirty, and his hair stuck up randomly as though he'd been yanking it. He paced back and forth, muttering happily to himself, his feet, as ever, silent. He spun to me and said, "I'm leaving my pets here with you, darling. Don't get any bright ideas." He scoffed, "Not that you have any possibility of escape."

He stroked my toes almost lovingly. "I have so enjoyed your company, sweet Simmi, but it's time to kill the Mers. Then, the humans. I may leave the Surfecti alive. They could be useful. I'm not sure yet. It depends. As of now, I'm not feeling terribly generous, with them helping Scyphozoa and all." He giggled. "When I return, I'll give you to my pets. I'd offer you now, but I would love to watch them feast on such a fallen masterpiece. Maybe I'll bring your brother back here to witness it. Or maybe I'll enslave Scyphozoa and make her kill him. Oh, so much choice! What will I do?"

He stroked his beautiful hands over his high cheekbones, his green eyes flashing with insanity. He giggled again. "Oh, now that is a lovely idea! Yes, yes, yes, I will capture him once I'm done with the Mers and let him watch you die while his lover changes into one of my creatures. Then I'll have her tear his throat out, ideally in front of your father. His poor heart will simply burst. How fabulous! Well, wish me luck! Ta-ta for now, darling!"

He vanished.

I strained against the straps to no avail and watched helplessly as Eators crept into the room, hissing and drooling over their fangs. Kindee jumped outside on his oleander branch. "No, no, no, this is not good, not good at all."

Something moved across my matted hair and settled, hiding behind my ear. Esmerelda said in her raspy, smoker's voice, "There are whispers on the webs, Simmi. A group arrived in Tom Moore's Jungle on the main island. They popped in from nowhere and scared the bejeezus out of my cousin Esperanza. One of them talked to her and said he was looking for his daughter. He's a giant fella, a Fae since he could communicate. He said they have to wait for the mermaid. But they're here. Take a deep, deep breath and exhale nice and slow if you understand what I'm telling you."

I slowly blinked my eyes and sighed a long breath, watching the Eators watch me. Esmerelda chuckled, "Yeah, that's what I thought. Okay. Hang in there. Sounds like they'll be here soon." She stroked the small patch of skin behind my ear with one leg. "We won't be able to feed you while the monsters stand guard. But we're here with you. Don't upset them. No sudden movements."

My throat dried from fear as the Eators paced near the entryway, their red eyes fixed and hungry. Drool dripped from their fangs, and they made screeching noises at each other as if yelling. One lunged at me; only to be struck back by another. They hissed and chittered, clacking their teeth, waiting to rip me to pieces.

THIRTY-FOUR

Anna took us directly to Nell and Jack's dock without further comment. The engine was running, and Nell waited anxiously, holding the only rope that secured the boat. Anna quickly hugged each of us. She said, "Come home safe, Mako."

She turned to me and Mori. "You two as well. Take care of each other down there." She crossed both arms and put her fists to her chest while bowing deeply, causing a lump to form in my throat. It was a Mers bow. We jumped on the boat.

Nell shouted to Jack and pushed off. She said nothing, simply passing us our armor and weapons. She handed Mako a facecloth and his dive mask. I wished he had armor and frowned apprehensively at his bare chest. Mori strapped on her whalebone stars, silently passing her metal ones to Nell. She and I held our swords on our laps, not speaking, our minds imagining the worst.

Jack hit the throttle hard, and I was grateful for Sophia's gift of a new boat. Once we were out in deep water, we became more tense. I shouted above the noise of the boat, "We're most vulnerable while transforming. Mako, I'm guessing you can do it on command?"

He said loudly, "Yes! And I'll bet you can, too, now that you have Fae magic!" I nodded, filing away that information for later. I wondered what else I could do. He moved closer so he wouldn't have to shout. "So, I probably should have told you this sooner, but I can only hold my Mers form for three days. I need to have legs for a day before I can change again."

I nodded. "I'm hoping we won't be here that long." He bit his lip and scanned the water, not replied to my comment. I squeezed his hand. "I assume you've never been down there. What are you feeling right now?"

He stared at the ocean, frowning as the boat plowed through miles and miles of debris. Weathered jugs, water bottles, fishing buoys, nets, and plastic bags parted for the bow as we raced for the reef. Mako leaned in close and gathered my hair at the nape of my neck, pulling my face to his. He looked angry, hovering on the edge of violence.

He growled, "Vengeful, Jelly. I want to rip off Terrun's head for taking Simmi. Yet, part of me wants him to wipe out the humans so this bullshit pollution will stop. But then that makes me furious that I'd even entertain that as a viable solution." His eyes shuttered. He shook his head slightly and dropped his voice, his eyes intense. "Mostly, I'm terrified that something will happen to you. That I'll never get the opportunity to just enjoy life with you and do something fun, something frivolous. Like watch you eat an ice cream."

He scanned my eyes with longing, a sweet emotion right there in his gaze. I wanted to promise him everything, but our future was uncertain, and it seemed unfair to dream. He smoothed back my hair, releasing his grip. "But I'm not frightened of what we might see or happen as we fight. I believe in you. And Mori, her father, and your shaman. I will be at your side as your guard. Nothing will hurt you so long as I breathe. I swear this to you, savage queen."

The engine cut to idle and then stopped. With both hands, I reached for his face and pressed his forehead to mine. Our lips were less than an inch away as I whispered, "Salted caramel is my favorite, followed by chocolate. We will have that damned ice cream."

A familiar face broke through the swamp of pollution, exhaling softly. No jumping and splashing this time. Hannah whispered, "The fightin' is at the West Gate. We've seen nothin' up here, but cover yourselves as dolphins and be as quiet as you can while you change. Jelly…it's chaos down there. I hope you're feelin' strong."

I asked, "Did they attack? Where is Synchi?"

"It just started. She's in the thick of it. Scared the scales off a few Mers when she showed up in her natural form. Said it was stupid to waste energy on young skin." Hannah cackled softly. "A Warrior drew his sword when he didn't recognize her. She slapped him so hard that he spun in a circle."

I hoped it was Gorn.

We slipped into the water without a sound. Mako's legs transformed with ease. Mori and I followed. She bit her knuckle so hard she drew blood, and I tore up my healed cheek. Mako was right; I didn't need the potion, and changing to my tail was smoother, like I'd been born to it, but it still burned like hellfire.

Mori and I pulled on our chain-mail and strapped our swordfish swords to our backs. We looked at each other morosely, wondering if we'd have to use them. Nell handed Mako a sword, whispering with a wink that it was hers and she wanted it back, suggesting she believed he'd survive. For the first time ever, I hated he was naked, my eyes scanning over his tattoos. We wrapped our faces in cloth and donned our eyewear. I hid us as dolphins, and we dove.

We swam to a cluster of rocks about two hundred feet from

the West Gate. "Dear Goddess," whispered Mori. "They're in a frenzy." We watched in horror as ten swordfish ripped at the bubble with their swords. They would stab and then swing their bodies, causing great gashes. The protection zone was full of trash, the magic almost entirely torn away.

One swordfish, a female based on the length of its body, attacked the central bubble while the others decimated the outer shield. I couldn't see her face, not knowing if we were friends. She slashed with her massive sword. Synchi held steady with raised arms, mending every fresh cut. Tro hovered like a giant behind her, his hands on her shoulders, pulsing his magic into her.

The other Warriors, the only Mers with impactful magic, raised their palms toward the bubble, feeding it their energy. Synchi's gnarled hands grabbed it and wove as fast as she could, her white locs flowing wildly around her head. Mako whispered, "What does the Shaman have around her neck?"

I squinted and gasped, "It's Oggie! What is he doing out here?" The little octopus waved his arms in the exact pattern as Synchi. "I think he's helping her! How?"

Mori whispered, "He's been living with you two for a while, saturated in magic, so maybe he's acting as a conduit or just giving her support like Toto. What should we do, Jelly?"

I chewed on my lip. I didn't want to attack. We were grossly outnumbered and on the wrong side of the bubble. Abruptly, two of the swordfish pulled back, shaking their heads. They spiraled and looped before hovering, staring at the bubble. Their heads turned in our direction. I reached for my knives. "Get ready."

One shot toward us and careened around the rock. His eyes were normal. I recognized him and sagged. It was Nevin. He whispered, "Jelly! We are so confused! We were on the surface, minding our own business, basking in the sun, and then the next thing, we're attacking the Mers! It makes NO sense!"

"Does everyone have black eyes?"

He nodded vigorously. "What does it mean? Is it what happened to the sharks?" He hovered above the rock, watching for a second before floating back down.

I coaxed him closer so I could whisper. "A Fae is controlling you. How did you break free?"

"It's like I just woke up. What do we do? How do I make the others stop?"

I peeked out. Another swordfish shook its head and shot for the surface. Then another. Terrun was losing his power. Somehow, Simmi had been successful. Only six remained. Three more pulled back, hesitated, and spun, swimming away as fast as possible. As some of the fastest fish in the ocean, they vanished within seconds.

The largest one turned to watch them escape, and my breath caught in my throat. It was Josephine. I knew her. Her eyes skimmed over our rock, and I realized what was happening a moment too late. Terrun was concentrating his efforts into one beast, and Josephine, already massive, grew even larger. Gathering strength, ripping and tearing, she was ruthless. As the last two swordfish took off, her vigorous attack grew more violent.

Tro yelled, "Josie! Stop!" She doubled her efforts under Terrun's control, and lashed so hard she overpowered Synchi's repairs. Josephine lunged for the Shaman. Tro whipped around to protect her, pushing her away. The swordfish's bill went straight through his torso, just above the hip. She jerked to the side, intending to tear him to pieces. He bellowed in pain and pumped his tail to match her movement. Mori screamed and bolted from behind the rock, throwing whalebone stars at Josephine. Mako and I were right behind her.

Fillian swung the killing blow, his great sword slicing straight through Josie's face. I screamed in shock. Horror rushed through me as her body sank to the sand, her bill still driven through Tro. Blood swirled and danced with the garbage.

Fillian turned toward me and slowly lowered his sword, his face grief-stricken at killing our friend. I reached Tro and spun the blood away, shouting for Synchi to help us. Mori and the Warriors sprang into action, holding Tro's wound and funneling their magic to keep him alive.

I turned sharply, frustrated that Synchi hadn't come. I cried out in terror as Oggie's eyes turned black. His arms constricted around Synchi's throat. He hissed in his squeaky, high-pitched voice, "Didn't I warn you, darling?"

"NO!" I screamed, "Let her go!" I bolted to her with my hand up, and Oggie's arms tightened, choking her. She pulled at his arms, her milky-white eyes wide with panic.

She shouted in my head, *Don't you dare give him the pearl!*

I yelled back, *He'll kill you!*

Oggie hissed, "I told you what would happen! You didn't listen! You went to the Surfecti! Tell me, little mermaid, how does it feel to see your nightmares come true?" He squealed with demented laughter.

"Stop," I gasped, "Please!" The Shaman loosened one of his arms, only to have another replace it.

Oggie sneered. "I've been watching the pearl for years, waiting to get it back." He spat, "You're untrained, helpless, and weak. She never should have gone to you!"

I shook my head, "Who? She? The pearl? Please! Please let the Shaman go!" I called for the pearl, but it had retreated, terrified of the monster in Oggie.

Oggie let his arms briefly slacken. Synchi coughed and caught her breath. As soon as she did, Oggie tightened again, and Synchi suffocated, thrashing her tail as she struggled fruitlessly. Oggie's voice turned venomous and ugly. "I don't want her dying too quickly. No fun in that."

He cocked his head, thinking of other ways to torture me. He sang my mother's song, twisting it. "Jelly, Jelly, eyes so blue, I'll kill them all before I'm through. Oh, oh, that was quite good! Let me try another."

"Please," I begged through a sob, "Stop!"

"Jelly, Jelly, eyes so blue, I killed your Da, that much is true!" He shrilled with laughter, "Oh, this is fabulous! Look at your face! I could do this all day!" I swam closer. Oggie slid an arm over Synchi's mouth. I halted, and he lilted, "But I have things to do, Mers to kill."

He sighed as if heavily burdened. "And then all of humanity. Give me the pearl, Scyphozoa. Give it to me, and I'll let this old bag go." Synchi's old, wizened hands grasped at Oggie, staring at me with wild fear.

Don't, she gasped in my head.

I clung to the words that had torn open my heart. "What do you mean you killed my Da?"

Oggie snickered, delighted to see my distress. "Your father? I was experimenting. I used so much energy that day. It took weeks to recover. I worked with a squid, not unlike this little one here. Although it was much bigger and far stronger. Wrapped your daddy up like a little present, pulling the ropes so tight he couldn't get free. I sucked the joy right out of him! He cried your name, begging me to leave you alone. I guess your mommy had told him about a dream she had where you were wearing the pearl. He died knowing that one day, I would come for what is mine!"

My body froze with shock. He had murdered my father. He'd taken the joy from my life. Synchi's face turned purple, and the life in her eyes dimmed. I blinked back tears. The bubble would fall if she died, and everyone would perish, poisoned by pollution. Strands of foreign magic filtered through my blood, calling for me, but my fear overwhelmed and dulled them. I couldn't grasp any, not even a single thread.

There was no choice. I'd failed. I'd failed them all. Biting my lip, I whispered, "Okay. You win." The pearl pulsed twice, aggressively. I shook my head again and croaked, "Let the Shaman go. Let the Mers live. You can have it. Just take it." I choked a sob and thought of the little girl at the store on the cracked seahorse. I had just condemned her to death. The pearl throbbed at my throat, repeating two beats as if screaming.

Oggie shrilled with delight. "Well, finally! You can take her place and hold this sham of magic together, under my influence and command, of course. Yes, that will do nicely."

Rage instantaneously lashed me away from my tears. "That wasn't the deal!"

Oggie giggled, "Oh, darling, don't you know not to make deals with the Fae? You said to let her go. You didn't specifically say whether she would still breathe."

I shook with anger. The pearl vibrated. He would never stop. I thrust into Oggie's mind, hoping some part of him could hear me. I whispered, *I love you, Oggie, and I'm sorry, baby. I'm so sorry.*

The black in his eyes retreated momentarily, and he blinked at me innocently, reaching out one of his arms. "Jebby?" His arms went slack as he looked around in confusion, allowing Synchi to gulp in a breath. Then darkness flooded his features, and he redoubled his grip, strangling her and shaking her body. I swallowed my sob and raised my hand, hoping my aim wouldn't kill Synchi as well. I inhaled, ready to scream, then choked, my eyes flying wide.

Mako sprang up from behind and gripped Oggie's small,

red head. He chanted a spell, and Oggie spasmed as the black in his eyes scattered like gunshot, swirling and breaking into pieces. I screamed, "Mako! What are you doing!" Black ink surrounded them, joined by a swirl of thick nurdles, sucked in through the torn bubble.

I spun a whirlpool so I could see and shrieked as Mako's eyes slowly turned from a beautiful blue to black. He was absorbing the possession. Oggie's tiny red arm loosened enough for Synchi to breathe. Life flooded back into her face. Mako's body shook as he shouted, "Jelly! It's too much!"

I yelled, "Mako! Stop! Don't do this! I'll give him the pearl!" I yanked at Oggie. His arms gave way entirely. I pulled him from Mako's hands and his small body slipped to the sand and lay still. Mako spasmed as the blackness engulfed his eyes.

Synchi bellowed in my head. *Help Mako! I have Tro!* I glanced over my shoulder as she grabbed Oggie by the arm, swooping Tro and Mori into a whirlpool and disappearing.

I spun back to Mako. His eyes were more black than blue. He choked out, "Too strong."

Without hesitation, I pulled Mako's lower lip between my teeth and bit hard, doing the same to my cheek, and then fisted his hair to hold his face to mine. I wasn't sure if we needed the blood, but I wouldn't take the chance to find out too late. As I kissed him, an oily, thick magic flowed into my body, seeking all the love I had, hoping to devour it.

Faces and memories flashed before me. I saw matriarch Juniper, and the cheeky little turtles, gorgeous Amira with her pod, saucy Hannah, and Oggie. My parents danced, holding me between them and laughing. Mori and Synchi cackled together, and Tro twirled me in his arms. I saw hundreds of sea creatures winking and smiling, as if thanking me and saying goodbye.

That was love. We'd been joyful despite our surroundings. I felt it all. The sweetness in my soul shimmered at the edges, as if fraying, and I clung to the love, willing it to be stronger, to hold on. Mako fought me, thrashing and struggling, trying to escape and break free. But it was Terrun, fighting for possession. As I pulled dark magic through the kiss, the pearl bounced manically against my skin. I shrilled to it in my mind. *It's too much! He's stealing Mako's soul! Help me!*

The pearl rose above my armor and hovered in the water at my chin. It pulsed over and over and over like a heartbeat. The pearl siphoned black oil from Mako, helping me absorb it. As it guzzled and gulped, it screamed a single word in my head.

Mine!

Mako groaned, and I jerked my head back to look at him. His eyes were blue, just peppered with black. But the veins in his face had turned dark, like a spider had crawled over his skin with black silk. "No! Mako! Give it to me!"

His eyes were listless and blank. He shrugged and slurred, "S'alright, Jelly. Payback for Leif."

I screamed, "NO! MAKO!" Terrun was stealing him right in front of my eyes. I snarled and spat, "You can't have him!" Absolute fury coursed through me. The pearl pulsed and jumped, electric and frenzied with fresh magic. I would not let Mako die, not now. I laid my hand on his chest, my other still fisting his hair. I didn't know what this would do or if it would work. It might kill us both.

I thrust out my magic, turquoise fire ringed in a Surfecti rainbow, pressing my hand to his heart. I cried, "MOKSHA!"

My head snapped back as an electric surge went through me. The mark on my back burned, searing and flashing, the blast of pain like lightning. Mako screamed in agony. The surrounding water exploded in turquoise and rainbow light, mixed with a thick, dark cloud of black.

Time stopped dead. The water stilled and turned solid around us. Mako's eyes flew wide and went blank.

THIRTY-FIVE

We fell through a tunnel of every hue of blue. We twisted and spun as I clung to Mako, one hand still gripping his hair, my other arm wrapped tightly across his smooth back. He dragged his arms around me and held on.

The spinning stopped, and we drifted for a while in cool water. Our eyes remained locked on each other. His were still sluggish, unable to focus, but they stuck to mine like glue. The tunnel faded and morphed into something else, and we settled onto a smooth surface, creamy in coloring and silky to the touch.

I laced my fingers through Mako's, watching his eyes, waiting for the return of the spark I so adored. When his eyelids fluttered closed, I stared at his skin, still traced with black lines. It had left his face to slide down his chest, spreading from shoulder to shoulder, as low as his navel, like a dangerous half-plate of armor. He looked ashen, drained. I stared anxiously until my eyelids grew heavy. Exhaustion finally took me under.

I woke to the sound of gentle humming. Water

rhythmically flowed over me. It was peaceful. I looked at Mako and found him still sleeping. I curled closer, pressing my body right to his, and closed my eyes again. A voice surrounded me, deep and sonorous, like a whale song.

You are safe in a Fae dimension, away from your time and events. That world is on pause. You flung the Fae far away, but he regathers himself. You lack the strength to confront him. You and your lover must bind. You cannot go back until you do.

Mako called to me sometime later, maybe after minutes or months, dragging me up from a deep sleep. "Jelly? Jelly, wake up. Oh, Gods, please let her be okay." I stretched and yawned. I blinked and stared at Mako as he hovered over mine. His eyes were entirely cobalt. I gasped with relief and tugged him toward me, my fingers on his cheeks as I stared.

He chuckled and lowered his face to mine, his kiss slow and sensual. Lazy, as if we had all the time in the world. He pulled back and grinned, tracing his fingers across my lips. "That was a hell of a kiss, savage queen. Why did you bite me? I'm not complaining, don't get me wrong, but what compelled you to do that?"

I laughed, so relieved to see him alive. "It helped your sister, and you were fading so fast, so I did blood magic, or at least, my form of it. It was instinctual."

His eyebrows raised. "You kissed Simmi like that?"

I nodded, grinning. "Mm-hmm. It strengthened her. I figured it would do the same for you."

He shook his head. "Then you did a forced fusion on me. Damn, Jelly."

"Are you okay? How do you feel?" I glanced at his chest, still covered in darkness. It didn't seem to bother him.

His eyes sparkled with joy. He looked at me tenderly and whispered, "So grateful." He kissed me softly, then traced his thumb gently over my lower lip. My heart bloomed like a thousand-petaled flower. His voice was soft. "Terrun was sucking the joy out of me, and I was so angry that I hadn't told you my feelings, that I was going to die without you knowing."

I whispered back, "I thought I'd lost you. I was furious at him for taking you from me."

He kissed me softly. "You risked dying by doing that magic."

I pushed his hair back. "You risked dying for Oggie and the Shaman. You knew it would hurt me if they were gone, so you let Terrun take you instead." I shook my head, traumatized by what had just happened. What I'd almost lost.

He smiled, and his chipped tooth made my breath hitch in my throat. I scanned his beautiful eyes. I bit my lip. I whispered, "So…there was a voice…"

He purred in his throat. "Telling us to bind?" His eyes simmered as his lips pulled up into a bigger smile. "Jelly, for all I know, I'm dead. But if I'm here with you, about to make love to you, I am the luckiest dead man alive."

His lips met mine with intention, and my back arched, suddenly frantic to remove my armor. He helped me with deft fingers. I trailed my hand down his chest, worry creasing my brow at the shadows on his skin. He kissed me, murmuring, "Forget about that. Let me love you, Jelly."

My heart beat faster as he slid his body over mine, pressing my skin to the soft silk. A flush of warmth spread through my body as we kissed, and I softly groaned as he nibbled and sucked along my neck. He paused, his voice low. "I've never done this in my Mers form." He slid his lips down, down, tortuously down, to hover above my chest.

My breath caught in a cry, and I wove my fingers in his hair. I looked at his broad back with the wave tattoos running down his arms. "Wait, Mako," I exhaled. "Before, in my room, you said you didn't want it to be transactional. Isn't this…aren't we?" I moaned as his tongue moved against my sensitive skin, cutting off my concern.

He looked up and held my gaze with dancing eyes. "Jelly, a disembodied voice told us we are in a Fae dimension, holding time still and not strong enough to return unless we bind. Now," he flicked his tongue, "I think," he sucked, making my fingers tighten in his hair, "we should honor and obey said voice."

I half-moaned, half-whispered, "It's different for Mers."

He chuckled and darted his tongue before his full lips made my breath hitch into a gasp. His voice growled, deep and aching, "I think I can figure it out." He was hard against my hip, pushing through the scales of his dark blue tail. His hands slowly roamed down my curves. "I imagine if I touch you right here…"

I startled a cry as his fingers brushed on the scales at the front of my tail. We moaned together as he explored; the scales sliding back as I panted. I clung to his shoulders, my eyes hooded as I watched the muscles in his forearm alternately tense and release. He whispered filthy, beautiful words against my ear until I shuddered, my fingernails digging into his skin. Power rushed through my blood, stealing my breath like a thief.

I pulled him to me and groaned, "I need you, Mako, I need…" His lips and tongue captured my words, and I cried out into his mouth, my tail tense as I held him so tightly my arms ached. A firestorm built between us, made of magic and power and longing. It flushed through my blood, coloring my cheeks as I gasped. I wanted to weep and laugh simultaneously as the delicious sorcery of him coursed through my body.

The graze of his teeth on my lips took me over, and I

exploded in turquoise light mixed with cobalt and aquamarine. His deep groan was music that I swallowed through kisses. Thick magic pulsed in my body, heavy and lush. He stroked my hair away from my neck and rested his face on my skin. Our fins flicked and tickled as we lay breathless and silent.

He rearranged himself on his side to face me. I turned my head and sighed lazily. I'd never felt *this* before. His face was solemn as he said, "I love you, savage queen. Since the moment you exploded into my world, drenched head to toe in soap, I have loved you."

"Mako," I whispered, my eyes filling as my heart overflowed. I stroked his stubbled jaw, my thumb rubbing over his lip. Love meant vulnerability—which led, inevitably, to pain. Grief clenched my throat as I held back. I hoped he could see the words in my eyes.

The feminine voice rumbled around us. *Your heart is like a pearl, Scyphozoa. There was an initial wounding, a severe one, and layer by layer, hurt by hurt, you coated that injury, creating a wall of protection made from fear. You have suffered enough.*

White light blinded us, sudden and intense, and I shrieked as my heart cracked open. Shadows poured from it, soaring into the light like thin oil. My back arched for different reasons, and I cried out as the shadows grew denser, the pulling sensation more intense.

Her chuckle rattled my deep bones. *So stubborn. Let go.*

I wanted to clutch at the shadows. If I wasn't my pain or my torment, who was I? I'd spent a lifetime crafting this persona, hard with skepticism and dense with disappointment. I'd worked for my layers. I looked at Mako in desperation, frightened. He took my hand, a silent witness, and wove his fingers through mine.

Taunts, jabs, and barbed whispers flew through my mind,

releasing into the light. Tears, so many swallowed tears, rose from my throat and escaped with a strangled cry. Beyond them, an ache pulsed in my chest. It was the seed. The grain of sand. The initial wounding. My parents' deaths. It throbbed, desperate for healing. In my mind, I could see the event and witness my reaction. The pain was too large for a child's small heart, and I had taken it personally. The seed was compact and crusted, thick with misunderstanding.

"Mako, it hurts so bad!"

His whisper was soft and sad. "I know."

The strange voice was kind. *You suffer so much because you loved so deeply.* Primordial power rushed into my heart, replacing the piece of sand. It flowed through every wound, erasing my armor completely. Deep loneliness twirled in a shadow before lifting away into the light. The voice sighed. *There. Now you can love fully.*

My mother's soft voice lilted through the water. "Jelly, Jelly, eyes so blue. No one loves you like I do." My heart leaped with sweet remembering. There was no pain, no sting, just joy. I'd had a mother who loved me absolutely. My father's deep chuckle resonated through the water, as the ghost of him kissed my cheek.

Euphoria engulfed me. I clenched my fingers around Mako's as the mark on my back pulsed, sending a forceful wave crashing through me. I split away from my body and stared down, seeing the magic inside me. A network of energy flowed in the shape of my figure, as though tracing along my nerves.

The thickest line was turquoise, followed closely by cobalt blue, winding itself around it. Electric blue zipped and darted, while the blood-red line was slow, as if thoughtful. The maroon energy traveled without care, going wherever it wanted. The purple thread floated and the orange one flamed, leaping to escape its confines. Green light thrummed and hummed, almost as if it were laughing. Surfecti magic flowed in my veins.

The voice said, *You're missing yellow.*

"Yellow?" I asked, hoping for clarification. She didn't respond.

When I opened my eyes again, Mako was close, watching me. I fell into the cobalt blue of his eyes and saw love, so patient and kind, allowing me to be exactly who I was without judgment. A noise escaped me, half laugh, half sob, as I gasped, "Mako, I…"

My words died in my throat as Mako's eyes squeezed closed, his body and tail startlingly rigid. I scattered my hands over him, looking for the source of the attack. "What? What's wrong? What now?"

His clutching fingers bruised my shoulder. He gasped as his jaw tightened and the veins in his forehead pulsed. The darkness on his chest shifted like shadows clawing for purchase. He couldn't hold back his roar of agony, and there was nothing I could do except tell him to breathe. His whole body shook, and his skin turned to fire. He yanked back and threw his chin to the sky. He screamed, and cobalt rays shot from his eyes. His body levitated like a balloon, and I grabbed his hand so he wouldn't float away from me. White light surrounded him, obscuring him from my view, but his hand was solid in mine.

He screamed inside the shroud, and I worried my cheek with my teeth, whispering, "Come back, come back, please come back." The light gently faded, and he trembled as he drifted and sank back down. I spun, hovering over him as he lay on the silk. I tore at my lip and kissed him hard, letting my blood flow into his mouth.

He responded gently, coaxing me to calm down, running his hands on my arms, whispering, "I'm okay, I'm here. It's okay, Jelly." I pulled away and stared down, my blood swirling away from my mouth. My eyes went wide. The black that had covered his torso had changed. Thick markings spanned his chest, all the way to his shoulders in the shape of waves.

Each carried patterned scales, gathering in a swirl of a whirlpool at the center. Inside the gray spiral, a dark circle nested, containing brilliant white shapes that glowed in the eerie light. A sliver of the moon guarded three stars, almost embracing them. I touched his heart, beating in time with mine.

"She marked you," I whispered. He craned his head to look down. He slowly swept his eyes from side to side. A soothing current of water washed over us, cleansing the shock from our skin.

The voice sounded around us, vibrating with its deep ocean song. *Mako Fields, I claimed Scyphozoa as my own with her marking, and now, I claim you. You acted impulsively, instinctively, to save an innocent from harm, and to spare Jelly from grief. Remember, magic is energy. How it is treated determines whether it is light or dark. You absorbed malicious magic with the purest of intentions. Thus, I have transformed it and given you its power.*

Mako asked, "But what does that mean?"

The voice chuckled, rattling my bones. *That is up to you, my child. Expect wondrous things. But Mako? You must reclaim your gift. It serves no one when hidden.* Mako looked shocked. His hand slipped across his throat as though seeking a vital part of him. He swallowed and nodded once firmly.

You were willing to die for each other. You embraced the ultimate sacrifice with love in your hearts. And so it shall be.

I looked at Mako blankly, not understanding what she meant. But he did. He wrapped his arm around my waist and held my face with his other hand, triumph and love in his eyes.

He captured my lips in wild abandon. I responded to his kiss in kind. The roar of energy that shot through us was so forceful it hurt, and the skin on my finger burned. We broke from the kiss, panting.

"What in the Goddess was that?" I yelled.

Mako shook his right hand in the water, and with a frown, lifted it up. His eyes flew wide. "Look!" He grabbed my hands to inspect them. We stared. A turquoise ring surrounded his index finger, whereas mine was cobalt and on my left hand. I peered closer. A thin black line ran through the center of the color. I wiggled my index finger, no longer burning.

I stared and stared. Mako giggled and kissed me, creating another surge of power that snapped to my tail. I stammered, "Mako? Are these...?" My jaw hung open as the impossible suggestion hung in the water.

The melodious voice answered my question. I could hear the smile in the words. *Mate rings.*

Mako kissed me again, and I wrestled him off as the power flushed my cheeks red. "Mako! Give me a minute! Did you say 'Mate rings?' or did I misunderstand?"

The voice simply hummed. All I could do was blink in shock while Mako grinned joyously. Mate rings. Mate. Fated mate. I expected anger, a fierce denial, but it never came. My soul was perfectly content with all this.

Finally, I whispered, "Do you have a name? What should we call you? Are you a Goddess?"

Call me Mother Kokuro. I am.

I waited for her to complete the sentence. She didn't.

Along the lining of my shell is sustenance. It will further restore you. Your journey together has just begun. You will need your strength. Eat.

Mako gently peeled the green phytoplankton from inside

her shell, and passed me a piece. It was crunchy like romaine lettuce and tasted like sun-ripened watermelon. Energy flooded to my cells. He looked at his finger and grinned at me, as if he couldn't believe his luck. I snorted and said, "Well, you're stuck with me now."

This time when he kissed me, it was gentle, and the magic between us a thrum.

I stroked the soft surface we lay on. "Mother Kokuro, thank you for caring for us, for healing us. Did the pearl bring us here?" The pearl pulsed once, a powerful presence at my throat. I asked, "How do we get back? Back to our time? We still have to get Mako's sister."

Kokuro's voice vibrated around us. *Scyphozoa, trust your magic. Trust the pearl.*

"Okay," I whispered. I asked the pearl hesitantly, "Do you want to stay? This is your home." There was a pause, then two slow pulses. The pearl spoke softly in my mind, her voice distant, like a butterfly's whisper in a hurricane. I felt it more than I heard it.

We must go.

THIRTY-SIX

JELLY

Without a goodbye or a warning, we twisted through a tunnel of cobalt and black and turquoise, moving so fast my eyes teared up and blurred. Our bodies shimmered and took form, my armor intact, weapons in reach. We were in Synchi's secret cave at the back of her bedroom.

"Sweet Goddess!" I shrieked as the world stopped spinning.

Mori yelped and reflexively threw a whalebone star at our heads. We ducked, and it landed with a sharp thunk on the cave wall. She shouted, "Jelly! Mako! Fillian said you just disappeared! Are you okay? Mako! You're marked!" She rushed to him and held him by the shoulders as she greedily stared at his chest, completely forgetting about me.

I asked Synchi, "Where is Terrun? What happened after we left?"

Synchi shook her head. "Fillian was closest. He said a black cloud, like a giant ink spot, vanished right after you did. I went back to get him, needing him to give Tro magic." She tipped her head and added quietly, terribly, "If Tro doesn't make it, he will be the next commander."

I glanced at Fillian, anticipating the burn of disgust in my chest. It didn't come. My eyes fell on Tro, who lay on a slab within the circle. Strips of kelp lashed small pearls to his wound. Fillian frowned, holding his hands over Tro's chest, which rose and fell out of rhythm. The inhale was too short and labored. His skin was gray, his tail color had faded, and his rich, red hair had no luster. Black lines crawled away from the injury, creeping toward his heart.

My ex-lover scowled when Mako pressed his body against mine, possessively circling my waist with his arm. I bit my lip to hold back a laugh, quickly introducing them. It was a frosty nod on both sides. Synchi joined us, her mouth tight and turned down. She looked depleted as she said, "I'm doing everything I can. Those pearls were for the shield." She shook her head, tears forming in her milky eyes. "They aren't ready. They're underdeveloped. The bubble is falling. It's failing. The destruction was too great. And now, Tro."

"I think I can help," I whispered, trusting my instincts. Kokuro said magic was an intention. I reached for the colored strands of power in my body, asking for their assistance. They perked up at my attention and swirled around my turquoise. I freed my knuck and slashed it across my palm. Swallowing thickly, I pressed my bleeding hand to Tro's wound.

The black lines writhed as if pained and squirmed from my touch like worms fleeing a hot pavement, pushing harder to get to his heart. The pearl thrummed, and with a snarl, I drew them back, sucking in the poisoned magic. It shot straight to my mark like an arrow, where it transformed. I spun it back out. Turquoise magic flowed steadily from my hand and into Tro.

Synchi gasped, "What in the blazes?"

Tro sat up with a roar, causing us to scream and scatter back. We watched in fascination as his wound sealed up, leaving a pale blue scar in its wake. He bellowed, "What the sweet Goddess?" He stared at me and shouted, "What happened to your eyes? Where the hell am I? Shaman! Where am I? Is he gone? Did we win?" He swung his face at Mako and yelled, "And who the hell are you?"

"Shh, Toto, you're safe," Mori said through a laugh and a sob, staring at me with wide eyes. "A possessed swordfish ran you through with her blade. And Jelly…Jelly just…just…what did you just do?" I stared at her mystified face, threw my head back, and crowed.

Cackling, I slashed my hand again and created a gentle whirlpool around Synchi, infusing it with my blood. She gasped and squealed, her skin shimmering and dancing with magic. I saturated her with it, soaked her in it, until she cried through a laugh, "Enough, Jelly, enough!" I dropped the whirlpool.

She looked at least one hundred years younger. She was still older than sand, but her energy was sprightly and mischievous. Her eyes were a clear blue, her tail snowy white, and her wrinkles didn't swallow her features. Best of all, silver sparks flew from her fingertips. She giggled, "I haven't felt this electric in centuries!"

Immediately weaving her hands in a pattern, a blast of energy burst from the cave, stretching out to the bubble. She swiped her palms on her tail, satisfied. "Right. That should do it." She grinned at me and crossed her arms, the skin hugging closer to her muscles. "Well, well, Warrior Jelly. Look at you."

My euphoria and brazenness sagged like a worn-out sponge. I'd spent too much, too fast. Dizzy, I sucked in my bottom lip, annoyed to discover I had limits. I slumped, but soon found myself in Mako's arms, his tongue seeking mine as he commanded a carnal kiss. Magic rushed back into me and blue light, turquoise and cobalt together, shimmered and swirled, cocooning us. When he released me with a growl, the light faded back, leaving me reeling from his power.

I stammered, "Whoa, Mako! What was that?"

Synchi cleared her throat, her head cocked to the side as she playfully pulled on her beard braid. She had a knowing smile on her face. "*That* was not a normal kiss. *That* was a mate kiss." She waggled her eyebrows roguishly. Simultaneously, we lifted our marked fingers.

Mori screamed and clapped excitedly.

I grinned. "How could you tell?"

Synchi chuckled. "Your magic curled together, like it can't bear to be apart."

I blushed. "We have a lot to tell you. But how much time has passed since the battle?"

Synchi frowned and looked at Mori. "Five minutes? We raced here, strapped on the pearls, and Fillian started giving Tro his magic."

I yelped and squeezed Mako's arm. "The Mother said it would pause! I didn't believe her! So much happened inside her shell, I thought for certain more time would have passed here."

Synchi's jaw dropped. "Mother? Did you meet Mother Kokuro? Did you become *mates* on Mother Kokuro?"

"Yes!" I shouted gleefully. "What is she?"

"She is," said Synchi, not at all helpfully, still staring at us in shock.

"What?" asked Mori impatiently. "She is what?"

Synchi's brighter locs swam around her as she shook her head roughly. "She just is. She is. There is no other way to describe it. She claimed you? Both of you?" Her eyes flew wide. "And you…? While with her?" She waggled her fingers between me and Mako.

Nodding vigorously, I grinned and snorted, weaving my

fingers between Mako's, somewhat embarrassed yet not. Mori flung herself at us, her arm muscles straining from the ferocity of the hug. "I'm so happy for you both," she whispered, crushing our faces together. I scanned the small cave. Tro was now up and swimming like he hadn't been shaking hands with death. Fillian hovered to the side with a grim expression, watching me and Mako. I took a moment to breathe.

A thumping noise startled us, wild and insistent, slamming repeatedly on the outer wall of the cave. Mako shoved me behind him, and I pushed right back, floating at his side. I slid my knives free, and Mori readied her stars, tossing one to her father. Fillian drew his sword and Mako lifted his hands. Synchi's magic snarled at her fingertips as she opened the cave wall.

Faster than lightning, a small, red body shot for me, and eight arms squeezed my face, suckers slapping tight to my skin. I sheathed my knives and returned his eager embrace, tears of relief in my eyes. He released four arms to wrap them around Mako's head, gripping him with so much strength that our skulls clacked together.

Oggie's face was at ear level. He whispered in his squeaky voice, "You are my family, my chosen. Thank you, Mako, from the bottom of my three hearts. Thank you. If I..." his words broke off. He squeezed tighter, almost choking me, "If I had hurt the Shaman..."

I stroked his head and nuzzled his skin. "You're speaking in sentences, Oggie."

"Yes, having the ink scared out of you will do that," he quirked. He drew back and gazed at us. "I can see your bond. And you, Jelly, have lost the permanent fog that surrounded you. Your energy is delightful."

I scowled, "It wasn't before?"

Oggie chittered a laugh. "No, it wasn't. I absorbed as much

of your pain as possible, willing myself to be bigger to take it all for you. You held so much sorrow." He sighed happily and patted Mako's face, the suckers lifting his cheek from his teeth. "Take good care of her. I love her."

Mako wrapped his arm around my waist. "As do I. I'm glad you're okay, Oggie." Oggie's suckers peeled off as he went to Synchi, landing on her head and turning white, two arms gently stroking her face.

Tro cleared his throat and called Mako over to speak with him in private. Tro floated with his hands on his hips, completely recovered, his vibrant red hair swirling his serious face. Mako squeezed my hand and swam to him. Mori and I grinned. Tro was doing the father talk. They were too far away to hear what they were saying. Mako nodded, solemn, and then smiled, his hands moving through the water as he spoke. Tro tipped his head back and laughed at something Mako had said.

Mori sighed wistfully. "I doubt Toto will ever have 'the talk' for me."

I spun to her. "What are you talking about? Of course, he will."

She shook her head; her freckles bunching up as she frowned. "No, I don't think so, but…We'll see."

We turned back to Tro and Mako. They were hugging, with no back-slapping or distance between them. Tears of joy flooded my eyes. Fillian watched them from the other side of the cave. Understanding dawned on his face. He turned to me and lifted his fingers to his temple, his voice sounding soft in my mind. *He was willing to die to save you from pain. He's a half-Mers, yet more courageous than a Warrior.*

I nodded, smiling softly, and replied. *He is.*

Mako turned away from Tro, immediately looking for me with delight on his face. He followed my eyes to see me communicating with Fillian. Cobalt blue eyes darted back and forth before he responded to something Tro said.

Fillian's voice was soft. *I see he loves you deeply. Jelly, I never apologized for how I treated you. I am sorry I used you. You deserved better. Looks like you got it.*

I sighed, finally getting my apology. *Thank you, that means a lot to me. When you get your seat at the table, and I'm certain you will, remember this moment. And when you find your mermaid, treat her well. I hope you have your family, Fillian. I truly do.*

Mako swam to me and kissed me gently. My tailfin curled underneath me as he whispered, "I have your father's blessing. I know he's not your real—"

I interrupted him. "He is. He is the best father."

As Tro approached, he spread his arms, and I went to him. He kissed my head and murmured, "I support whatever you choose to do. I'm guessing you'll stay on the surface." I hesitated for a split second before nodding, worried about how he'd respond. But this was my life. I wanted to go back up.

Tro sighed, "I'll miss you, sweetheart." I blinked back happy tears as he gruffly cleared his throat, breaking our hug. He said, "You make me so proud, Jelly. Now, there's still a girl you still need to rescue. Best get on with it."

Synchi put her hands on her hips. "We're fine here. I just received a message from Nell through Hannah. You are to go to Bermuda and meet Asherah, the leader of the North Atlantic Mers. It turns out that Bermuda rock has a naturally high lead content. Terrun must have known somehow and chosen to hide her there. That's why no magic could find her. The lead hid her from us. I'm still not sure how you reached her, Jelly."

I slowly shook my head. "I think the pearl tracked Simmi. It needed to find her. It, she, the pearl, is Fae or some relation to the Fae. At least, I think that's what she is." The pearl pulsed once in reply.

Synchi peered at my eyes and smiled. "I see the Fae rings. Let me see the mark." I raised my eyebrow. I hadn't told her about it. She said, "Sophia told Nell, who told Hannah, who told me." I chortled at the fishy grapevine.

I released my chest plate and turned around, pulling my hair to the front. She traced the mark with a steady knuckle. "You are one of the most powerful creatures on the planet. The pearl bonded with you and gave you its magic. Incredible." She spun me around and cupped my cheek. "You didn't have to overpower it at all. You learned to work with it. And you successfully absorbed the magic of seven Surfecti. Quite a feat, Jelly. I'm proud of you."

I sighed, "Thank you, Synchi, but I'm back at square one. I am completely clueless about what I can do." The pearl vibrated at my throat. I'd learned this was her way of laughing at me.

"Oh, you'll figure it out. Somehow. And Jelly, you deserve everything good in this world. You've given so much of your soul to the sea creatures. It's about time you found happiness for yourself. Mako is a good man. I saw what he did for you, for us." She stroked my cheek. "He loves you like deep water, all the way to the bottom." Her voice wobbled. "But he cannot stay for longer than three days."

I smiled sadly. "No. He cannot." I slipped my arms around her and hugged her close, hearing her deeper question. "I can come back, though, right? What about the Trident? I want to be allowed to travel here freely. No restraints, no loss of magic." I shuddered. "No hole."

When Synchi pulled back, her clear eyes sparkled. "I wouldn't be too concerned about the Trident." She stroked her beard mischievously. "Expect major changes."

"Changes?"

She chuckled darkly. "After what just happened?" She nodded to Mako. "A Surfecti willingly sacrificed himself for the Mers. That deserves changes. No, we can't stay hidden in our bubble, leaving the Surfecti to defend the planet alone. It's high time for a revolution. I'm sick of those old farts dictating how we should live." She patted my cheek. "You're our Ocean Emissary, are you not? Well, go on and do it then. Do what you've always wanted. Defend the ocean and work from the surface, where you can actively change things. Your choices won't have any repercussions. *Your* choices."

Mako slipped up beside us, weaving his fingers in mine. Synchi smiled at him and said, "And you, dear Mako, take good care of her for me."

"I will, Madam Shaman. We will come back soon to visit."

She tutted and patted his cheek. "Call me Synchi." She suddenly shivered, her eyes flying open. "You must go, Jelly, now! The Goddess said to make haste. Terrun is regathering himself!" I slipped on my armor in alarm. Mori kissed her father's cheek and shot across the cave to us. Synchi handed her a small bundle containing several bottles of the transformation potion.

I opened my mouth, assuming she'd want to stay. I snapped it shut when Mori stated bluntly, "I'm coming with you."

"Mori, are you sure? You don't want to stay with Tro?"

She nodded firmly. "Where you go, I go. We have to call Nell. How are we—"

"Hold on!" I shouted, grabbing her arm.

Her words cut off in a scream as I yanked us into a whirlpool, my mind imagining pink sand, turquoise water, blossoming oleander trees, and red hibiscus. I shouted to the pearl in my mind. *Bermuda! Find Sebastian!* If my assumptions were correct, Fae would find Fae. If I was wrong, well, hopefully, we'd be okay.

We gasped as the water spun around us, settling almost immediately in the purest, prettiest water I'd ever seen. It was pristine and tasted divine. We swam for the surface, and Mori's voice bounced off the cave walls. "You did a whirlpool across the ocean? From the Pacific to the Atlantic? Is this Bermuda?"

I shrugged and bit my lip nervously. "I sure hope we're in Bermuda. The pearl took over. Like I said, I'm just along for the ride."

Mori gasped, "This place is gorgeous! Look at these things! What are they?"

Mako answered, "Stalagmites and stalactites. The stalagmites are on top and drip down to form the stalactites below. It takes a century to grow one centimeter."

Mori, about to touch one, hoicked her hand back. "Better keep my curious fingers to myself."

I sensed a mild thrumming in the water, like a heartbeat. "Do you feel that?"

Mako nodded. "It's magic of some sort. Old magic."

A melodic voice startled us from behind. "Welcome." Mori spun with a yelp. I grabbed her wrist, already drawn back with a star.

"Mori, take a damn breath!" I hissed. "You can't just go killing people!"

"Jelly," she whispered, "Look at their ears."

A small group gathered, all of them smiling. Except their teeth were not square. Every tooth narrowed to a sharp point, as did their ears. Ancient Fae-Mers, emphasis on the Fae. I immediately bowed reverently. Mako and Mori followed suit.

The voice belonged to a glorious creature. She immediately reminded me of Synchi. I couldn't help but stare. She was wizened, of an impossible age, her facial features almost entirely consumed by wrinkles. Her hair was snowy white and floated softly in curls around her head despite it being soaking wet. She beamed at us, and her smile reminded me of a moray eel, all sharp teeth. Her eyes were a kaleidoscope of colors, shifting and changing with each blink.

"My name is Samara. I am the Seer. We have been waiting for you. We've been waiting for centuries." I opened my mouth to speak, but she held up a hand. "Please, Scyphozoa. I have so much to say. A prophecy long ago stated that a blue-haired warrior would heal the schism between the magics. And here you are."

She smiled at Mako. "At the time of the prophecy, the races only mated with their own, bound by law, forbidding mixing. And then love changed that. Surfecti fell for Mers, Fae for Mers, Surfecti for Amphibi, Amphibi for Fae. On and on it goes. The offspring bloomed from love. As it should. Nothing else matters. Imagine if we all kept to ourselves. There would be no new magic. No blending. No…surprises."

"Amphibi?" I asked. "I'm not familiar with them."

"Ah. They are reclusive. Changelings. Able to live on the land or in the water, both fresh and salt. They have been hunted for their potent magic, driving them to hide to avoid extinction."

She swam to me and rested her hand over my heart. "And it was told that one day, a Mers with a true love for the ocean and all of her creatures would take on an impossible assignment. She would bear the Spirit of the Fae. She would take the pain of its magic, and if courage prevailed, she would absorb it and belong to all."

In my mind, I whispered to the pearl. *Spirit of the Fae? What are you?* The pearl rumbled at my throat. Samara turned to Mako. "And there would be a match for her. With a love so deep it would make the oceans blush. And through his love, his Fae would rise so that he might join her on her path."

Mako bowed. "I sincerely hope you are speaking of me, Samara." He lifted his twinkling eyes. "For if not, I fear I may have to hurt someone."

She laughed joyfully and swam to Mori, touching her cheek. "And the blue-haired warrior would have a faithful companion," she smiled, "with hair of fire and eyes of gold, one who would join her journey to strange lands."

She pinched Mori's cheek. "And yet, one more," she winked. "But I do not wish to ruin the surprise for you."

Mori huffed with a mix of laughter and impatience. "Can you give me a hint, Seer Samara?" She shrugged, "To ensure I don't kill them before knowing them."

"Ah," Samara smiled. "He will make himself known, Fire Maiden. We see you having a powerful influence on the world of magic. Do not forget that. Even when all seems lost." She tipped her head at Mori, her eyes turning a startling green. They shifted to purple in the next blink as she looked at me. "You, dear child, are missing yellow."

I frowned. "What does that mean?"

Samara smiled through sharp teeth, her eyes shifting to the color of the sun. "You must seek it. It will not come easily, but with determination, you will find it. Ah. The others are ready. Asherah will be here in three, two…"

A gorgeous mermaid popped up right beside the Seer. She was pure Mers. "Jelly! My Goddess, you look exactly like your mother! I'm Asherah." She flung her arms around me like we were old friends. Spirals of dark, shiny curls surrounded her face, and her tail was a brilliant orange, highlighting her luscious, dark skin. She wore a crown of white starfish and a breastplate of giant blue crab shells. Her body was exceptionally curvaceous and lovely to hug.

She unapologetically wiped tears from her eyes. "Your momma, Jelly. I'm so sorry. I met her as a child. She was exceptional." I nodded, my heart full of remembered love. She spun to Samara and asked, "Seer? Are we good to go?"

"Swim fast. Terrun in limbo, but he's fighting to get back here." Samara winked at me, her eyes shifting to candy pink. "You knocked him far away, Scyphozoa," she chuckled. "We delayed him as much as possible, throwing obstacles in his path. Be swift. He is spitting mad and intent on killing the girl as revenge."

Without further conversation, preparation, or any semblance of what we were doing, we dove with Asherah. We swam only a short time, popping up in another cave, this one smaller, the water even bluer. "Mako!" His name echoed and reverberated around the walls. We spun, searching for Sophia. Anna dropped her invisibility shield, and the Surfecti shouted and waved. I sighed with relief. They were here.

Sebastian boomed, "Son! You're marked!"

Sophia dove into the water, fully dressed, and hugged Mako, laughing and crying simultaneously. "Honey! Let me see what she did to you." She held him at arm's length and marveled at his chest.

Mako laughed and said, "It happened like a minute ago! How could you possibly know?"

She said breathlessly, "Samara told us. Mother Kokuro sent a message to the ocean's Seers, telling them a prophecy has begun, starting with the marking of a Fae-Mers, in love with a blue-haired mermaid." She turned to me and dissolved into tears of joy. "Jelly, sweet girl, thank you for saving him." She drew back and hiccuped. "If I'd lost him…"

"No one is losing anyone, Sophia. But he saved me first," I said, beaming at Mako. "A few times, actually." He pulled me to him snugly, his arm around my waist. Sophia noticed his possessiveness and how much I liked it. He stroked back my hair, and she gasped, seeing his index finger marked with a turquoise ring. She grabbed for my hand and lifted it. "Mates?"

Mako and I grinned, becoming more easy with the word. Sophia's eyes filled with tears. Mako said, "We'll tell you everything later, promise."

She smiled and wiped her eyes. "That's beautiful. I knew you had something special." She turned to me. "Jelly, I'm sorry for how I behaved. I put you in an impossible position."

I wrapped my arm around her, squeezing her against me and Mako. "Shush, Sophia. Never apologize for a mother's love. We're here, we're alive, and we're going for Simmi. We made it."

Asherah broke our moment. "Samara said to hurry. Anna, you remember the coordinates I gave you?" Anna nodded.

Asherah turned to me and grinned. "Your traveling whirlpool will save us time. I have warriors stationed in the waters around Castle Island. There's only one beach. Otherwise, it's limestone cliffs. Anna, we'll see you there. Goddess speed."

THIRTY-SEVEN

JELLY

Anna and the others grabbed hands and vanished as soon as Sophia reached them. "All right, then," I said. "No reunion." We left the beautiful cave behind, making our way toward Castle Island via whirlpool. We surfaced cautiously.

It was weirdly quiet; the stillness was unsettling. The sun rose sleepily over the horizon, and I was grateful for the light. I didn't want to battle on unfamiliar terrain in the dark. We swam silently, staying back from the only beach on the island. If it was a trap, it was masterful. Effectively corralled into one place, it was perfect for an ambush.

Heads popped up, and Asherah nodded to them. She called softly over her shoulder for her captain. "This is Max, my Head Guard. I must return to my people. Samara and I will watch through her glass. Good luck, Jelly."

I bowed to Asherah before turning to the dark-skinned merman, his thick chest and bright green tail resplendent in metal armor. He had a beautiful broad face, and his eyes were kind, contrasting the overall picture of the menace he portrayed.

He fisted a wickedly sharp machete, curved at the tip, and an assortment of knives hung in holsters fashioned to his armor. On his back, he carried a trident, the three prongs glinting in the morning light.

I gave him a Warrior salute, a fist to my chest, and a chin nod. "Max, do you know what possessed fish look like?"

Max had a thick islander accent, and it took me a moment to understand him. "Vee dun seen a dark cloud envelop a whole big school of parrot fish. Lionfish killed 'em straight away and den de cloud disappeared."

"Lionfish? What are they doing here? They live in the Indo-Pacific region."

"Some dodobird human released 'em from a fish tank. Dey been killin' ary-ting. But dat means dey ate de bad fish too. Snapped 'em up quick like." His lips curled into a violent smile, creating an immediate kinship. But my heart hurt from the loss of balance, again from human stupidity. Lionfish weren't indigenous to the Atlantic. They must be decimating the local reefs.

I said, "Don't let the fish with black eyes cut your skin. And there could be monsters called Eators. Don't let them cut you, either."

"Ya got it," Max replied, relaying the information to the ten warriors with him. With no time for personal introductions, I bowed to them before scanning the beach for our land crew. Anna and the others appeared seconds later, crouched in fighting stances at the far end of the beach. Gray split away from the group to scout. Roan came into the water to speak to us.

I swam to him and kept my voice low. "Do you hear anything?" He shook his head and looked at Simon on the beach, his eyes focused intently. Simon spun in a slow circle and with a snarled frown, his blue eyes bored into Roan's.

Roan said, "Simon hears crying. A woman." I strained my ears, but the only sound I heard was the melody of tree frogs singing to the fade of the night's humidity. When I looked at him, puzzled, he whispered, "Ye think yer the only ones with telepathy? How else would Shifters speak when changed? He's strong enough to do it in human form." I shrugged. Roan's voice was deep. "Ye need yer legs."

We shimmied out of our chain mail but kept on our chest plates. We handed our swords to Roan. Mori took out her potion and necked it, Roan offering his hand to her for support as she shifted, squeezing her eyes and mouth shut from pain. His green eyes were keen on the surrounding waters, watching for an attack. Mako and I nodded to each other and turned our tails into legs. I was as fast as him, and it barely hurt anymore.

"Thanks," Mori gasped as Roan let her go.

He grinned almost shyly, and said, "I brought ye a gift." He handed her a strap of metal stars, different from the ones Mako had given her. These had six prongs, each viciously sharp. "Thought ye might like them." She fisted and pumped her hands, looking at him with wild glee. She slung the strap over her chest plate and put her hands on his shoulders, kissing his cheek.

He blushed. Roan…blushed. Then I realized why.

I flexed my toes and frowned. "Roan," I hissed, "We're naked except for chest plates!" Roan's eyes darted to Mori's body and lingered as though he couldn't tear them away. I scolded, "Roan! Focus!"

He turned his startled eyes to me and rubbed his beard with a grin. He whispered in a deep growl, "Sorry, lass. Can't help it." He tipped his head, handed us our swords, and crossed his arms. "Ye don't need yer fanny covered to fight."

I scowled at him. "No. But…I'd rather it weren't hanging in the breeze."

Roan stifled a laugh. "Ye ain't got no bits in the air, lass."

Mako chuckled behind me and shrugged when I turned my scowl on him. He whispered, "The woman of my dreams fighting wild and naked…The Goddesses love me. They're making my every wish come true." I elbowed him in the ribs to sober him, but he moaned in mischievous delight.

Sophia swam up to us, grinning despite the impending danger. She whispered, "I have bottoms for you." I threw a fake glare at Mako, who pouted as I pulled on the bikini bottoms. His mother nudged him. "Put on your shorts, Mako. You can flirt with her later."

Mori swam to my side, and Roan slowly turned away from us. I caught a smile on his face as Mori pushed her long legs through her bottoms, stretching them around her other stars. She whispered, "I don't like this, Jelly. It's too quiet."

"I agree," I replied softly.

With a nod from Roan, we swam toward the beach until we could touch down. He stopped us again, and the waiting made my pulse jump erratically. Nothing was around us save the long stretch of pink sand, the early sun catching it with a beautiful sunrise fire. The ocean was still, almost glass, as if the world were holding its breath. I bit down on the inside of my cheek.

Where were they? Where was the enemy? They had to be somewhere. Terrun wouldn't make it this easy. I'd been certain the place would crawl with Eators.

The fort was in the distance. I lifted my hand to signal that we should proceed. A sting slashed my shoulder, partially protected by my hair. I immediately recognized the signature of the burn. Portuguese man o' war were not individual creatures, but a siphonophore, a colony that worked together to survive. Magic hid this one.

"Man o' war!" I screamed in warning, shattering the eerie silence. With my shout, the glamor concealing their stealthy approach dropped away. They were everywhere.

Sebastian and Gray splashed into the water to help clear a path to the beach. Deadly tendrils reached out from the translucent blue and purple bubbles, and I slashed at them, watching as everyone else cut and dove, trying to avoid getting stung. I looked down at my hand and saw turquoise magic coursing through my blade.

We were making little headway as the colony closed in around us. With horror, I saw Gray get tangled and go under, his short knives having little reach. Max yelled at Gray's cry of pain, "I'm comin' to you!" He spun his trident into the long tendrils like a fork in spaghetti, and snapped his trident in the air, flinging them away. "Okay, mate, you're okay," he barked, helping Gray find his feet.

I swung my knife wildly, and terror clawed at my throat as the wall got closer and closer despite our frantic fighting. There was no way we'd survive if they surrounded us. I screamed at the ocean life in my head. *HELP! Man o' war attack! If anyone hears this, come! Come to me! Please!*

I slashed my knives faster, hissing as a tendril wrapped around my calf. Max looked past me, and his face lit up. "Vee got company!"

A bale of Loggerhead turtles sped toward us. Their leader yelled in a female voice, *Eat the bubbles, ladies! Chop, chop! Gather up the strings as well!* They zoomed through the man-o-wars, inhaling them as they cackled with glee. But we were still in trouble. Too many blocked our access to the beach.

Max caught my eye, winked, and pointed over my shoulder. I turned as a fever of Spotted Eagle Rays gracefully swept in, further destroying Terrun's ocean attack. Max whooped and shook his fist over his head. "Yas gurl! And look o'er der! Blue dragons!"

My jaw dropped as a fleet of Blue Glaucus arrived. Little sea dragons, three inches long, fed on venomous prey, ingesting the stinging cells to become tiny toxic monsters themselves. They squealed. *Delicious! Such a feast!* High-voiced cheers rose from the fleet, and I crowed joyfully as they assailed the Man o' war.

The ocean had answered my call.

Max waved me toward the shallow water and yelled, "Go, gurl, go! Vee got dis! Get to de beach! Go get ya gurl!" He spun with a flick of his green tail and charged back into the fray. I took a step and startled as a school of barracuda almost knocked me over, their sharp, fang-like teeth bared as they honed in at twenty-five miles an hour. They whizzed past and latched onto a moray eel behind me, just about to strike my legs.

I dropped under the surface to see more stealthy morays executed by the barracuda, all menacing, gnashing teeth. The turtles, rays, and dragons tore at the man-o-war. The rising sun showed dark red blooms in the water, highlighting the destruction battling around us. It was utter carnage, but the Bermuda forces had us covered.

Roan shouted, "Get to the beach!" Our sea allies created a path for us, and we pushed through the water as fast as possible. We were almost there when a voice rang out. My body froze to ice. It was a treasured voice. One that had been missing for years—my mother's. "Scyphozoa! Come to me, sweet one! Let me see what a beautiful mermaid you've become."

I shook my head to clear the voice as it crooned to me. My mother was dead. This was dark magic. Again, the sound sang, "Zoa! Come here, child! You have my pearl, sweetness. I need it back. Let me see you. Come to me, my darling little jellyfish."

A vision shimmered on the sand, perfectly capturing my mother. Her arms were outstretched, and she had a beautiful smile on her face. She looked young and healthy. But it made no sense. She was Mers. She didn't have legs. Or did she? Confused, I sobbed her name as she called to me. The temptation of her was overpowering. My rational mind screamed at me to stay where I was, but my legs moved of their own volition, striding for the hallucination. Mako reached out, but I snarled and threatened him with my knife.

Roan jumped in front of me, and I raised my blade, ready to gut him. He spoke in my mind, *Lass, it's not her!*

Mori's voice collided in my head with Roan's. *Jelly! Fight back! Don't go to her! It's not your mom! She only called you Jelly! It's not real!*

I wanted to touch her so badly. Every bone in my body ached for her. My heart bounded in my chest, desperate for a hug from those familiar arms. I would give her the pearl. I would give her everything. She would leave my friends alone if I gave her the pearl. Just one hug. Just one.

Sophia grabbed my shoulder. "It's not her! Sebastian! Help her!" I swung around, almost slicing her across the stomach. She jumped backward, and I snarled as Sebastian pressed me to his body from behind, wrapping thick arms around me so I couldn't use my knives. I panted as the voice seduced me, thrashing to get loose.

Sebastian's arms went slack when the voice changed, and a second hallucination formed. "Daddy! Daddy, help me! He's hurting me! Help me, Daddy!" Sebastian dropped me and roared, rushing forward. Roan grabbed him and wrestled him back, the two of them falling in the water. Sophia sobbed as Simmi's voice shrieked and begged. Gray restrained her, locking her in muscular arms. Simmi was in the castle, yet seeing her perfect mirage collapsed all sense. I banged my hand to my head, trying to dislodge the fake images and sounds.

Mako bolted for the beach, no one to stop him. He fell with a shout as an enormous white wolf tackled him to the sand, and then everything descended into chaos. The voice multiplied, playing on our distress as it morphed to each individual's fear. Mori cried, "Toto! Toto, I'm coming!"

Roan gasped in agony, "Yer dead! Yer dead! Yer not real!" He released Sebastian, his arms wrapped around his waist as he buckled over. Mori wrestled in the hands that held her. Anna and Richard stood staring at each other, hands grasping each other's faces as they fought to withstand the magic. We choked on tears as the voices and visions of the past sang to us, calling us home, back to one last embrace, back to a chance to say a proper goodbye.

My heart fractured from the broken sorrow in Roan's voice, in Mori's wails for her father, all of us keening with some version of grief. Sebastian and Sophia screamed for Simmi while Mako battled the wolf, blood flying from their inflicted wounds.

Terrun was feasting on our pain.

I did the only thing I could think of. I raised my hand toward the beach and screamed into the void, aiming for the hallucinations. Jangled, I shot with no focus. It hit Mako and Simon, and they rolled with entangled limbs before coming to a stop, their bodies as still as stone. Terrun's spell broke, and the visions and voices fell dead. I roared with fury, "Move forward!" Mori screamed with blue murder, furious that Terrun replayed her worst fear.

The pearl beat against my throat, thrumming with power as I pushed through the water with my hands raised. To my astonishment, I found Max beside me on sturdy legs. "Daddy ain't a Mers," he grunted, his machete lifted, acting as my guard. Mori was on my other side. My head snapped up. The smell of tar cut through the fragrance of salt and flowers.

"Jelly! Eators!" Roan roared. Max, Mori, and I stalled in the surf, red-stained waves kissing our thighs. Two Eators raced toward Mako and Simon, mouths open, fangs dripping with venom. They closed in on the unconscious pair. I wouldn't get there in time with my knives, but didn't dare scream again in case I hurt them further.

A whistling shriek made me instinctively crouch, an arm swinging over my head. My jaw dropped open as Branko's claws wrenched off the heads of the two monsters, lifting to the sky with the grisly globes clutched firmly in his talons. He was enormous, an ivory-colored beast with vicious claws and broad wings. His head bore curved horns, and fangs jutted up over his lip.

The freshly decapitated Eators wavered mid-stride. Blood and black liquid spurt from their mangled necks, spraying and drenching Mako and Simon. Then, the headless bodies dropped to the sand like felled trees. An oily sheen took shape above the fallen bodies. The cloud dissipated without a trace, retrieved back to its evil source. The glamor hiding the Eators lifted. They were everywhere. Terrun had amassed a small army, ready for our attack.

Branko swung back with a blood-curdling roar and used the heads as bowling balls, flinging them into a nearby cluster of Eators, knocking them to the sand. I sprang from the water and collapsed on my knees beside Mako and Simon, both of them unconscious and soaked in blood. I frantically pawed at them, searching for injuries. Anna sprinted to my side and raised her shield, creating a bubble around us. She turned manic eyes to me and shouted, "Go! Save your strength! Find Simmi!"

Sophia's scream pulled me back to the present as I'd stalled over Mako's still form. The sound was terrifying, even to me. Everyone stiffened in place, disabled by her powerful voice. It wasn't a sound of fright. It raged. Richard drove a sword through the heart of the Eator, frozen from her power. She licked her lips, looking for her next target. I chuckled darkly. Never mess with a mermaid's anger. Even if she hadn't had a tail in years.

Further down the beach, Gray roared ferociously, orange flames ripping, and Mori threw her stars into the eyes of the Eators they battled, watching with satisfaction as they dropped to the sand. With a grimace, she yanked out her weapons and turned to the next. Richard's purple magic shot through the stomach of an Eator creeping up behind her.

Branko dropped out of the sky again. He snapped off two more heads. He was silent when he approached, never giving the Eators a chance to defend themselves. Branko twisted for the sea, dropping his load for the fish to eat before looping back around.

Max swung his machete and lopped the head off a monster like he was cutting down papaya for dinner. He slapped his palm to Sophia's. The Bermuda Mers warriors battled in the ocean, using their blades swiftly and efficiently as the lionfish and blue dragons paralyzed the swimming Eators with their venom. Heads bobbed in the water, washing up on the beach like buoys. The lionfish feasted on the bodies, and my stomach rolled in protest at the gore.

Anna's eyes flashed as she seethed, "Get your tail out of here and find Simmi! Go, Jelly!" I scanned the beach and found no sign of Roan or Sebastian. They must have left during the chaos. I looked at Anna, and she jerked her head toward the fort, her hands working over Mako and the wolf. With my heart in my throat, I left them and ran.

Six Eators jumped in front of me, but I was ready with my left hand raised, my right firmly gripping my knuck. I screamed at the top of my lungs, aiming for the heads of the dark creatures. Like candle wax, they melted under turquoise flame, their faces sliding off their skulls before they slumped to the ground.

I tore into the fort, my heels bruising on the stone stairs as I nearly tumbled down them in my haste. "Roan!" I bellowed, spinning down the spiral staircase toward the grunts and screams below me. "Roan! Where are you?" The lower level of the fort was a maze of small rooms. The sound of their fighting echoed and bounced against the stone walls, misdirecting me as I raced from room to room.

Every wasted second was one I couldn't afford. Neither could Simmi.

THIRTY-EIGHT

SIMMI

Esmerelda hissed behind my ear as the solitary Eator prowled closer, its fangs clicking together ominously. The others had bolted to defend the fort, leaving this solo monster to guard me. Shouting and screaming came from the beach, carried on the cool ocean breeze, causing my heart to hammer with hope.

The Eator guttered, "So pretty. I want. So. Hungry. Master not here. All mine."

I squirmed and shrieked, fruitlessly tugging at the straps and cuffs that bound me to the bed. "No, no, no!" I wailed, thrashing with terror as saliva hovered from its fangs before crashing to the floor. The Eator was almost upon me.

A flash of yellow dove through the window, a small beak driving straight for the eye. The monster turned and swatted the air, but my feathered friend was agile. He swooped away from the claws, threatening to slice him to ribbons. With a shout, he struck the Eator in the back of the neck, making it hiss and twist.

Kindee cried, "Now!"

Birds swarmed the room, beating their wings against the

Eator's face, their tiny feet tearing at its eyes and throat. There were kiskadees and bluebirds, sparrows, and starlings, all turning the Eator's attention away from me.

"Ha!" cried Esmerelda, running from her hiding place, her furry feet skidding across my cheek. She bunched her legs and launched herself from the bedframe. I held my breath as she landed on the Eator's face amidst the flurry of feathers. She moved so fast I could barely follow, binding its mouth and nose in thick webs.

It choked and grappled with the webbing, but Esmerelda was brave and darted between the claws to its neck, racing in circles, creating a hurricane-strong scarf with the ends dangling down the back. I watched in awe as the birds clutched the loose strands and flew sideways away from each other, tightening the noose. The Eator let out a surprised snarl as it stumbled and fell. A chorus of small voices cheered from the floor. The lizards had stood on each other's backs to trip it.

Esmerelda made a small slash across the webbing over the monster's mouth. From the shadows in the ceiling, the five huntsman spiders zipped down thin ropes and landed straight in the Eator's mouth. It screamed in abject horror. I retched as Esmerelda cackled and wove the Eator's jaw shut, reinforcing the web in its nostrils. It ripped at its face, slowly suffocating from the mass of spiders in its throat. Esmerelda moved like a nimble ninja, avoiding the deadly talons, laughing maniacally while repairing whatever it slashed.

The Eator finally succumbed. A dark cloud shimmered away to leave a plain man with thin hair lying on the floor in khakis. He wore a white-collared shirt. A pocket protector defended the fabric from a red pen, boasting the name of an accounting firm. His human mouth remained grimly sealed.

Esmerelda swiftly tore back her webbing, and the furry

brown spiders ran free, shouting with disgust at the smell of the man's breath. I giggled hysterically as spiders swapped multiple high-fives, forty-eight feet joyfully slapping together, and birds swooped in circles above me. The lizards sat on the window shelf, puffing orange throats, while ants formed a V shape for victory on the wall.

Kindee landed on my thin mattress with a bump. He shook out a wing before wincing and pulling it tight. I blinked at him, tears streaming down my cheeks. His small, beady eyes glittered with pain he tried not to show. "They're on the beach, Miss Simmi. Shouldn't be long now. We're ready if any more come." He accompanied his words with a determined nod, although I feared for his damaged wing.

Esmerelda ran back up the bed and collapsed joyfully where my ear met my neck. She patted my face gleefully with three arms. "Did you see us, Simmi? Did you see what we did? Kindee and I planned it all." She wiped away my tears, tutting at me.

I shuddered. "Thank you, Esmerelda. That was the most horrific yet satisfying thing I've ever seen. You were incredibly courageous. All of you were."

She cackled and coughed, tucking in her legs and rubbing her belly. "I will need at least four fat cockroaches after all that. I used up every last drop of my webbing." She looked at Kindee. "I'm of no more use, bird. I'm about to pass out." She folded herself in my hair, just behind my ear.

Heavy footsteps pounded toward us. I cringed, fearful of a battle where all of my small friends would die. But footsteps also meant it wasn't the Fae. Green light knocked out the spell at the entrance, and a furious giant consumed the space, his face a menace, inked muscles tight and ready to battle. He snarled when he saw the dead man on the floor. Roan was feral with rage and lifted his hand, aiming at Kindee. He stood bravely on my chest, his good wing shielding my face. I screamed, "Don't hurt the animals! They're mine!"

My father rushed in behind Roan and froze, witnessing the room. On seeing me alive, he exhaled. He took a moment to bow to the birds, the ants, the lizards, and the spiders. Each one tipped their heads in return, even the army of ants. He ran to me with tears in his eyes, and I broke down sobbing. He cradled my face, wiping my tears with his thumb. Kindee stayed where he was, a protector to the end. Dad's face flooded with gratitude, and he gently lay his hand on Kindee's broken wing.

Kindee ruffled his feathers and nodded his head. "Oh! That's much better! Are you Miss Simmi's father? I can see the resemblance. We've been keeping her as healthy as possible, all of us feeding her." Kindee turned to me with a wink. "Although I don't think she'll ever eat escargot again."

I hiccupped through tears, sobbing, "You found me!"

Dad freed my straps, far gentler than Terrun had ever been. "Of course we did, sweetheart. And we'll tell you all about it. Once we get you away from here." He looked over his shoulder to Roan, who stared slack-jawed at the spiders. They spun on the wall with their arms in the air, dancing with the ants, tossing them to each other like bean bags. The ants shrilled with delight.

His eyebrows bunched together in confusion. "Why are they not eating the ants? Why are they bloody playing?"

I sniffled. "Because they're allies. They came together to help me."

Kindee perched on the headboard and laughed in three raucous syllables. Dad grinned at his dumbfounded friend, his inked head tipped to the side as he watched the spiders and ants. "Roan! Can you undo these cuffs?" Dad glanced at the ceiling and grimaced at the thick brown symbols covered in flies.

Roan shook his head and crossed to me. "Sorry, lass. I got distracted." He laid his rough hand on my cheek and jumped back when Esmerelda hissed at him. He peered closer at the eight angry eyes staring back. Chuckling, he said, "Ye made ye some friends, eh, Simmi?" He nodded to Esmerelda. "I'm no threat, wee spider. No need to fear me." He studied the metal cuffs and shouted in a deep voice, "Dhíghlasáil!" The locks shuddered and clicked, and Roan gently pulled them away from my skin. "Yer not as chafed as I thought ye'd be, lass."

"Thank Jelly for that," I moaned, lowering my aching arms. "Where is she?" Just as I uttered the words, the blue-haired mermaid flew into the room, her eyes wide and wild.

"SIMMI!" she shrieked, bounding toward me and sweeping me into her arms. She clutched me and whispered, "Goddess, Simmi. You're a bag of bones." She turned to Dad and Roan, her eyes brimming with tears. "Let's get out of—"

She seized, her muscles clenching me painfully as her back arched. "Jelly, what's wrong?" I squeaked, wincing from the power in her mighty biceps. She let me go, dropping me in a heap as she staggered backward. The pearl at her throat pulsed and writhed until it pulled the chain tight. Her eyes flew open, and we watched breathlessly as her eyes changed. I scuttled close to Dad as the black ring thickened around the turquoise.

"She's getting possessed!" I gasped, terror making me want to crawl out the window. I curled into my father's arms. He tensed, ready to snatch me away in an instant.

"No, lass. Look." Roan's face was a mixture of awe and reverence.

My eyes stretched enormously as Jelly curled over on herself. She ripped at her chest plate and flung it away from her. Turquoise light shot from her back, illuminating the cold gray wall behind her. It projected a symbol, a yin-yang of sorts, the two halves swimming in endless circles like a signal.

I screamed as a flash of turquoise light blinded me, and when my vision cleared, my jaw dropped open as I stared at my friend. She stood taller by at least six inches, and her thickened muscles flexed as if chiseled from stone. She threw her head back and laughed, her voice deeply sonorous. I leaned forward on the bed, dropping to my hands and knees in amazement.

She winked at us and smiled. Fangs hung over her bottom lip. She chortled, "Thiff iff a furpriffe." When she pulled her hair back, it tangled on the tips of her…pointed ears. She opened her jaw wide, stretching it twice before trying to speak again. Her tongue gently teased across one sharp tooth, and she enunciated each word carefully. "Wow. I have to be careful not to slice my tongue off with these. Mako would be furious."

"Mako?" I whispered. "Is he here? Is Mom?"

Dad kissed the top of my head. "The whole family is here." I looked up at him and saw the lie in his eyes. We would never be whole without Leif.

Jelly rolled her head and growled, "We have to end Terrun. I can sense him." She looked at Dad and Roan. "You've got her?" They nodded.

I said, "Jelly, be careful. He's completely unhinged." She snarled and sprinted away.

Dad bundled me in his arms and twisted to leave. I gasped, "Wait!" Kindee stood in the window, his yellow breast puffed out, his beak lifted proudly. Esmerelda sat next to him, rubbing a foot across her jaw. I swallowed thickly. "I will never forget you. You saved my life. Thank you."

Dad gasped, embarrassed by himself. "Goddess, yes, thank you. But tell me. Why did you help?"

Kindee bowed until his beak scraped the stone. "My grandmother taught me that even the smallest kindness can have a significant impact. Two years ago, one of my fledglings fell from the nest. My wife and I spun in circles, dive-bombing the local cats, even though we knew it was futile. We flew until we almost collapsed. A human girl saw us and chased away the felines, carefully lifting my boy back to the nest. A girl saved my baby. And now I've saved yours."

He flapped his brown wings. "It has been an honor, Miss Simmi. May your life astound you with marvelous events. Remember us. Remember that every small creature matters."

Esmerelda rasped, "Stay brave, Simmi. And when the winds blow, weave low. But keep weaving. Always keep weaving."

THIRTY-NINE

JELLY

I could feel him lurking, as if breathing down my neck. The pearl was heavier and vibrating. I stormed out of the old fort and onto the pink sand, my eyes narrow and scanning for danger. Corpses lay everywhere, primarily men, many gruesomely decapitated. Branko landed at my side as if summoned, causing a spray of sand from his massive clawed feet.

"You're a damned masterpiece," I said, reaching over to slap his shoulder. He recoiled before I could.

"My skin is dry ice," he explained. He looked me up and down appreciatively. "You found your Fae form." I nodded. "Has it ever happened before?" I shook my head, still awestruck, as I stared at him.

His wings hung heavily on his back, resting. They had talons on their ends, crusted with black and red stringy pieces like spaghetti. I shuddered. I wasn't entirely immune to gore. He put his hands on his hips and stretched back, his clawed feet digging into the sand. He was a stone monster with muscles that would make Mew envious. Branko was thick…everywhere, something Mori quickly noticed as she careened around the corner.

"Oh, thank Goddess, there you are. Whoa! Fae! Nice!" She was speaking to me, but her eyes roamed over Branko. She jiggled her head. "Sorry, I'm staring, Branko. I've never seen Shifters up close, and you're...you're..." Her eyes slowly devoured his body. She dropped her voice, husky as she spoke. "You're a dark horse, aren't you?"

He bowed his head, his lips stretching over his thick fangs in a flirty smile. Mori blinked at him vacantly. His head suddenly snapped up as he tilted his ear toward the sea. "You need to be near the water, Jelly. As much as you're now Fae, you're primarily Mers. You'll be stronger in your element." His eyes squeezed shut for a moment. Mori took advantage and gawked before winking at me.

Branko growled, "I'm going back up to scan. There's a shift in the air." He lifted his chin and shot into the sky.

Mori exhaled, "He's... well, he's something special."

I tipped my head to the side. "For someone who kept going on and on about shagging everyone up top, you've been remarkably hesitant."

"Oh, right now? Just trying not to get killed. But over all, I've been a little busy with Eator attacks, ancient rituals, kidnappings and the sort. At the moment, I'm distracted by my best friend turning into a damned Fae after finding her fated mate." She crossed her arms with the last words.

I frowned. "Stop deflecting. You're notorious for your quick hookups. What's different?"

She squinted into the sun, uncomfortable with the conversation. "Can we discuss it later? Now isn't the best time, with a rogue prince on the loose and all."

I pushed my hair behind my pointed ear. "Fine. But we're circling back to this." She snorted at my ear and twirled her stars in her fingers.

Her head swiveled back and forth. "I lost track of everyone. Once the Eators were down, I went to the fort to look for you. I couldn't find you. It gave me the creeps in there, so I came back out."

I frowned, looking around. Where did everyone go? "Do you know where Mako is?" The pearl jumped on the chain, alarmed at something. Nails scraped down my back in a shiver.

A menacing voice slithered from behind us. "I do. He's tied up, darling. And if you want to see any of your Surfecti friends again, you'll give me the pearl."

We turned toward the dark, melodious voice. Both of us sucked in a breath. Mori sighed, "Dear Goddess, he's phenomenal." Terrun stood before us, ravishingly flawless. He was so exquisite it was almost painful to look at him. He oozed sensuality and dark promise.

His silky hair draped his sculpted face as he stood with a hip cocked to the side, displaying his impressive girth in tight, low-slung pants, his sinewy arms folded across his bare chest. Veins twisted along his lean body, and he casually swept a hand through his hair, flexing his wiry muscles. He was slinky and feline. Dangerous. He licked his lush lips, and Mori involuntarily groaned. He took advantage of our stunned shock to step closer. I raised a hand to stop him.

His electric green eyes brightened with excitement. "Ooh, threatening me with Fae magic? I'm a Prince of the Fae, my sweet girl. Royal blood." He paused and rolled his snaky hips temptingly, drawing Mori's eyes toward the motion. Gray was right to test my mettle against Fae seduction. Terrun was incredible. I kept my eyes resolutely on his face. He pouted his lips as if shushing a petulant child and dropped out his hand, palm up. "The pearl. Or everyone dies."

The pearl hummed at my throat. I asked quickly, *Can you*

beat him? The pause before the single pulse was too long for my liking. I needed more backup than Mori, especially as her tongue was practically hanging out of her mouth. Branko was somewhere in the sky. I didn't dare look up and take my eyes off Terrun. I stalled. "Why don't you help the humans? You could influence them to do better. Use your royal magic and work with the Surfecti."

Terrun rolled his gorgeous eyes. "The planet doesn't have time! Surely, you understand. You live under a trash pile." He scowled. "It's disgusting. I didn't realize just how awful it was until I attacked your little fortress. How do you bear it?"

I snarled, "I'm working on it."

Terrun tsked. "Ants against a dragon. The pollution is too dire. Humans are greedy little monsters and they will destroy everything. No. They need to die. All of them." Mori clung to his every word, nodding her head in agreement as if in a trance.

I screamed at her. *Snap out of it, Mori!*

She straightened as if I'd slapped her. I shook my head, saying, "Can't let you kill them, Prince Terrun. We have to give the humans a chance to change. If you want the pearl, you'll have to kill me first." Mori made a desperate noise in her throat and bent her knees. Power raced toward my palm. He felt it.

Terrun cocked his head, causing his hair to spill away from his long, pointed ear. He cooed, "So potent; more than ever. I can sense her." He spoke to my throat. "Come, my darling, be with me. You remember how good I can make it. We can rule together. Just you and me."

The pearl strongly pulsed twice. I raised my other hand and asked, "Are you talking to the pearl?"

Terrun tipped back his chin and laughed. It sounded like a wind chime with one short string. His eyes were a delighted madness as he purred, "She hasn't shown herself to you? She doesn't trust you with her truth. Has she even spoken to you?" I bristled. She had. Less than five words, but she'd spoken. Besides, we talked through the language of pulses.

He took another step forward on his slinky legs. Mori and I stepped back. "She is mine," he hissed, "Mine! The Fae could finally overcome all other magic with her ancient power." He stroked his fingers through his hair, ruffling it distractedly. "All the races interbreeding have diluted the magic, disturbing the natural order. Like your lover," he spat, "half Mers, half-Fae. Disgusting! Sebastio needs to be set on fire for his crime—making halfling children!"

Mori gasped, putting it together far faster than me, "Sebastio? Sebastian? Wait. Do you know each other?"

Terrun seethed. "He hasn't told you? Ha!" He put his hands on his hips, his fingers wiggling in agitation. They stilled as he smiled, his canines exposed. "No, I suppose he couldn't. That silencing curse held nicely." His eyes narrowed again.

Mori tapped her fingers to her chin, the other one holding a star. "You hate that he's had children outside of the Fae. But...if I'm right... you're not strong enough to fight him directly. So you took Simmi. Why? Her blood is familiar? Or even perhaps familial? I assume you have a history with the pearl. Somehow, you used Simmi's blood to locate it. So there's a deeper connection between you, Sebastian, and the pearl. Does that sound right?"

She took a step toward him, making my eyebrows raise in alarm. Her finger jabbed the air menacingly. "You want the planet exclusively! What? Just for the Fae? But you can't do it because Sebastian won't allow it, seeing as how his family is mixed. But if you had the pearl...you'd be stronger than Sebastian."

Terrun licked his lip so sensuously that I shivered despite

myself. He purred to Mori, "My, my, you're a clever little fish, aren't you?"

Mori pushed further. "And you keep threatening Jelly, but you haven't made the kill strike. You've hurt everyone around her…wait…*can* you kill Jelly?" She tipped her head. "Unless…if you kill Jelly, the pearl dies with her…because they're bound to each other?"

He hissed. "You talk too much."

She snorted. "I'm just getting started. Now, this isn't adding up." He ran a smooth hand down his chest, letting his fingers trace lower and lower, distracting Mori. Her words stuttered, but she shook her head and carried on, speaking despite watching him touch himself. Mori's eyes widened as the pieces slotted into place. Blood streamed from her palm from where she'd dug in a star to keep her focus.

She said, "You referred to the pearl as if *she* were a person. Killing Jelly might prevent the pearl from reverting to corporal form. She couldn't change into a person again. If you want the power *and* the person, Jelly has to give it to you willingly!"

Terrun snarled and raised his hand so swiftly I missed it, but the pearl didn't. A shield of turquoise light surrounded us just as Terrun hurled a black bolt of magic. The two energies collided, shooting a flare of twisted magic into the sky like a beacon. The mark on my back flared to life, and I squeaked when my fingers sprouted five-inch claws.

Tactical information from the pearl flashed through my mind. I confirmed, *His hamstrings?* One pulse.

I held my knuckles to my temple. *Mori, his weakness is the back of his legs. We have to get behind him.*

How?

No idea. Distract him. Keep dazzling him with your brain.

Mori chose a more direct route and whipped a throwing

star at Terrun's head. She frowned as he effortlessly moved to watch it fly past him. He chuckled, "She's smart, and she's a fighter. It's Mori, right? I might take you with me, pretty fish. I could use you in my army." He looked at my claws appreciatively. "And you…you're getting help. Is it the pearl or a result of your little ritual?"

Mori snarled, drawing his attention back to her. "I'll never work with you. You've been bleeding an innocent woman for selfish reasons. You're no better than the greedy humans you turn." We slowly approached him, splitting apart so he couldn't attack us both, although, given that he was a Fae Prince, it was entirely possible.

Mori kept talking. "And what? Someone took her away from the Fae? Away from you?"

As Terrun grew angrier, his fangs became longer, more wicked. "My father stole her! He sent her back to the ocean, where it would be more difficult to track her, but I knew she was there. I was close to having her during the humans' piddling little wars, but then she disappeared again, silent as the deepest waters." His head swung in my direction as I tried to slip behind him. "Then you lost your temper!"

Mori laughed derisively, and he faced her again as she said, "She didn't want to be with you, did she? She sacrificed herself to live as a pearl. You keep blaming your father, but maybe she begged to be changed to be rid of you. Ever think of that? Ever think that she *hates* you?"

Enraged, he morphed into his true Fae form, similar to Sebastian's in size. Yet Terrun was pitch black, as though coated in tar, and the smell of him choked my lungs. His brilliant green eyes turned the color of fresh blood and flashed with the promise of violence. He looked like the Eators. Only much, much larger.

Terrun's glamor had been so beautiful. Perhaps he had looked like that once, but the darkness of his soul turned him into a monster. We gawked at his gruesome transformation. Mori slipped her hair behind her ear. *I'm going for the jugular, Jelly. Be ready. This is our shot.*

Mori laughed in his face. "Typical Narcissist! You made your monsters in your image! Goddess, no wonder the pearl doesn't want you. What happened to you? You're not at all handsome like Sebastian. He's like, *gorgeous*! But you?" She wrinkled her nose in distaste. "What made you so…so…ugly?"

Enraged with Mori's words, he threw back his horrible face and yelled foreign words at the sky, his body trembling with anger. I blasted him with turquoise light, power flaming from my hands toward his throat. He staggered from the magic but didn't fall. But it had its intended effect of distracting him. Mori darted behind him and sliced into his thigh with a star. He howled and violently backhanded her, flinging her to the side. Black vines crawled across her chest toward her heart, writhing under her skin. Mori gasped, choking, her hands at her throat as if being strangled by invisible fingers. Her legs started to spasm, digging into the sand, her hazel eyes staring blindly at the brilliant blue sky.

"Let her go!" I screamed. I hit him again with my magic, but it wasn't enough. Even with the pearl sending me surge after surge, I wasn't enough. He laughed as I sent blast after blast, swatting it away while Mori convulsed behind him.

Terrun hissed, "Clever little fish figured it out." He turned to me, staring at the pearl. "I wanted her flesh again. Her blood is extraordinary. Such a shame. But I will settle for her power. It isn't as strong as her blood, but I'll make do. So, to answer your dying friend's question. Yes, I can kill you. And that is what I shall do." He snarled and lifted his hand. I gritted my teeth, praying the pearl could defend me.

The ocean roared at my back. The gentle Bermuda waters rose high in a wave, bearing Samara and the other Fae-Mers on its crest. Their combined energy was a kaleidoscope of color, a spear of swirling, flashing light. Samara's hair stood on end in a white halo of fury, her fangs exposed as she shrilled at him in a foreign tongue. They shot their magic at his heart. I added my magic with ferocity. Terrun froze, his horrible body shaking as though plugged into a live wire.

Behind him, Mori's eyes went blank, her body still and lifeless in the sand. Thinking the Fae-Mers had him trapped, I dropped my magic and ran to her. My poor judgement allowed Terrun a reprieve, one he used to his advantage. He struck at the Fae-Mers, shooting a lance of thick black. A wave lifted to block his dark magic, cutting off their attack. I gasped as the ocean and black cloud clashed. He reached a hand toward me and made a tight fist.

I staggered forward as the chain bit into my neck, causing a warm wetness against my skin as my blood spilled fast. The chain wavered and pulled tighter, edging deeper into my neck. The pearl pulsed twice, thrashing against him. I took another step to relieve the chain's pressure, my claws scrabbling and slicing through my skin as I protected the back of my neck. The claws disappeared, and I squirmed the fingers of one hand under the chain. I bit back a cry as I immediately lost sensation in the tips. With one hand trapped, I panicked.

I called forth the Surfecti magic within me, begging it to respond. I lifted my free hand and demanded it. My hand sprouted white fur and orange flames burst from my fingertips, spitting sparks out onto the sand. Purple light flared, and I levitated, my feet hovering an inch off the ground. More fire shot out from my fingers, scattering in every direction.

Fear stole my courage, my magic fading to nothing, silent

under my skin. Terrun cackled and pounded his good leg, thoroughly enjoying my failure. He sneered, "All that magic for nothing! You stupid, stupid girl!"

From nowhere, Anna appeared, her face grim and pale. She nodded to me once, her eyes sorrowful, as if saying farewell. She took Mori's hand, and they vanished. Tears filled my eyes. Terrun giggled, squeezing his fist tighter. I lurched forward, a sob escaping my throat. I called to the pearl. *I'm so sorry. He's too strong. I'll fight to the death for you, but I don't think I can win.*

Her voice spun through my head, along with a vibration at my throat. She was laughing at me.

You aren't alone.

Crackling blue lightning struck Terrun from the side, startling him and spinning him around. His clawed hand wrapped around his splintered ribs, and hissing, he yanked his fist hard. I stumbled as I jumped forward to counteract the pressure, falling to my knees, my head bowed as the pearl fought and thrashed against his force. I screamed in pain. The chain sawed through my fingers, finding bone.

Mako and Sebastian charged toward us as Fae. Sizzling ropes of cobalt and electric blue magic whipped from their hands. The pressure on my neck eased as Terrun swung to face them, needing the full force of his magic for defense. Cobalt blue flame shot from Mako's eyes, searing into Terrun's skin.

Scorching red lasers came from the sky as Branko aimed directly for Terrun's chest. Gray's orange fire intersected it, setting Terrun's black skin up in flames. His feet left the sand, seized within Richard's purple levitation, while a massive white wolf paced aggressively, waiting for the chance to join in. Terrun blurred at the edges of his body, as if a careless finger smudged a charcoal drawing.

The Fae-Mers bolstered the Surfecti, beaching themselves to get closer, hands lifted, fangs bared. Hope panted in my heart. Together, we could do this. Blood gushed down my back, the flow coming from my fingers and neck. Mako's voice was otherworldly and called to the core of me. "Rise, my savage queen! You kneel to no one!"

His words bolstered me and I staggered to my feet, dizzy from the pain and the blood and spent magic. Mako screamed, "Wrath, Jelly! Give us your wrath!" Every moment of biting my tongue gathered in my mouth. My cheeks burned in fury, thinking of how often I'd gnashed them to silence myself. No more. Rage accumulated, making me spin with its potency. The pearl's memories collected in a storm, her moments of abuse under this Fae remembered. She thrust her magic into me in one typhonic blast, flooding every cell in my body. I raised my hand, and on an exhale, I screamed. Turquoise fire exploded from my hand, hurling straight for Terrun.

He wailed in pain as it hit him. My savage heart relished the sound. I screamed again and again and again. His body vibrated as he shrieked. He squirmed and shimmered from our collective force, his body flashing in and out of being. Sebastian lifted his hands, murmuring a spell in a foreign tongue. With a roar, he tore them toward the sand. His voice was a force of nature, as fearsome as overhead thunder. He shouted, "AD FONTES EXILIUM!!!"

The world held its breath, sucked into a vacuum of silence until there was an outward blast of such proportion as it flung us away. We tumbled across delicate pink sand. The Fae-Mers were thrown into the sea.

I coughed and opened my eyes, but my vision was blank white. When I blinked against it, trying to see, I panicked, thinking I was dead as I couldn't hear or see or feel, but then she materialized in my mind.

A statuesque Fae stood before me. She was massive, at least six feet tall, if not more. She immediately bent over, heaving for breath, resting her claws on meaty thighs. Her skin was vantablack, the darkest pigment I'd ever seen. She would make the darkest night sky seem shy.

Her wild eyes glowed as she stared at me. They were electric purple, ringed in a turquoise band, the pupils a shocking pink. They sparkled with joy. Pure white hair streamed to her hips and flowed like liquid silk around her tall, pointed ears, capped with shiny silver tips. She drew back her lips and smiled, displaying deadly, long, sharp teeth. Her voice was an orchestra of sound, encompassing the heavy vibration of a double bass while tinkling with the starlight of bells. "Hello, Jelly," she sang.

The sound was glorious, causing the bloody, tangled hair on my neck to prickle and stand up, my entire body erupting in goosebumps. She stood and flung her head back and laughed from her belly. Her fisted hands pumped into the sky as she screamed elatedly.

I recovered my shock and laughed with her, hot tears streaming down my face. She bent over again, panting from all she'd spent. I opened my mouth to ask her a thousand questions, but she stopped me with a raised hand, speaking into my mind.

I must practice speaking with a tongue again. It's been a long time. I am Leoht. I will return to the pearl now, but Mori needs you. She's in the Sliver and slipping fast. Hurry!

FORTY

JELLY

I blasted back to reality, waking to shouting as Sebastian pulsed healing magic into the wound on my neck. Mako held my fingers in his warm blue fire and yelled at me to wake up. My eyes flew open, and Mako's face sagged with relief. I said over a raw throat, "We have to go to Mori!" I no sooner said the words, and Anna materialized and seized my hand, she and I vanishing from the beach.

Our bodies landed in a strange house, the walls painted bright white, and a large ceiling fan ruffled sheer curtains. I crawled on my hands and knees to Mori. She lay still on the floor. Roan cradled her head in his massive hands and exhaled when he saw us. "Thank fook. I'm holding her soul here, but only just. Be quick, lass!"

My fang tore open my lip, and I pressed my mouth to Mori's. It was like kissing ice. She didn't respond at all. I looked at Roan frantically. "She's not coming back to me."

Anna barked, "Vision walk! You don't need the ceremony as you've done it together once before. Hurry!"

Without hesitation, Roan said, "Bite me." I would have

joked if it weren't for Mori's perilous state. I sank my fangs into his shoulder and grabbed the wound with my damaged fingers. Our blood mixed, and Roan whipped us away into Mori's mind.

At first, it was dark, but as I called for her, it brightened slowly with a faint reply as she whispered my name. I noted where I'd arrived and ran toward her voice to find her nestled inside a hollowed oak tree. Her body tucked into a tight, rolled ball, and her hazel eyes looked at me mournfully.

"Mori?" I whispered, "Mori, come back. Terrun is gone. We sent him back to the Fae. Or somewhere. Sebastian did it. It's safe. I promise."

She shook her head and retreated further into the tree. Not seeing an option, I squirmed in beside her, my feet sticking out. She whispered, "I can't feel anything, Jelly." Her smile was sad. "Mom is here. She tells me I'm in the Sliver. It's when you straddle both worlds, neither dead nor alive."

Her eyes filled with tears. "She says only people who love you can reach you in the Sliver. People from either side. I don't say it enough, but I love you, Jelly."

I choked, "I love you too, Mori. But you're not saying goodbye. Not today."

A tear slipped down her cheek. "Tell Toto I love him."

I retorted, "Tell him yourself. You can't die, Mori. I don't have anyone else."

She shook her head. "You have a mate now, Jelly. And Simmi. The village. You have the pearl. You don't need me."

"That's not true! I need you like air! Like water! Goddess, Mori! I need you like salt!"

Another tear slid silently down her cheek. She sniffled. "It's like when Mom died. Just this hole inside. Leave me, Jelly. Let me go."

My voice broke. "Who will help me with the humans? You like them far more than I do. I'm likely to kill them when I get angry."

She snorted, eyes downcast.

I tried a different approach. "You said you wanted to sleep with a Shifter. There's Branko. He's keen, you saw. And Gray's hot. He might be bisexual. Simon might be too. You could jump into bed with both of them and see what happens. You and a mage and a shifter. How fun would that be? And we can meet more. We can meet all the Shifters. If there are gargoyles and wolves, there's bound to be others…A dragon! We can find a dragon for you to shag!"

Thunder sounded outside. Or maybe it was Roan.

She chuckled, lifting lightened eyes before sighing heavily. "I'm going to miss you, Jelly. I'll never find another friend like you."

"Then don't go," I begged. I scrambled for something that would make her want to stay and live. "Remember what Samara said? She said you were going to kick ass with magic, and to keep your shit together when everything seemed bleak."

Mori grinned. "That's not even close to what she said."

I huffed. "That was the gist of it." Mori made a humming noise. I stroked her cheek with the back of my hand, my fingers still sore and raw. "I need you, Mori. I can't do this without you."

She tipped her head to the side, curious. "Do what?"

I sighed. "Work up top with the Surfecti. Bridge the gap in magic. I can make a difference here, but it won't work without you. You're so smart. You figure everything out way before anyone else does. Please, Mori, please. You're so powerful. Your brain is incredible, and I seriously cannot do this without you."

She said wistfully, "Sebastio. I think Sebastian and Terrun

are relatives. Brothers or cousins, maybe?" She sucked her teeth, annoyed. "I wanted to ask him about that. I guess I won't have the chance now."

I hiccuped, forcing my voice to stay steady. "You can still ask him. I love you, Mori. You're my soul sister. I can't...I can't live here without you. Please, Mor. Come back with me. Samara specifically told you to hang in there. Mori, you're supposed to live."

She hummed, weighing her options. I bit my cheek to stop myself from dragging her out. She had to make this decision herself. I prayed. *Goddess Kelbazi, please help me. All I do is ask for help, but she's my best friend. Give her a push.*

Kelbazi answered in a tattooed man's voice, sounding all around us. "From the moment I met ye, I knew ye was special. But when ye split me lip open...oof. Such sass. Very sexy. Come back, Mori. Yer not done here, lass."

Mori bit her thumbnail then shouted to the wind, "Roan? Can you hear me?"

"Aye."

"How much magic are you using to access the Sliver?"

"A fook of a lot, lass. And I can't hold it much longer."

She grinned. "Will you teach me telepathy like yours?"

"Aye. If ye hurry the fook up."

Her eyes sparkled, her mind excited by the possibilities. My voice held an urgent edge. "Your physical body is...well, it's almost gone, Mori. You're like ice. We don't have much time. We're holding you by a thread."

She looked at me hard and then shoved me toward the entrance. "Better run, then."

We sprinted for the entry point, whipping back to the room with the lazy fan. When Mori sucked in a breath and coughed, Roan sighed, his entire body sagging. I sat back with a thunk, wanting to yell at her for scaring me half to death, but so, so happy she came back. I swept her red curls from her face. "Need a blood kiss?"

She choked. "I love you, Jelly. But not like that. No. I just need a minute." Anna crouched down beside us.

"Mori, this is a potent tonic from the local Seer. She must have expected this because she gave me a vial with your name on it." She turned to Roan. "Carry her to the bed, please."

Mori was alert enough to joke, and her eyes rolled up loosely to Roan's. "Not how I pictured this, Surly Bear. I should at least put some enthusiasm into it. Not act like a dishrag."

He grunted and lifted her as if she were a feather, holding her propped up so Anna could tip the tonic down her throat. He covered her with a blanket and kissed the side of her head, causing my eyebrows to raise while Mori grinned through an alternate grimace from the tonic. "That's so strong…" Her eyes fluttered closed. Roan stroked a knuckle on her cheek.

Anna nodded. "She'll be out for a while. Let her rest."

Roan cleared his throat and left without saying a word.

Anna pulled the door shut and motioned me toward the kitchen. I limped down the black and white tiled hallway, admiring the pastel yellow on the walls, and inhaled the heady perfume of frangipani on the breeze. "Whose house is this?" I asked.

"It belongs to a Bermudian Walker. Asherah contacted her. She's gone to stay with her cousin, and said we could have it for as long as we needed. I'm hoping we won't need to linger, but Simmi is too weak to travel to either my home or hers. She needs time to recover."

We entered the open kitchen. Sebastian had commandeered the gas range, flipping pancakes and stirring scrambled eggs. All the chatter stopped. I said, "Mori's sleeping.

She's alive." Sighs of relief flooded the air. A ferocious kiss stalled my steps as Mako pounced on me. He pushed back my hair and kissed me more gently before showing me to the table.

Simon was on coffee duty and asked, "Cappuccino?"

I nodded to the shifter. "Simon, yes, please. I'm sorry you didn't get to rip out his throat. You looked annoyed as you paced. Like you were missing out on all the fun."

He sighed. "So true."

Simon handed me a steaming cup and pulled out the chair beside me. I smiled as Mako piled my plate and passed along the eggs. Sebastian put a platter of pancakes on the table and groaned heavily as he sank into a chair next to Sophia. He kissed her blond hair. He whispered in her ear and she smiled shyly, glancing at me and Mako.

She cleared her throat. "So, I don't know if you noticed, but Mako and Jelly are mates."

There was a second of silence before the table exploded with noise, everyone clamoring for the story. We told it through pancakes and coffee, smiling and laughing, and leaving out some details that weren't for sharing. Mako squeezed my knee under the table.

Anna passed out healing potions, courtesy of the Fae-Mers. I shuddered as the unfamiliar dark liquid burned down my throat. I coughed, "Goddess! That's like firewater!" Anna only chuckled as she tipped hers back.

Exhausted, Surfecti quickly collapsed onto the beds and sofas in the borrowed house. Mako took my hand, and we wandered to the beach, looking for privacy. Asherah popped up from the water. "Samara told me to find you and tell you about a special place. It's hard to get to from land. It's very secluded," she added with a wink, glancing at our intertwined fingers. "Take a blanket." With a coy smile, she gave us directions and disappeared under the waves.

I giggled. "Handy having a Seer, huh?"

We gathered supplies from the house, hurriedly shoving them in a waterproof bag. We left a note saying where we'd gone and ran for the ocean. When we arrived, we changed from tails to legs, slipping on our suits in case we encountered any humans.

"Are you nervous?" Mako asked, pushing my hair back over my rounded ears. "We could wait. Do this in a bed. It's your first time with legs and all."

I answered him by sucking his lower lip between my teeth. "Nope, I can't wait anymore. I want this, Mako. I want you. I want you here by the ocean. It seems fitting, although I'm glad we have a blanket for when we actually do it. I don't want sand in my—"

He cut off my words with another kiss, magic racing up my spine and curling my toes.

I moaned into his mouth and whispered, "So, there's a thing that women with legs have that the Mers don't. Mori calls it the power dot. I've only just discovered it, having played with it once, and it's electric. I know what it is, technically, but I swear the thing's magic."

"Mmm," Mako growled, slipping his warm fingers down my wet belly. "I know exactly what you're talking about. It's your—"

"Hey there!" A voice shouted from down the beach. "You two! Give us a hand, will you?"

We turned to see an elderly gentleman struggling with a loaded trash bag. I giggled as Mako cursed under his breath. We strode through the shallow water, holding hands. The man blinked at me, his jaw slack as if he'd seen a ghost.

"You!" he said, his voice rough. "Well, I'll be damned. She said I'd see you."

I smiled, shading my eyes with my hand. "Who said? Have we met? I'm sorry, I don't remember."

"Nah. It was years ago. I was about twenty-five and knocked myself out. I got drunk on my boat, and the boom swung around and clocked me. I'll tell you, I was all but dead, sinking for the ocean floor. And this little…it sounds crazy. This mermaid…swear to God…I'm not lying. She had hair and eyes just like yours. She gave me the kiss of life under the water and dragged me back to the surface. She told me that if I stopped drinking, I'd marry the woman of my dreams. I'd have a family that would love me till my last breath. Well, I listened. Never touched another drop."

My heart was in my throat. Mako slipped his arm around me, holding me close as my knees buckled. I whispered, "Did she tell you her name?"

He shook his head. "No. But she said I'd meet you. She had a message for you. Now, hang on, I haven't thought of it in years." He closed his eyes, and the few strands of hair he had left twisted in the ocean breeze. "Ah, I got it. She said, 'Jelly, Jelly, eyes so blue, the love you share is pure and true.' Does that mean something to you?"

He squinted in the sun, chuckling at our stunned faces. "I guess it does. Good. Those look like happy tears. That warms my old heart. Now, help me drag this trash to my car, would you?"

FORTY-ONE

JELLY

I wasn't alone this time. As the bus steamed down the road, I held hands with Mako. Simmi and Mew sat on the bench across from us. We watched silently as people boarded, heading to where it all started. We'd planned to meet Mori and Roan when we were done, and weren't sure if our sushi dinner would be for congratulations or commiserations.

Mew broke the silence. He said in a low voice, "It makes sense to change our focus." When I glowered at him, he laughed, his massive shoulders shaking. "Damn, girl, get that scowl off your face. Hear me out. There are organizations with money behind them. Humans already doing good things. We can piggyback and jump onboard."

I crossed my arms, dropping my voice to a hiss. "There you go again, talking about humans like you aren't one. Unless you'd like to share?"

He grinned. "Five seconds, girlie. That's the deal. I'll tell you everything if you can hold me down for that long. Now, I've been reading about The Ocean Cleanup. They make a good point about the plastic."

"And what's that?" My voice had a bite, annoyed that he wanted to go off-plan. I'd made myself crystal clear that my priority was ocean pollution. Also, I stewed from his comment. I still couldn't pin him in sparring. My best was a second and a half. He was something other because I could sense it. But no one would tell me what he was. Not even Mako.

He shrugged. "We need to clean up the rivers. Makes sense. Stop the pollution before it gets to the ocean."

Mako nodded. "I've heard of them. They say that eighty percent of the ocean pollution comes from just a thousand rivers."

"A thousand? No biggie, then. Where do we start?" I said sarcastically.

He smiled at my grumpiness. "Mew's not wrong. I mean, we have to start somewhere. At least, if we work on the rivers, we stop it early."

Simmi peered around Mew's colossal body. She'd regained her lost weight, and her cheeks were a healthy, rosy pink. She said, "We're not giving up on the ocean, Jelly. Never. Just think about it."

"You too?" I said, throwing my hands up.

The bus wheezed to a stop outside the dump. We stared at the mountains of trash, seagulls racing each other to pillage the rotten bounty inside. Giant dump trucks offloaded, waiting patiently for their turn like a line of ants. I snarled and turned away as the brakes of the bus eased, lurching us forward again.

We were silent, Mako stroking my hand as I flailed, overwhelmed by the sheer volume of work before us. Simmi straightened and said, "Okay. We're here. You good?"

I nodded as the pearl pulsed once. "Yeah, we're both good. We got this."

I laughed as a cute, scruffy man waved me over to his

rickety table outside. He said, "Do you want to make a donation to our foundation, Save Our Oceans? You can get a stainless steel water bottle for a twenty-dollar donation, or one of these outstanding canvas bags for thirty." He stared at me with shining eyes, hopeful. "Gosh, I'm sorry if this sounds weird, but your hair is beautiful. I've never seen a blond like you. It's like it's spun with gold. It's almost magical."

Mew chuckled and handed him fifty dollars, swiping up a bag printed with the foundation's name and the image of a breaching humpback. He winked at the man. "Keep the change."

We entered through the front door of the superstore, Mako's grip on my hand almost bruising. I chewed on my lip, intentionally keeping my eyes from aisle six. A familiar older lady bustled up to us with a smile and said, "Welcome! Can I help you find something?"

Her breath sucked in as she looked at me. I froze, praying she wouldn't recognize me. "My, what extraordinary eyes! I don't think I've ever seen rings like that! And they go so beautifully with your blond hair!" She raised her hand, as if to touch it, dropping it with a shake of her head. "Gosh, I swear I've seen your face before. Are you a model, sugar?"

I swallowed my grin and said, "Thank you. It's kind of you to say, but no, I'm not a model. Can you point us toward the manager's office, please? We have an appointment." Mako kissed my temple hotly.

The lady stared at me for a beat, trying to place me, and murmured, "Strangest thing." Then, in a chipper voice, she said, "Follow me." Thankfully, she skirted around the outside edge of the store. She knocked on a door, still puzzling over my face. A voice told us to come in.

The man at the desk stood and shook our hands, pausing

briefly as I introduced myself. His eyebrows furrowed before he waved us toward the two chairs across from him. Mew faded into the background inconspicuously as Simmi and I sat, and Mako stood at my side.

Simmi said, "Thank you so much for meeting with us, Mister Bunt. My partner and I have been working on a product we think will interest you. I've run multiple tests against the leading detergents on the market, and these are just as effective. Plus, they take up less shelf space, giving more room for other items, which helps your bottom line."

He nodded, "Okay, good opening. Let's see what you have."

Simmi rustled through her bag and pulled out our sample, neatly displayed in a cardboard sleeve, the packaging colorful and fun. She smiled with pride as she slid it across the weathered desk. She said, "These are *Ocean Lover Laundry Strips*. No need for bulky plastic containers. No dripping mess on the laundry room floor." She winked at him. "And no clean up on aisle six."

Mr. Bunt's eyebrows shot up. I blinked innocently, cursing Simmi in my mind. I'd told her not to mention the explosion. Of course, no one knew it was me, and it had been on the news, so it wasn't a secret, but I'd argued that we shouldn't bring it up and distract him. She'd disagreed, saying that it helped our cause.

She fought back a grin as she watched me squirm in my seat. I cleared my throat, proceeding with my part of the presentation. "People increasingly worry about ocean pollution, and they're changing the way they shop. Environmentally friendly companies are gaining traction in the market. We're already stocked in the smaller stores in the area. We wanted to approach you as our first superstore."

The manager's eyes narrowed. "Why?" he asked suspiciously.

I said confidently, "Because if the large stores stock it, we'll get more exposure."

He chuckled. "And more profit. What does it cost?"

I clenched my jaw. I appreciated it all came down to money, but we needed to play his emotions more. The finances worked against us. Simmi shrugged casually, sliding around his question. "Tell me, Mr. Bunt. Do you have children? Grandchildren?" He did. We'd stalked him on social media before securing this appointment.

He smiled softly and leaned back in his chair. "I do. Three children and seven grandchildren."

Simmi went for his heartstrings. "Aren't you worried about what kind of world you're leaving them?"

Mr. Bunt swallowed thickly. He reached for the laundry strips and held them to his face, sniffing. Meticulously, he opened the cardboard sleeve, the teeth of the serration separating smoothly. I sighed with relief. It had been a bugbear in our production.

He pulled out a strip and rubbed it between his fingers, his mouth turned down in a frown. "How do I stack them? Laundry jugs line up neatly on shelves."

"We have wooden racks to display them. They're the same width as a standard jug," Simmi stated.

We worked in tandem. I followed. "They're free of all known carcinogens, unlike most commercial laundry soaps. Our strips are free of formaldehyde, which can cause dermatitis, and they don't have phthalates, which can cause endocrine system problems. Not good for anyone. Laundry soap making us sick - who would imagine?"

Simmi came in as smooth as silk. "We also have a fragrance-free option for people with allergies, meaning it's also perfect for babies. We're working on dryer sheets. Obviously, it's better to let your clothes dry in the sun, but not everyone has that option. Commercially produced dryer sheets leave a chemical coating on clothing."

I piped in, "Quaternary ammonium compounds, to be precise. Linked to various health concerns, like asthma, rashes, and burning eyes. Standard dryer sheets are made from polyester, which is petroleum-based. Who wants that on their skin?"

Mr. Bunt looked annoyed, like my facts were causing him discomfort. I went off track from his expression. "Personally, I think our laundry strips are so effective that you don't need dryer sheets. But until the humans—" My brain stalled. "Um, until *the public*," I cleared my throat, "When the public tries our laundry strips, they'll see there's no need for dryer sheets."

Simmi shot me a sideways look. I prayed that Mr. Bunt hadn't caught my fumble. I cursed myself inside. I'd gotten too carried away, letting myself slip into my natural way of thinking, seeing the humans as separate. We sat back nervously, letting him absorb everything we'd just thrown at him.

He held the strip up to the sunlight streaming through his window. His voice was patient, but it was hard to judge if he was interested. "All of that is important. What's my cost?"

Mako twitched at my side. We'd debated whether to wheedle the manager, to persuade him with a small zap of magic. I imperceptibly shook my head. No manipulation. I wanted to see if we could change humanity without it. Simmi said, "Well, sir, we want to be transparent with you. It's twice as much as the leading brand."

I huffed and added, "But the big companies charge more for baby soaps, which is ridiculous. They contain fewer chemicals. Wouldn't that make them less expensive? But gotta play on those new mommas! Our strips are only thirty percent more expensive than the commercial baby soaps, giving it a more favorable margin. But let me ask you, do any of your grandbabies suffer from eczema?"

They did. His daughter constantly lamented on social media, saying it was impossible to find pure cotton clothing for her eldest. He quirked an eyebrow suspiciously and nodded. I copied his nod and said, "Ten percent of the population has eczema. Horrible. Ten million kids in this country scratching until they bleed. They can't sleep or find clothes that don't aggravate them. And soap burns like acid. And if their little bodies get overwhelmed, for example, with chemicals? Well, it can develop into more complicated diseases."

Simmi soothed, "We're not saying that laundry soap *specifically* causes eczema or other illnesses, but it can't be good to have all those aggravates against that poor, sore skin, now can it?"

The manager smirked, seeing through our bleeding heart campaign. He asked, "What is your marketing budget? No matter how viable the product is, we won't take on those costs for you." He glanced at the packaging. "Can you run with the big boys? Corporations have millions to throw at advertising."

Mako cleared his throat. This was his department. I'd recently discovered that my handsome lover had a finance degree. He said, "Our funds are more than enough to support the marketing. Stock the product, and we'll ensure your name is all over it." He added, "And we have a social media expert already on board."

"She's amazing," I grinned, thinking of what Sophia had done to cover up my explosion.

Mr. Bunt chuckled to himself and took another sniff of our laundry strips. He looked at us and cocked his head. Then he sat back in his chair, which squeaked as he shifted his weight.

He looked at the packaging again before tossing the sleeve on his desk. I swallowed.

He rubbed his jaw, squinting at us. He leaned forward and placed his elbows on his desk. "Well played, ladies, well played. Preying on an old man's weakness. That was well done. Good presentation."

We gave him our best innocent faces with big, hopeful eyes. He smiled. "All right. I'll give these to my daughter to test. She's the one who decides what's used in her home. If she likes them, I'll give your laundry strips a shot. But…if I stock them, I'll need a better price."

We needed as many humans as possible to see our strips. Moreso, we needed them to pause and think about what they were using on a daily basis. Ideally, they'd seek a better alternative to plastics and toxic chemicals. Mako said, "We will run a promotional price for a determined amount of time. We'll eat that cost until it gains traction."

So unfair, I thought sourly in my head. A small company like ours wouldn't see the light of day without the family's financial backing. Mako continued, "Our primary motivation is environmental awareness. But we require profit for growth. As our operation becomes smoother, we'll likely be able to reduce our costs and give you a better price."

Mr. Bunt smiled at him appreciatively. "Very well, son. I'll be in touch with you to discuss it further."

Mako smiled. "Oh, no, Mr. Bunt. I'm not in charge. My sister is. You'll be working directly with her."

The manager nodded graciously at Simmi. "My apologies, Miss Fields. I'm an old man. Forgive my presumptions."

Simmi grinned. "Thank you, Mr. Bunt. I look forward to hearing what your daughter thinks of our strips."

We grinned from ear to ear as he stood. We shot out of our

chairs to shake his hand. He didn't release mine, holding it as he looked me in the eye. He dropped his voice low, as if he were fearful of being overheard. "It took us three days to clean up after the explosion. It was disgusting. The soap burned my staff. Peeled off layers of skin. A few got worker's comp because of it. We had to hire a special crew with protective gear, practically hazmat suits, to get rid of it."

He let go of my hand. "Craziest day of my life." He stroked his hand across his chin. "I'll never forget your eyes, Miss Vetula. They're a little different now with that ring. It's nice to have a name for the face that still haunts me. That rage of yours burned into my soul."

His eyes dropped warily to the pearl at my throat. He sighed heavily and spun a picture on his desk. It was a beautiful photograph of a thriving coral reef. "I'm a diver, and I love the ocean. Ladies, I'll be frank with you. I hate plastic, but I haven't had the balls to stand up to corporate and suggest we make changes. Your laundry strips are the perfect opportunity."

I grinned savagely. We had an ally. He grinned back and said, "Still can't figure out what happened to our security footage. It vanished, then returned, but changed. I keep a backup system. One that no one knows about." The blood drained from my face. He chuckled. "I destroyed the evidence. Your secret is safe with me."

I gasped. "You saw it all? You didn't tell anyone?"

He shrugged. "Like I said, I hate plastic. We're only just recognizing the damage it causes. But I still don't understand how you caused the explosion. I'm guessing the pearl around your neck had something to do with it. I've never seen anything like it, pulling up as if on a string. And then you walked away without a trace."

"Actually, I ran as fast as I could," I breathed.

"Hmm," he grunted with a wry smile. He held out his arm and showed us to the door. Mew stepped forward, startling Mr. Bunt, who shuffled backward in fright. "Christ, you're a big fellow. How did I not see you standing there?"

Mew winked and rumbled with laughter.

We left the store, tripping over ourselves with joy. I pressed my fingers to my temple. *We did it, Synchi! We got our tail in the door.*

She cackled and shouted, *Well done, Jelly! I will tell Tro. He'll be so pleased. Come back and talk to the Trident. It's being reorganized. They'll see this as a successful mission—Ocean Warrior. Keep going, Jelly. Keep changing the world. But, more importantly, has Mako proposed to you yet?*

I made a raspberry noise with my lips. *Goddess, Synchi. Drop it. It will happen when it happens. If it even does. I don't need a human ceremony.*

She grumbled, *No, but you do need a Mers one. Until, my dear Jelly. I hope to see you soon.*

Later, I lay in bed with Mako, both of us sweetly satisfied, power pulsing through our sweaty, thrumming bodies. He kissed me until I had to pull back for breath. "I'm so proud of you," he whispered. "You did great today. You and Simmi both."

I rested on his chest. His fingers played in my hair. "Yeah, we all did. It's just the start, too." The pearl vibrated softly and pulsed once. "Leoht agrees." I yawned so wide my jaw clicked. "I can't believe Mr. Bunt recognized me."

Mako snorted. "You're kind of unforgettable, sweetheart." He kissed me softly. "Sleep well. I love you."

My heart flipped over. I'd never tire of hearing him say that. I snuggled into his chest, murmuring, "I love you, too." I'd said it to him for the first time after we dragged away the old man's trash and laid out our blanket under a tree, the shadows dappling over our skin. I smiled at the memory.

Mako's breathing evened out, and I fell asleep, slipping into a dream instantaneously. Water flowed over me peacefully. A gentle humming noise colored the background, and I stretched on the creamy silk sheets below me. I blinked and frowned. Mako and I slept in blue sheets. I propped up on my elbows and scattered my gaze, recognizing where I was. I called out, "Mother Kokuro?"

Scyphozoa. I have searched, and I have found him.

I rubbed my eyes sleepily and asked, "Found who? Who's missing?"

Her answer was so soft that I almost missed it.

Leif.

I screeched, "LEIF?"

I scrambled up to kneel on her smooth flesh, my heart beating out of my chest. "He's been gone for years! Can you take us to him?"

In my real world, I could sense Mako trying to wake me. I'd probably screamed his brother's name. "Quickly, please, Mother. Mako is getting upset."

Tell Mako to retrieve his necklace. Leif is not dead, but he is lost and cannot find home without help. Careful, daughters. It is a treacherous place. Jelly, you and Mako will not be welcome. Neither of you is pure Fae.

"How do we get there?"

Leoht, my love, my precious daughter, you must show yourself to enter. To retrieve Leif, you must take them to the Hellhole.

The pearl pulsed twice in rapid succession.

I pleaded, "Leoht, he's been missing for so long. Please… Wherever this place is, we can handle it. We can do anything together."

The pearl hummed at my throat and reluctantly, ever so softly, throbbed once.

There is more. Scyphozoa, you must find your yellow before you attempt to enter. You will not survive without it.

I sighed impatiently, frustrated by the vagueness. "My yellow? You said that before. Samara did as well. How do I find it?"

Ask your witch.

Unable to resist Mako's panic, I felt myself pulled from the dream. "We'll be back soon. Thank you, Mother. I'll contact you when we're—"

Mako's worry ripped me from the dream, his magic and love pulling me back to him.

"JELLY!" Mako's eyes were manic. He'd hauled me up to lean against the headboard, straddling my thigh as he cradled my skull. "Jelly, you were dreaming. The pearl was jumping. You shouted Leif's name! What did you see?"

I slammed my hands to his face and kissed him ferociously. Magic made his hair float away from his head. I stared into his cobalt-blue eyes, my excitement barely contained. My words tripped over in a rush. "Leif needs us to get home. Have you ever heard of the Hellhole?"

The End…for now.

AUTHOR'S NOTES

At the time of writing, September 2024, the scientific facts and figures in the story are accurate, carefully and methodically researched. Yes, a mako shark can swim at almost fifty miles an hour, and a single sucker of a Great Pacific octopus can support thirty-five pounds in weight. Yes, some turtle groups are nearly all female, up to 99%.

Sadly, the pollution data is also current.

According to the United Nations Environment Programme, we produce 400 million tonnes of plastic waste every year. Annually, eleven million tonnes flows into the oceans, a number that may triple by 2040, a mere fifteen years away.

And as much as the statistics are grim, and have given me black and bleak thoughts, I also have hope.

Countries are coming together to tackle the crisis. Supposedly, by the end of 2024, the Intergovernmental Negotiating Committee (INC), with delegates from over 160 countries, will implement an internationally legally binding agreement to address the lifecycle of plastic, and what we can do to halt the madness.

Some plastic manufacturers oppose this progress. They fight small communities, aimed at reducing their plastics. They influence governments via lobbying. They pour money into preventing a loss to their revenue. At our expense. At the planet's expense.

What is one person to do? We're just ants against a dragon, right?

Here's where it gets exciting. When you buy your mayonnaise or peanut butter in a glass jar versus plastic, it has an impact. Someone is crunching the numbers, and takes notice. If more glass sells, they will produce more glass jars. It's just business.

Remember that you have power. Your one small thread makes a difference.

Keep weaving.

ACKNOWLEDGEMENTS

Where do I start?

Mark, my ever supportive husband. He has listened to countless pollution statistics, gasped appropriately at multiple random facts, and offered many magical suggestions on our dog walks. Thank you, love.

My friends. You've listened to me warble on for months. You fell in love with Jelly before she fully developed. This book reflects every one of you, whether in a character or in a detail. Thank you so much. Your support means the world to me.

Thanks to Kenneth Zink, my editor, who read my second draft and told me to start again. Hurt for a nanosecond, I took his excellent advice and rewrote the story.

Richard Ljoenes created the gorgeous cover, magically turning my vision into art.

And you.

Thank YOU for taking a chance on my first novel, a modern-day environmental fantasy. My hope is that this book changes the way you look at the world.

There are many more adventures for Jelly and the Surfecti. Keep in touch and sign up on www.andieholman.com

Find me in my private Facebook group - Jelly's Scream Team.

If you ever see a flash of colored light, just catching the corner of your eye…Who knows? It could be magic. It might be yours.

www.ingramcontent.com/pod-product-compliance
Lightning Source LLC
Chambersburg PA
CBHW031056130726
47906CB00008B/415